We Hold These Truths

Victor Fleming

Black Lake Press
TELL YOUR STORY
BLACKLAKEPRESS.COM

Published by Black Lake Press of Holland, Michigan. Black Lake Press is a division of Black Lake Studio, LLC. Direct inquiries to Black Lake Press at www.blacklakepress.com.

ISBN 978-0-9883373-3-6

Dedication

To God's little angels everywhere and to William and
Nicholas near here.

Table of Contents

Acknowledgements

Many thanks to Greg Smith for his knowing assistance with the story, to philosopher Alvin Plantinga for his unknowing assistance with the argument, and to the all-knowing Designer for the case.

Chapter One

In The Beginning
Wednesday, May 13, 2009

Fifteen year-old Michelle Taylor reached for the garage door opener with her right hand, swinging her long left leg and slender, under-developed hips over her bicycle in one continuous motion. "Goodbye George," she said matter-of-factly to George Chavez, her mother's chauffeur, as she pushed out of the garage and wobbled past him into the driveway.

While remaining over the hood of a black Mercedes, George looked up, only slightly slowing the pace of his circular waxing. "You be careful on that bike, Ms. Taylor," he warned. George kept Michelle in his gaze as she straightened the bicycle and picked up speed, leaving the driveway and entering the side street. He smiled and shook his head sideways, returning the velocity to his burnishing. "That girl is always on a mission," he muttered under his breath. After four or five spins of the waxing pad, he suddenly looked out, his smile dissolving and a vague anxiety settling. Michelle was already beyond his view.

Michelle arced onto Lake Drive, the two-lane thoroughfare that connects the leafy residential streets of wealthy East Grand Rapids, Michigan, to the slowly gentrifying commercial district called "East-Town" and then merges into Fulton Street at the entrance to the Heritage Hill District, the repository of dozens of turn-of-the-century lumber baron mansions. At the top of Fulton Street hill, Michelle stopped peddling, working to break her speed as she descended into downtown Grand Rapids, nestled on the banks of the Grand River two hundred feet below the Heritage Hill bluffs.

Michelle covered the four mile trek in twenty minutes with a pace neither fast nor leisurely. She carried a face neither sad nor happy. Several times drivers honked as Michelle drifted abnormally into the traffic lane. Michelle paid little attention to her swerving and even less to the drivers' reactions.

Eventually she reached her destination, a bench on the Calder Plaza in the heart of the downtown government complex–a windswept plaza from the nineteen sixties that hosts city hall, the federal courthouse, and the Calder stabile that is the emblem of the City. Hewn by Alexander Calder, the renowned European artist who brightened several American downtowns in the nineteen sixties with his large creations, La Grand Vitesse is a forty foot wide, thirty foot tall, brilliantly red steel sculpture that abstractly depicts the now tamed rapids for which the city was originally named.

Michelle and her father, Frank, often came to this bench on summer Sunday afternoons to contemplate the "Calder" in particular and life in general. "No one ever looks at the centerpiece of our community," Michelle remembered her father saying the last time they visited this spot, several months before he died.

"What do you mean? The Calder is everywhere; it's even on the side of the garbage trucks," she joked.

Michelle remembered her father expelling his deep belly laugh–the one only she could cause. "In all the times we have come here, my love, have you ever seen anyone studying it? It's just like the big issues in life. Few people spend much time thinking about how we arrived? How our brains were forged? How our intrinsic values were formed?" Michelle recalled her father's smile drifting away as he turned to her with tears filling his pensive eyes. "Life is so short, sad, and mysterious."

We Hold These Truths

Michelle sighed as the memory faded. She looked down and pulled out the first of the two items in her backpack, her iPod, set it to one of her father's favorite songs, Ella Fitzgerald and Louie Armstrong singing their rendition of "Summertime" from the musical *Porgy and Bess*:

> Summertime and the live'n is easy
> The fish are jump'n, and the cotton is high,
> Your daddy is rich and your mama is good look'n
> So hush little baby don't you cry
>
> One of these mornings, you're gonna rise singing
> You'll spread your wings and take to the sky
> But until that morning, there's nothing can harm you
> With daddy and mommy stand'n by.

Michelle reached into her backpack and extracted the second item. "Sorry dad," she sighed, "this is the morning I'm gonna spread my wings and take to the sky. I miss you..."

One hundred and fifty yards away, Nico Lahr hoisted the twenty-five pound television camera onto his shoulder like a bazooka and aimed it at Alex Ross's well-coiffed head, "Ready when you are, Alex." In response, Alex closed his eyes, deeply inhaled, and shrugged his shoulders, hoping his pre-taping ritual would wipe away one more time the complete boredom his face would otherwise reveal.

"Behind me—in its chambers—the Grand Rapids city commission will be poised tonight to take up the long awaited restaurant smoking ban that has caused such a local uproar..."

Alex instinctively ducked from the camera's view as the shot rang out.

The television camera was too heavy for Nico's own startle to register. "Jesus Christ!" Nico exclaimed, as he instinctively focused his camera's lens and his own eyesight beyond the space that Alex's head had occupied and on the slumping teenager in the background. "Oh my God, Alex..." he shouted. "I think that girl just shot herself."

Alex did not hear Nico. He was already running. He was twenty-five yards into his sprint before he realized he was running towards the gun fire. "What in the hell are you doing?" He thought to himself. "You crossed busy Ottawa Avenue without looking, and what are you running towards? A sniper victim?" His mind was trying to process the scene, but he didn't seem to be in control of his legs.

Before he could conjure another thought, he saw the gun in the teenager's hand and the pool of blood forming behind her head on the plaza. "No! No! No!" he exclaimed. He was standing above the girl, staring directly into her open blue eyes. Her legs were neatly tucked beneath her torso, as if she had staged her fall. He knelt. "Don't touch the gun," he thought to himself, as he gently pulled the revolver out of her right hand. After casting the gun aside, he sat, clasping the girl's hand between his, hoping he could keep it warm. Instead, a cold chill shuddered down his spine.

* * *

Owen Austin stared at the United Nations-blue colored sky. It was ten o'clock in the morning on a perfect day in May. Owen was prone on the grass in his East Grand Rapids backyard, his front absorbing the growing heat of the sun and his back slowly soaking in the cool moisture of the retreating dew.

What would he do if in a blink of the eye gravity gave way? If he was quick and his hands didn't sweat and his fingers could hold, he might be able to snare the leafy far branches of his giant beech tree as he floated past. He could then compose himself and gradually shimmy up the flowing branches. After he rested on the backside of a tree fork, maybe he could jump into his open second floor bedroom window and live for a while confined within the four walls and the ceiling. But how long could he survive that way? Just one mistake would catapult him into the azure abyss. Even without such a mistake, surely he would eventually starve. And, what would be the point, even if he located the pantry's contents? Certainly, his family might not be as dexterous and survive the first fateful transitional moments. Life without them would be empty. Maybe he should just let himself go, but where would he end up? Was he destined to freeze or burn as he reached the earth's outer atmosphere?

Owen smiled slightly for the first time that day. Sixty years and two miles as the crow flies separated him from the last time he had pondered such questions. The earthy smells of the well-manicured lawn had transported him to his days as a young boy when he had spent hours on his back staring into the sky. Like all mysteries he had pondered in that position, the "gravity quits" dilemma had never been resolved, abandoned in favor of school, sports, girls, and the work-a-day world of his mature life. He realized now the conundrums of his sixty-ninth year would be much closer to the concerns of his ninth.

He should get up. The dampness was penetrating his four thousand dollar handcrafted Italian suit, and his dog Caesar had begun licking his cheek. He should get going. He had a mountain of briefs to read in his office. Yet the Honorable Owen Randolph Austin, chief judge of the United States district court for the western district of Michigan, one of the most disciplined and purposeful men on the planet, could not will himself to move. Only ten a.m., but already it was a fateful day. Soon he would be forced to confront the age-old dilemma of what lies beyond the light blue sky.

Strangely, Owen could not force his mind from the moment to the momentous. His thoughts would not focus on the present, or worse, the future, but returned to the start of his life. The wafting spring smells transported his memory to his mother's garden, and for a moment he could smell her skin close to him, though she had been dead for twenty-five years and had not held him close for over fifty years. For a second, he thought he could recall lying in his baby carriage, staring at the sunlight moving through the oblong, translucent green beech leaves in his parents' backyard.

Suddenly returning to the present, he stared at his beech tree's leaves dancing almost twenty yards over his head in the mid-morning breeze. The space between the branches of his memory and leaves of the present did not matter, nor did the ensuing joy and sorrow, the toil and play, the accomplishments and disappointments, the gains and losses—even family or friends. Conservative or liberal did not matter, nor did Christian or Jew, Democrat or Republican, plaintiff or defendant, Yankee or Red Sox fan. Whether life was purposeful or meaningless did not matter. Owen could force no thought except that after the long winter the beech leaves were dancing again.

Lightheaded and dizzy, everything was familiar but nothing was the same. Everything seemed the same, but he knew everything soon would be different.

* * *

"Life is good" was thirty-eight-year-old Dexter Bussey's second thought as he looked out the lobby window of Kingman Walker's fiftieth floor lobby on West Wacker Drive in downtown Chicago. His first thought was to marvel at the view of Michigan Avenue's "Magnificent Mile" in the foreground and at least ten miles of Lake Michigan in the background. During his second year at the University of Michigan Law School, Dexter had interviewed at Kingman Walker, one of the top three law firms in size and prestige in the Midwest, but had not been offered a job. He settled for an associate's position at one of the top three law firms in Grand Rapids. Now, thirteen years later, Kingman Walker was recruiting him for a partner's position with an opportunity to work as the "first chair" litigator in major cases across the country and to be head of its soon-to-be-opened Grand Rapids office.

"Dexter!" A booming voice exclaimed from behind. "Enjoying the view?" Dexter turned to see the familiar face of Robert J. Johnson, a blue blood from one of Chicago's oldest and wealthiest families and the head of the firm's litigation department.

"Robert!" Dexter turned. "It's been too long." Dexter smiled and extended his right hand, prompting Robert Johnson to slowly raise his own right hand. "Can you believe it has already been three and a half years since we tried the Ductile Steel case?"

Johnson smiled only slightly to acknowledge the memory of the Grand Rapids auto supplier tangling with one of Detroit's major automakers. Johnson defended the automaker when Ductile Steel sued for breach of contract after the automaker terminated Ductile's supply contract, killing the small company and costing two hundred and fifty Grand Rapidians their jobs. Dexter served as local counsel to the automaker and as "second" chair to Johnson during the trial. Halfway through, the automaker's highly attractive jury consultant worried the jury, naturally sympathetic to the local company, was reacting coolly to Johnson's patrician style. She convinced the company's vice president to use Dexter for the key witness cross examinations and for closing argument, producing a slow burn in Johnson.

On this morning's flight, Dexter wondered if Johnson's past wounds had been forgotten. "You could share this view with me on a regular basis as we savor the memory of our mutual victory three years ago and welcome many more in the future." Johnson positioned himself next to Dexter and glanced lovingly towards Chicago's gold coast of million dollar residences.

Nope, Dexter thought to himself, the scabs are barely healed. Dexter offered a sly smile and said, "Well, I wouldn't be here if that prospect didn't hold some interest."

"Good," Johnson smiled wryly back, "Then let's get to it." He curled his arm around Dexter's back, ushering him into one of the ultra-chic conference rooms spiking off the marble floored lobby.

* * *

At the same time back in Grand Rapids, fifty-nine year old John Cleaver was slouched in a tenth floor conference room of Riley, Dickson and Farhat, P.C. "This year is unlikely to be a very good for me, but that's entirely due to the depression in the Grand Rapids commercial real estate market," Maxwell Bennett complained to John, chairman of the firm's compensation committee. Also serving on this year's committee was Gary Pickett, a corporate lawyer in his early fifties, and Greg Jones, a young litigation partner. Of all John's managing partner duties, chair of the comp committee was his least favorite by far. Every May the committee met with each partner to assess his likely performance and entertain his compensation demands.

Maxwell Bennett continued his pitch: "You will recall three years ago, I knocked the ball out of the park. Unfortunately, there was little firm profit to provide a fair bonus. If my four-year numbers are averaged, I am underpaid compared to my peer group."

John sighed. As you would expect of forty-five accomplished lawyers, every partner presented a compelling case for underpayment, carefully selecting statistics to demonstrate his self-serving conclusion. Each year at the end of the interviews, John marveled that every partner had argued he was relatively underpaid and—John had no doubt—each truly believed in the merits of his cause.

"Thanks Max, we will certainly take these points into consideration." John rose slightly, waiting for Max to stand before he completely stood. John always terminated these meetings because the partners never knew when to quit. "You know how difficult our job is, especially this year, with revenues down." John wrapped one of his large paws on the outside of Max's shoulders, ushering him out of the conference room.

"I know, John. I think you are doing a fine job in this capacity and in your managing partner leadership," Max pitched on the way out. John rubbed his eyes after closing the door behind him. Another interminably long day stretched ahead of him. It didn't help that it was already June and his golf clubs had yet to feel the grass.

"We'll be lucky to have an average year," Greg Jones offered dejectedly after Max left, concluding the partner interviews. Jones was in the firm's receivership group, which was having a banner year. The firm's workers compensation and bankruptcy practices were also booming due in no small measure to Michigan's seemingly endless recession, which had lasted almost a full decade. But the rest of the firm was struggling.

After pouring his third cup of coffee, John squeezed what was left of his six foot five, two hundred and twenty-five pound frame into one of the modern new conference room chairs recently purchased to update the firm's image. "It's not all bad, Greg. It is truly painful when we don't make our draws and there are no bonuses, but a great financial year is actually worse. The bickering, politicking, and hurt feelings are three times as bad. It's success that kills the large law firm, not failure," John pontificated to a bored Jones.

"Are we going to evaluate each other?" Gary Pickett asked.

"Good Lord, no!" John responded quickly. "It's a given we are going to screw ourselves; why magnify the injustice?" John was referring to the compensation committee's traditional sacrifice of its own wage increases. The gesture was less altruistic than pragmatic. Typically, among the first compensation "awards" the partners scrutinized—after their own—were the committee members' compensation.

"There is a lot of discord in the younger partnership ranks." Jones ventured carefully.

"I am aware of that, Greg," John sighed in a resigned voice Jones took as encouragement to push further.

"There is some sentiment, certainly not shared here, that you are significantly overpaid." Jones stared at John for a reaction.

"That's bull shit, Jones!" Pickett rushed to John's support.

"What is, Greg? The sentiment or my assessment of the sentiment?" Jones fired back, taking advantage of the forensic edge he had over Pickett, who hadn't seen the inside of a courtroom in a quarter century.

Pickett slightly reddened before rallying. "There isn't a major law firm in this state that wouldn't gladly pay John what our firm is paying and more. He's taken a home team discount for years, and the last two and one-half years has carried his full weight professionally, while steering the firm through one of the toughest bear markets the legal profession has experienced. John was winning some of the biggest cases this town has seen before these Young Turks were born—how ungrateful and shortsighted!"

John sighed again. Both men were right. John was by far the highest paid attorney in the firm, but also carried the biggest reputation. Yet, it had been almost five years since John had tried a major case. Law firms were the ultimate: "what have you done for me lately" organizations. When John started in the practice, a sixty-year-old litigator was in his prime, his grey hair commanding courtroom authority. Now, litigators were in their prime at age fifty, maybe even earlier. Few cases went all the way to trial. Cases were now exhausted in pretrial depositions, document discovery, and summary disposition motions, which placed a premium on tedious attention to detail, aggression, and a minimum on strategy and wisdom. John held a sneaking suspicion the big cases were passing him because the corporate in-house lawyers who had previously sought him were now looking for a more energetic, hip presence.

"Thanks, Gary. I appreciate the support, and Greg, thanks for the courage to bring these concerns to my attention. It's only natural the one making the most money draws the most attention in tight times. It's an issue we will have to consider, but let's break for the day."

John lingered as Pickett and Jones left the conference room. He turned to the Grand Rapids skyline. Did he want the big case and the energy it took? Should he cash in on his reputation and transition his book of business to another firm, or stay to take on the young bucks who would eventually take him down? The window on the first option was closing and the pace of the second was quickening.

* * *

"The district court is the trial court system of the United States government. All federal trials occur here. In a sense, it is one court, but administratively it is organized into 'districts.' Many states have several districts. Michigan has two. The 'western district' includes the western half of the lower peninsula and the entire upper peninsula. By some measures it is the largest district in the country. From the city of Watervliet in the southwestern corner of the state to the village of Watersmeet in the far western tip of the U.P. is a five hundred and ninety mile trip."

Owen Austin had slipped into the back of his courtroom behind the class of eighth graders gathered in the front pews. At the head of his courtroom with her back ramrod straight stood the lecturer—his secretary, Sarah Lewis. Sarah had served as his secretary during his last ten years in private practice. She continued as his secretary on the federal payroll since President George H. Bush appointed him a federal judge in 1987.

As Owen silently sat in what he hoped was an unobserved position, Sarah moved to her left and stood next to Owen's court reporter. "Say hello to Kelly Vandervelde, our court reporter."

Sarah waited for Kelly to smile. "Kelly swears in the witnesses, who sit above her in the 'witness chair.' She transcribes all of the lawyers' questions and the witnesses' answers and produces a transcript that looks like dialogue in a book."

"Standing against the back of the wall is Frank Callahan, our bailiff. Frank takes care of security." Frank Callahan stood at attention in his formal soldier's stance. "He's not as mean as he looks, and we are softening him with coffee cake." Frank smiled and then leaned forward and glared, making the kids laugh.

Owen smiled at the scene. Despite his Irish surname, Frank was an African American ex-marine drill sergeant working on his second federal pension as a United States marshal. Frank carried the easy physical presence that never abandons great high school athletes, in Frank's case a sure-handed football tight end. Callahan was intuitive, especially adept at sensing when a courtroom customer—whether lawyer, spectator or party—was about to lose his composure. He was equally savvy at sensing which office on the seven floors of the Gerald R. Ford federal building was serving sweets, and now carried an extra ten pounds across his midsection reflecting that skill. But neither that bulge nor the discomfort he endured because of his sport coat would slow Frank down if a physical crisis presented itself. Owen could not think of anyone he would rather have protecting his staff.

"Most importantly, at the top of the podium, which we call the 'bench,' sits our judge." Sarah continued. "He controls this courtroom. He decides what questions may be asked and what matters will go to a jury. If someone gets convicted, the judge will sentence him to jail. A federal judge must be appointed by the President of the United States and then be confirmed by the United States Senate. Once confirmed, he remains a judge until he dies. Our judge isn't on the bench right now, but," Sarah moved towards the class and leaned forward to whisper, "that doesn't mean he isn't here." She lifted herself on her tippy toes and smiled at Owen. "Kids, look behind you and meet the

Honorable Owen R. Austin, chief judge of the United States district court for the western district of Michigan."

Although slightly jarred by the unexpected introduction, Owen rose. "Good morning young ladies and lads," Owen slowly intoned in his deep baritone as he ambled down the corridor and through the swinging door of the proverbial "bar" separating the spectator and working areas of the courtroom. He slowly spun to face them. "I hope I never see any of you in my courtroom again." They looked at him wide-eyed and startled. They softened only when Owen smiled. "Actually, that isn't true... I hope to see some of you right here," Owen pointed to the chairs at the lawyers' tables, "as young lawyers in my courtroom; or maybe as witnesses; or perhaps performing your valued civic duty as jurors."

"But, if you are ever a 'party'—and that is what we call a person whose case will be decided in this courtroom—I want you to remember one thing, but before I tell you that thing, let me ask you this..." Owen adopted a pensive pose with his hand under his chin. "Does anyone know how the Declaration of Independence starts?"

A blonde girl with a pony tail shot her arm up. "I do sir—I mean, Judge..."

Owen smiled; only the girls dared respond to this question. "Go ahead," Owen encouraged. "Give it a try."

The girl paused but didn't lose her confidence, starting slowly but picking up the pace: "We hold these truths to be self-evident, that all men are created equal, that they are endowed by their creator with certain inalienable rights, that among these are life, liberty and the pursuit of happiness!"

"That's it exactly! Now I will tell you that one thing I want you all to remember: our country is dedicated to the notion that every person is equal. It doesn't matter what color you are, what religion you might believe in, whether you are rich or poor. Every person is on the same level as far as our government is concerned. Everyone is to be treated with the same dignity, fairness and respect. The judge and juries sit higher than the spectators in this courtroom only because they are deciding the case and receive a position of honor. All parties and the spectators are on the same footing. And, when I am not on that bench, I am just like all of you. No better, no worse; free to pursue my own life, liberty, and happiness." Owen stepped forward. "Do you each promise me you will remember this principle?" He stood tall with his hands on his hips and surveyed the starstruck students' eyes, each trained on him with awe. After all heads had nodded in agreement, he stepped back and nodded to their teacher.

"Thank you Judge Austin," said the teacher on cue. "Class, let's thank the judge and his staff for taking the time in their busy day to show us the courtroom." The students politely applauded, led by the blonde. "Now let's exit and let them get back to their important work, deciding the kinds of cases we studied in our civics class." The class shuffled out the back door, leaving Owen with the bitter reality he would never see any of these eighth graders in his courtroom as lawyers, jurors, or parties.

"Judge! What happened to your suit? It has grass stains and mud, and it's a little wet!" Sarah exclaimed as soon as the students left the courtroom, and she wiped a dirty blade of grass off Owen's right should blade.

"It's nothing, Sarah," Owen frowned.

"You must have fallen? Are you all right?"

"You're right. Caesar's chain tangled around the sprinkler and as I struggled to free it, I snared my leg, slipping on the wet grass. I'm without a bruise. Something else will surely kill me," offered Owen.

To the women in his family—his deceased wife Susan and his two adult daughters, Mary and Megan—this was Owen's most annoying habit. He always disguised his lies in a larger truth, confusing fact and fiction.

"I'm glad you are all right... Guess what?" she quickly transitioned. "It arrived this morning. I think the artist finally has it right. Come check it out." Sarah walked quickly to the back door of the courtroom.

"I will be there in a moment, Sarah." Owen said, lost in his thoughts, not ready to return to his chambers, to his work, to his sanctuary from life's many disappointments.

"Oh come on, Judge, you have been waiting for this painting for twenty-five years. It's finally here!" Sarah was unable to contain her excitement.

"I'm not entitled to a moment in my own courtroom anymore!" Owen bellowed in frustration. The shock, dejection, and then embarrassment in Sarah's face shook Owen out of his mood. Owen seldom raised his voice. His temper now quickly dissipated. He paused. "I am sorry Sarah, I'm just nervous to actually see the final version. You are right; I have spent far too much time anticipating this moment. Let's go."

Sarah took a second to recover from the unexpected, unusual sleight and looked deeply at her boss. After a moment, she brightened and opened the courtroom door for him. Owen strode past Frank and Kelly, who silently remained at their stations—Kelly fussing with her steno-machine, which wasn't even on, and Frank staring intently at Owen, who wouldn't make eye contact with him.

One of a long sitting federal judge's perks is the eventual installation of an oil painting portrait in his courtroom. The federal government did not buy the portraits. Instead, a committee of former law clerks would form to facilitate the task of picking an artist and commissioning the portrait. Only a retired, deceased, or sitting judge who has been on the bench for at least twenty-five years is eligible for a courtroom portrait.

To Owen, this portrait represented his place in the court's history—the culmination of decades of hard work and the sterling reputation he had so carefully cultivated. Three previous versions of the portrait had been returned for rework because the expression was flawed. In the first, Owen was too dour. In the second, his demeanor was frivolous. In the third, he looked dense. As Owen examined the last rendition, he thought this was easily the worst. He looked—"loopy" was the only description coming to mind.

"I think the artist captured your thoughtfulness," beamed Sarah.

"It is the perfect amalgamation of the artist's previous efforts," Owen stated obliquely. "Thank you Sarah, for your persistence. Make sure you fire off a letter of gratitude to Robbie Goldman and his committee today."

Robbie Goldman had been one of Owen's favorite law clerks and was now a forty-year-old partner at Simon and Strong, one of Chicago's largest firms. Robbie proudly volunteered to organize the portrait committee and raised the portrait's funding in less than a week.

Owen employed two law clerks, always for a two year period and always right out of law school. One was usually a graduate from the University of Michigan law school, Owen's alma mater. Law clerks perform indispensable research and writing assistance for a judge. A federal clerkship, particularly with a judge as respected as Owen Austin, was a plum—the perfect start to a legal career, particularly for a litigator.

Of the nearly fifty clerks Owen had mentored during the quarter century, a current clerk, Jack Gooters, was one of his least liked. His other clerk, Mary Lou Shurlow, was among his favorites. Gooters was certainly bright, as was reflected in his number one class ranking at Michigan. However, Owen considered Gooter's know-it-all attitude a cardinal sin for all lawyers, especially the inexperienced. Owen took guilty pleasure in knowing someday lady justice would bring Jack Gooters to his knees. All lawyers ended there sooner or later.

"Sarah, will you take that picture and hide it in the hall closet until the installation ceremony? Give me fifteen minutes to organize my desk, and then send Jack in to review the docket." Sarah proudly left Owen's office and was only too happy to secret the painting until the prized moment.

As Sarah closed the door, Owen dropped his head into his hands, his elbows propped on his oversized desk. After learning the magnitude of Susan's cancer and had she completed her first round of treatment, Owen had taken a leave of absence. Susan and he traveled to London, Paris, Berlin, Madrid, and Rome—the continental capitals in their travel bucket. They cut their dream vacation short after four weeks, however. Susan had been too tired, and they couldn't escape the weight of her illness and the tragedy impending. After forcing time with their daughters and their families, they discovered what they most enjoyed was their usual routine. Sunday church and the following family brunch never seemed more satisfying. Reading the paper and listening to popular music, sitting in their backyard garden—savoring all of life's simple pleasures proved to be their most rewarding final activities as a couple.

Owen was through with the cancer patient scene. He was long resigned to the knowledge he would not recover from the death of his wife. The loneliness of the last five years had driven him deeper into his work. There would be no travel, retirement or new routine for Owen Austin. He would spend his remaining time at his home, his office, and his work.

With that thought, he began wracking his brain over his current docket of cases. What he needed was not an oil portrait but a good trial. The phone on his large mahogany desk rang. "Did you like this rendition, your honor?" the pleasant voice of Robbie Goldman asked.

"How did you know it arrived, Robbie?"

"You don't like it, do you?" Robbie responded quietly.

In his mind's eye, Owen could see the faint smile on his protégé's face. Robbie was nearly unflappable and keenly perceptive, just two of the endearing qualities Owen appreciated in his younger charge. "Sarah must have sent you a picture of it." Owen offered, again ducking the question.

Robbie laughed. "We can have it redone again. In fact, why don't we find a new artist and start over?"

"No, Robbie, it is fine. Have you ever seen a photograph of yourself you liked?"

"Oh! I have almost never seen a photograph of myself I didn't like," Robbie answered.

Each man laughed. "I can't decide if that makes you more or less vain than me?" Owen pondered.

Robbie pressed forward. "You know, Judge, I have commitments from all eleven of your former clerks in the Chicago area. We are all taking the day off, chartering a small bus and coming up to Grand Rapids for the installation ceremony between Christmas and New Year's."

"You're kidding me!" Owen was truly surprised and delighted.

"Why wouldn't we want to celebrate a judge who hasn't gotten a single case wrong in twenty-five years?"

"What are you talking about, Robbie? I have been reversed four times."

"I have read all four of those cases, Judge, and like I said, it's amazing you haven't been wrong in twenty-five years."

"Well," Owen reflected, "who's counting anyway?" At that, they shared a hearty laugh.

* * *

Monday, May 18, 2009

"Vicki, please stop!" Ross Wagner pleaded. "Not today. You are burying her this afternoon for Christ's sake."

Mrs. Frank Taylor quietly ignored the advice of her deceased husband's long time lawyer and her lover of almost the same duration. Instead, she continued lovingly packing her daughter's clothes into boxes for transport to the Goodwill charity. Every so often, before packing a particular item, she would bring it close to her nose and take a deep draw. Taylor was beyond tears, beyond fatigue, beyond heartache. She was operating only on a raw force of will. She had never been stronger.

* * *

"Alex, you are not going to cover this poor girl's cemetery ceremony."

"Of course not! I am attending the funeral for myself, Dan. After all, the poor child died in my arms. I need to pay my personal respects," Alex Ross explained to his editor, Dan Busman. "But I would like your permission to develop a generic piece on teen suicide. It's a close second to car accidents for premature death among teenagers. It is a huge problem no one in the media, much less local television, wants to profile."

Busman sighed. "Honestly Alex, do you think an exposé on teen suicide is going to buttress our flagging ratings?"

"Maybe following the right stories—the important stories— will slow our ratings decline, and if not, at least improve morale."

"Are you trying to sell me on this piece or just hell bent on pissing me off?"

"You are right, Dan. I apologize. Honestly, I can't get out of my mind the damn sight of Michelle Taylor laying there with her eyes open and her life draining away. I need to make sense of it and am hoping this piece will give me a few answers." Alex's knew he was playing a winning hand. His boss was a sucker for the complete truth even though his TV station hadn't found it on a significant issue in years.

Chapter Two

Monday, November 2, 2009
(Morning of the Opening Day of Trial)

Five and a half months later, an anticipatory crowd gathered in front of the federal courthouse. "Today, November second, is a cloudy, overcast day in Grand Rapids, Michigan, with a hint of the season's first snow in the air," intoned Cox Cable News Network's star, Joe Block, attempting a poetic air. "To the immediate south of our position is the Calder stabile where Michelle Taylor, the fifteen year-old child, committed suicide. To the near north is the Gerald R. Ford courthouse where her mother will seek justice. Today is the first day of trial, where the federal district court will entertain the radical prospect that public schools in this country should be free to suggest that human beings are not the happenstance product of evolution, but the designed result of a supernatural God. When I put it like that—and I think it a fair recitation of the issue in this case—the answer seems so patently obvious that the question seems absurd. After all, this is not the godless Soviet Union, but the United States of America."

Block raised his right hand and pointed to the courthouse, "Yet, the courts and the public schools in this country are frustrating the moral curiosity of our children, sometimes—as here in Grand Rapids—with tragic results. In this case, we are sure to hear that the humiliation Michelle Taylor received at the hands of her high school biology teacher played a role in the depression which took her life. This humiliation, good people, resulted simply because she dared argue natural selection might not explain the moral compass embedded in each of us. Incredibly, this mother is not looking for money from the perpetrators of this travesty. She simply wants her deceased daughter vindicated. She wants federal district court judge Owen Austin, a Bush One appointee, to declare the public schools a place where the most cogent theory regarding the origin of life, 'intelligent design,' may be openly taught. We cannot fathom how Judge Austin could rule any way not fully supportive of the requests of this grieving mother. And, we are going to stay here—right here—to report on each day of this significant trial."

* * *

John Cleaver grabbed last night's newspaper as he headed to his favorite breakfast haunt—something he always did before starting a day of trial. His blood began to boil as he read the editorial while sifting through his scrambled eggs:

"Tomorrow an important trial starts in our community. This is a trial in which the protections of the First Amendment will be put to the test. The First Amendment is often vulnerable to popular passions and such could be the case here. Mrs. Frank Taylor deserves our sympathy and our community's support, having been touched by two recent tragic deaths in her immediate family. However, we cannot support her efforts to compel the teaching of intelligent design in our public schools. Undoubtedly, the East Grand Rapids high school biology teacher could have been more diplomatic and more empathetic in dealing with Mrs. Taylor's daughter's religious beliefs about creation. But on the basic question in this case, the teacher was right and so is the school district in supporting him. The divide that separates church and state isn't always easy to discern, but it must be divined and it must be respected with nothing short of religious zeal. Evolution and natural selection are accepted biological precepts. Whether a god or the God set those forces in motion is worthy of discussion and debate in our churches and in our living rooms, but not in our schools, as countless other cases have already determined. Federal district court judge Owen Austin is well respected in our community for being a man of the law. We can only hope that his reputation will not be tarnished through this case by outside forces or momentary passions."

John picked up his cell phone and dialed a Chicago number. "Robert, I am eating breakfast, finally reading last night's editorial in *The Grand Rapids Press*."

"What a coincidence. I am reading it online as we speak. Isn't it wonderful? I couldn't have written it better myself," Robert Johnson answered.

"Your associate on loan suggested that the Press' editorial page editor was an acquaintance of yours from American Civil Liberties Union conventions. I assume this editorial was published as a result of your encouragement," John's voice revealed no hint of the sarcasm he would have liked to exhibit.

"I spoke; he spoke; it came up; he made the decision; he wrote it. I had no editorial involvement at all."

"Robert. Anyone who tries to intimidate Owen Austin makes a mistake. I know this all too well. This could easily backfire, but you know that isn't the point. This is my case. I am the captain of this ship, and my right to steer it strategically must be respected. Next time, clear any move like this with me beforehand."

"There won't be a next time, John. I apologize. Yours is exactly the spirit we want in the head of our future Grand Rapids office. Now finish your eggs and clear your head for your opening, which I am sure will knock Judge Austin on his can," Robert added with minimal levity.

Victor Fleming

* * *

Vicki Taylor hated to admit it, but she was excited by the full courtroom. As is customary in federal trials, Owen had banned all cameras, meaning the only way to view this spectacle was in person. Every seat was filled. There were a few people Taylor recognized, including Paul Kingston, Michelle's biology teacher, who was pouting and refusing to make eye contact with anyone. William Morris, the old principal of the high school, caught her attention, offering a warm smile, and she saw William Reichel, the superintendent, projecting an air of studied nonchalance. The rest of the audience appeared to be media. The district's lawyers entered the courtroom and began to unpack their many briefcases. She thought John Cleaver and his young partner, Greg Jones, looked handsome. They were organizing piles of exhibits and other papers at their table, a task in which young Mr. Diamond, one of her lawyers, was also busily employed. Her principal lawyer, Dexter Bussey, sat with his arms and legs crossed nonchalantly, studying the judicial portraits lining the courtroom walls.

At a little past nine a.m., Sarah Lewis entered and asked the lawyers if they were ready, and then almost immediately, Frank Callahan popped out of the chambers' door and announced, "All rise, the United States district court for the western district of Michigan is now in session, the Honorable Owen R. Austin presiding." Everyone in the courtroom immediately stood and Kelly Vandervelde and a trailing Owen entered, the latter's simple black robe flowing. As he was sitting, Owen with one extended hand directed the crowd to be seated. He glanced in Sarah's direction without focusing on her. "Ms. Lewis, would you call the case."

Sarah Lewis addressed the courtroom and declared, "Vicki Taylor, personal representative of the estate of Michelle Taylor, versus the East Grand Rapids school district," rattling off the case number. With that, Owen addressed the entire courtroom, with his attention focusing on the lawyers.

"This is the time and place scheduled for trial in this case. Counsel, will you state your appearances for the record?"

Dexter Bussey stood first. "Dexter Bussey and Peter Diamond for the plaintiff, your honor, and I would also like to introduce you to our client, Mrs. Victoria Taylor, personal representative of the estate." Dexter pointed his right hand towards Taylor and then sat.

John Cleaver stood when Dexter sat. "John Cleaver and Greg Jones of the law firm Riley Dickson, your honor, for the defense." He too quickly returned to his chair.

"Thank you, Mr. Bussey and Mr. Cleaver. Before we take opening statements, I want to remind everyone in the courtroom this is a serious proceeding. There is no audience participation. I expect everyone to be quiet. There will be absolutely no clapping, hollering, or any other audible reaction to the arguments or testimony. You should not have been able to get a camera, audio recorder, or even cell phone past the marshals downstairs. If you have, I warn you they may not be used or even seen in this courtroom or they will be confiscated. Any talking should be kept to a minimum and to a whisper so as not to disturb these proceedings. No deviations from these rules will be tolerated, and if someone materially violates them, they will be removed from the courtroom and not permitted to return during this matter. Okay, Mr. Bussey, the court will take your opening statement."

Dexter stood, buttoning his jacket while walking to the podium. "Thank you, your honor, and good morning. Eight months ago, Michelle Taylor, barely fifteen years old, entered a freshman biology class at East Grand Rapids high school carrying the fresh scars of having lost her beloved father to the cruel dual fate of ALS and an accidental encounter with a bus in downtown Chicago. In that class, she met her teacher's cynical suggestion that premature death is but nature's way of cleansing the gene pool. Rising to that insult, Michelle forcefully pointed to the metaphysical values all of us who are sane carry, such as a longing for love and a respect for human equality. To Michelle, these inherent traits were evidence nature's amoral cruelty does not exclusively control our existence but rather portends a creator who has birthed us into something more than our temporal, physical lives. These feelings were at the core of Michelle's religious beliefs.

"Oblivious to the sensitivities before him, her teacher belittled these beliefs as 'magical thinking' unworthy of any rational mind, ignoring not only the testimony of millions of human minds, but also espousing the nihilism of 'metaphysical naturalism,' a religious philosophy that has co-opted evolution.

"The United States Constitution's First Amendment is commonly described as a 'two-edged sword.' One edge, the 'anti-establishment clause' or 'entanglement clause,' prohibits public entities from encouraging religion. The other edge, the 'anti-discouragement clause,' prohibits the discouragement of religious thought. The estate alleges the East Grand Rapids school district has impaled itself on each edge of the sword in its biology class.

"Regarding the entanglement clause, the estate's claim is similar to that of the plaintiff in the 2005 *Kitzmiller* case involving the Dover, Pennsylvania, school district. In *Kitzmiller*, a United States district court found intelligent design theory intertwined in the public's perception with Christianity. As a result, the school district's curriculum statement supporting intelligent design and criticizing evolution as a gap-filled alternative violated the establishment clause. The *Kitzmiller* court enjoined the district from teaching intelligent design as an alternative to the theory of evolution.

"But if the federal courts posit such an unconstitutional linkage can occur with the intelligent design cosmological theory, they have to concede the possibility such an unconstitutional linkage could happen to the evolution cosmological theory as well."

His posture ramrod straight, Dexter was not reading from his notes but was looking directly at Owen. He did not move from the waist down, only occasionally moving his arms to make a point.

"In our case, pollster Milton Hileman will establish that evolution has become intertwined in the public's perception in East Grand Rapids with atheism, which the law recognizes as a religion. We will further establish that this link between atheism and evolution is intentional. You will hear one of the nation's leading evolutionists, professor Leonard Devoneau, a distinguished biologist, attest that Charles Darwin and the current leading proponent of evolution, Richard Dawkins, each proudly assert that evolution proves atheism is correct and no God exists."

Dexter paused to take a drink of water and to give the court a break in his presentation before restarting.

"Where we differ from the plaintiffs in *Kitzmiller* is in the remedy we seek. Ms. Taylor on behalf of her daughter's estate is not asking this court to enjoin the teaching of either theory. Our position, your honor, is that no religion can take ownership of a cosmological theory so as to enjoin its teaching in the public schools. When a religion—whether Christianity with respect to intelligent design or atheism with respect to evolution—substantially co-opts a cosmological theory in the public mind, the solution is not a reactionary censorship such as the *Kitzmiller* court employed, but an enlightened uncoupling of the linkage so impressionable youth understand that the mere teaching of a biological theory does not mean the school district advocates the religion embracing the theory.

"Because of the common perception that evolution and atheism are the same, the East Grand Rapids school district must take affirmative action to uncouple the science from the religion. There are perhaps many ways in which the district could accomplish this. What we propose is a statement the district would read before its students are taught evolution. The statement would simply state that the science of evolution and the monotheistic religions of Christianity, Judaism, and Islam are not incompatible.

"As the court knows, Mrs. Taylor offered the district an opportunity to avoid this suit and to adopt such a statement. As the court has already concluded, the district made the conscious decision to reject this request. Accordingly, this court must conclude that the East Grand Rapids school district has a practice of rejecting any curative instruction on evolution's distinction from atheism. As such, the district has failed its fundamental constitutional obligation to maintain lofty neutrality and has encouraged atheism.

"As for the discouragement claim, the expert educator, Alvin Henry, will testify the roots of modern education lie in 'methodological naturalism,' often called the 'scientific method.' The scientific method holds that for any theory to be called 'scientific" it must be testable through either deductive reasoning alone or through empirical observation. Empirical observation requires a statistically significant sample to defeat subjectivity.

"The *Kitzmiller* court required testing through deductive testability to be the sole threshold test for the teaching of any cosmological theory. There are several problems with this reliance on deductive testability as the sole threshold test for cosmological discussion in the public schools. First, it ignores the role induction plays in creating hypotheses later tested through the scientific method. For instance, there are at least three seminal questions in cosmology for which there are at present no testable theories: where the mineral matter in the universe came from before the Big Bang origin of our universe thirteen billion years ago? Where, when, and how the first biological or plant life developed from mineral matter? And, where, when, and how the first animal life emerged? If deductive testability is the threshold for discussion in the public schools, none of these questions may be acknowledged, much less taught.

"The second problem with the *Kitzmiller* test is evolution is only slightly more scientifically testable, if at all, than intelligent design. In fact, a father of the scientific method, philosopher Karl Popper, considered evolution only a scientific speculation, not a scientific principle, because it cannot be physically tested. The truth is intelligent design and evolution are theories— perhaps even consistent with one another, since many evolutionists believe a supernatural force created the laws of natural selection and the matter and life upon which it operates.

"Third, the *Kitzmiller* test fails to acknowledge the commonly understood distinctions between the 'hard' and 'soft' sciences. 'Hard sciences,' such as astronomy, physics, math, and chemistry, and to a lesser extent, biology, are testable through objective sensory experimentation. 'Soft' sciences, including the behavioral sciences of history, sociology, philosophy, and psychology, are dependent on empirical observation and collective reasoning. Many philosophers have criticized the *Kitzmiller* decision for embracing a view of the scientific method eliminating behavioral sciences as 'science.' Expert philosopher Alvin Henry will testify the metaphysical concepts of human equality, right and wrong, good and evil, love and hate, joy and sorrow, although not capable of physical testing or even sensory observation, are empirically verifiable through common experience, reasoning, and logic.

"The presence of these values in the human mind is at present only explained by three theories: one, that human beings biologically transmit these values orally through repetition. A second theory is they are mere components of our biological draw to those genetically close to us. The third theory is they were impressed upon our biology by a supernatural designer. None of these theories can be scientifically tested in the manner required by *Kitzmiller*.

Victor Fleming

"While the United States Supreme Court in *Jaffree* left no doubt that a public school cannot teach God exists, it also expressly precludes public school teachers from denying God exists. When a teacher states there is no empirical evidence of the metaphysical, he is saying there is no empirical evidence of God. When a teacher states belief in afterlife is 'magical thinking,' he is denying God exists. When a teacher tells a young student who has lost a parent to a horrific disease that premature death is only nature's way of selecting the gene pool, he is denying the very possibility our fate lies within an omnipotent will. Paul Kingston, Michelle Taylor's biology teacher, made each of these statements and in this manner advocated his own belief in metaphysical naturalism and discouraged Michelle Taylor's Christianity, thereby violating his constitutional obligation to remain religiously neutral. The institutional failure of the East Grand Rapids school district to discipline this teacher or to instruct its teachers against endorsing their own religious beliefs allows individual transgressions to become corporate First Amendment violations.

"We ask for an injunction restricting teachers in the East Grand Rapids school district from making any comments suggesting there is no empirical evidence of the metaphysical. We ask the court to restrain any opinion that science and religion don't mix and that belief in another world unconstrained by time and physical limitations is merely magical thinking. We ask the court to declare that the postulate that physical matter, biological life, and values may have been created by a supernatural being is perfectly permissible in the public schools, as long as teachers do not endorse the worship of that designer. Any suggestion to the contrary, your honor, violates *Jaffree* and the anti-discouragement clause of the First Amendment.

"This brings us to the tragedy behind this case. We can say with certainty that Michelle Taylor's constitutional rights were violated by the East Grand Rapids school district through its discouragement of her Christian beliefs. What we can also say with certainty is this violation of her constitutional rights was traumatic to an adolescent who was clearly troubled and who tragically committed suicide just a few weeks after this troubling encounter in the classroom. While our client asks for only nominal damages because it cannot prove the proximate cause of Michelle's suicide, in no way do we suggest the district's biology class played no role in her death. What Michelle's death underscores is that cosmological discussions have serious impacts on the lives of our impressionable children. It is critical to our Constitution, but more importantly, to the mental health of our children that we get these issues right."

Dexter let his words echo in the courtroom, and slowly sat down.

"Thank you, Mr. Bussey," Owen responded, "But before you sit down, I have a few questions regarding your position."

"Yes, your honor."

"Is your client asking this court to order the East Grand Rapids school district to teach intelligent design theory as a competing theory to evolution in biology class?"

"No. The estate agrees the district's policy makers should decide its biology curriculum. This court should not compel the district to teach evolution or even biology itself. The estate asserts the district is wrong to believe it may not present intelligent design theory, as it would be wrong if it believed it could not teach evolution theory. Our client merely claims if the district offers either, it must take positive steps to uncouple the scientific theory from its religious connotations and it must acknowledge that science cannot yet explain the mystery of life's emergence, thereby negating any impression that science is incompatible with creation or that evolution is incompatible with the possibility of an intelligent designer who may have set it in motion."

"But isn't intelligent design theory inherently religious?" Owen asked.

"No. We recognize the *Kitzmiller* court found intelligent design theory to be creationism sanitized to pass constitutional muster. The Dover school board's disingenuity notwithstanding, the truth is First Amendment law requires sanitization. After all, sanitization is the difference between teaching that some people believe in God—which under *Jaffree* is perfectly permissible— and suggesting students should believe in God, which is clearly unacceptable. Let me come at your question, your honor, a little differently. Suppose there really is a God who created original matter and biological life, and let's further suppose the devil witnessed the creation and hates everything about God. Are we saying that the First Amendment would prohibit the devil from appearing in an East Grand Rapids biology class and describing how creation occurred? Would we worry that the devil would endorse Christianity? No, the speculation that a supernatural being, perhaps the personal God of Christianity, perhaps a now deceased being, or perhaps a now disinterested or hostile being, created matter, life, and the process of evolution is in no way an endorsement of a particular religion, nor is it a violation of the First Amendment."

"Isn't this the 'teach both creation science and evolution' edict struck down by the United States Supreme Court in *Edwards v. Aguillard*?"

"No, you honor, we do not request either theory be mandated, nor if either is taught, that the other be presented as competing or compatible. We advocate only the district must teach all facts—both what we know about evolution and what we know about the human mind which appears to be inconsistent. No cosmological theory should be banished from the discussion. No cosmological theory should be offered without being stripped of its religious connotations."

"Thank you, Mr. Bussey. Mr. Cleaver, you have the floor."

We Hold These Truths

"Thank you, your honor." John Cleaver rose and walked to the podium. "I will confess one thing up front: as a philosopher, I cannot compete with Mr. Bussey. I am a mere defense lawyer. What I know is the estate carries the burden of proving our client, the East Grand Rapids school district, has committed the serious act of violating the tragically deceased girl's constitutional rights by refusing to give a statement no school district in the country is giving on the science of evolution. That is a heavy constitutional burden the estate cannot carry.

"I appreciate the concession evolution has scientific proof and should be taught in our public schools as the one scientific theory, albeit imperfect, explaining the origins of life. That some scientists might draw religious conclusions from the science should not concern this court any more than the belief that East Grand Rapids school district, with its multiple state football championships, has made football a religion. Should the school district be compelled to warn that football can become an obsession and engender religious-like fanaticism? Should the district be obligated to disclaim it's endorsement of football for fear of religious consequences if doesn't?

"I appreciate the concession that policy makers at the East Grand Rapids school district do not have to teach intelligent design and if they do, they would be compelled to uncouple it from its Christian roots. Frankly, our client chooses not to teach a theory that has no scientifically testable support and would require a complicated constitutional disclaimer. Rather, it will leave the theory to the realm of personal religion where it belongs and apparently where the estate agrees the district is free to leave it.

"Likewise, I am happy for the concession that love and hate, right and wrong, good and evil, or other metaphysical concepts do not have to be taught in the public schools. If popular opinion is correct, our schools have a hard enough time teaching the core courses of reading, writing, and arithmetic. Whether viewed as hard science or hard fact, the truth is there is no sensory verification of love or hate, right or wrong, goodness or badness and, therefore, there is no empirical evidence these concepts exist. Even if one is to disagree with that conclusion, this is a matter of opinion. Although they have tentacles into religious thought, these concepts are not owned by religions. For a teacher to opine that no empirical evidence of such concepts exists is neither a denial of God's existence nor a discouragement of religious practice. Indeed, to discipline this teacher for expressing an opinion not verifiably wrong would itself violate his First Amendment rights to free speech, something the East Grand Rapids school district properly refused to do.

"In short, the district will prove through its own expert testimony that evolution is neutral to the metaphysical and the metaphysical is by its very definition incapable of sensory verification and, therefore, to deny there is empirical evidence for these concepts is fact and if not fact, then mere opinion which does not discourage religion.

"Finally, I appreciate the concession that neither teacher Paul Kingston nor the East Grand Rapids school district was the proximate cause of Michelle Taylor's tragic death. Much of the public has scornfully accused each of being the cause of her death, unfairly maligning the reputation of Mr. Kingston and the district, which likewise cannot be restored with any monetary damages.

With all due respect, the case should be dismissed without relief of any kind." John Cleaver half turned to his find his chair and settled in.

"Thank you, Mr. Cleaver. Gentlemen, your openings were very helpful to the court. We are off to a good start. Now, let's take our morning break before the estate calls its first witness. I would like to see counsel in chambers." Owen stood and Frank Callahan quickly directed the entire court to rise as Owen swept through the door behind the bench.

Dexter and John stepped forward, shook hands, and walked into Owen's chambers, but not before John shot a frown at Kingman Walker's associate, Chad Bachman, who was sitting in the first row of the gallery.

"Gentlemen, please sit down. Very good job. Your openings were superb representations of your positions." Owen sat down in his desk chair, still draped in his robe, a condition John Cleaver took to be a negative sign.

"Thank you, your honor," Dexter and John responded simultaneously.

"I want to remind you this case is to be tried in my courtroom, not the media. I have never placed a gag order on counsel in a civil case and don't intend to start here. However, *The Grand Rapids Press* and the national media are working overtime to distort the issues in this case, and I will not be pressured by such outside influences. Is that understood?"

"Yes, your honor," Dexter and John chimed together.

"Good," Owen smiled and stood. "I have you singing in unison already. Are you sure you cannot settle this case?"

"Yes, your honor," Dexter and John voiced nearly simultaneously again, as all three men chuckled. Dexter and John exited the judge's office together, then went their separate ways.

Dexter paused as he left chambers, looking at the exiting crowd waiting for the elevators. He spotted Bachman and Jones anxiously waiting for an update from John Cleaver. Dexter frowned slightly. A quick trip to Kingman Walker's website last night confirmed his suspicion. Bachman was Robert Johnson's associate. Makes some sense Kingman might be interested in Cleaver as head of their planned office. Maybe they will let Judge Austin pick the winner, he thought to himself.

Dexter knew he should enter the side door to the courtroom and brief Vicki Taylor and Peter Diamond on the chambers' discussion, but found himself pausing. This had been the most momentous four months of his life, and his thoughts returned to the day it had started...

Chapter Three

Seeds Taking Root

Monday, June 8, 2009

"Any messages, Amy?" Dexter slowed only slightly as he neared his secretary's desk.

"Yes. I need your time, or I am leaving." Amy Gainer did not look up from her typing, handing Dexter a stack of pink messages with her left hand as he passed.

Dexter grabbed the messages, but Amy's comment stopped him in his tracks. "Why does every significant relationship I have with a beautiful woman end in the same line?"

Amy looked up, turned to him and deadpanned, "I can't speak for the others, but for this woman, it's just about the money."

Dexter took one long step of his six-foot-three-inch frame back to the front of Amy's cubicle. "Money...?"

"New firm policy—unless a timekeeper has recorded all monthly billable time entries into the firm's billing system by the middle of the next month, his secretary is docked her pay."

"Bastards!" Dexter exclaimed, half impressed with the creativity of the firm's management committee, since previous efforts to withhold his paycheck had produced no results. "That's blackmail. Are your sure this is a firm-wide policy or just directed at me?"

Amy sighed. "It is law firm wide, but I'm the only one presently affected." Amy paused on the contraction "I'm" for dramatic effect.

Dexter emitted a short soft laugh—it was all he dared—deferring to her humor, which always exposed at least one of his character flaws. "I'll go back to my desk and input all my May time before returning one of these messages."

"You have two things to do before you do that." Amy responded. "The second is to tell me all about your weekend with William."

"And... What could be more important than that?"

"You need to deal with Mrs. Frank Taylor, who is in your office," Amy whispered.

"Mrs. Frank Taylor? Mother of the young girl who..."

"Quiet..." Amy raised her forefinger to her mouth, nodding her head in agreement.

Most lawyer's offices are now only for working or "chewing the fat" with other lawyers. Typically, attorneys no longer allow clients to see their personal offices, much less enter them. Client meetings are usually held in sterile conference rooms strategically sprinkled across the office floor. As in so many things, in office approach, Dexter was a throwback. Dexter typically used his office for client meeting and carefully staged its decor. He hung only modern art—anything accessible might brand him as traditional. He tolerated no clutter—any papers might expose other client matters. He had no personal items—any pictures or diplomas might reveal his personal life.

Dressed in black, Mrs. Taylor was sitting with her back to his doorway in one of the four modern swivel chairs that adorned the small coffee table. Dexter knew that Taylor had moved to the coffee table on her own. As instructed, Amy always sat new clients in one of the two leather chairs facing Dexter's desk.

"Are you comfortable, Mrs. Taylor?" Dexter slid behind his desk, dropping his paper and carefully setting down his coffee.

As much as he sympathized with Mrs. Taylor, whom he knew had also lost her husband a few years earlier to a tragic accident, Dexter was not willing to lose control of his office. He chose to sit at his desk with the intention of inviting Taylor back to one of his client chairs.

"Most comfortable, Mr. Bussey. Thank you for asking." Taylor swiveled slowly towards him, her legs strategically crossed to draw attention to her still perfect calves, her blonde hair warmly contrasting with the color of her dress. "You don't mind if we sit here, do you," she asked, fully opening her eyes at Dexter. "I sprained my ankle over the weekend and it is painful to move."

Scanning Taylor's flawless ankles, Dexter felt flushed. He hadn't even introduced himself and was now making the first concession. "Of course not. Sorry to hear of you injury. Dexter Bussey," Dexter said weakly as he slipped around the desk and extended his hand.

While maintaining eye contact, Taylor patiently extended her hand without standing. After she left Dexter standing above her for a moment, she released his hand, "Sorry... You remember... The darn ankle?"

Feeling out of sync, Dexter took a seat and decided to defer an offer of coffee or water and plow into the substance. "What can I do for you and your ankles, Mrs. Taylor?"

"My fifteen year-old daughter Michelle was victimized, and I would like you to sue the perpetrators, Mr. Bussey."

Dexter blushed at the realization he had offered sympathy to Taylor for her ankle but not her daughter's death. "I am aware of your daughter's tragic death, Ms. Taylor. I am very sorry for your loss. I can't imagine your pain." Dexter looked straight into Mrs. Taylor's eyes.

"Thank you, Mr. Bussey, but I don't need your sympathy. What I need is to right an injustice contributing to the toxic mix of emotions that confused my daughter into believing death was preferable to life."

"And who were the perpetrators of this injustice?"

"A biology teacher and the administration at the East Grand Rapids high school," Taylor said matter-of-factly.

"I have often believed my career would not be complete unless I sued the scofflaws in the East Grand Rapids school system," Dexter tried to lighten the mood without appearing insensitive. For a second, he thought he had crossed that line.

Taylor was nonplussed. "I was told you were very handsome and disarmingly charming." She revealed a brief smile then reassumed a serious demeanor.

"What do you think so far?"

"An understatement on the looks, overstatement on the charm."

Dexter chuckled spontaneously, but also felt flushed again. "What did an East high school teacher and the high school administration do that could have contributed to you daughter's unfortunate death?"

Taylor paused for a minute, carefully choosing her words. "The teacher advised my daughter that the existence of creation is not evidence of a creator, denied there is any empirical evidence of the struggle between good and evil in the world, suggested her beloved father's untimely accidental death was a result of the positive forces of natural selection, and implied her belief in an after-life is magical thinking. The administration backed him on all fronts."

Dexter paused to let Taylor's recitation sink in and formulate an equally calculating response. "Let me be equally direct: I am not as religious as your daughter, the First Amendment may protect or even require the teacher's comments, the law requires a thick skin, and—although you have my full sympathy—a lawsuit is no salve for a broken heart. Shouldn't this be worked out with the administration informally?"

"I am not particularly religious myself and am a big fan of the First Amendment," Taylor's eyes burned into Dexter's, "but the last time I checked, the First Amendment also prohibits the discouragement of religious belief. I tried unsuccessfully to work this out informally with old man Morris, the high school principal, back when the school's corrective action may have made a difference to my daughter. I could care less about getting any money from EGR. I don't care about the education of anyone else's child. I am doing this for two reasons only: I want my only child and the only person whom I have selflessly loved to have the last word in this argument, which was so important to her, and I want the bastard teacher who was so insensitive to my daughter's emotional state to twist on the stand. I don't care how much money the case costs and will never agree to a settlement. I want a trial and I want to win."

"Lawsuits are an imprecise tool for retribution, Mrs. Taylor. Your daughter sounds like a sensitive, value-driven young lady. Wouldn't Michelle's memory be better served by building a homeless shelter?"

Taylor emitted a sarcastic cackle. "My husband Frank just turned over in his grave. He regularly railed at how college boys —which is what he would have called you—assuage their guilt by contributing money, although never time, to soup kitchens."

"So your husband was a self-made, religious man?"

"You just caused Frank to complete a three-hundred-and-sixty-degree turn. Frank was born into wealth and earned a PhD in molecular biology. He added to his family's considerable wealth through shrewd business practices. He was Michigan's richest oilman. You might say that Frank was a lifelong student of the human condition, but he wasn't charitable and he sure as hell wasn't religious. He was nothing if not a stubborn, original thinker. His only child, Michelle, was exactly the same way, except at this stage of her life anyway, she was deeply religious and very charitable."

Suspicious as to how this calculating woman had ended up in his office, Dexter probed: "Wasn't Ross Wagner your husband's attorney? His firm has a very competent litigation team. I would recommend Jack Seidman."

"Wagner's firm helps the scofflaws finance themselves. Besides, he said you were my 'man.'" Taylor arched her back, recrossed her legs and continued: "Wagner considers you to be the finest litigator in western Michigan, and you are his only recommendation for a case of this complexity."

"I'm flattered," Dexter offered without surprise. "Nonetheless, I don't take a case unless I know I can win, and floating around in the back of my head is the belief there is case right on point which won't let a public school teacher suggest there is an intelligent designer."

"Look, Mr. Bussey," Taylor leaned closer to Dexter, "I know you are busy lawyer and don't need this case. But your law firm does. Those legal beagles whose neat little offices I passed were merely polishing their newly framed sheepskins. They look hungry for meaty work. Your firm's transactional lawyers haven't closed a major deal in a year. And let's not even mention the commercial real estate lawyers. This case means hundreds of thousands of dollars in billable time you can't afford to turn away. So, I suggest you take one for the team."

Taylor paused and took a deep breath before continuing. "As I said, I don't want a dime in compensation from East Grand Rapids. In fact, the notion sickens me. And let me make this perfectly clear..." She leaned in for emphasis, "I don't want you to claim the classroom confrontation was the cause of my daughter's unfortunate suicide. I merely want my daughter vindicated and that bastard teacher to account for his insensitivity. Do I make myself clear?"

Taylor leaned back, satisfied.

Dexter marveled at Mrs. Taylor's poise. He also realized she had rehearsed her lines with a lawyer, probably Ross Wagner. "Let me take a five thousand dollar retainer as a sign of my good faith. I'll turn two of those little legal beagles lose and see if they can sniff a claim through the relevant law. And I will want to interview your daughter's friends. Then we can meet to see if there is a case to be made."

"I like a man who is in control," Taylor said while writing out a check. When she finished, she stood and handed it to Dexter. She pivoted and began walking out of his office, turning at the door to face Dexter. "I can find my way out. Don't forget to quickly spend that retainer. Before you start, let me fix your tie–the back half is facing the front." She walked back to him, straightened, pulled his tie up to his neck, and almost imperceptibly drew him close enough so he could feel her heat. After locking her eyes into his, she slyly smiled, turned, and sashayed down the hall as if it were a fashion show runway.

As Dexter emerged from his office, he chastised Amy, "Damn it, Amy. How could you let me go in there with a screwed up tie?"

"What did Mrs. Taylor do to you?" Amy questioned, open mouthed. "You went in riding on cloud nine and a half hour later you come out underneath a storm cloud."

"Never mind. Call Michelle Taylor's best friend and ask if she would be kind enough to meet me to discuss her friend," Dexter directed, as he gave Amy a note with a name and phone number that Taylor had shared with him, before taking a step back towards his office.

"I certainly will in a minute. But, first, I am dying to know about your overnight with William." Amy attempted to steer Dexter back to his former mood while also satiating her curiosity.

Dexter brightened. "The little fellow figured out on his own that I was his father. I took him to a monster movie, which I shouldn't have. Then back at home, I turned out the lights on him, which I shouldn't have. Together these mistakes drove the little fella into my arms seeking sanctuary, complaining that his 'daddy scared him.' Comforting my little tike was unlike anything I have ever experienced." Dexter beamed. "I may be a paternal savant."

"You sure it was the thought of monsters and not the realization you were his father that scared him?"

Dexter ignored the remark, unwilling to spar with another strong-willed woman. "Give me five minutes to recover and call Peter Diamond and Joe Stein. Ask them to come to my office for an assignment," he said as he retreated to the comfort of his desk chair, if no longer his office. An unsettled feeling had fallen over him—the kind that makes a man wonder if his life is getting off track.

* * *

John Cleaver smiled at the confirmation of his hunch. He knew his former partner well, he thought, as he had pulled alongside Keegan Riley's BMW in the Department of Natural Resources' parking lot outside of Baldwin, Michigan, along the banks of the Pere Marquette river, a little more than an hour north of Grand Rapids. Keegan Riley was a founder of John's law firm and almost exactly ten years older than John. Riley had retired from the firm and from the practice of law in a complete fashion. In fact, John wasn't sure Riley had graced the firm's lobby since leaving his retirement party ten years ago. Twice divorced without any children, Riley decided he had acquired enough money and retired to a life of fly fishing, traveling, and chasing any woman who tickled his fancy, making her part of a large and ever-changing set.

John had intended to invite Riley to lunch. When he didn't answer his cell phone, John surmised his mentor would be fly-fishing in his favorite spot on his favorite river. So, John grabbed his own rod, which hadn't seen any action in at least five years, and headed north for the morning. He was half hoping Riley wasn't there so he could enjoy the solitary effort of working the river.

John threw on his waders and began sloshing down the river, figuring Riley had at least an hour head start on him.

Forty-five minutes later he was still looking down river for Riley when he was startled by a gravely brogue directed from the river bank. "What do you want Cleaver?"

John had walked right past Riley, who was drinking a large cup of coffee from a tall silver thermos, but his camouflaged outfit blended into the fallen oak tree on which he was perched. When he saw the surprised, startled look on John's face, Riley roared with laughter.

"Glad I can still amuse you, Keegan," John responded good-naturedly but not without a twinge of annoyance.

"Sorry to do that to you, John. Then again, you know what they say, the older a man gets the more childlike he becomes."

"Who says that, Keegan? You would think that after forty years you would know your bull shit doesn't work on me."

Riley roared again. "You know, John, you are the only one at the firm I miss."

"A couple of young secretaries and me is what you really mean."

"Who says I am not still seeing them?" Keegan chuckled devilishly without missing a beat. "Actually, they aren't so young anymore!"

"And not nearly as naive," John added.

Riley stashed his thermos in his backpack, heaving both over his shoulder. In five large steps he met John in the middle of the river and the two men started gingerly picking their way across the bottom, careful to avoid both fallen tree limbs and the deeper holes in which the brook trout were hiding.

After twenty minutes of casting their lines on either side of the river and without looking at John, Riley said, "You didn't take the morning off to hassle me or to fly fish, John. What's eating you?"

"Oh, I guess the practice is just getting a little repetitious," John replied weakly.

"Fly fishing is repetitious. Doesn't seem to bother either one of us. Let's see, I suspect you have just finished this year's compensation committee meetings and are getting ready to pay the upcoming year's college tuition. You are wondering why you are stuck in a rut?"

John smiled for a moment, startled by the accuracy of his former partner's insight.

"If you want my advice, the moment after you write the last tuition check you will hand in your resignation from the firm and quit the legal practice. You should be close enough to that day to start coasting."

"But what about the law firm, Keegan? The firm you started, by the way," John wondered.

"You don't think I give a rat's ass about a law firm, do you John?"

"Not since we finished the last of your founder's fund payments three years ago." John smiled, returning his gaze to the river.

"You were stupid to make those payments. That was a scam Farhat and I put together. We never expected you guys to pay it all out."

"Now you tell me!"

Riley looked to the sky and bellowed.

"You guys deserved that money. You built the entire organization," John responded defensively after Riley had settled down.

"John, if you haven't figured this out yet, there is no organization. A law firm is merely a collection of individual lawyers bound together by last year's budget and this year's compensation pledge. It has no lasting identity or intrinsic purpose. Even the law is a scam. It is only a human construct designed to keep the masses in line and the pockets of the politicians and lawyers well lined."

"What was in that coffee? That's an extra jolt of cynicism even for you, my old friend."

"Well why did you get wet if you think I am all wet?" Riley smirked. "Eat, drink, and be merry, my buddy, because tomorrow we are dead and as cold as the river."

"Do you really believe there is no more to life than that?"

"Well... If there is a God, why has he blessed me?"

"Maybe he just can't figure out what to do with you," John answered with a wry smile.

"Maybe so, John... But he's just honored me with another 'brookie' while he was thinking about it."

* * *

Thirty miles to the west, Owen Austin found himself howling into a fairly stiff breeze. "Run free and enjoy our day at this beach, 'ole boy,'" Owen directed his seven-year-old west highland terrier as he released him from his leash and the dog sprinted down the beach after a sea gull. Owen sat on a beached white log ten feet from the surf and smiled to himself, amused by Caesar's unbridled enthusiasm. Although he had never owned a dog in his youth, as an adult he had become a dog lover. He admired the reliability of their affection and their consistent appreciation for even the smallest attention—a walk, a treat, a scratch behind the ear. Dogs were able to see into the human soul with their big, intense, usually friendly brown eyes. Dogs also never seemed to strive to become something that they weren't. Dogs showed no desire to evolve.

Caesar was his fourth dog and his second "Westie." He had owned a golden retriever when the girls were young, and after the first terrier, a Shetland sheep dog—a "sheltie." None were favorites. All were loved.

This was one of his favorite places—the "doggie beach," part of Pere Marquette beach, the pride of the city of Muskegon. During the May to September beach season, there weren't many public beaches that permitted dogs and their attendant issues.

His favorite hiking location was just to the north across the Muskegon River channel, Muskegon State Park. Traversing the steep wooded dunes never failed to transport him to a youthful mood, especially when he broke into the open dune land that separated the beach from the woods. Maybe after his lunch with Megan he would head to the state park.

Owen smiled slightly. He felt free from many of the concerns occupying his free time over the past few years—whether to find a condominium in Florida, whether the backyard should be re-landscaped, or whether it was worth fixing the dent in his Chrysler's rear quarter panel.

Still, there were a few new concerns. Owen had always taken his dogs to the doggie beach the day he put them down, giving them one last, gloriously free experience among earth's basic elements—wind, water, waves, and sand. He kept close memories of his three prior dogs on their last hoorahs, sometimes bounding, but usually at that point, ambling against the endless horizon. To Owen, the lazy Lake Michigan surf and beach framed the perfect goodbye portrait, a lasting tribute to his friends.

"Everything you need today is around you; everything you need tomorrow is beyond the horizon." Owen uttered softly but out loud in the general direction of Milwaukee, fifty miles across the lake.

"What brilliant philosopher is behind those wise thoughts?" Owen heard a voice from the beach behind him answer, and he turned to greet his daughter without getting up.

"Hi Judge," Megan said, not waiting for Owen to answer the question, the answer being familiar to both, since it had been one of Owen's favorite pontifications to his girls during their summer treks to the Lake Michigan shore.

Owen's smile turned south. "Can't you call me 'dad'?"

"This was a pleasant and unexpected surprise." Megan ignored her father's question, but lightened the mood as she had referred to Owen's invitation to meet for lunch. Megan, who was now past forty, lived with her husband and two boys, aged seventeen and fifteen, in Grand Rapids, but worked as a food services representative with a sales territory of tourist restaurants along the lakeshore. "It's not like you to take a day off in the middle of the work week."

"I have been neglecting Caesar, which you know is what I do to those closest to me. Besides, I haven't abandoned my work. I'm trying to figure out which case I am going to accelerate for trial and which lawyers are going to have their summers ruined." Owen smiled lightly as he picked up a written summary one of his clerks had prepared. He wasn't quite ready to give up his displeasure with the way this conversation had started. Megan's longstanding refusal to call him "dad" was a major sore spot to him and her last youthful rebellion. For some reason, she couldn't give up this little dig even after Susan had died. Her persistence surprised Megan as much as Owen.

"Let's review the candidates," Megan noted as she took the papers from Owen, sat down next to him, and quietly scanned the two page memorandum for thirty seconds. "Case number one looks like an anti-trust case. One party trying to unfairly squeeze out a smaller competitor and the competitor, in turn, trying to take the shorter path to riches. Case number two is obviously an environmental case. Government officials nobly protecting God's creation, irrespective of the damage to Michigan's floundering economy. Case number three is a prisoner suing the police for beating him up. Looks like the plaintiff deserved a beating, but not the one he got. Three pretty poor candidates, if you ask me," Megan concluded as she pinned the summary under the log so it wouldn't blow away.

"I'm afraid you are right," Owen said pensively as he located Caesar's position on the horizon. "You would have been a very good lawyer, Megan, but I'm now glad you didn't go into the practice."

"Wow! You are full of surprises, today." Megan was thinking of the heated battles with her father while in the throes of her decision to quit the University of Michigan's Law School after acing her first year. Megan had never seen her father so angry, so obviously disappointed she was throwing away her best chance for professional success and at the same time, declining to follow in his footsteps.

"Yeah. There was a time I thought the practice was better suited to women than men. Women better understand the human condition; men typically don't even understand themselves," Owen reasoned. "But now I realize that a woman's biological clock and the calendar for partnership in most law firms are incompatible. The practice takes too much time and energy away from parenting, a task at which you are superb."

"Overlooking the sexism, was there an apology buried within the compliment?"

Owen smiled and put his arm around his daughter. "Maybe there was, but if so, I have to confess I didn't intend it. Come on, let's round up Caesar and get some lunch. There's a bad hamburger joint on the beach. It isn't one of your accounts, is it?"

Looking up the beach, Megan smiled back, "No, your honor, you can't blame that one on me."

* * *

Back in Grand Rapids, Alex Ross was developing a story, only slightly guilty in the knowledge his real hunt was to solve a mystery for an audience of one. "Why do high school students with the whole world in front of them choose death over life, doctor?" Ross asked Dr. Adam Lambert, one of the area's foremost psychologists, as Nico turned on his camera.

"It is usually an impulse rather than a well thought-out decision," Dr. Lambert mused.

Struggling to get the images of May 13 out of his mind but also strangely energized, Ross had convinced his reluctant producer to allow him to follow up on Michelle's suicide with a generic piece on adolescent suicide.

"Are there warning signs that parents and friend should look for?"

"Well, there are the general signs of depression—loss of appetite, lack of interest in exercise and other routines, melancholy," Dr. Lambert listed, "but then again, the teens who kill themselves don't fit a particular pattern—some are loners, some are class leaders, some are followers—hence the phenomenon of copycat suicides. As an act, it is extremely hard to predict," Dr. Lambert added, causing Ross to wonder whether he was collecting anything his audience might find useful.

"If I had to look for a predictor, I would look to a significant loss—a loved one, a friend, the loss of a dream, of getting into a particular college or making an athletic team. Some fixture in their past or something they expected to be in their future is removed, shaking the psyche. And, then there's the trigger." Dr. Lambert paused. "There is usually something that drives the youth into action. Could be something seemingly trivial; could be something of momentary significance: a break up; a crush gone badly; some negative temporal event to which they over react."

"That's on the inside. Is there any common characteristic that all suicidal teens exhibit?" Ross wondered.

"The young people who commit suicide tend to be more serious than their peers, but I would say despair, alienation, and a loss of hope for the future are the principal characteristics they all share."

"And what causes human despair, alienation, and a loss of hope in the future?"

Dr. Lambert's eyes widened and an incredulous look fell over his face. After a moment, Nico turned off the camera.

* * *

Friday, June 13, 2009

"The intelligent design theory is a 'dog that won't hunt,'" smirked one of the legal beagles, Joe Stein, seated at Dexter's office table with his fellow associate, Peter Diamond. After a week of research, they were briefing their boss on *Kitzmiller v. Dover Area School District*, a case decided in November of 2005 in a federal court in Pennsylvania. "In a one-hundred-and-thirty-nine page opinion, Judge John E. Jones III clinically exposed intelligent design as nothing more than the repackaged creation science ruled unconstitutional in the nineteen-eighties. The judge held intelligent design isn't science because it postulates supernatural causation and because it isn't testable under any scientifically recognized methodology."

"Don't start with the conclusion, Professor Stein. What was the controversy? What did the school district do to prompt the lawsuit?" Dexter quizzed just five days after his initial meeting with Mrs. Taylor.

The chastened Stein started over. "The Dover school board approved a statement to be read to all ninth grade biology students. The statement noted the State of Pennsylvania requires the teaching of Darwin's theory of evolution and to take a standardized test about it. The statement characterized evolution as a theory still being tested with gaps for which scientists have theories, but no fossil evidence—the so-called 'missing links.' It implied intelligent design is a more viable alternative explanation for the origins of life, encouraging students to read a book called *Of Pandas and People* to learn more about intelligent design. It encouraged students to keep an open mind about all theories on the origins of life, implying that it had no choice but to teach evolution as an educational standard imposed by the state."

"That sounds fairly innocuous," Dexter responded. "I can't imagine how the court could tease a one hundred and thirty-nine page opinion out of a statement that could not have consumed a single page."

"It took a while to wade through the deceit of the statement's proponents, who wouldn't reveal their funding sources or motives in denigrating evolution and elevating intelligent design as a scientific principle on an equal footing," Stein offered.

"Judge Jones concluded the statement was a product of the 'contrived dualism' behind the creation science movement in the nineteen eighties," Peter Diamond interjected, assisting his peer. "Contrived dualism assumes evolution is incompatible with the existence of a creator, and therefore, the concepts of creation and science of evolution are mutually exclusive."

"What did that have to do with the plaintiff's cause of action in Dover?" Dexter wondered, his brow furrowing.

Stein continued. "Having found intelligent design to be a religious, not scientific, doctrine intimately associated with the origins of life as described in the biblical book of Genesis, Judge Jones found the statement violated the First Amendment's establishment clause by implying evolution was only being taught because the State of Pennsylvania required it and that it was filled with 'gaps,' while admitting no flaws in intelligent design and encouraging its further study and not evolution's. The totality of these features, Jones concluded, would clearly signal to a reasonable student that intelligent design was favored by the Dover district and evolution was an incompatible, disfavored alternative. In this manner, the statement failed the so-called 'endorsement test,' meaning under the totality of the circumstances the challenged practice conveyed a message favoring religion."

"The case was a forensic route," Peter Diamond said, picking up the analysis. "The plaintiffs were represented by the prominent Pepper Hamilton law firm headquartered in Philadelphia. They had a cogent strategy—cast intelligent design as a supernatural, not natural, explanation of the origins of life, and argue that by attacking the science of evolution, intelligent design was actually a threat to Christianity itself."

"How did they pull that rabbit out of the hat?" Dexter questioned.

"They were careful in calling expert witnesses not openly hostile to Christianity. In fact, their chief biological expert and first witness was Kenneth Miller, a Brown University professor and ardent Christian who set the stage perfectly. He excoriated intelligent design as a specious theory devoid of scientific support, and in a brilliant paean to the scholarly but also Christian judge, Miller ended his testimony by positing that as a committed Christian who dearly wanted his daughters to retain their faith, Miller feared that if his daughters were placed on the horns of the Dover statement's dilemma, which was to choose either science or faith, the likely victim would be their faith. Without a doubt, Professor Miller's scientific intellect and the clarity of his Christian parental fear was deeply influential on Judge Jones. In fact, I don't think it is an exaggeration to suggest the forty day trial was effectively over after the first witness."

"Where was the defense?" Dexter inquired.

"Good question," Diamond offered rhetorically.

"Peter is right," Stein added. "The defense was a conflicted mess. Start with the fact that the school district was represented for free by the Thomas Moore Law Center."

"The Tom Monahan sponsored society from Ann Arbor?" Dexter interjected, referring to the pizza chain founder.

"Yes. Can you imagine trying to argue intelligent design is not tethered to religion when you are an out-of-state, special interest Christian lawyer working for a fundamentalist Christian organization?" Stein posited. "Then, as if the legal team realized their conflict of interest at trial, they largely abandoned the intelligent design cause by spending their energy arguing the statement wasn't objectionable because it didn't teach intelligent design, implicitly conceding that such a teaching would be unconstitutional. In trying to save the statement and the district from their own cause, they argued the Dover statement only taught that a controversy existed between Darwinism and intelligent design. This tactic clearly angered the judge, who called it 'disingenuous' and found it either a canard or a reheated leftover of the 'teach both creation science and evolution' school board edict struck down by the United States Supreme Court in 1987 in *Edwards v. Aguillard*."

"The Pepper Hamilton troupe cross examined the intelligent design biologists with cellular tests that seemingly provided scientific support for the validity of evolution," Peter added. "The defense counsel obviously failed to prepare their experts for such a cross and failed to engage the plaintiff's experts on the differences between evolution and evolutionism, only exaggerating the rout."

"Why wasn't the matter tried to a jury?"

"Another brilliant strategy by the plaintiffs' counsel," Stein answered his boss. "The plaintiffs only asked for declaratory and injunctive relief and no significant damages, eliminating the district's Seventh Amendment right to a trial by jury."

"Was there an appeal?"

"One final example of quality lawyering," Diamond responded. "As the losing public party, the district was facing a two million legal bill and all the proponents of the statement were swept out of office during an election after the decision. Pepper Hamilton offered to cut its fees in half if the district did not appeal. The new board snapped up that offer."

"It wouldn't have mattered. Jones' analysis is air tight. An appeal would have gone nowhere. In fact, the case is so definitive, there hasn't been a serious second effort anywhere," Joe concluded.

"So where does that leave us?"

"Up shit creek without a paddle," Stein smugly concluded. "Judge Jones was the fundamentalists' best shot. A conservative Republican—an appointee of the younger Bush. The truth is that the EGR biology teacher was right: intelligent design is just magical thinking in the face of the scientific truth of evolution."

"Maybe," Peter Diamond agreed. "But, maybe not..." He slowly revealed a knowing grin that promised a strategy.

* * *

"Look Mr. Ross, your television station has been very good to the food pantry over the years. I can remember years when you were the face of the holiday spot, featuring our end of the year call for contributions, but I wasn't pleased with the piece you ran on Michelle when she died—a tragic death like that should remain a private matter." The director of the Wealthy Street Food Pantry, Aubrey Carpenter, crossed her arms and shot Alex Ross a look he hadn't seen since grade school.

"I understand completely, Ms. Carpenter. I really do," Ross agreed. "Michelle's death was only newsworthy because we accidentally captured it on our television spot. You know we intentionally blurred the pictures and we never released her name. That disclosure was the work of the national tabloids. I was deeply affected by her death and I am honestly trying to make some good of a senseless loss. Please help me in that task." Ross hoped a little honesty would advance his case again.

"How are you going to use this information, Mr. Ross?" a still skeptical Carpenter replied, not unfolding her arms.

"To be perfectly honest, I don't yet know. As you may be aware, right now I am doing a general piece on teenage suicide and this information may give me greater insight into the behaviors parents need to look for in children who might be considering harming themselves."

"You mean to suggest sensitive, serious children like Michelle who volunteer at the food pantry must have a screw loose?" Carpenter bristled.

"Of course not! But a prominent psychologist in town advised me suicidal teens are often more serious and sensitive than their peers. Those are wonderful traits, but perhaps they portend a troubled soul?"

Aubrey Carpenter sighed deeply and unfolded her arms, "Certainly, I never saw the pain Michelle must have been experiencing. She was a model volunteer. She was thoughtful, caring and dedicated in the two years she volunteered here. And she always made sure her mother donated generously to the cause. I often thought how proud I would be to have her as a daughter."

"What about her relationship with her mother?"

"What about it, Mr. Ross?"

"Did it appear to be a healthy relationship?"

Carpenter tightened her lips and her shoulders again.

"Ms. Carpenter." Ross softened. "I promise you all of these details about Michelle Taylor are only background and will only be used generically. If you have any doubts, think of the army of lawyers that Mrs. Taylor could dispatch against me and my station if I said anything negative, and from what I have heard about her, she wouldn't hesitate to do that."

Carpenter smirked, the argument obviously making sense to her. "Vicki Taylor is a beautiful woman with the kind of carriage even a gay man would notice. She knows it. She uses it to full, calculating advantage. I suspect, however, the more one gets to know her, the less attractive she becomes. Michelle was the opposite. Average looks, but the more time you spent with her, the more beautiful she became. I don't get many rich girls who choose to spend their free time stocking shelves and making small talk with our downtrodden clientele."

"So, there was tension in the mother-daughter relationship?"

It was Aubrey Carpenter's turn to soften. "Look, Mr. Ross, this poor woman has lost her husband and her daughter to tragedies. I have no doubt whatsoever Vicki Taylor loved Michelle very much. But they were as different as night and day. That is all I am saying."

"Thank you, Ms. Carpenter. I appreciate this very much. I don't seem to be able to eat lunch while on this story, so can I put twenty dollars into your collection jar?"

"Mrs. Taylor was kind enough to list our charity in Michelle's obituary, and I would be glad to add twenty dollars to the healthy total we have received in her honor."

"Perfect!" Alex Ross smiled as he left.

* * *

Dexter Bussey darted his convertible in and out of the late Friday afternoon traffic. He was already annoyed. There aren't many good days in Michigan to drive around topless, and this was definitely one of the few. Dexter felt like a geek driving through this perfect early summer weekend evening with his hard top up, but he was picking up his son for their first solo weekend together. Dexter wanted to show mom he was thinking only about what was best for their son.

This noble objective did not stop Dexter from daydreaming about mom's legs. Melissa Connelly owned the long, trim legs that supported an all-star collegiate volleyball career. As his car slowed in traffic, Dexter's mind wandered from Melissa's legs to the image—just three years old now—of a downcast Melissa waiting for him on his home stoop, as Dexter paid off the cabbie who had driven him home from the airport, returning from an out of state deposition. On that occasion, Dexter had slowly and quietly walked up his front sidewalk, sizing up the situation. Up until that moment his relationship with Melissa Connelly had been casual and, for Dexter, recreational.

As Dexter neared the stoop, Melissa blurted out, "I'm pregnant, Dex," without looking up. Before he could respond, she cut him off. "Yes, I'm sure. Yes, I'm also sure it's yours. No, I will not abort. No, I don't need you or your money. Yes, I am capable of handling this on my own."

We Hold These Truths

Dexter kicked out his right leg and knocked over his bag, "Well then why in the hell couldn't you have waited until I was in my kitchen and into two fingers of whiskey?" He could still remember thinking at the time that Melissa was close to bolting, but she regained her resolve and stayed moored to the stoop. Dexter remembered being impressed by her steadfastness and asking her, "So I know your plan for yourself. What is your plan for me?"

Melissa refused to look at him. "I don't want to see you during my pregnancy. When the baby is born, I would like two years to get him on a solid foundation. We could introduce you slowly over that time, but not as the father. After he is a toddler, we can reassess your role." Deferring to the fact he was the father and, probably more to the point, a lawyer, she added, "That would be my ideal approach to the situation, if you, of course, concur." She had offered plaintively, looking up at Dexter for the first time.

Dexter accepted Melissa's plan. Burying himself in his work and a small stable of reliable ex-girlfriends, he nevertheless regularly attended to Melissa throughout her pregnancy. Once William was born, he would periodically spend time with Melissa, pushing the stroller in the park or at the mall, and later, lounging at their favorite weekend breakfast haunt. William David Bussey displayed his father's full forehead, button nose and, most prominently, his big brown eyes. He carried his mother's thin, straight hair.

From the beginning, William was a charmer. People stopped to admire his physical attractiveness and marvel at his sunny disposition. Most unlike Dexter, William was fascinated with all things mechanical, so much so that Dexter nicknamed him "WD," short for the popular lubricant WD 40. After he learned to talk, as they had traveled around town in Melissa's small SUV, William would call out from his car seat, "crane!", "dump truck!", "bowdauser!" (for "bulldozer"), or his favorite, "cement truck!"

Victor Fleming

He was introduced as "Dexter," and William asked no questions about his relationship with Melissa. Dexter enjoyed these familial visits, learning to change diapers, feed, bathe, and dress the little one. Melissa and Dexter spoke on the phone regularly. She didn't ask him about his sex life and he didn't probe about hers, although he paid enough attention to satisfy himself she wasn't seeing anyone else. To date, Dexter hadn't been much inconvenienced at all by this style of parenting and was content to play a character to Melissa's starring role, even leaving to Melissa the job of preparing William for this weekend's new chapter.

As Dexter completely stalled in the Friday night traffic, his thoughts returned to the how quickly his life was changing. Fatherhood and now a chance at the brass ring with a Chicago firm. He was certain Melissa would be warm to the proposal of his opening an office in Grand Rapids and, hopefully, thereafter moving to the larger stage of Chicago. After all, Chicago owned a variety of fantastic restaurants; there were dozens of places for kids to visit—like the Shedd Aquarium, the Adler Planetarium, great museums and major league sports; and what woman wouldn't enjoy regular trips to the "Miracle Mile" on Michigan Avenue or an occasional evening in live theater? Melissa could easily land an even more rewarding position as a psychiatric nurse in Chicago.

These thoughts lightened Dexter's mood. He smiled with satisfaction as the traffic loosened and his sports car picked up speed. Yes, things were opening up perfectly.

* * *

Owen decided to close the work week with a stroll downtown. Everyone else seemed eager to flee the workplace to enjoy the summer weekend. Owen was carrying a contrarian mood. While on the bench in his courtroom earlier in the day, his thoughts were dominated by the memory of the eighth grader reciting the Declaration of Independence. "We hold these truths to be self-evident; all men are created equal..." How could the man penning these stirring thoughts own slaves? Owen thought to himself.

Without consciously heading there, he found himself at the Park Church doorway, heartened to find the back door open. The dark, stone-lined corridor was refreshingly cool. Quickly finding the columbarium where Susan's ashes were interred, he sat on the bench facing her remains. "I'll be joining you before you know it, sweetheart," he mumbled quietly, looking up at the stone etchings above the columbarium boxes. "Love the Lord with all your heart and your neighbor as yourself." Owen smiled, recalling the passage in Luke where this Old Testament phrase was repeated by the lawyer who, after impressing Jesus with his succinct summary of the Golden Rule, threw the good impression away by asking Jesus who his "neighbor" was, prompting Jesus to tell the parable of the Good Samaritan, foreshadowing Jefferson seventeen hundred years later—all men are your "neighbors."

"Didn't expect to see you here today, Judge."

Thoughts interrupted, Owen turned to see the warm face of his old friend, Reverend Maurice Felch, Park's senior minister.

"Maurice. Good to see you. Join me." Owen patted the empty end of the bench.

Felch slipped into the columbarium and sat next to Owen.

"I am taking a break from my Sunday sermon; you taking a hiatus from crafting some groundbreaking legal opinion?" Felch asked, breaking into a sly smile.

"Something like that..." Owen smiled.

They stared silently at Susan's columbarium niche, studying her memorial plaque.

"Time doesn't offer much solace, does it?" Felch broke the silence.

"Actually, Morris, that time moves so fast is of great comfort. Can you give me a hint as to Sunday's sermon?" Owen hoped to change the subject.

"My sermons have so little thunder, why would you want to steal it in advance?" Felch chuckled. "But, I can offer you the title: 'Socrates and Plato, the Lord's Apologists.'"

Owen strained to remember his Greek philosophy. "Ah... You are referring to the teleological argument for the existence of the supernatural: the presence of logic and scientific laws reveals the existence of the supernatural. I see something like that in the common sensibilities of most juries."

"Yes, you could argue that Socrates and Plato were the founders of intelligent design theory."

"What happened to Aristotle?" Owen asked, reaching the end of his memory.

"Aristotle believed the world has always existed, and therefore, its laws are a scientific given embedded in everlasting nature. Aristotle was the great naturalist of his time."

"I am not sure we have advanced the debate much in the last two millennia, have we?" Owen noted.

"Ironically, Aristotle's reason for the rejection of the supernatural is the one argument that science has subsequently disproved."

"How is that, Morris?"

"Modern physics has traced time and beginning of the universe to the Big Bang, some thirteen billion years ago. Prior to that explosion, time and the physical world as we know it did not exist."

"Interesting... Am I now free of my Sunday obligation?"

"That's what I think you call a 'loaded question.' Certainly, I am not going to answer it." Felch chuckled as the two men rose and walked out of the columbarium, the minister shutting off the lights. "Have a great weekend either way, Judge." Reverend Felch palmed Owen's back before shuffling into the deeper, darker recesses of the cool basement.

Owen stepped out of the stone church into the warm sunlight. He stood and waited for a moment as his eyes adjusted. He was tired, his head hurt and his spirit flagged.

We Hold These Truths

Enough thinking for a day—enough thinking for the week. Time to go home and feed the dog.

Chapter Four

Close Testimonies

Monday, November 2, 2009

(Afternoon of the Opening Day of Trial)

Nearly two seasons later, the weather was fifty degrees cooler outside and ten degrees cooler inside his courtroom when Owen returned to the bench after the opening arguments and his morning recess.

Dexter Bussey called Madelyn Wysocki to the stand as his first witness. After establishing certain background facts, Dexter probed her relationship with her good friend Michelle Taylor:

Q.   Were you a friend of Michelle Taylor?

A.   Best friend.

Q.   What was Michelle like as a friend?

A.   Loyal, caring–cool.

Q.   What was Michelle like as a person?

A.   Michelle was the best. She was smart but never talked down. She cared about people. She never dissed anyone.

Victor Fleming

There was no sound in the courtroom. One could have heard a pin drop.

Q.   Was Michelle religious?

A.   Yes. After her father died, she got into my church and became a serious Christian.

Q.   What was your perception of Christianity's influence on Michelle?

A.   Gave her life meaning. She was looking for meaning—for something real, especially after what happened to her dad.

Q.   You mean her father's death?

A.   Yup.

Q.   When did her father die?

A.   He died about two years before Michelle did.

Q.   How did he die?

A.   A bus hit him when he was on business in Chicago and was crossing a street, but he also had ALS... Bad.

Q.   What aspect of her religious belief do you think gave meaning to Michelle's life?

A.   It gave her hope—that she would see her father again. Religion explains that good beats evil.

Q.   Did you attend freshman biology class with Michelle?

We Hold These Truths

A.   Yes, sir.

Q.   Where you present when Michelle had an emotional discussion with your biology teacher?

A.   Yes. You're talking about the day Mr. Kingston taught evolution?

Q.   Yes. What happened, in your observation, that triggered Michelle's emotions?

A.   Mr. Kingston said that premature death is a part of natural selection; that it is part of the 'survival of the fittest' thing.

Q.   Did Michelle react to that?

A.   Yes. It obviously pissed her off.

Madelyn looked to Owen. "I'm sorry, your honor."
Owen looked over his glasses and stared at her, breaking his serious look with just a hint of a smile. "You may continue."

A.   It set her off. She said that death is here because there's evil in the world. Death is not natural.

Q.   What response, if any, did she get to that argument?

A.   Mr. Kingston said she was talking about religion, and public school teachers can't talk about religion. He said he could only talk about stuff that can be proved by science. He said there is no scientific proof of God or even that good or evil exist.

Q.   Did Michelle appear to accept this explanation?

A.   No. She was pissed.

Nervous laughter spread through the taunt courtroom, which Owen gaveled down. Madelyn turned beet red and turned to Owen. "I am so sorry, Judge... I am really nervous," she pleaded.

"Apology accepted," Owen said sternly, this time without a hint of a smile.

Dexter quickly moved on:

Q.   Did Michelle saying anything to Mr. Kingston?

A.   She wanted to know if Mr. Kingston was implying that the Holocaust wasn't evil.

Q.   Did Mr. Kingston respond to that question?

A.   Yes. He said that you can't scientifically prove that murder is wrong—that these are just value judgments that have evolved over millions of years like our biology.

Q.   What did Michelle say, if anything, to that declaration?

A.   Michelle asked Mr. Kingston who created the first plant or animal.

Q.   How did your teacher respond to that question?

A.   He said that there is no science on those issues and public school teachers cannot speculate on those questions.

Q.   Is that how the discussion ended?

We Hold These Truths

A.   No, Michelle wouldn't give up. She asked him if he was saying that there is no God or no afterlife.

Q.   How did Mr. Kingston answer those questions?

A.   He said he was just saying that there isn't any evidence of God or any other creator of the world. He said there just isn't any proof of a soul or afterlife. We can't talk about it further in the public school.

Q.   Did the discussion end there?

A.   Mr. Kingston explained that science and religion don't mix and said that scientists believe that of all human fantasies, the hardest to give up is the belief that consciousness exists after death.

Q.   Did you observe how this affected Michelle?

A.   She became even more upset. She said something like, "Are you calling religious belief 'fantasy?'"

Q.   And how, if in any way, did Mr. Kingston respond?

A.   He said, "Dear..." I remember he said it like that, which I didn't think was cool. He said, "I am not calling it 'fantasy,' but we can't speculate about beliefs in biology class. We can only talk about things that are real. We can't speculate about the possible existence of a creator." Then Billy Fowler, who was also in that class, said, "Yeah, this isn't Sunday school, Taylor."

Q.   Did the rest of the class react?

A.   They laughed.

Madelyn's voice rose and thinned, and her eyes began to well up.

Q.   Did Michelle react?

A.   Yes. She dug in. She said something like, "Hitler was the ultimate evolutionist and thought he was just helping the natural selection process along with the Holocaust. Maybe the world should have just let him keep killing, and we wouldn't have global warming." She was very emotional. Not crying, but on the verge.

Q.   How did Mr. Kingston deal with that?

A.   He said, "Michelle, there is no scientific evidence of the struggle between good and evil in the world. We have to concentrate on real things, not magical thinking."

Q.   Did this comment seem to affect Michelle?

A.   She wouldn't give up and asked if he was saying values don't exist.

Q.   What, if anything, did Mr. Kingston say in response to that?

A.   He said something like, "Scientifically, social values are not from a creator but come from" something he called 'memes'—I think is how he pronounced it. He said memes are values lessons transferred verbally from generation to generation until they become biologically encoded.

Q.   Did Michelle ask any more questions?

A.   She asked Mr. Kingston if he was denying that we are born believing that all men are equal. And he said something like, "Right and wrong and good and evil are man-made values encoded by repetition."

Q.   How did Michelle react, if at all, to that statement?

A.   Michelle's voice was high pitched and she was starting to cry. She asked Mr. Kingston where his scientific proof was that good and evil, right and wrong, and human equality are only created by humans and only transmitted by humans to one another through repetition.

Q.   Did your teacher respond?

A.   Yes. He said, "Dear, you provided the evidence yourself —the evidence is testimony that only people can give. 'Social science' and our experience are the opposite of magical thinking."

Q.   What happened next?

A.   The class laughed again, and Michelle bolted out of the classroom.

Q.   What did you do?

A.   As soon as school got out for the day, I went straight to Michelle's house to see how she was doing. By this time, her mother had already been to talk to the school.

Q.   What was Michelle's mood when you saw her?

A.   She was stoical. It was strange. She wasn't mad at Kingston. She blamed the problem on the school. She said something like, "The school has the teachers who believe in God so afraid to mention religion that we can't even talk about how we got into this world or how we got values or where we are going when we die." She thought this stuff was all relevant to evolution. She was mad at the school, not Kingston.

Q.   Did she say anything that concerned you about her mental state?

"Objection, your honor." John Cleaver bolted out of his chair. "That question asks the witness to speculate and draw conclusions."
"I will rephrase, your honor?" Dexter responded.
"Please do," Owen admonished.

Q.   What do you remember her saying, if anything, after she blamed the school district?

A.   I remember her clearly stating, "If Kingston is right, there's no point to life. Nothing at all matters."

Q.   When did she kill herself after that statement?

A.   Two weeks later, she went downtown...

At that, Madelyn broke down and cried softly.
"Let's take a ten minute break," Owen said as he looked to Sarah, who was already reaching behind her for a box of tissues for Madelyn. Owen swept off the bench and out the rear door behind his chair.

Frank Callahan moved towards Madelyn with a glass of water. "Take this, young lady," he said as Sarah stood up and left through the back door.

"You did great, Madelyn," Dexter offered. "Just a few more minutes when we resume."

Fifteen minutes later, court resumed with Dexter formally passing the witness to John Cleaver, who spoke gently:

Q.   Ms. Wysocki, I'm looking at your scholastic record. You have received all A's at East Grand Rapids, is that correct?

A.   Yes sir.

Q.   Do you know what you want to be when you complete your education?

A.   No sir. Although I am thinking about law.

At this comment, there was a general chuckle from the audience. Judge Austin immediately gaveled it down and chided the spectators, "The gallery will remember my instructions."

Q.   I think you should continue to give the law thought. We can always use more thoughtful, smart people entering our profession. Coming back to your academic record, I note that you received a straight 'A' from Mr. Kingston in the class that you are describing, is that correct?

A.   Yes sir, that is correct.

Q.   You saw Michelle several hours after the incident, and by that time she was calm, is that true?

A.   Yes, sir.

Q.   And she wasn't mad at Mr. Kingston, correct?

A.   Correct.

Q.   And she had directed her frustration at some policy of the administration, correct?

A.   Yes.

Q.   Did you know what policy she was talking about?

A.   No, sir.

Q.   Do you know today what policy she was talking about?

A.   No, sir.

Q.   Have you ever witnessed any similar conflict in the classroom about evolution and Christianity?

A.   No, sir.

Q.   Have you ever witnessed any similar conflict in the classroom about the scientific method and Christianity?

A.   No.

Q.   I know this is tough for you, Ms. Wysocki, but bear with me. Although Michelle Taylor was a serious girl, and despite the upset of this day, which had calmed when you saw her, you didn't suspect that she would take her life, did you?

A.   No, sir.

Q.   You don't know why she took her life, did you, even
       though you were her best friend?

A panicked look immediately fell over Madelyn. She froze.
Finally, Owen straightened in his chair and then leaned forward.
"Ms. Wysocki. Can you answer Mr. Cleaver's question?" Panic
was replaced with fear and then horror on Madelyn's face.

A.   No. I can't.

Without making a sound, she suddenly bolted from the
chair, burst through the swinging doors at the bar and sprinted
down the center aisle and out the courtroom door. The audience
gasped.

One of the marshals followed her to the doorway, looking
anxiously at Owen, waiting for instructions as to whether he
should catch and fetch Ms. Wysocki.

Owen stood as the crowd began to buzz. Owen looked at a
startled John Cleaver, still at the dais. John regained his
composure, shrugging his shoulders.

Owen looked up and shook his head sideways, and the
marshal retreated. He then struck his gavel so hard it bounced
back into his arm. "Ten minutes. Counsel in chambers in five."
He swept out the door with a frustrated glance at Dexter Bussey.

Dexter was still recovering when a calm, low voice next to
him said softly, "Let her go. She'll be fine." Vicki Taylor was
staring straight ahead, her eyes unfocused.

Meanwhile, Alex Ross was on the run... Again. He had
sprung from his seat next to Keegan Riley in the last row in the
courtroom, where he had been furiously scribbling notes, and
followed the marshal into the lobby.

"She headed down the steps, Mr. Ross. Someone should go
after her," the marshal declared.

"Same thought here," Ross responded as he hit the stairwell door. He could hear Madelyn's steps at least two floors ahead of him. Ross was surprisingly fit for a fifty-four year-old, heavy-smoking, hard-drinking journalist who relied only on a nervous metabolism and haphazard diet to stay trim. He used his right arm on the stairwell railing to project himself down chunks of stairs at one time. He could hear Madelyn's heels clicking at a hurried, rhythmic pace that nevertheless told him that she was taking one step at a time. He caught her the moment she crashed through the stairwell door to the Calder Plaza. As Ross reached for Madelyn's right bicep with his left hand, he was surprised to find that she fainted in his grasp. Fortunately, he was able to slightly toss her up with his left arm, then skip behind and catch her in a bear hug before she collapsed. She immediately came back to consciousness, although Ross' quick glance at her eyes showed them to be more than slightly glazed.

"Come on, Madelyn. Walk with me. My car is in the open lot fifty yards away. I have a bottle of scotch in the glove compartment. We could both use a shot..."

* * *

"Damn it, Bussey! Don't you have your witnesses prepared for the courtroom?" Owen turned and burst, startling Bussey and Cleaver.

"I'm sorry your honor," Dexter offered plaintively. "That came totally out of left field. She gave me no indication that she would react so emotionally."

"She is a teenager, your honor," John Cleaver cut in, rising to Dexter's defense and earning a grateful glance from Dexter.

Owen stood and leaned over his hands, which were each firmly planted on his desk. He exhaled deeply and closed his eyes for a moment, which further startled the two lawyers standing in front of him.

"All right." Owen opened his eyes and regained his composure. "Are you finished with Ms. Wysocki, gentlemen?"

"I am, your honor," John said softly.

"I am as well, Judge," Dexter offered.

"Okay. Who's next? Mrs. Taylor?"

"Yes, your honor," Dexter said, relieved that the judge had calmed.

"Be out in five minutes, gentlemen," Owen offered weakly. "Thank you. Let's push through lunch and finish one more witness and then break for the day." He rubbed his forehead and turned toward the window, signally the end of the conference.

As they moved into the secured hallway outside of Owen's chambers, John turned to Dexter. "Dexter, do you have any idea what happened to Wysocki?"

"Honestly, John, I've asked her the very same question several times and she never lost her composure. Truly, I have no idea."

"Well, I compliment you for not pursuing damages so we don't have to push this issue.

"Compliment the next witness, John, not me."

"Maybe I will, Dex, maybe I will." John smiled and gently slapped Dexter on the back as they entered the courtroom and moved to their separate tables.

Dexter met Taylor's eyes as he neared the table. "Five minutes and you are on, Vicki. Are you ready?"

"Of course," she offered stoically before breaking into the slightest of smiles.

"Mrs. Taylor, do you swear to tell the whole truth and nothing but the truth, so help you God?" Owen asked ten minutes later after rescaling the bench.

"Yes, your honor."

"Mr. Bussey, your witness," Owen commanded.

Q.   Thank you. Would you state your whole name for the record?

Victor Fleming

A.   My name is Victoria Taylor.

Q.   Can you describe your family situation?

A.   I am a widow, my husband Frank having died a little over two years ago. I had one daughter, Michelle, who died earlier this year. Michelle, as we know, had just completed her freshman year at East Grand Rapids high school.

Q.   What was your daughter like, Mrs. Taylor?

A.   I would agree with Madelyn Wysocki's general assessment. She was serious but very loving and caring. She could seem tough, but she was a very sensitive soul.

Q.   How old was Michelle when her father died?

A.   She was thirteen years old.

Q.   How did he die?

A.   My husband contracted ALS, which is a devastating neurological condition. As you may know, it is a cruel disease that eventually paralyzes the entire body. He was fifty-six when he was first diagnosed, and it progressed steadily until he died at age fifty-eight when he accidentally stepped in front of a bus in Chicago and was killed instantly.

Q.   Was Michelle close to her father?

A.   She was very close. His illness and the tragic way he died were devastating to her.

Q.   How did she respond?

A.   As Madelyn testified, she became very religious—very serious in her Christianity.

Q.   What is your understanding of why she turned to religion?

A.   She was trying to make sense of life—to find meaning in life. She saw the world in terms of good and evil and wanted victory over that evil. She also viewed it as the only way to have hope of seeing her father again.

Q.   Do you recall the day of her confrontation with Mr. Kingston?

A.   Of course. I will never forget it. She came home mid-day from school crying and rushed to her bedroom.

Q.   What did you do?

A.   I went with my housekeeper Anna, who was a second mother to Michelle, to find out what was wrong.

Q.   What did she say had happened?

A.   She relayed much of the dialogue to which Madelyn described in detail.

Q.   What was her mood?

A.   She was very emotional.

Q.   What was your response?

A.   I was furious. I left Anna to comfort Michelle and headed to East Grand Rapids high school to see the principal.

Q.   What made you so angry?

A.   I was furious that a public school teacher would deny the existence of God, suggest that there is no evidence of good and evil in the world, and imply that belief in an afterlife is magical thinking. And the crack about premature death being the tool of natural selection to clean out the gene pool was beyond the pale to a young woman who had recently lost her father to a cruel disease.

Q.   What response, if any, did you receive from the school?

A.   The principal reported that Mr. Kingston was simply following the district's interpretation of the First Amendment and refused to discipline the man.

Q.   How did you respond to that?

A.   Well, I contacted our family's lawyer and then, eventually, retained you and your firm to investigate and pursue the issue.

Q.   What, if anything, resulted from that?

A.   A statement separating evolution from atheism was presented to the school board, which apparently refused to implement it, necessitating this lawsuit.

Q.   Was your daughter alive when you presented your statement to the school board?

A.   No. She took her life a little over two weeks after the incident.

Q.   Was she apprised of the school's support for Mr. Kingston?

A.   Yes. I informed her of the principal's refusal to take any action against the teacher or to redress the situation.

Q.   What was her reaction, if any?

A.   She was stoical. She did not seem surprised. In fact, as Madelyn testified, she blamed the administration, not the teacher.

Q.   What was her emotional state between the incident and her death?

A.   She was never emotional again after that date. I suppose I should have been concerned, but frankly, I was relieved that on the surface she seemed fine. In hindsight, she must have been depressed.

Q.   Are you asking the court to find that the incident with Mr. Kingston was the cause of your daughter's death?

A.   No, I am not. Who knows what causes a fifteen-year-old with her whole life ahead of her to take that life? I am not asking for damages or a causal finding because I don't think we can sufficiently prove that. However, that doesn't mean it wasn't part of the toxic stew that contributed to her decision. I very much believe that it was a contributing factor to her suicide and a very traumatic event that should not have happened.

Q.   What are you asking of the court?

A.   I am asking for the court to find that my daughter's constitutional rights were violated because her religious beliefs were discouraged. I would ask the court to order the district to utilize something like the statement that my lawyers' drafted and that I authorized for presentation to the district.

"Thank you, Mrs. Taylor. Your honor, I have no further questions at this time," Dexter reported.

"Thank you, Mr. Bussey," Owen said. "Mr. Cleaver, your witness."

Chad Bachman immediately approached John Cleaver and Greg Jones and whispered, "You should ask her if she's a Christian."

"What for?" John asked in a slightly irritated tone.

"If she says 'yes,' it goes to her motivation and suggests that she's aligned with the Joe Blocks of the world. If she says 'no,' it will suggest that she isn't serious about the suit and that it's merely to extract retribution," Bachman argued.

"Makes sense to me, John," Jones chimed in.

"I don't like it. It's only marginally relevant, if at all, and it seems too personal. My instinct says no."

"Two to one." Bachman smiled in a way that John found disrespectful.

"Mr. Cleaver?" Owen asked, looking over his reading glasses.

"Ready, your honor... Mrs. Taylor, good afternoon."

"Good afternoon, Mr. Cleaver."

Q.   I have only a few questions. Your daughter was deeply affected on all levels by her father's horrific death, is that true?

A.   I would agree.

Q.   I appreciate your concession that you cannot establish the cause of your daughter's tragic decision to end her life, but would you also agree that whatever impact the incident in biology class had, the loss of her father was far greater in its impact?

A.   I would not disagree with that proposition.

Q.   Prior to the incident that brings us to court today, had you daughter ever complained about the East Grand Rapids school district's curriculum as it related to her faith?

A.   Not to my recollection.

Q.   And the incident was not repeated in the two weeks or so after the incident to your knowledge, correct?

A.   Not to my knowledge.

Q.   So, this appears to have been a one-time incident?

A.   Yes, although the school district refused to treat it as such.

Taylor's eyes did not waiver from John's, and her face revealed no emotion at all. The courtroom was completely hushed, without a sneeze or cough in the gallery. Owen leaned back slightly in his chair and was taking no notes, just watching

Mrs. Taylor testify. John Cleaver stood erect at the lectern, occasionally glancing at his notes, but also taking none and trying to make as much eye contact as possible. However, he was obviously uncomfortable with the intensity of Mrs. Taylor's gaze.

Q.　Your original intention in going to the school was not to change the curriculum, but to have Mr. Kingston reprimanded, is that true?

A.　I wouldn't quibble with that description.

Q.　The statement that you authorized to be sent to the school board—the one that triggered this lawsuit—you didn't prepare it, did you?

A.　No, sir.

Q.　Who did, if you know?

"Objection, your honor. That question calls for privileged communications."

"Based on Mr. Bussey's representations, I will withdraw that question, your honor."

Owen nodded.

John Cleaver paused. "Mrs. Taylor, are you a Christian?"

John expected an objection, but he received none. Vicki Taylor paused, gathering her thoughts.

"I hope you aren't offended by that question," John added, disquieted by her pause.

A.　I am not offended, Mr. Cleaver. I haven't seen much evidence of a loving God. But, then again, I know I loved my husband and my daughter, and I don't see nature engendering much love, either. So, I would say that, like the First Amendment, I am neutral on the subject. I certainly don't see any reason why the public schools cannot consider all creation theories.

"I have no further questions." John smiled as he sat down, but inside he was seething, resolving that this would be the last time he would trust Jones or Bachman over his instincts.

"No redirect, your honor," Dexter joined.

Owen did not respond. He was staring at the portrait of Jonas Drummond, an early-twentieth-century judge, on the side wall above the empty jury box behind Dexter. Taylor's last comment had given him pause. He had often entertained the thought that there was no God, but it surprised him to think that he had never seriously considered the possibility of a creator God who was non-loving or disinterested. Given what Mrs. Taylor had been through and what Susan went through, the prospect of an uncaring creator suddenly struck him as depressingly possible. Only the realization that a fidgeting crowd was watching him shook him out of his reverie.

"Thank you, gentlemen. I think we will rest for the day. We will see you all at nine a.m., sharp." As he passed through the jam of the door to his chambers, Owen stole one last glance at Jonas Drummond and had to suppress a desire to laugh out loud at the absurdity of the former judge's grossly dated countenance.

* * *

Alex Ross slipped into the soft light of the Lumber Baron Bar in the stately Grand Plaza Hotel and quickly located Keegan Riley nursing his second whiskey sour at the bar.

"I've been in this bar in a hundred locations," Riley mused without looking at Ross. "They must share the same interior decorator. There's always a menagerie of black-and-white photographs of urban buildings and urbane movie stars and then one stiff figured oil painting of a fox hunt. I wish just once that they would install oil paintings of movie stars and buildings and a black-and-white photograph of a fox hunt."

"Keegan, you need to go back to work. The things you think about are scaring me away from retirement," Ross said as he slid onto the stool next to Riley.

"What do you mean? I worked in the courtroom all day today. The only thing that's changed is the compensation. I'm only working for drinks now." Riley chuckled into his whiskey.

"Thanks for the text report on Mrs. Taylor's testimony."

"Like I said, I'm working for drinks now, and I wouldn't want to compromise your expense account." Riley turned and smirked. "Nice report on the evening news. I almost forgot you missed half of the testimony today. How's the kid?"

"I'm afraid high school students aren't kids anymore, Keegan."

Riley burped. "High school students have never been kids. So tell me, why did Ms. Wysocki bolt out of the courtroom?"

Ross looked towards the bartender, pointed to Riley's drink, and put two fingers in the air. When he realized Riley hadn't broken his stare at him, he said, "I guess the reality of the loss of her friend and the intensity of the courtroom experience just overwhelmed her."

"Never lie to a lawyer, Ross, you should know that by now. Actually," Riley corrected himself, "never lie to a lawyer who isn't a tax or criminal defense lawyer, of which I am neither."

Fortunately for Alex, the Joe Block Show came on the television and sucked up their attention.

"Michelle Taylor wasn't asking her teacher to embrace or teach intelligent design," Block started slowly, "and it wasn't the teaching of evolution that caused Michelle Taylor's emotional distress. It was the teacher—Kingston's belittling of her beliefs about human equality and the inherent dignity of man, and his saying that good and evil are inconsistent with science. Even worse, he discouraged her religious beliefs by belittling her belief in an afterlife as magical, unsophisticated thinking. Gregory Morse joins me. Gregory is a prominent constitutional trial lawyer. My friend, what do you think of this first day of trial?"

"Well, Joe, lawyers learn in first-year constitutional law class that the First Amendment is a two-edged sword. A public school cannot endorse religion, but it also cannot discourage religious beliefs. This should be an encouragement action, but I'm afraid after today, despite claims to the contrary, the plaintiff is really limiting herself to a discouragement action. What I mean by that is that it doesn't appear that the plaintiff is going to employ a frontal attack on the New Darwinists. All she asks for is a statement neutralizing the evils of evolution, not an injunction neutering the amoral pseudo-science."

"Amen, brother." Block nodded. "This is the same milk toast mistake the Dover school district made four years ago."

"Exactly. The problem with evolution as it's presently presented in the public schools is that the dualism Judge Jones found in *Dover* isn't only contrived by the advocates of intelligent design. Imagine if the *Dover* plaintiffs had called Richard Dawkins or Jeffrey Coyne as their first witness. You know, the eminent English biologist and University of Minnesota biologist, respectively. These are the leaders of the so-called 'New Darwinists.'"

"Assume for the moment that we don't recall these biologists' arguments," Block interjected.

"They believe that the principles of Darwinism have proved that a personal God does not exist," Morse explained. "They belittle all Christian evolutionists as pantheists who believe that nature and God are the same thing. They turn intelligent design on its head, arguing that because the capacity for design comes later in the evolutionary process, there couldn't have been a designer present at the beginning of the process when all the elements of life were simple. They are openly hostile towards all things religious."

"This is exactly what I have been saying for years. Don't fight with one hand tied behind your back. The evolutionists are promoting science and atheism as the same thing. They are prophets of atheism."

"Exactly, Joe. These biologists are as zealous as any Christian lawyer in the Thomas More Society," Morse continued. "They have disdain for the language in First Amendment law that prohibits the discouragement of religion. In fact, they consider religion to be behind all terrorism and the conflicts of the Middle East and, therefore, the root cause of the current threats to national security. They would want the public schools to actively discourage 'magical thinking,' as the East Grand Rapids teacher was bold enough to describe religious thinking."

"Evolution is bunk," Block nearly shouted, "'man came from the Almighty, not a monkey!' That's the 'statement' Bussey should be focusing on, not this mealy-mouth, wimpy statement that he has drafted and is passing off as the cornerstone of his case!"

"Exactly," Morse intoned.

Riley upended his rock glass and then slapped it on the bar as he turned to Alex Ross. "These TV lawyers have never tried a case. What a sham. Bussey's statement is brilliant, Alex; it's the transmission that drives his case. Without it, there would be no school policy in play."

"Yeah, but laymen don't get the big deal," Ross answered as he upended his own glass. "I'll bet it seemed a little tame to Vicki Taylor when it was first presented. She looks like a woman more interested in action than words."

"You've been spending too much time with me," Riley chuckled.

"So you think Bussey has a chance?" Ross wondered, tuning out Block and his sidekick.

"No way. Austin is too intelligent, too traditional, too strong a jurist. Besides, he relishes his reputation. To rule in Bussey's favor would make him a laughingstock to the men whose opinions of his intellect matter most—like me." Riley returned to his drink and smiled.

When the last jab failed to get a rise out of Ross, who was staring straight ahead and whose mind had drifted away, Riley rose from the bar, slapped Ross on the back, and leaned close to his ear. "You'll tell the Irishman the truth about Wysocki's flight eventually. Everyone tells me the truth in time." With that, Keegan Riley ambled out of the bar, the lobby of the hotel, and into the chilly November air.

* * *

Ross Wagner stood on the Taylors' expansive wooden deck, sullenly scanning the still lake shimmering in the crescent moonlight. He could not bear to focus on Vicki Taylor, who was a hundred feet below him sitting on the beach, dry sobbing. Although she would never admit it, he knew she was agonizing over whether she had made a mistake in bringing this lawsuit and exposing herself and her family to this form of public scrutiny, especially so soon after Michelle's death. Non-lawyers never understood the difficulty of testifying, especially on a subject so close to one's emotional core. He had known the lawsuit was a mistake, but Taylor was committed to casting this ship into uncharted waters. Wagner knew that it was now best to maintain his distance and wait to be summoned.

Chapter Five

Cultivating the Case
Monday, June 16, 2009

Four months earlier, the suit's risks did not seem emotional. Dexter was seated at his desk facing Mrs. Taylor one week after their first meeting. "Here's the deal. We don't yet have a lawsuit. We may never have a lawsuit to file. I don't think we can sue Mr. Kingston personally, which is probably just as well because I am quite sure he didn't know he was violating a clearly established right. As a result, his good faith immunity protects him from liability. We can't effectively sue the district at present since we cannot articulate, much less identify, a district policy or practice violating Michelle's constitutional rights. The best way to achieve your goals is to present a statement differentiating evolution and religion reflecting what Michelle wanted to discuss and ask the district to embrace it as policy."

"I told you I want a lawsuit and a trial." Taylor glared.

"Don't worry. The chance East Grand Rapids will accept our statement is slim to none."

Taylor paused. "How do you know that?"

"It's East. It is proud of its sophistication. And, our statement would almost surely provoke a lawsuit from the American Civil Liberties' Union, because it is going to appear right winged and inconsistent with modern First Amendment law. The district's lawyer will surely convince the school board if they have to be sued, better to be sued by the fundamentalists than the ACLU—much better to be sophisticates than Bible thumpers. That rationale will control—mark my word," Dexter explained, his logic resonating with Taylor.

"So what happens when they reject the request?" She softened.

"We will have teased out an actionable claim. We will have received an official decision. We will have crossed the threshold of a having a school policy to challenge," Dexter explained.

Taylor paused, again deep in thought, her eyes locked with Dexter's. Then a smile slowly spread. "I like it—you are setting them up... You are cute and devious."

"Great!" Dexter said, spinning in his chair and leaning towards the right side of his desk. "Amy," Dexter buzzed on in his intercom, "could you ask Peter Diamond to join us?" Dexter stood, inviting Taylor to his conference table. As they left the desk area, Dexter explained, "Peter Diamond is a lifelong Grand Rapidian. He is a graduate of Catholic Central, Aquinas College, and Notre Dame law school." Dexter pulled back one of his conference table chairs for Taylor and they sat down.

"That makes him perfect for the job of tweaking a public school's curriculum?" Taylor asked sarcastically as she sat back in her chair and crossed her perfectly hosed legs.

"Look, like Michelle, he is a true believer. He has traveled the same paths only accompanied by Thomas Aquinas. He is perfectly qualified to draft our statement," Dexter explained, impressed with his own plan. "Also like your daughter, he is a young idealist. I would prefer we not let him know that we don't actually want East Grand Rapids to accept our statement."

"Gotcha." Taylor smiled conspiratorially.

A gangly, thin, six-foot-two-inch, mop-haired young associate with sandy colored hair knocked and opened the door, smiling at Mrs. Taylor. "Hello, I am Peter Diamond." Peter extended his hand towards Taylor, who did not rise to greet him.

"Peter, this is Mrs. Frank Taylor, our new client," Dexter said, also without getting up. Taylor shook Peter's hand as he sat down beside her.

"Mr. Bussey asked me to draft a curriculum statement you could review, and if it meets your approval, we could send to the East Grand Rapids school district."

"I have explained our general strategy to Ms. Taylor. She is waiting with bated breath to review your statement." Dexter leaned back in his chair.

"Have you reviewed it, Mr. Bussey?" Taylor inquired.

"Well... I was in depositions yesterday, so I am just as anxious to hear as you are. It is a first draft and, of course, we welcome your input, Mrs. Taylor." Dexter squirmed.

"First, let me say, Mrs. Taylor, how sorry I am for your loss." Peter interjected sincerely. "From what I know of your daughter she was a wonderful person, and I tried my best to put myself in her position. I think I have a good handle on Michelle's concerns, because, frankly, I share them."

"Thank you, Peter," Taylor said. "That means a lot to me."

Peter exhaled. "With that introduction, here's what I have:

> "The theory of evolution, which involves random mutation and natural selection to explain the development of animal species, has scientific support. However, evolution must be distinguished from 'naturalism,' which is a religious viewpoint that evolved nature is all that exists and there is no supernatural creator. Some scientists are naturalists. Some scientists who adhere to the theory of evolution believe a supernatural being or God used mutation and natural selection to unfold the living world and are not naturalists. Neither evolution nor any other scientific theory yet explains the original emergence of minerals, plant or animal life, nor the existence of metaphysical concepts such as love, the struggle between good and

evil, and the uniqueness and equality of human life, all of which are commonly understood by human beings. Science can only speculate at present at how the human mind embraces and understands metaphysical concepts. Some postulate that it is the result of imitation and repetition, passed down from generation to generation. Other scientists postulate the brain's ability to differentiate right and wrong and good and evil is programmed by an intelligent designer. Science has been unable to prove, disprove, or even test either postulate. The mind's condition remains one of the greatest mysterious in life. The East Grand Rapids school district encourages its students to learn the science of evolution, but also its limitations in explaining the origins of life itself, as well as the existence of metaphysical concepts."

Taylor smiled at Peter. "Thank you, Mr. Diamond. Yours are my daughter's words. I wouldn't change a thing."

Dexter gazed at Vicki Taylor. "Well then, we have our play book. It's time to take the field." Dexter realized too late the shallowness of his sports analogy. Still, he was proud of this game plan and looking forward to the notoriety of this case and its potential for healthy fees.

He was still savoring those feelings in the afternoon when Robert Johnson called. "Dexter, my partners are very impressed. They would like you to come to Chicago next Wednesday for dinner and drinks. We are prepared to make you an offer you will not refuse."

Dexter paused. "Robert, when have I known you to be wrong?" He said ambiguously. "I am honored and humbled at the same time. Wednesday, you say?"

"Yes. And feel free to bring along a significant other. Knowing you, deciding which one to choose will require more effort than deciding how to phrase your acceptance."

"You've left me speechless, Robert," Dexter scrambled.

"Good. Until you are billable, that's exactly where I want you. Meet us in the lounge at Sixteen, the signature restaurant in the new Trump Tower, at five-thirty central time. We will have a grand evening; a great kickoff to what I am sure will be a mutually beneficial relationship."

"See you then," Dexter offered weakly as he hung up the phone, stood up, and looked out his window to the Calder stabile. "Something about the gaudy sculpture is starting to get under my skin," he thought to himself as his cheerful mood soured.

* * *

"Ms. Wysocki!" Alex Ross shouted as he saw Madelyn Wysocki leave the East Grand Rapids high school tennis courts, racket in hand. Alex was purposefully without his sidekick Nico, realizing that the cameraman would certainly shut Madelyn down before his interview even started.

Nevertheless, Madelyn picked up her pace in the opposite direction. "I have nothing to say to you, Mr. Ross."

"Can I call you Madelyn?" Alex asked as his longer strides quickly caught Madelyn's.

"I know you are doing news reports on teen suicide, Mr. Ross. I don't want to talk about that."

"I can understand given what you have experienced, Madelyn. I am not looking to put you on camera. This is just background. I won't even use your name. I am only doing research, honest."

"Not interested..." Madelyn grimaced and began to trot.

"Aren't you interested in making some sense out of Michelle's suicide?" Alex slowed slightly, not wanting to create a scene as they garnered the attention of others alarmed at seeing an adult male chasing a high school girl. Alex knew he had one chance, so he resorted to a low blow.

"Don't you want to help other friends out in Michelle's position so maybe the next teen suicide can be prevented?" He called out after Madelyn as he stopped. "Don't you owe it to your friend that something positive might come out of this?" Alex's stomach turned as the words left his mouth.

Madelyn slowed and then stopped as if shot in her tracks. Alex wasted no time and quickly crossed the nearly empty soccer field, sweat from the warm June morning forming on his brow.

"Not going to use my name? Not going to put me on camera?"

"That's right, Madelyn. I'll put it in writing if you want. Just background, that is all," Alex said as he caught up to her.

"You don't see it coming Mr. Ross—that's the truth."

"Well, that's a point of my piece, Madelyn. You don't if you aren't trained in what to look for—which you certainly weren't," he quickly added. "But the ultimate point of my piece is that there are signs. There are always signs."

"It had nothing to do with Mr. Kingston's class," Madelyn sneered.

"Yeah... Well, adults need time and space to process too..." Alex knew by now about the classroom episode, Mrs. Taylor's confrontation with the school administration, and growing community rumors she might sue the district. "It's a difficult thing for anyone who loved her to comprehend."

Madelyn softened as the two walked in silence for a few paces. "Being a teenager sucks, Mr. Ross. Especially when one parent dies and the other doesn't understand anything about you."

"You mean Michelle's Christianity?"

"That and other things..." Madelyn trailed off.

Alex waited. "Other things...?"

Madelyn sighed. "Michelle was a tomboy. She didn't want to learn to walk like Mrs. Taylor or use make-up or shop—stuff like that."

"Hmm... Sounds like pretty ordinary stuff to me." Alex pushed.

"Not if you just lost your dad to a possible suicide," Madelyn huffed.

"Is that what Michelle thought?"

"I don't know. We didn't really talk about it. But it wasn't hard to think that way. He was dying of ALS, a god-awful disease, and then walks right into the path of a bus... What do you think?"

"But that was two years earlier, and like you said, suicide in the face of ALS even makes some sense. The doctors tell me there is usually a trigger right before the suicidal impulse. If it wasn't Kingston's class, what do you think it was for Michelle?"

"I don't know. I gotta go. Nice talking to you Mr. Ross..." Madelyn stuck out her hand and didn't even wait for Alex to react before she withdrew it and started jogging away, leaving Alex at the edge of the field, slightly out of breath, a little light-headed and with an upset stomach.

* * *

Tuesday, June 24, 2009

"Here's the situation." John Cleaver addressed one of one of Riley Dickson's best clients, the East Grand Rapids school board. "If you re-enter open session and vote to accept Mrs. Taylor's invitation to use this statement, you will likely be sued by the American Civil Liberties Union or the Americans United for the Separation of Church and State. If you vote to reject it, you will hand Mrs. Taylor the official policy she needs to sue the district. If you simply follow my recommendation and do nothing with it, you will still likely be sued by Mrs. Taylor, but I stand a chance of getting the case quickly dismissed because there is no official district action she can attack."

Victor Fleming

The seven elected members of the East Grand Rapids school district board were meeting for the only time in June. Michigan's Open Meetings Act provides few exceptions for a public body to exclude the public and enter "closed" session. One of the excuses was to consider the written legal opinion of its legal counsel, although no decision may be lawfully made in closed session. John Cleaver had been engaged by the district's superintendent to provide a written review of Mrs. Taylor's correspondence. The board, of course, understood Mrs. Taylor had the resources to pursue a legal claim against the district, and her correspondence was obviously written by a competent lawyer.

"I don't see the harm in Mrs. Taylor's proposed statement," complained board member Brent Peek. "I don't see where it suggests the district is endorsing Christianity."

"You wouldn't, Brent, because you are regular church-goer," scoffed board member Jordan Shipley.

"What do my religious beliefs have to do with it?" Peek replied angrily.

"They don't," gaveled Gerald McElroy, the board's president. "Mr. Shipley, that comment was out of line. We are going to conduct this discussion with civility and without any personal attacks. Is that understood?" McElroy stared at each of the other six members of the board until he received an agreeable nod from each.

William Reichel, the district's superintendent, signaled McElroy and was recognized. "Mr. Shipley's and Mr. Peek's comments demonstrate how divisive this statement would be in the community. The subject is too emotional, too close to our closely held opinions on religion."

"My concern, Mr. President, is that it will hurt the prestigious reputation of the district, which we have worked so hard to maintain," youthful board member Matt Ingram argued. "This statement sounds like something the Byron Center school district would approve," he added, referring to a rural public school district known to be located in a religiously conservative community.

McElroy jumped. He was resolved to suppress character attacks of any nature no matter how slight. "Ladies and gentlemen, I am not going to remind you again, no attacks on any person or organization will be tolerated."

"John, I would like to know the ACLU's chances if we adopt the statement and it sues," Brent Peek asked.

"That's a good question," John soothed, trying to appease the one perceived holdout. "The Taylor statement is remarkably similar to a statement the Dover, Pennsylvania, school district used. As here, that statement was designed to point out gaps in evolution, encouraging cosmological alternatives like intelligent design. The ACLU sued in a case called *Kitzmiller*. A conservative judge presided over a forty-day trial full of expert witnesses on evolution and intelligent design. After two million dollars in legal fees were incurred, the judge excoriated the district for being inane, finding the attack on evolution designed to advocate a supernatural being, in violation of the establishment clause of the First Amendment to the United States constitution."

As always, John saved his winning argument for the close—the "kill," as he liked to explain to young associates. "All of the school board members were defeated shortly after the trial. The new board gladly accepted the ACLU attorneys' offer to split their fees in half if the district did not appeal. It still cost the district one million dollars in legal fees and ignominy in the annals of public school constitutional law."

McElroy knew this was his signal to end the discussion and execute the strategy he, Cleaver, and Reichel had developed at a pre-meeting dinner. "This is a highly technical area of the law. We have to follow the good counsel of our attorney. We entered closed session so you could quiz Mr. Cleaver about his written opinion. Anyone of you has the right when we go back into open session to put this issue to a vote. My hope is no one will do that.

Is anyone intending to do that?" McElroy waited until everyone had shaken their heads. "Good."

"Who will communicate with Mrs. Taylor?" Peek asked, signaling his acquiescence.

"I will take care of that," Reichel stated.

"What will you say?" Peek wondered.

"I will thank her for her correspondence and note it was thought provoking—which is true. Nothing more." Reichel answered.

"Okay, do I have a motion to go back into open session?" McElroy asked. A motion was made and approved. Reichel and McElroy lingered with Cleaver after the meeting.

"Great job John, as always." McElroy tapped Cleaver on his back.

"What's wrong?" Reichel queried, puzzled by Cleaver's countenance.

"Dexter Bussey is what's wrong," Cleaver responded. "Rumor on the street is he's representing Mrs. Taylor."

"I have heard of him," McElroy intoned. "He is a hotshot young plaintiff's lawyer, isn't he? I have a friend who raves about him; says he obtained a million dollar settlement for a cousin on a personal injury matter. Haven't we cut out his legs tonight?"

"It was the right play. Nevertheless, nothing is simple in court anymore, especially when a well-funded, creative young lawyer is on the other side. This isn't the end, gentlemen; it's the beginning," Cleaver exhaled.

* * *

Tuesday, July 8, 2009

"Anything interesting filed while I was gone, Jack?" Owen asked as he walked into his chambers, returning from the four-day July Fourth holiday spent with his oldest daughter Mary and her husband and two teenage girls on their farm in southwestern Minnesota.

"No, Judge. All the new cases assigned to you are dogs. Three pro se suits, two by prisoners and one by a tax protester," Jack Gooters referred to lawsuits filed by individuals without a lawyer.

"There is one case filed by a lawyer, but it is about as frivolous as the pro se cases. Some fundamentalist claims her fifteen-year-old daughter's First Amendment rights were violated because the East Grand Rapids school district is promoting secular humanism by teaching evolution. The complaint even suggests the deprivation was a contributing factor in the fifteen year-old's suicide."

Owen was about to scoff, but lingered on the last clause. "Who is the lawyer on the complaint?"

"Let's see," Jack flipped back to the last page of the complaint. "Dexter Bussey."

"Bussey! Let me see that." Owen reached for the complaint, walked into his study, sat at his desk, and began reading. "Vicki Taylor!" Owen exclaimed, prompting Jack to scurry into the study behind his boss.

"Who is Vicki Taylor?"

"The second wife of Frank Taylor, a wealthy oilman who died a couple of years ago. I knew Frank from the tennis club. He certainly didn't exhibit religious tendencies. I know Vicki, his second and much younger wife, only by reputation. Sharp dresser, sharp tongue, sharper figure," Owen said, devouring the complaint. "I also remember this poor child's death a few months ago." Owen looked out his window. "She committed suicide at the base of the Calder, not more than a hundred yards from chambers."

Owen's comments about Vicki Taylor piqued the interest of Sarah and Kelly, who were gabbing outside the doorway and were not used to Owen Austin referring to anything sexual. Frank heard the comment too, and observed the women's interest. He smiled to himself. As he was leaving the chambers, he leaned over and whispered to the two ladies, "The old man isn't dead yet," chuckling to himself as he returned to his desk. Unbeknownst to anyone in the office, when alone, Owen and Frank sometimes enjoyed the contents of the liquor cabinet Owen kept in his office, a reminder of the vastly different conditions under which Owen had practiced law privately. During those moments, they often shared a guilty of pleasure of ranking the secretaries in the office according to a number of categories that would have shocked Kelly and Sarah. Frank relished this minor indiscretion he alone shared with the judge.

"She doesn't sound like a fundamentalis, and is this Bussey any good?" Jack asked, genuinely puzzled.

"I can't imagine Vicki Taylor is a fundamentalist." Owen chuckled. "Yes, Dexter Bussey is a very good lawyer," Owen added, and then to himself more than Jack Gooters said, "I wonder what the two of them can be up to—fascinating."

Owen finished reading the Taylor complaint, looked up and asked Jack, "Has anyone filed an appearance for the East Grand Rapids district?"

Gooters checked his notes. "John Cleaver."

"Bussey and Cleaver..." Owen drifted off, thinking to himself. Not much of a factual controversy... "Jack, can you pull up a case from the middle district of Pennsylvania involving intelligent design and evolution? I am quite certain the court determined the teaching of intelligent design in public schools violates the establishment clause."

"Yes, sir. I will get right on it. Like I said, your honor, this case is a dog," Jack shot back as he left to confirm his own opinion.

"Maybe..." Owen said to a departing Gooters. "May be not," He said under his breath. One thing was sure: this case held the prospects for a more interesting trial than the environmental case he had accelerated before he left for the holiday weekend. The lawyers alone promised an interesting battle. On the other hand, there was the topic. Did he want to spend time listening to experts mull the prospects for an afterlife? What would a constitutional case like this do to his reputation? If he ruled against the grieving mother, finding the district did nothing hostile to her poor daughter's religious beliefs, he might be branded an insensitive sophisticate. If he ruled in the estate's favor, he could be considered an ignorant rube, perhaps by his colleagues and the judges on the sixth circuit court of appeals whose opinion of his intellect he savored.

He was the chief judge. He could easily reassign the case on the premise he was a long time resident of East Grand Rapids and he and his daughters were proud graduates. He immediately experienced a flash of guilt; the thought he might use his power to benefit his own desires seemed self-indulgent.

Outside Owen's chambers the telephone rang. Because Sarah was away from her desk and Jack on the computer searching the computer database for the Pennsylvania case, Frank Callahan answered the phone and greeted Megan Austin Manning, his favorite of the Austin girls.

"Hi Frank," Megan warmed as she recognized Frank's voice. Frank was likewise her favorite member of Owen's staff. "You didn't burn your garage down with your fireworks on the fourth?"

"Fireworks! We are too smart in my neighborhood to shoot fireworks; someone would return the fire." He laughed. "Besides, fireworks are for yuppies in Ada Township to use when they want to burn the neighborhood down," he declared, taking Megan's bait, which had been a self-deprecating reference to last year's traumatic incident where her two teenage sons' fireworks accidentally started a grass fire that almost torched their own house.

"Is the judge in?" Megan laughed in response.

"Your father is in his study." Frank replied, emphasizing the word "father." "Why can't you call him 'dad'?" Frank asked. "You know it would mean a lot to the old man."

"I don't know, myself, Frankie," Megan replied. "It's complicated. Wasn't there a wall between you and your father?"

"Yes," Frank answered, "but there is a big difference between my dad and yours. Your father may be the finest man I have ever known, although I don't want you telling him I said that; it might impair our relationship." Frank laughed.

"He may be a great man, an exceptional boss, and a distinguished judge, but he is an average father," Megan said, surprised at her own defensiveness.

"Just remember, sugar, you won't have him forever, and once he's gone, there's nothing you can do for him," Frank counseled.

"Why do you say that, Frank?" Megan asked.

"No reason in particular. Other than he is sixty-nine years old and has experienced over forty years of above average stress," Frank answered. "But now that you mention it, his color has been off a little over the past few months."

"You would call me, wouldn't you, Frank, if you noticed something serious?" Megan inquired.

"You betcha. Yours would be my first call, and you know I am not shy. On that note, I will put you through."

"Thanks, Frank."

Megan soon received the judge's firm voice on her phone. "Hi Megan! Good to hear from you."

"Hi Judge," Megan said, surprised again by the spontaneity of her response despite the conversation with Frank. "How was Minnesota?"

"Had a great time, Meg, thanks for asking. Didn't you get a full report from Mary?" He was referring to the girls' well known penchant for checking in with each other, especially when the subject was their father demeanor after Susan's death.

"Yes. As a matter of fact, I did, which is why I am calling. What's wrong with you?"

"Wrong?" Owen responded, perplexed, since he had been careful to project a good mood during the four day holiday. "I don't know what you are referring to, because genuinely, I had a good time."

"Mary said you had too good a time. She is concerned. You helped Hal and the girls bale hay. You took a hike with the girls through the cow pasture, and Mary caught you by yourself up in an old tree house in the grove. You hate the farm. Plus, Frank says you look pale." Megan rattled off her list.

Owen laughed. "We all look pale to Frank. And, if Mary is concerned because I had too good a time, then Mary is the one you better worry about."

Megan was surprised at Owen's mood. He did seem rejuvenated and her "judge" reference didn't even register.

Owen had hoped that Mary's feminine intuition might have been suppressed by the toughness of farm life. He had always expected quicker intuition from Megan. Now he felt challenged on all fronts.

"Mary said you wouldn't commit to Thanksgiving. You and mom always went to the farm for Thanksgiving."

Owen paused for a moment. "Ah... Megan, you know the end-of-the-year holidays are still tough. Tell Mary not to worry when you talk to her tomorrow. Will you do that for me, Meg? I hate to cut you off, but Jack and I have to conclude some business."

"Sure, Judge. I understand." Megan felt reassured as she hung up. Mary was wrong; her father was no different.

Owen slowly rose from his leather chair and stood staring at the Calder six floors below. His thoughts were interrupted by Sarah's voice on his intercom, "Robbie Goldman, Judge. I am sure he wants to talk about the portrait investiture," she added excitedly.

Owen ignored the excitement. "Put him through, Sarah," he said.

"Well, the bus is full, your honor."

Owen laughed. "Robbie, you are a force of nature. The installation ceremony is still six months away! A lot can happen in six months."

"Nonsense. Everyone I talked to is as excited as if it were next week. We will have a grand celebration."

"Did I ever tell you, you are my all-time favorite clerk?"

"No. You haven't but I did assume it."

Owen chuckled again. "Have a great summer, Robbie, and remember to take your son somewhere on vacation—just the two of you. You will never regret it. Listen to your old boss."

Robbie laughed. "I have never disregarded one of your instructions."

Owen didn't laugh this time. "Don't start now, my son," he said, carefully choosing his words.

"My secretary is frowning, which means I am late, again. I will talk to you later, your honor."

"Please call anytime, Robbie." Owen hung up, looking out the window again, this time past the Calder to the clear blue sky, which reclaimed his thoughts.

A couple of minutes later, Owen picked up the phone and dialed interoffice to Jack Gooters. After thanking him for pulling up the *Kitzmiller* case, Owen advised he was reassigning the environmental case to him and Taylor to Mary Lou Shurlow. Owen had anticipated Jack would assume the reassignment was because the environmental case was more difficult but would nevertheless protest his unpreparedness for the impending trial date. When the expected occurred, Owen allayed the concern by instructing Jack that his first task on the file would be to reschedule the trial for January of the following year. He then asked Jack to send Mary Lou to Owen's study.

Mary Lou Shurlow, a blonde pixie who had graduated from Northwestern law school, popped into his study five minutes later. Owen instructed, "Mary Lou, I want you to call Dexter Bussey and John Cleaver and ask if they can meet next week for the scheduling conference in the Taylor case."

"Certainly your honor, but isn't that Jack's case, and isn't a scheduling conference premature?"

"It was Jack's case, and technically the scheduling conference is early, but I am reassigning the case to you. There is no reason a judge cannot hold the scheduling conference before the first responsive pleading. Every once in a while, young lady, I like to demonstrate a little unpredictability. Keeps the lawyers from getting an edge on me." Owen smiled, producing a shy smile in return from Mary Lou.

"Oh... Mary Lou," Owen added, as Mary Lou had risen and was walking out the door. "After the scheduling conference you may want to take your summer vacation now if you are planning one. We might be getting busy."

"That's okay, Judge," Mary Lou responded. "I was planning to save my vacation time for a warm weather vacation next January."

"Perfect, Mary Lou." Owen looked down to finish reading the *Kitzmiller* case.

* * *

"Is it a problem he likes little girls' underwear?" Dexter asked Melissa as they followed William through a children's store in the shopping mall. Enticed by the see-through plastic pouch with a handle, William had picked up a package of toddler girls' underwear and was vigorously resisting Dexter's efforts to get him to put them back on the shelf.

"Kids at this age are asexual, so I wouldn't get too alarmed." Melissa soothed, demonstrating her psychiatric nurse's knowledge. "Besides, he may be exercising his genes." She smiled.

"Very funny. I guess I deserved that," Dexter responded.

"He told me he found a pair of my underwear in your couch, but you assured him they weren't mine. How thoughtful!" Melissa only slightly suppressed a smile.

Dexter actually blushed. "I'm sure they were a couple of years old."

Melissa laughed. "That is even less assuring. Is it possible you haven't cleaned your couch in a couple of years?"

Dexter blushed again. "Couches need cleaning?" he asked, smiling. "By the way, I'll have you know I have a cleaning lady."

"Hard to supervise a cleaning lady when you don't know what needs cleaning," Melissa teased.

Dexter and Melissa were deviating from her script. Now that Dexter had begun taking William on solo overnight visitation, the plan had been for Dexter and William to spend time bonding without Melissa until William felt comfortable with Dexter as his father. In part because William, being a perceptive little boy, had quickly figured out Dexter was his father on his own, and perhaps because Dexter and William bonded so easily, Melissa felt comfortable in spending time with the two of them. At least, that was her justification.

"William, we have to put the underwear back. It's for little girls, not boys." Melissa said as she bent down and gently guided the package back to its display.

"Hey WD," Dexter interjected before William could protest. "How about this cool hat? Look at the embroidered hawk on the front." He handed William an orange toddler baseball hat, which William quickly put backwards on his head the way he had seen the older boys wear them. Dexter turned to the cashier, handing another cap to her. "My boy over there has already taken possession. Can you scan this one for me?"

After they had paid for the cap, they went to the center of the mall where there was a play area for little children. Melissa and Dexter sat on the circular couch surrounding the play area. As they watched William chase a girl a year older, Melissa brought up the Taylor case. "I was surprised to read about your new lawsuit in *The Grand Rapids Press*."

"Why, because you didn't think I had any intellectually challenging cases?"

"No, but a lawsuit challenging whether the teaching of evolution promotes a religious point of view was something I would have never guessed you would be behind."

"And why is that?" Dexter asked, raising his eyebrows.

"You never struck me as a religious person."

"How did you come to that conclusion?"

Melissa laughed. "Try lifestyle. Try the fact that you have never asked me if I am religious."

"I suppose that's fair. Although, I don't recall you ever telling me if you were religious, either."

"Touché, counselor. For the record, I am Catholic, although I must confess I don't follow all the rules or always meet my Sunday obligations."

"For the record, I'm not certain." Dexter smiled. "I would have told you that I was an agnostic a month ago, but my deceased fifteen year-old client and a thoughtful twenty-eight year-old associate have me thinking. Also, for the record, *The Grand Rapids Press* did not get the case correct. We aren't contending the teaching of the evolution is improper. However, because so many proponents have made a religion out of it, we contend that the school district has an obligation to point out the distinction between evolution and atheism. Did you know that there are many Christian scientists who believe evolution is true?"

"Really?" Melissa answered. "I did not know that. I would have thought the two are mutually exclusive."

"I rest my case. Don't you see how simply brilliant I am?"

Melissa laughed. "Brilliantly simple, maybe. But doesn't the Bible say God created the universe in six calendar days and then rested on the seventh?"

"You probably shouldn't look to me for biblical scholarship. However, my colleague, Peter Diamond, who is Catholic and graduated from Aquinas and Notre Dame, would say that God is beyond time. Yesterday, today, and tomorrow are all one to him. The long evolutionary processes to him would be nothing more than the spinning out of species in the blink of an eye," Dexter explained. "Like the materialization occurring on Star Trek when Scotty beamed people and things around."

"I am not sure I follow the Star Trek analogy." Melissa chuckled.

"Well, I added that. It is what I visualized when Peter was describing Thomist creation theory to me. But I just learned a lesson—I am going to stick to Peter Diamond's script in this case." Dexter laughed.

"So let me see if I understand who your client is. You say she is a deceased fifteen-year-old, but I thought the newspaper described her as a 'Mrs. Taylor'?"

"You are right on both fronts," Dexter explained. "Mrs. Taylor is suing as the personal representative of her daughter's estate. Michelle Taylor was a fifteen-year-old freshman at East Grand Rapids high school, but she tragically took her life earlier this year at the base of Calder after having her religious beliefs belittled in a high school biology class."

"How sad... I think I remember reading about the suicide in the paper," Melissa mused. "How can her mother afford to sue? Are you taking the case on a contingency basis?"

"The tragedy for Mrs. Taylor doesn't start with her daughter. Her very wealthy, older husband died after being struck by a bus while in the latter stages of ALS just two years before their daughter committed suicide."

"Wow! That poor woman," Melissa said. "And Mrs. Taylor is an angry, grieving, old mother and widow with enough money to pay you a lot of money to fully pursue her cause?"

"Sort of. You have most of it," Dexter stated.

"What does Mrs. Taylor look like?" Melissa asked, staring at Dexter.

"Well..." Dexter fumbled.

"No... Now I understand all of it," Melissa quickly interjected, smiling as Dexter blushed again.

* * *

Wednesday, July 9, 2012

"Mr. Bussey and Mr. Cleaver, thank you so much for coming in on such short notice." Owen Austin rose to greet Dexter and John at the door to his chambers. Owen knew Dexter and John well enough to use their first names in any other context, but the formalities of the legal practice require lawyers to address even their best friends by their surnames in court or in judicial chambers.

Dexter was accompanied by Peter Diamond and John by Greg Jones. After introductions of the younger lawyers, all four took a seat at the table where Owen and Mary Lou Shurlow were settling. "I am very pleased to have lawyers of this caliber on this case, which I note has drawn more than a little interest in the Press. It is important to handle this matter expeditiously and with sensitivity to the subject. I hope you agree with me," Owen started.

Dexter and John looked at each other a little apprehensively, then nodded in agreement.

"Great!" Owen exclaimed. "I knew I could count on you. Of course, I don't have the benefit of the district's responsive pleading, so I am not exactly sure of its position, but I have thoroughly reviewed the complaint and the attached statement you want the district to adopt and have a couple of questions for you, Mr. Bussey, if you don't mind?"

"Not at all, your honor, fire away," Dexter replied, at little bit surprised.

"Good. Your case appears to be like *Kitzmiller* in that you want a disclaimer offered in science class, but it appears to be like the *Jaffree* in that you claim that the district is endorsing evolutionism and secular humanism? Am I generally correct?"

The second case to which Owen was referring was *Jaffree v. Board of School Commissioners*, which was heard in the United

States district court for the southern district of Alabama between 1982 and 1987 and traveled three times to the Eleventh Circuit court of appeals in Atlanta, and once to the United States Supreme Court. Initially, the case had been filed by Ishmael Jaffree, who objected to school prayer in the Mobile, Alabama school district. After it became apparent that Mr. Jaffree would prevail and school prayer would be banned as violative of the First Amendment's anti-establishment clause, certain school teachers and parents joined the lawsuit as plaintiffs, challenging the district's textbooks as advancing atheism and secular humanism at the expense of theistic religions.

Mr. Jaffree, having won on his claim, dropped out and the case proceeded as *Smith v. Board of School Commissioners.* During several weeks of trial, educational theorists and theologians testified as to whether secular humanism was a religion and whether the forty-two textbooks approved by the state of Alabama advanced secular humanism and inhibited belief in the supernatural. The Mobile school district actually flipped sides and supported the new plaintiffs, contending its own state-required textbooks violated the anti-establishment clause, leaving the defense to state education officials.

The district court agreed with the new plaintiffs and enjoined the use of the textbooks. The eleventh circuit court reversed, finding even if secular humanism was a religion, the textbooks had a secular purpose: their primary effect was neither to advance nor inhibit any religion and they did not cause an excessive entanglement between religion and government.

"Yes, your honor, that is true if by *Jaffree* you mean the *Smith* portion of the case," offered Dexter, suddenly thankful that Peter Diamond had spent time thoroughly prepping him on the *Jaffree* case while they were drafting the complaint.

Owen smiled. "I stand corrected. Yes. The *Smith* prong of *Jaffree.* Let me clarify. You aren't asking that intelligent design be taught at East Grand Rapids high school?"

"That's correct and incorrect. We think *Kitzmiller* correctly found intelligent design is not physically testable. On the other hand, no public school can thoroughly address speciation without addressing the cosmological questions of how minerals and life started and how the human brain ended up able to differentiate right and wrong and other metaphysical principles. On those subjects, there is no theory meeting the rigors of the scientific method as outlined in *Kitzmiller*. All we have at present are speculative theories, unsupported by scientific testing. One of these speculations is an intelligent designer created matter and life and hardwired the human brain. When these topics are addressed, the speculation of whether there is an intelligent designer or the new Darwinists' speculation that there is no designer may be presented without endorsement. In sum, we aren't asking for a mandate that intelligent design be taught, but a declaration that it may be taught if without endorsement." Dexter was pleased with his articulation.

"You apparently admit evolution is sufficiently scientific—as many other courts have found—to be taught in the public schools, at least if a warning label such as you have prepared is attached to it?" Owen pressed.

"Well, I might characterize our statement differently, but that is close enough for present purposes," Dexter responded. "The problem is evolution has evolved as well, Judge. Its leading proponents such as Richard Dawkins are unabashed in their belief evolution can lead to only one conclusion: namely, there is no God. They actively proselytize this position in their bestselling books. These leading biologists and the intelligent design advocates on the Dover school board in *Kitzmiller* share the same view of evolution—that it is absolutely incompatible with belief in God. They just divert on the ultimate conclusion to be drawn from that dualism—prominent biologists saying it proves there is no God; the *Kitzmiller* intelligent designers saying it proves there can be no scientific truth to evolution because they presuppose the existence of God. Because evolution is now so closely linked with 'evolutionism'—a variant of atheism—some caveat is necessary to maintain the 'lofty neutrality' mandated by the United States Supreme Court in *Jaffree*."

"Interesting," Owen conceded. "But speaking of the eleventh circuit's opinion in the *Jaffree* case, didn't it set the bar very high as to what constitutes educational support of secular humanism?" Owen was careful not to encourage Dexter Bussey's case at the expense of John Cleaver's, particularly since John had yet to express it.

"That may be true, your honor," Dexter conceded. "However, even the defense experts in *Smith* conceded public school teachers could not deny the existence of the supernatural without violating the requirement of neutrality. In the present case, we will produce evidence this is exactly what the East Grand Rapids biology teacher denied. Moreover, we believe in the nearly quarter of century since the *Smith* portion of *Jaffree* was decided, evolution has now been co-opted by the atheists the same way the *Kitzmiller* court found intelligent design to have been co-opted by Christian fundamentalists."

"Mr. Cleaver, this Court values 'lofty neutrality' above all else. You haven't had a chance to respond to these allegations, and I don't want to put you on the spot, but if you are ready, how do you respond to Mr. Bussey's claims?" Owen turned to John.

John plowed into the discussion. "Unlike either *Kitzmiller* or *Jaffree*, no official decision is being challenged by Mrs. Taylor. No matter how well intentioned, she hasn't been elected to set East Grand Rapids high school's curriculum. There hasn't even been an official decision on what to do with her statement, nor any district endorsement of any off-the-cuff statements the teacher might have made."

"I am glad you started with that point," Owen interjected. "Mr. Bussey alleges in his first count that the EGR school board at its most recent meeting made a closed session decision rejecting Mrs. Taylor's statement. Did such a closed session occur and was such a decision made?"

"A closed session was held. Legally, I can't divulge what was discussed therein," John responded defensively.

"Fair enough—for present purposes," Owen responded. "But let me ask this question: Did the discussion have nothing to do with Mrs. Taylor's request to the district? Because if it was on another subject, it is of no concern to us. If you cannot confirm it had nothing to do with the issues in this case, we have to take the inquiry to another level. I trust you, Mr. Cleaver, to be fair in your response. Mr. Bussey, do you?"

"Yes, your honor. If Mr. Cleaver says there is no connection that is good enough for me as well," Dexter stated, believing John Cleaver under most circumstances would answer truthfully, convinced he would do so in this setting under the examination of a United States district judge.

"Thank you, Mr. Bussey. Mr. Cleaver, can you offer me such an assurance?"

John knew he had been backed into a corner. He shifted his weight slightly and in resignation answered, "Your honor, I cannot give you that assurance."

"Thank you for your candor, and I apologize for my aggressiveness. I think you know me well enough to know this is not my typical approach to case management. In this matter, however, I am concerned about two things: One, I know the *Kitzmiller* and *Jaffree* cases cost their respective school districts millions of dollars. Second, and equally important, the cases tore the two communities apart. I am determined not to let the first, and hopefully, not the second consequence occur. I think we all agree the East Grand Rapids public schools are, if not the premier public school system in West Michigan, certainly among the very best. I will give Mrs. Taylor and Mr. Bussey a full and fair opportunity to prove their case, but I will also do everything in my power to minimize the damage to the district from this dispute."

"Thank you, your honor, for those sentiments." John smiled graciously, but warily.

"Now, Mr. Cleaver, I would like to review the minutes of the closed session in camera," Owen directed, referring to the process where the judge reviewed material privately to see if there was any possible, potential use by the opposing party. If not, the material could be disregarded from the case. "Do you object to such a review, John?" Owen intentionally softened to the colloquial, hoping to induce acquiescence.

"Sooner or later, I suppose we would get to that point, so no, your honor, although it is a little unusual since I haven't even filed my responsive pleading. I will acquiesce to the court's requirement."

"Dexter, is this procedure acceptable?"

"No problem here, your honor—at least as a first cut on the issue. I want to reserve the right for discovery if need be."

"Very well." Owen leaned back, pleased. "My second question, John, is whether the district intends to answer the complaint or file a motion to dismiss."

"We intend to move to dismiss, your honor."

"Then let's set a briefing schedule now. I am assuming, Dexter, with my in camera review of the closed session minutes there isn't any need for discovery on the motion?" Owen turned his gaze to Dexter while realizing that once he had gone informal, he could not go back.

"Yes, your honor," Dexter and John said in unison.

"Alright, then the last thing to do here is set the schedule. John, how quickly can you file?"

John looked at Greg Jones and they whispered together. "Four weeks, your honor."

Without blinking, Owen said, "How about three weeks?"

"Fine, we'll do it."

"Dexter, two weeks thereafter to respond, since you already know half of what will be in the motion?" Owen pushed.

"Yes, sir."

"Okay, Mary Lou, where does that take us and how quickly thereafter can we schedule oral argument?" Owen asked.

Mary Lou Shurlow ran her finger across the calendar, landing in the third week of August. "Your honor, I have Monday, August twenty-fifth at ten a.m."

"Gentlemen, there you have it. I am going to work as hard as you are. I intend to be ready with a decision on the motion at oral argument, so be prepared for one of two things that day: to work on a final order for appeal or a pretrial conference where we will set a trial date. For the reasons stated, I am placing this case on my own rocket docket, and if it survives motion we will go to trial quickly, so you should be thinking about witnesses during the next five weeks. Thank you very much, again, for coming on such short notice and for your cooperation." With that, Owen stood and extended his hand. All four lawyers quickly stood in response, quickly forming a receiving line to shake Owen's hand and exit his chambers.

After the lawyers left, Owen asked Mary Lou to prepare a summary of the meeting and have it on his desk by the end of the day. When she had left and closed the door, he slumped, immediately reaching for his aspirin and exhaling deeply. He thought of the old saw, "run fast enough and death will never catch you." He was tired but adrenaline was coursing through his veins for the first time since that beautiful but awful day just a few months earlier.

* * *

"What do you think?" Dexter asked Peter as soon as they were out of earshot of John Cleaver and Greg Jones, who walked off in a different direction as all four passed through security and exited the Gerald R. Ford courthouse.

"I don't think he likes our case. He seems to want to rush it. I was surprised at how active he was," Peter responded.

"Can you blame him if he hasn't warmed to our case?" Dexter responded. "After all, unlike *Kitzmiller* and *Jaffree*, we aren't challenging a policy as religious. We are challenging comments and the failure of the district to adopt a policy as being irreligious. We don't even have an agitated parents group. Our plaintiff is committed to the case but not to the cause."

"Doesn't that make our case stronger than *Kitzmiller* and *Jaffree*, where it wasn't clear the kids cared a lick? It was all parent driven," Peter argued. "Here, our student truly felt slighted and the experience played some role in her end of life decision."

"Maybe the motives of our deceased student are pure, but the motives of Vicki Taylor may not impress Judge Austin, even if he is sympathetic to her loss. Make a mental note: I need to prepare her on that subject before her testimony."

"Why did you so readily agree to the in camera inspection of the minutes? Won't Cleaver and Jones have those minutes sanitized?" Peter wanted to know.

"He's going to grant us relief on the open meetings act count and deny their motion to dismiss. He wants to clear the ring and get to the main event quickly," Dexter explained.

"Really, how did you read all that? And, isn't that good news?" Peter asked.

"No, it isn't good news. You should know what appears up is typically down in court. He wouldn't want to give us an appealable issue on a minor issue in the case, so he will find the district decided not to adopt our policy statement. Then he will bend over backwards to find Kingston's comments were made as we represent and that they constitute de facto policy positions. He will give us as much trial time as we want. Thereafter he will conclude the district's curriculum and teacher's statements— although not perfect—are sufficiently in line with the lofty neutrality required under the First Amendment and toss us out of court." Dexter depressed himself as he recited his thoughts. "I hate losing, especially to Riley Dickson, and particularly when

The Grand Rapids Press covers the loss. I knew I shouldn't have taken this case." Dexter's disposition was darkening.

"What experts do you think we are going to need?" Peter inquired, hoping to shake his boss out of his funk.

"I have been thinking about that. I want you to find an atheist evolutionist—an eminent biologist who is a disciple of Dawkins and believes evolution proves there is no God. We are going to follow the brilliant Pepper Hamilton playbook in *Kitzmiller*, only in reverse."

"How are we going to convince someone like that to serve as our expert witness?"

"You leave that task to me."

"But won't Mrs. Taylor find that disturbing? It will appear as if we are advocating there is no God despite her daughter's religious beliefs."

"Don't worry. When it is his turn, Cleaver will put on a Christian biologist who believes in evolution." Dexter laughed. "Let's see... We will need a statistician linking evolution with atheism in the average mind. The net result of this testimony will be that while evolution is scientifically religiously neutral, the work of Darwin and evolution's most prominent adherents since has sufficiently linked it to the religion of atheism so that the public schools have a duty to warn the science of evolution is different from the religion of Darwinism. Hence, part one of our statement."

"What about the metaphysical aspects of the statement? What do we need there?" Peter wondered.

"Make a trip to see some of your Aquinas or Notre Dame professors, or check out Calvin College here in town. Surely there are philosophers, psychologists, ethicists, or anthropologists who can attest to the empirical evidence for the concepts of love and hate and good and evil and the inexplicability of those concepts in the human mind as developed through evolution," Dexter responded. "Hopefully they can also attest to the deepening divide over the last twenty-five years between religion and science."

Peter frowned. "That's a lot to do in ten weeks."

"I will talk to the firm's management. I'll have all your other work reassigned. You are to work on this project full time. And grab as many summer associates as you can find. Make sure you each bill ever minute spent. This case will lift the firm's bottom line."

"So you are going to try to prove the existence of the supernatural?" Peter wryly smiled.

"Isn't that close to what you Christians call 'blasphemy'? God can take care of himself. My objectives are modest. I just want to prove the need for a modest disclaimer, make some money, and win a lawsuit."

* * *

"Thoughts?" John Cleaver asked Greg Jones as they parted from Bussey and Diamond.

"I've never seen Judge Austin so aggressive, but I'll take him at face value. He doesn't want to see this case take apart a good community. We are going to win this case on motion," Jones predicted, then he paused, troubled by John's frown. "What's the matter?"

"I don't know. Something's not right. I can't put my finger on it." John was thinking about Owen's approach, which although reasoned was extraordinarily rushed, unlike the man John had known even before Owen assumed the bench. Owen Austin never acted impatiently. It was a perceived strength as a lawyer he never lost as a judge. Although it wasn't unlike the judge to be concerned about the costs of litigation to the participants, everyone knew that Mrs. Taylor was well-heeled, and if any defendant could afford the costs of a lawsuit, it was East Grand Rapids. No... Something else was lurking.

"Do we need to retain the service of an expert this early into the case?" Jones asked.

"Yes. We cannot wait, which is one of the reasons I don't completely buy Austin's stated concern about this rocket schedule saving costs. I want a Christian biologist who adheres to the science of evolution. Perhaps Professor Miller, who testified in *Kitzmiller*, or someone like him. We want to neutralize this 'evolution equals atheism' argument before it gets any traction," John instructed. "Also, call Peter Diamond to see if he will consent to a release of Michelle Taylor's medical records. Let me know if he gives you any trouble. I would love to get that back to Judge Austin. We need a psychologist who can point to suicidal causes more likely than a bad day at school."

"I also assume you want me to sanitize the closed meeting minutes," Jones stated.

"That won't be necessary. Reichel is sufficiently savvy to be cryptic and inconclusive in his minute taking."

"But he isn't a lawyer, John. He may not realize he has offered up a decision. I should look just to make sure."

"No, Greg. Any changes now would expose Reichel on cross examination. Bussey will certainly ask about changes and, as you well know, we have an obligation to preserve all drafts." John wanted to add that it would also be inappropriate now that the suit had been filed to tamper with the evidence, but he didn't want to appear soft to his young partner. "I'll take care of reviewing and securing the minutes for delivery to Judge Austin."

"We could be offering up a victory on count one right out of the blocks. How will that look in the paper?" Jones looked away from John, afraid his face might reveal his skepticism.

"Even if that is true, it's part of the sideshow. It isn't critical to our position on the merits," John rejoined.

"True enough, but we worked hard to underscore the need for the school board to avoid making a decision on the statement. We'll lose credibility if it follows our advice and still loses the point."

"So be it," John weakly demurred.

They walked the rest of the block in awkward silence before Greg begged off for another meeting.

John knew Jones was partially right. He should have edited the minutes before the suit was filed, certainly before the scheduling conference. The window had closed on his ability to edit the minutes now, since it would be disastrous if an edit were uncovered after the judge had requested the minutes.

John sighed. He knew there was a bell curve in a lawyer's attention to the myriad of details required in effective litigation. Young lawyers missed details due to a lack of experience. On the downward slope, older lawyers started missing details due to fading memory, mental fatigue, or simply—as John suspected in his case—a loss of interest. Sloppiness lost cases, maybe not this one, but eventually.

The sweat was seeping through John's suit from the two block walk in the midsummer heat, if not from his conversation with Jones. Trudging up the steps to Riley Dickson's office building, John steeled himself to the prospects of dictating a couple letters, answering multiple calls, and worrying about the details of a dozen other cases.

Chapter Six

The Scientist
Tuesday, November 3, 2009
(Second Day of Trial)

On just the second day of trial, almost four months after John had struggled in the summer sun, Dexter Bussey was the litigator who was feeling slowed. The reason had nothing to do with his general physical state and was almost entirely due to the wine he had enjoyed the night before while dinning with the two experts he planned to call today. He had only lightly prepared Professors Devoneau and Hitchcock, mostly letting the two men entertain each other. It turned out they were correspondents and close friends from attending various academic conferences together over the years. Devoneau was in his late fifties and had a rosy complexion. His hair had been blonde but was now turning white, skipping the graying stage entirely. His lively eyes and broad, round forehead dominated his face, which was angular. His demeanor was patrician. In appearance he resembled a hawk.

After Owen emerged and called the courtroom to order, Dexter rose to greet the Court and begin the day's session.

"Your honor, the estate calls Leonard Devoneau to the stand," Dexter announced as the second day of trial began. Devoneau strutted to the stand, raised his hand, and was sworn in by Kelly Vandervelde.

Q.   Sir, would you state your name for the record?

A.   My name is Dr. Leonard Devoneau.

Q.   You are a professor of what subject and where?

A.   I am a tenured professor of biology at Harvard University

Q.   What is your educational background, professor?

A.   I have a bachelor's in science from the University of Chicago, a PhD in biology from Princeton University, and I have also studied at Oxford University.

Q.   Have you ever testified as an expert in biology?

A.   Yes, on numerous occasions, most of which are listed in my twelve-page curriculum vitae, which you have in your hand, sir.

Q.   Your honor, I would propose Leonard Devoneau as an expert in the science of biology and its teaching.

"No objections, your honor," John Cleaver stated.
"Very well," said Judge Austin. "The Court will receive Professor Devoneau's testimony as expert in the field of biology and its teaching."

Q.   Professor Devoneau, are you familiar with the theory of evolution?

A.   I am familiar with the *fact* of evolution. It is no longer a theory.

Q.   Well, that answer is worthy of further exploration, but before we do that, how would you define "evolution?"

A.   "Evolution" is the process whereby animal organisms develop into ever more complex species through random genetic mutation and natural selection.

Q.   What would you say is the difference between a "theory" and a "fact?"

A.   The difference is one of degree and level of scientific testing and acceptance. Evolution before Charles Darwin was speculation, or a postulate of how things worked without any empirical evidence. Charles Darwin took the postulate of evolution to the level of theory with scientific proof. In the one hundred and fifty years since the *Origins of Life* was published by Darwin, the theory has become accepted scientific fact.

Q.   What was the scientific proof?

A.   When Darwin was in his early twenties in 1831, he signed on as a biologist on a British sailing ship called the *Beagle*. Eventually, the ship landed in the Galapagos Islands in the eastern Pacific off the coast of Ecuador, where he observed species found nowhere else. He was particularly fascinated by slight changes in finches from island to island—mostly their varying beaks. He eventually attributed the changes to the different kinds of environments and the isolation of each breed of finches. This led him to the concept of adaptive radiation, which is the micro-evolution of species to better suit the environment, which eventually led him to his grand discovery, natural selection.

Q. That evolution is a fact, not a theory: Is that just your opinion, professor?

A. Heavens, no. It is accepted as fact by every prominent biologist in the field The most prominent biologist in the world, Richard Dawkins, has opined that evolution is fact, not theory. Even the Christian biologist who testified at the *Kitzmiller* trial, Kenneth Miller, has so opined. We are relatives of gorillas, sea-life, and bacteria. That is not a theory; it is a fact.

Q. Would you describe evolution?

A. Life on earth evolved gradually from one self-replicating molecule more than three and a half billion years ago, branching out over time through the tree of life, and the mechanism for all evolutionary change is genetic mutation and natural selection.

Q. What scientific disciplines have confirmed the fact of evolution?

A. I'm glad you asked that question, because it is not just biology. I have read scientific papers in the fields of genetics, anatomy, molecular biology, paleontology, and geology that have all observed the process of evolution in either laboratory tests or through empirical scientific observation.

Q. You mentioned the *Kitzmiller* case. Are you familiar with it?

A. Intimately. A great triumph of the American judicial system, I might add.

Q.   Thank you professor, for that endorsement, but I want to focus on the concept of "contrived dualism." Do you recall that term?

A.   Yes, I do. I believe it was Judge Jones's description of the intelligent design proponents' efforts to discredit evolution.

Q.   What were the two concepts that were found to be in duality?

"Objection, your honor," John Cleaver interjected. "This witness is a biologist, not a law clerk. We can all read and interpret Judge Jones' opinion."

"Mr. Bussey, your response?" Owen asked.

"This line of questions is just foundational, your honor, and since Mr. Cleaver admits that we can all read and interpret *Kitzmiller*, there is no harm. I would ask for a little leeway."

"A little leeway is given; the objection, at this point, is overruled."

"Understood, and thank you, your honor," Dexter said. "Now, professor, do you remember the question?"

A.   Of course I do. The answer is that Judge Jones found Christianity and evolution to be the subject of the contrived dualism.

Q.   And by "being in contrived duality," what did you understand Judge Jones to mean?

A.   Christianity and evolution are supposedly incompatible when they are not.

Q.   Do you believe that they are incompatible?

A.   Absolutely.

Q.   So you would disagree with Judge Jones on this point?

A.   Yes, I supposed I would, Mr. Bussey. In a one-hundred-and-thirty-nine-page opinion, one cannot expect a judge to get everything right. No offense, your honor.

"I can't speak for Judge Jones, but I took no offense, professor," Owen interjected.

Q.   Why do you think Christianity and evolution are incompatible, professor?

A.   It is not just me who think this way, Mr. Bussey. I dare say that over ninety percent of the biologists in the world today believe that evolution has proved that there is almost certainly no God. The leading proponent of this view is, of course, the great Richard Dawkins, Oxford professor of biology.

Q.   Can you summarize why biologists such as yourself and professor Dawkins contend that evolution serves as a proof that there is no God?

A.   Yes, I most certainly can. It is simply that the ability to rationalize and design only appears late in the evolutionary progression. Because it arrives late and requires millions of years of molecular and biological evolution, there could be no designer-creator present at the beginning, and without the presence of a creator, there could be no creation.

Q.   But what if God were present from another world?

A.   Then God would have to have evolved in that universe, and again, he would not have been present at the beginning in that world.

Q.   But didn't Stephen Gould, the preeminent scientist, lay the foundation for the premise that religion and science are separate spheres when he coined the phrase "non-overlapping magisterial," or NOMA?

A.   Yes. For years scientists have feared the Catholic Church and its prejudices, but again, whether or not there is a supernatural God that is ordering or affecting nature is a scientific proposition that must be tested, because if true, it would affect everything. Thus, it cannot be off limits to scientific inquiry. NOMA is a giant fallacy. Science must make probability judgments on this question, and it has. God and the tooth fairy have the same probability for existence.

There were gasps in the courtroom at this comment, but Owen immediately gaveled them down.

Q.   So you see incompatible tension in the concepts of evolution and Christianity or any monotheistic religion?

A.   Yes. All rational proponents of evolution do. The real war is between rationalism and superstition. Science is rationalism; religion is superstition.

Q.   Let me ask you this question, professor: As a biologist and man of science, what do you think of the preamble to the Declaration of Independence? "We hold these truths to be self-evident, that all men are created equal, that they are endowed by their creator with certain unalienable rights, that among these are life, liberty and the pursuit of happiness."

A.   As science, it is mostly poppycock. As social convention, I ascribe to it.

Q.   The poppycock is what?

A.   That men are created.

Q.   How about their equality under the fact of evolution?

A.   They have similar DNA.

Q.   But are they evolving equally?

A.   No, of course not.

Q.   Does evolution value one species over another?

A.   Of course not.

Q.   So, scientifically, humans are of no more value than horses or whales?

A.   True.

Q.   The right to pursue happiness, is that inalienable scientifically?

A.   The drive to pursue happiness or stasis is inherent to all plants and animals.

Q.   So you wouldn't describe this as a right inalienable to humans?

We Hold These Truths

A.   No. It is a drive that is inalienable to all creatures; the right is a social convention.

Q.   Do these social conventions, as you call them, promote or impede evolution?

A.   Ultimately, they are a part of it.

Q.   But could they destroy it?

A.   You mean does respect for the equal drive to stasis of other humans produce overpopulation that threatens global warming and the potential collapse of the population?

Q.   Yes, that is where I was headed. Could that be possible?

A.   That could be the ultimate biological fate of the human race; we don't know yet, do we?

Q.   Yet you personally subscribe to these conventions.

A.   At this point, yes.

Q.   What could change your mind, personally?

A.   I don't know. I suppose if the convention seemed to be counterproductive to the survival of the race or the planet.

Q.   Would you call yourself, sir, an "evolutionist?"

A.   If by that term you mean that I believe that evolution disproves religion and, therefore, is explanatory of the cosmos, I am proudly an evolutionist.

Q.   Do you draw any distinctions between "evolution" and "evolutionist?"

A.   Only that evolutionism is the study of evolution.

Q.   As an evolutionist, how do you feel about the First Amendment as a social convention?

"Objection, your honor. This man is not a legal scholar," Cleaver said indignantly.

"Sustained," Owen ruled without giving Dexter an opportunity, signaling that he wanted the testimony more closely linked to biology, not the law.

Q.   Professor, what effect, if any, have you observed in your students after they have learned the fact of evolution as it might relate to their religious views?

A.   Religion is superstition. The enlightenment that comes to the young mind when it learns about the true origins of the human species and casts off the superstition through the teaching of evolution is as rewarding as the teaching of physiology must be when it disproves the possibility of a virgin birth.

"Thank you, professor. I have nothing further." Dexter sat down amid audible grumbling in the courtroom, and John Cleaver took his turn at the podium.

Q.   Good morning, Professor Devoneau. My name is John Cleaver and I represent the East Grand Rapids Public Schools.

A.   Good morning, sir.

Q.   Professor, have you read the statement that the plaintiff is seeking to force upon the school district?

A.   Yes.

Q.   Do you in anyway support the East Grand Rapids school district having to issue such a statement before, after, or during the teaching of the science of evolution?

A.   Absolutely not.

Q.   In fact, I take it from the firmness of your response that you find it somewhat offensive, would that be correct?

A.   Yes.

Q.   What about it offends you?

A.   There are a host of things. First, no other scientific fact requires a warning label. This was a point of Judge Jones in *Kitzmiller*. So it sends the wrong signal to students—that evolution is dangerous stuff, which is wrong. Second, evolution isn't a theory, it is fact. Third, there is no difference between evolution and evolutionism, as I have already testified. Fourth, those few evolutionists who still call themselves "Christians" are self-deluded. Fifth, these so-called metaphysical concepts are all human behaviors that are physically explained by evolution. Finally, once again, evolution disproves religion, and any suggestion to the contrary is just false.

Q.   Well, sir, if you don't share the plaintiff's ultimate objective in this lawsuit, why did you agree to testify for the plaintiff?

A.   I share Michelle Taylor's desire to see the discussion progress to its natural and logical conclusion. To the extent she was cut off in her discourse, her freedom of speech was infringed, and freedom of expression is essential to the scientific method.

Q.   Are you also being paid for your testimony?

A.   I am being compensated for my time, if that is what you mean.

Q.   How much would that be, sir?

A.   Twenty-five thousand dollars.

Again, there was a rumble in the audience that Owen had to gavel down. He also warned the gallery that if he had to employ the gavel one more time, he was going to position his bailiff in the back of the courtroom and remove anyone reacting to the testimony. After letting that admonition settle over the crowd, John Cleaver announced that he had no further questions. When asked if he had anything further by Owen, Dexter said he had nothing, and Owen excused Professor Devoneau while also announcing the morning break.

As Dexter shook hands with Professor Devoneau, who gave John Cleaver the evil eye as he left the courtroom, Vicki Taylor ambled up to Dexter and whispered into his ear while keeping up a perfect smile for appearances. "I can't believe you spent twenty-five thousand dollars of my money on that disagreeable human being."

Dexter smiled back, leaned over, and whispered into her ear. "Mrs. Taylor, he was worth every penny."

After the morning break, Dexter called Karl Hitchcock, associate professor of philosophy from the University of Minnesota. Hitchcock was in his mid-forties and sported a wad of unkempt brown hair resting over his bushy eyebrows and wire-rimmed glasses which bridged a large, wide nose that was slightly hooked. Behind his glasses and under his brows were deep-seated, penetrating blue eyes. He wore a tweed jacket and carried an easy smile that belied his obvious intellect.

Q.   Professor Hitchcock, can you tell me your field of expertise?

A.   I am a philosopher of naturalism.

Q.   What are your credentials?

A.   I have a PhD in philosophy from Yale University. I am an associate professor at the University of Minnesota, where I have taught for ten years. I have given numerous lectures and published numerous articles on naturalism, the scientific method, epistemology, and public education.

"Your honor, I propose Professor Hitchcock as an expert in philosophy and its teaching," Dexter stated.

"No objection, your honor," John responded.

"Very well. Professor Hitchcock's testimony will be received as an expert in philosophy and its teaching."

Q.   Are you familiar with the terms "methodological naturalism" and "metaphysical naturalism?"

Victor Fleming

A. Yes, I am familiar with how some philosophers would seek to separate those fields, much like how some would attempt to parse evolution into the science and the so-called religion of "evolutionism."

Q. Let's concentrate on how some in your field would separate methodological and metaphysical naturalism. How do they describe the so-called differences?

A. They would describe what I call "naturalism" to be "methodological naturalism," namely, the scientific method, which in a nutshell is the epistemological view that is concerned with practical methods for acquiring knowledge. It requires that hypotheses be explained and tested only by reference to natural causes and events—by observable effects. "Metaphysical naturalism" was a term coined in 1983 by Paul de Vries, a Wheaton College philosopher, to describe the position that nature is all that there is and that all basic truths are the truths of nature.

Q. Do you consider the fields to be distinct in this fashion?

A. No. Nature is all that there is. There is no supernatural and no metaphysical. If there were, there would be evidence of it and there isn't.

Q. What about concepts such as love, good and evil, altruism, and self-sacrifice, things that some would call the "metaphysical?"

A. They are all evolutionary behaviors. One engages in such behavior because it supports him, gratifies him, or makes him feel connected, like a dog to a pack.

We Hold These Truths

Q. Are one's beliefs of any importance to evolution?

A. No. Natural selection doesn't care what you *believe*; it is interested only in how you *behave*.

Q. Do you see science and philosophy as essentially one?

A. Absolutely. I support B.F. Skinner, Edward O. Wilson, W.V. Quine, George Santayana, and Emanuel Kant. The mind is rooted in self-serving behaviors which are discernible and explicable in modern biology and evolution science.

Q. Is this the dominant epistemological view in modern education in America?

A. Without a doubt.

Q. Is there any room for God in this equation?

A. There would be if there were evidence of God in the world, but there isn't.

Q. So there is no absolute good or evil?

A. No, I would not agree with that. Certain behaviors seem to be conducive to the species and certain behaviors are destructive.

Q. One of those destructive behaviors would be to sacrifice oneself for the sake of another?

A. Not necessarily. That trait may be self-perpetuating to the species.

Q. But why should I care about the species if I am only here to advance my own self interests?

A. Biology seems to drive us to protect the species.

Q. Why? Why should anything drive us to survive?

A. We can't answer that at present; we can only say that it is observable.

Q. Why would I ever rationally risk my life to save a drowning man?

A. It may make you feel better if you do.

Q. Well, I won't think at all if I don't survive.

A. True. It isn't a rational activity; it is only a biological impulse.

Q. Are there any absolutes except the laws of nature?

A. No, there aren't. By definition, the only absolutes are the laws of nature.

Q. How did the laws of nature get set in place?

A. No one set them in place; they just exist.

Q. And they are determined to exist by reliance on our faculties?

A. Yes—on empirical evidence as determined through our faculties.

Q. So would you contend, sir, that the public schools should confine themselves to what you have described as methodological naturalism or the scientific method as the universal font of knowledge?

A. Absolutely. This was the finding of Judge Jones in *Kitzmiller*, based on the unimpeachable testimony of philosopher of epistemology Robert T. Pennock.

Q. Do you know what Planck time is, professor?

A. Yes. I am not a physicist, but I know what it is.

Q. What is it, professor?

A. It is the time it would take a photon—the smallest body of matter—traveling at the speed of light to cross a distance equal to Planck length, which is the smallest distance possible in a gravitational world.

Q. So, if one moves beyond Planck time, he or she moves outside of our laws of physics and outside of the ability of our faculties to perceive, correct?

A. Yes.

Q. Do quantum physicists, to your knowledge, believe that there is something beyond Planck time and therefore beyond the limitations of time, space, and our physics?

A. Yes.

Q. So, in effect, physicists commonly postulate that there appears to be a world that we cannot perceive or understand through methodological naturalism or the scientific method?

A. Yes, although I would argue that it was the scientific method that got us there.

Q. So, you're saying that the scientific method impeached the scientific method, at least as the sum total of our human knowledge?

A. I can't agree with you there, counselor. The most I will say is that the scientific method has revealed something that the scientific method cannot yet explain.

Q. And that something which we cannot yet explain does not appear to be subject to the physical laws as we presently understand them?

A. Yes. That would be fair.

Q. Thank you, professor. Are you familiar with the *Scopes* trial?

A. Yes—the 1925 trial wherein a biology teacher, John Scopes, was prosecuted and convicted of violating a statute prohibiting the teaching of evolution.

Q. Do you know what textbook on evolution Mr. Scopes taught?

A. Hunter's *Civic Biology*, I believe.

Q. Very good. Are you familiar with page one hundred and ninety-six of that textbook on evolution?

We Hold These Truths

A.   I'm afraid I need my recollection refreshed.

Q.   Very well. Here's a copy, professor. Please read the subject entitled "Races of Man."

A.   All right. Beginning under that subheading: "Races of Man—At the present time there exist up the earth five races or varieties of man, each very different from the other in instincts, social customs, and, to an extent, in structure. There are the Ethiopians or negro type, originating in Africa; the Malay or brown race from the islands of the Pacific; the American Indian; the Mongolian or yellow race, including the natives of China, Japan, and the Eskimos; and finally, the highest type of all, the Caucasians, represented by the civilized white inhabitants of Europe and America."

Q.   That would be an application of faulty faculties, right, professor?

A.   Yes, in parts.

Q.   What parts, professor, would you consider faulty?

A.   The conclusion that the races are different in "instincts" and "structure" and that Caucasians are the "highest type of race."

Q.   And why is that faulty under present science?

A.   I think from a molecular, biological perspective, the races are largely the same in structure, and from a behavioral science standpoint, similar in behavioral instinct.

Q.   So, science has established the relative equality of the races?

A.   From a biological standpoint, yes.

Q.   And that makes the statement that Caucasians are the "highest type" scientifically incorrect?

A.   Yes. Absolutely.

Q.   What if science was to determine biological differences. Would that change the scientific principle of equality?

A.   I can't answer that in the abstract.

Q.   It may or may not; you would have to have more empirical facts?

A.   Yes.

Q.   Are you aware that scientists can ascertain genetic differences between normal humans and those with Down's Syndrome?

A.   Yes.

Q.   Would you say that those with Down's are equal to normal humans?

A.   The differences are not material.

Q.   You would tell parents of an unborn child with Down's Syndrome that the differences are not material?

A.   They are immaterial to the worth of the baby.

We Hold These Truths

Q.   The worth that social conventions would place on the baby?

A.   Yes.

Q.   Does nature draw those value distinctions?

A.   No.

Q.   How do scientists believe such values are communicated across society?

A.   Biologist Richard Dawkins has theorized that memes carry value systems between human beings.

Q.   What are "memes?"

A.   Memes is a method whereby values are passed from generation to generation by repetition.

Q.   Is there any empirical evidence using the scientific method to support this theory?

A.   Nothing other than the empirical fact that human beings carry such values, which is recognized in the Declaration of Independence.

Q.   That is the same empirical evidence that intelligent design advocates cite in support of their theory that a supernatural entity has encoded human beings with those values?

A.   I suppose; I don't know how they think.

"I have nothing further, your honor," Dexter stated.

John Cleaver rose but stayed at the defense table.

Q.   Professor, I just have two questions. First, do you think the court should order my client, the East Grand Rapids Public School district, to caution its students about the teaching of evolution with the statement that the plaintiff wants to impose on them or any statement of similar content?

A.   Absolutely not.

Q.   Why is that, professor?

A.   I would endorse Professor Devoneau's testimony on this point in its entirety. The Taylor statement's qualification of the scientific method and the impact on religion is not scientific and is not considered true by over ninety percent of the scientists in this country.

"Thank you, professor. I have nothing further."

"Mr. Bussey, anything further?"

"Yes, your honor, one or two questions." This time, Dexter did not stray from the plaintiff's table.

Q.   Professor, like Professor Devoneau, have you observed the teaching of evolution having an effect on students' religious views?

A.   Yes, in the same way that Galileo's teaching that the world was round dispelled the Christian view that the earth was flat. It dispels magical thinking and, therefore, attacks the notion of a supernatural father-creator, the basis of Judaism, Christianity, and Islam.

"Thank you, nothing further." Dexter stood, and John Cleaver passed the witness.

Dexter's last witness for the day was Milton Hileman, a statistician who was qualified by the court as a pollster without objection. Hileman, a robust, rotund man in his early forties, testified for less than half an hour, establishing that seventy percent of the one hundred adults he randomly polled in the East Grand Rapids school district considered the theory of evolution to be inconsistent with the possibility that the God of Christianity, Judaism, or Islam existed. He also testified that sixty-five percent of the one hundred high-school-aged students in the East Grand Rapids school district likewise considered the theory of evolution inconsistent with the possibility that a supernatural being existed.

Dexter was humming as he and Peter walked back to their office at three p.m. after grabbing lunch with Vicki Taylor.

"You're in a good mood for the middle of trial," Peter offered. "Do you think the trial is going that well?"

"Well, so far our plaintiff client has denied having any damages, our two principal experts have emphatically rejected the propriety of the injunctive relief we are seeking, and our secondary expert has opined that sixty-five percent of the people in the relevant school district reject our proposition that evolution and Christianity are not incompatible. In short, the scientific method must be bullshit, because despite all of the objective facts, I think our case is going swimmingly."

Peter laughed. "I think so, too. Maybe hell is freezing over?"

"Could be," Dexter replied. "After all, the polar ice caps are melting and tomorrow we try to establish that evolution is the strongest proof of an intelligent designer yet developed."

* * *

"What is Bussey doing?" Alex Ross wondered as Riley and he retired to the Lumber Baron bar, as was becoming their post-trial ritual. "He's got experts that should be playing for the other team. They're belittling Michelle Taylor's position, not sustaining it. They are ardent New Darwinists, for Pete's sake."

Keegan Riley leaned away from Ross on his bar stool, shooting him a sidelong look. "Do you play poker?"

"Yes, why?"

"I'm hosting a high stakes game on Sunday night. I think I want you at the table."

Ross looked down into his drink. "Too bad I only make a reporter's salary."

Riley looked at him and smiled. "Yes, that is too bad."

After a minute of silence, Ross became impatient. "Come on, Keegan. Explain the strategy."

Riley shook his head. "Now I remember why I didn't have children... Weren't you paying attention during Bussey's opening? He's reversing the playbook in the *Kitzmiller* case where the ACLU lawyers called Christian evolutionists to establish the religious neutrality of evolution. Here he's calling the radical naturalists in order to draw a link between evolution and atheism."

"I thought he wasn't going to attack evolution."

"He isn't attacking evolution. He's attacking the New Darwinists—the atheists who are trying to co-opt evolution the same way that creation science has been co-opted by the Christian evangelicals who believe the world was created in six calendar days."

"So he's calling these experts to discredit them?" Ross wondered.

"Close. He's calling them to expose them. He's trying to convince Judge Austin that if intelligent design theory can be co-opted by the young-earth creationists, as Judge Jones found in *Kitzmiller*, then it's possible that evolutionary theory can be co-opted by atheists. If he wins that argument, he's halfway home to convincing Judge Austin that First Amendment law may require the curative statement he's touting."

"So I suppose Cleaver is going to call a bunch of Christians?" Ross smirked rhetorically.

Riley lowered his chin and looked up at Ross. "Are you sure you aren't available Sunday? I would consider floating you a loan."

Chapter Seven

First Responders

Tuesday, July 15, 2009

Synthesizing evolution and Christianity was nowhere on the national media's radar in early July when the Taylor case first caught national attention.

"Here's an interesting case to watch," intoned Joe Block on the Cox Cable News Network. "Some leftist science teacher in Grand Rapids, Michigan, ridiculed a poor fifteen-year-old high school freshman's religious beliefs, driving the poor child to kill herself. The young girl was grieving over the recent death of her beloved father to accident and illness, and this wacko teacher suggested her belief she will be reunited with her father in glory is just magical thinking... That the only things real are those we can see, hear, and touch. Hey wise-guy, have you ever seen a radio wave? Do you need to touch the radiation coming out of Chernobyl before you believe it could kill you?"

Block smiled at his logic, knowing he had a full five percent of the American television audience in his back pocket. "Hey, Supreme Court justices, if you are listening, this is what you get when you force feed Darwinism down our children's throats—nihilism, insensitivity, and death."

He was going for the jugular now. He lowered his voice, looking straight at the camera, which he knew loved him. "Folks, it is time to take back our courts. We have been taking it on the chin since the original Scopes trial. Can't talk about God. Can't talk about the creator. Can't talk about the very values that built this great country of ours. Let me ask this simple question: How does our Declaration of Independence start?"

Block leaned in to the camera, adopting a monotone:

:We hold these truths to be self-evident. All men were C-R-E-A-T-E-D equal..."

He backed up and resumed his normal voice. "Not all men E-V-O-L-V-E-D equally, which is impossible, by the way..." He then leaned into the camera and reassumed his monotone:

"...endowed by their C-R-E-A-T-O-R..."

He backed up, using his normal voice. "Not programmed by their monkey ancestors..."

He stopped, letting the silence become uncomfortable, concluding in his normal but hushed voice, "Yes, liberal judiciary, you have blood on your hands in Michigan. We'll be watching to see if you finally wash it off."

* * *

"I don't care about Joe Block's rantings," Robert J. Johnson scoffed as Bart Baron, the partner at Kingman Walker who worked the Americans for Science Studies' files with him, fumbled with a stack of papers. AFSS was the perfect client—it was a nonprofit set up by Kingman Walker, exclusively funded by one of the corporate partners at Kingman, who conveniently persuaded a now long deceased multi-millionaire client to appoint him as the trustee for the client's charitable trust. AFSS and that beneficial trust had no purpose other than to finance lawsuits seeking to preclude religious teaching from creeping into America's public schools, although the million dollars a year they poured into Kingman Walker's pockets annually might suggest otherwise.

"Maybe you care that his ratings have increased ten percent since he started to obsess about cosmology in the public schools," Baron argued.

"He will eventually flame out. They all do. That's a scientific corollary of evolution," Johnson laughed.

"Maybe this will move you? Read this complaint and look at who authored it." Baron sneered, slowly smiling as he played his trump card.

Johnson snatched the complaint and immediately flipped to the last page to see who had signed it. "What in the hell?" Johnson blushed. He did not look up but steadied himself, spending the next ten minutes digesting the complaint.

Still not looking at Baron for fear Baron would be gloating, Johnson continued, "This is a dangerous complaint. It doesn't directly tackle *Kitzmiller*, but subtly undermines it. 'As intelligent design has been co-opted by the evangelicals, evolution has been co-opted by the atheists,'" Johnson read.

"If Bussey establishes this proposition, and he might, he is halfway home to turning *Jaffree* on its head and allowing intelligent design in the back door," Johnson continued. "Worse, Bussey isn't over-reaching. His goals are modest. I don't like this at all."

"He's certainly holds a strategy, but he's a fool if he thinks he can work this case while holding our lucrative offer in his back pocket." Baron unsuccessfully stifled a gloat when Johnson finally looked at him.

"Block is an ally in killing this case," Johnson declared. "He'll demand the entire enchilada—that the public schools be allowed to teach creationism. Let's help him along. Crank out some anonymous letters to the East Grand Rapids school district urging it to do the right thing and return school prayer and creationism in the classroom. Meanwhile, I'll take care of Bussey."

"Goddamn it!" Johnson mumbled under his breath as Baron shut the door on his way out. Johnson picked up the phone and dialed Dexter Bussey.

"Dexter!" Johnson exclaimed, positively without a hint of his true mood. "What's new?"

"Hello, Robert," Dexter replied. "Work... Old and new. How about with you?"

"Me? Nothing ever happens in Chicago. Have you made a decision on our offer, Dexter?"

"Truthfully, no. I've been preoccupied by a new case on a fast track."

"The Taylor case," Johnson interjected. "I know all about it. The boning you've been doing on the First Amendment will come in very handy, Dexter. One of the firm's best clients is Americans for Scientific Studies. You can help me in cases like Taylor across the country, only on the smarter side of the issue, of course. But I am sure that won't bother you. What's the delay? We are offering you three times your current salary and cases that will make Taylor look like child's play."

"It is a wonderful generous offer, Robert, as you know. I hate to quit on a job unfinished. Taylor is on a rocket docket. The trial will be over in ten weeks."

"I admire your determination, Dexter. I really do. Come to Kingman Walker and you will never have to quit another project. However, my young friend, this offer can't wait ten weeks. Call me next week with your positive response. We will send a team down to scout out local office space in Grand Rapids and assign you some challenging national cases."

"I will call you next week," Dexter promised weakly.

"Damn the timing!" Dexter mumbled under his breath as he hung the phone up.

* * *

Wednesday, July 30, 2009

"Do you believe in God, Frank?" Owen asked Frank Callahan at the end of the day as Owen poured each of them a scotch and soda from the crystal decanter, otherwise locked in the mahogany cabinet in his chambers

We Hold These Truths

"Yes sir, I do," Frank responded from his seat in the client chair across from Owen's oversized mahogany desk. "I most definitely do. I believe in truth and love."

"What does truth have to do with God's existence?" Owen wanted to know as he settled into the wine red leather chair behind his desk.

"God is love. God is truth. If there were no God, there would be no love and no true path." Frank inhaled a sip of scotch.

"But is God interested in your personal well-being?" Owen loosened his tie while longing for the cigar he used to enjoy at this point in the day but had to give up after the building went smokeless five years ago.

"Absolutely. Throughout time men have sought power, money, and sex. What they really seek is a reunion with God," Frank explained. "We are in a mess only because we rebel. Did you ever consider how strange it is that people swear? You hear a lot of swearing in the military. I've seen men of every rank, color, and creed swear. I've even seen men who claim to be ardent atheists take God's name in vain. You don't see them taking Charles Darwin's name in vain. People pick on the Lord. Got to be the work of the devil. Got to be a product of our rebellion."

"I have to admit, Frank," Owen offered as he took another sip, "I have never heard anyone suggest swearing is a sign of God's existence. But it makes some sense as you explain it. Let me ask you this, though: If there is a personal God interested in your well-being, why does he allow natural disasters, disease, accidents, wars, and poverty?"

"You know the answer to that from the parade passing through your courtroom. Most human misery is entirely manmade, caused by selfishness and greed. As I said, the rest is a result of man's pact with the devil—the product of our choice to be independent from God. God doesn't cause pestilence. He just allows it as a result of our choice. Our time on this earth is short, your honor, you can't fret too much about losses. Whether your time on the stage is short or long, happy or sad, life's play doesn't last but a blink of the eye. No, sir! Not more than a blink of the eye." Frank laughed lightly into his glass.

"Truth is an important concept in your culture, isn't it Frank?" Owen leaned back in his chair.

"That's the truth!" Frank chuckled. "'Stay true,' is maybe the most popular expression in the Black community right now. Sums up a lot. Lots of bad decision-making occurring in the world. It's easy to get off track with drugs, prostitution, crime, gangs, violence. Staying true to the right path; staying true to your family; staying true to yourself is the only way to survive it all." Frank sat ramrod straight in his chair, a vestige of his Marine drill sergeant days.

"What do you think of evolution?" Owen asked.

"Don't matter to me what means God used to create man or animal. That's his business. My business is to stay true and love those around me. Truth and love don't come from a rock—that much I know for damn sure." Frank downed his scotch.

Owen leaned over and poured another half glass and then wryly smiled. "You must not think too highly of lawyers."

Frank shook his head. "Your honor, you have the patience of Job. I can't stand them. They're an arrogant breed, pontificating like they have a corner on the truth, but they are always spinning it to serve their purposes. The truth couldn't be less important to them. You are the only lawyer I like."

Owen chuckled. "I am very glad to hear that, Frank." Then he leaned forward in his chair and became more serious. "Let me ask you this: Do you think the right decision is usually made in my courtroom—and I don't mean just by me, but by the juries?"

Frank sat back and pondered the question for a moment. "Yes, now that I think about it. I do think the right decision is usually made."

Owen's chuckle continued. "Well, I won't ask you to break down the mistakes. But let me explain something and maybe you will have a better appreciation for lawyers. Our system of justice is built on the premise that if both sides distort the truth in opposite ways the truth will emerge. Seems kind of crazy when explained that way, but it is the design. You are right that each lawyer is not looking for the truth. That isn't their role. Their limited role is to present their client's position in the most favorable light, and if each does the job well, the truth will be apparent to the decision-maker. It isn't perfect. Still, it's the best system man has ever developed to get to the truth, Frank."

"I'll trust you on that, Judge. It does make some sense now that you have explained it. Still doesn't explain all the spinning lawyers do outside the courtroom."

Owen smiled. "I will take a small victory today."

"Misses wanted me home at six." Frank emptied his glass and set it on the judge's silver serving tray. "Say, Judge, do you have a place for dinner tonight? We would be honored to have you join us."

"Thank you, Frank. I am honored by the invitation and will take a rain check. But it has been a long day and an even longer day for Caesar. I am going to finish a couple of emails to my daughters and then head home to feed and walk the dog. Thanks again."

"Anytime, your honor. Anytime." Frank sidled out of Owen's office, softly closing the door behind him.

After pouring a second scotch, Owen pulled out the empty banker's box Frank had hauled from the courthouse basement that morning. Owen began sifting through the contents of the bottom drawn in his desk. He flipped over the neat stack of legal documents so he could turn over the oldest documents first. Owen was amused as he extracted a yellow, onion papered document. This was a carbon copy of the first legal opinion he authored when he was a twenty-five-year-old lawyer almost forty-five years earlier. He hadn't read the opinion in forty years. He tossed it into the trash.

The next document in Owen's inverted stack, a letter written on bond paper bearing the watermark and the letterhead of the Peter Peerless Paper Company, carried the date of May 11, 1970. The letter was addressed to the senior partner in Owen's firm, complimenting Owen's work. Owen smiled. "What a great guy— Peter Peerless," Owen said to no one. "I haven't thought about you in thirty years. What a thoughtful letter," Owen marveled as he dropped it into the bottom of his box. "God Bless you, Peter, wherever you are."

Owen next pulled out a June 20, 1974 opinion written by the then-elderly, now-deceased Wilbur Miller of the western district —the culminating event in the first big federal trial Owen had won as a young lawyer, a high-profile case under the Federal Meat Inspection Act. Through the opinion, Owen had obtained a permanent injunction restraining the United States Department of Agriculture from installing permanent inspectors in the deli department of a local grocery chain. Owen noted that even almost forty years later it was possible to figure out the typewriter's corrections. After barely glancing at it, he tossed the ruling in the trash.

Owen carefully picked up the next document, knowing what it was before he turned it over. It was a handwritten letter dated January 15, 1975 on the personal stationary of Charles Ash, the domineering senior partner of Mead Snell, the oldest firm in Grand Rapids. The letter advised Owen that the partners had unanimously elected him to partnership status and invited him to join the "club." Owen paused, remembering how much this letter had once meant to him, and smiled ironically at how insignificant it seemed today. He pitched the letter into the trash.

The next document was a 1986 fax from the office of the local congressman advising Owen he had been nominated by the President as a federal judge, subject only to Senate confirmation. Strange; Owen pondered for the first time why the congressman would send such a significant message by fax.

Owen shrugged, dropping the fax into the box, wondering when he had last received a fax.

A chime on the computer denoted the filing of John Cleaver's motion to dismiss the Taylor case. Even though it was close to eight p.m., a lawyer could now simply electronically paste the document onto the court's webpage and it would be automatically posted in the electronic file, which could be accessed online by anyone at any time.

From carbon paper to electronic filing, Owen's forty-five-year career had seen greater technological changes in the legal practice's mechanics than the previous four hundred years. Owen felt the throbbing of his headache. His headaches were getting more constant and more severe.

Owen reviewed the East Grand Rapids' closed door meeting minutes, which had been sent confidentially to him for private inspection as requested. As he digested the minutes, he thought again about disqualifying himself. He vaguely believed Megan had been taught by Paul Kingston, and he almost remembered meeting Kingston at a parent-teacher conference.

Owen rubbed his own temples. He looked out at the Calder. Suddenly, he laughed at himself and bottomed his scotch. Who was he kidding? He wanted to hear this case. He looked forward to refereeing two very good lawyers warring for his attention, trying to shape his thinking. Damn the timing. Screw the consequences. He was going to be true to himself to the end. He was nothing if not a judge.

* * *

"Tonight, we are privileged to have the lead lawyer in the Michigan case attacking evolution in the public schools, Mr. Dexter Bussey. Welcome to the program Mr. Bussey, how are you tonight?" Joe Block intoned as the studio camera remained glued to him even after he turned to face the large television monitor on which Dexter's face appeared.

"I am fine, Mr. Block," replied Dexter. "But we are not really attacking the teaching of evolution in the public schools..."

"Aren't you arguing evolution has been linked with the new atheists?" Block quickly interjected, his famous temper already rising.

"To be sure," Dexter explained, "but we are merely asking the court to force the public school to decouple evolution from the atheism with which it is now entangled."

"Let's back up a minute, Mr. Bussey," Block answered. "Aren't you trying to revisit that wrongheaded decision in Pennsylvania—*Kitzmiller*, isn't that what they call it? Just so our viewers recall, *Kitzmiller* is the case where a George W. Bush appointed federal judge turned traitor and found evolution to be scientifically demonstrable and creationism not. He therefore concluded only evolution can be taught in the public schools and intelligent design may not be mentioned. Isn't that the case we are talking about, Mr. Bussey?" Block asked rhetorically.

"Yes, but we are using *Kitzmiller* to bolster our case," Dexter tried to interject. "As Judge Jones found intelligent design entangled with creationism, we contend evolution has become entangled in the public mind with evolution. They must be uncoupled or the public schools will have violated the First Amendment's anti-establishment clause."

"So you want all public school teachers to read a disclaimer that evolution is atheistic tripe. That's good," Block responded. "Aren't you also arguing creationism is a permissible subject for public school teaching?"

"Well..." Dexter paused, wondering whether to challenge Block on the first declaration, then deciding to merely answer the second. "We are asserting the origin of life and the condition of the human brain cannot be explained by evolution and, therefore, the speculation of an intelligent designer is perfectly acceptable in the public schools."

"Speculation? There is nothing speculative about where the human mind came from, Mr. Bussey!" Block roared. "Why don't you ask those monkey lovers why they haven't found a monkey that can talk in the heart of Africa? The problem with evolution is not missing link fossils, it is missing link live animals. The evolutionists point to crocodiles and say they haven't materially changed in one hundred million years because they are content and haven't had to adapt. Well, by that same logic, if we all evolved from monkeys, why can't they find one monkey who evolved to the point of talking and decided, like the crocodiles, to stop evolving at that point? Where are the half men, half monkeys, Mr. Bussey?"

Except for the cameraman, Block's crew were all laughing at the question. "I can't help you with that one, Mr. Block," Dexter smiled. "I am not a biologist—just a lawyer. My goals are a little less ambitious. I am not attacking evolution as a science; I am just saying the public schools must advise their young students that there are Christian scientists who also believe in evolution, as there are atheistic scientists who subscribe to it."

"There you go, Mr. Bussey!" Block leaned back, "You just found me an example of a half man, half monkey—a 'Christian evolutionist,'" Block blasted, forcing even his cameraman to stifle a chuckle, lest he jiggle the studio camera. "Bussey," Block continued, dropping any appellation, "I think you need to bone up a little on this subject before trial. Let me ask you this: Do you know who Karl Popper was?"

"A philosopher who was a father of the scientific method?" Dexter asked, having no idea where he had come up with that.

"Exactly! Very good, Mr. Bussey. Karl Popper, the father of the scientific method, understood evolution is not falsifiable and, therefore, is not scientific. You can't be into this game halfway, Mr. Bussey. You want to know how the human mind was formed. Just use your common sense. Did it come from a monkey or from an intelligent designer? Present that question to the judge so that every parent in this great country can see their kids properly taught creationism in our public schools.

There's your case, Mr. Bussey, and I won't charge you a dime for the consultation!"

"Thanks for the advice" was all Dexter could add.

"You are most welcome, sir, and good luck. We are way overdue for a commercial, folks," and with that Dexter's face blackened, replaced with a dishwasher soap commercial.

* * *

"I enjoyed you on the Joe Block show tonight," Robert Johnson smirked as Dexter picked up the phone

"I could hardly get a word in edgewise," Dexter moaned.

"What did you expect, Dexter? You can't appear on a cable ideologue's show and expect a fair hearing," Johnson lectured. "But he was right about one thing. You can't be half into things —such as our offer."

Dexter sighed. "I need more time, Robert. I am just digesting the EGR's school district's motion to dismiss."

"Time is a lawyer's rarest commodity."

"Funny, I bill enough of it in a year." Dexter fought to regain an edge.

"Get your case beyond the dismissal motion and you will have done your client a great service or disservice, depending upon your point of view. Then quit. Or, if you lose the case, there won't be a case to quit. Either way, our timing will be perfect. When is oral argument?"

"Three weeks," Dexter offered weakly.

"Perfect. There's your extension. You have three weeks. I will call you then." Johnson hung up.

This was not a good day, Dexter thought to himself. He had hoped to control his message with Block and string Johnson out. He had struck out twice. He had better call Mrs. Taylor and schedule cocktails after the court hearing.

* * *

Monday, August 25, 2009

Dexter Bussey strode through the ten-foot-high double doors guarding Owen Austin's two-story courtroom, Peter Diamond trailing him. He walked purposefully through the swinging, waist-high gate marking the entrance to the bar and stood at the plaintiff counsel's table on the right side of the courtroom nearest to the jury box. After flattening his brief case on the table, he turned to greet John Cleaver, already seated at the defense table on the left side of the courtroom. A lectern divided the two tables.

"Hello John, good to see you," Dexter said cordially, extending his right hand.

John turned, looking over his reading glasses to make eye contact with Dexter. "Good morning to you, Dexter." John rose to greet him. "Ready for an interesting hearing?"

"Undoubtedly." Dexter smiled while rummaging through his brief case to pull out his notes.

John sidestepped to Dexter, close enough to whisper. "Dexter, I must say, I was surprised to see your name of this file. I wouldn't have linked you with this subject matter, and although Mrs. Taylor can certainly afford your fee, I know you don't lack for high paying work. Pray tell, what's your real motivation?"

Just then the double doors to the courtroom burst open and all occupants turned. Vicki Taylor strutted across the threshold, stopping all conversation. She looked stunning in a perfectly cut, trim black suit, her blonde hair and large breasts bobbing as her hips swayed, her ankles sharply pointed as one lovely glam followed the other in a straight line. At the bar's threshold, she perfectly pivoted into the first row behind Dexter.

John leaned over and whispered into Dexter's right ear, "Never mind." He chuckled as he returned to this seat.

Frank Callahan emerged from one of the courtroom's back doors, squared his shoulders, and announced in a deep baritone, "All rise." Through the other back door, Owen swept in and quickly scaled the steps to his seat on the bench. "Please be seated." Turning to Sarah, who had entered the courtroom along with his court reporter from the right hand back door, Owen directed, "Ms. Lewis, would you read the call?"

Sarah took her seat and called out, "The Estate of Michelle Taylor versus The East Grand Rapids School District, 09-cv-0361-cz.

"Gentlemen, I have reviewed the minutes of the district's closed session." Owen started the hearing on the district's motion to dismiss. "There is nothing sufficiently confidential to keep them out of the record. Ms. Shurlow, would you circulate a copy of them to Mr. Bussey, and for convenience we have another copy for Mr. Cleaver as well."

Sarah approached the counsels' tables and distributed a page to each lawyer.

Dexter read the minutes, which were two sentences in length:

> "Attorney Cleaver's opinion letter regarding a constituent letter was circulated and reviewed by the Board. The letter will be accepted for information only."

"For the sake of this hearing, I conclude the constituent letter is Mrs. Taylor's request for the district to approve the statement attached to her letter. Mr. Cleaver, may I make this assumption a finding of fact at this time?" Owen asked, looking to John Cleaver.

"Yes, your honor, you may," John answered, only half-rising from his seated position.

"Thank you, Mr. Cleaver. I appreciate your cooperation. The court finds the letter discussed in the closed session at the June twenty-fifth meeting of the East Grand Rapids school board was

Mrs. Taylor's correspondence, which is attached as Exhibit A to the complaint. Given the definitive word 'only' in the second sentence in the closed session minutes, I conclude the school board made a decision it would not adopt the letter's statement as requested by Mrs. Taylor. Mr. Cleaver, your reaction to that finding?"

John rose quickly to his feet. "I object to it, your honor. You are clearly reading into the minutes a conclusion not apparent. Since we are here on the district's motion to dismiss only, such a finding is premature and procedurally inappropriate." Growing agitation crept across John's voice. His hand gesturing and higher pitched voice revealing his sudden anger.

"I recognize it is early in the case and the district has yet to answer the complaint," Owen soothed. "The Taylor estate alleges the board made such a decision at that meeting. You are free to deny this allegation if you choose, Mr. Cleaver, but if you do, it will open up your board members to discovery on whether a consensus was reached and whether they intend to do anything with the letter other than receive it for information. I will let you mull that possibility. For the present motion, I am obligated to accept all well pled allegations in the complaint as true, and I limit my finding to the present motion. And, for this motion only, I find that the board has made a negative decision on the estate's statement. Is that fair, Mr. Cleaver?"

"Yes, your honor," John answered as he sat down, his temper cooling only slightly.

"All right, I have thoroughly reviewed the complaint and the motion to dismiss and supporting and opposing briefs. As I indicated, my obligation is to construe the allegations in the complaint and all reasonable inferences to be true, and then to determine whether they state a plausible cause of action. Mr. Bussey has stipulated the estate is not seeking to compel the district to teach intelligent design as an alternative to evolution's tenets of natural selection and speciation, but rather only as a speculative explanation for how matter and life emerged and how the human brain is wired. Moreover, the plaintiff contends that as intelligent design has been co-opted by Christian evangelicals, evolution has become entwined in popular opinion with atheism, which is a religion. As a result, the estate asserts this public school must advise its students of the distinction between the science of evolution and religion atheism or it effectively promotes atheism in violation of the First Amendment. Mr. Bussey, have I accurately stated your claims?" Owen asked, turning his attention on Dexter.

"Yes, your honor, you have." Dexter rose to his full frame.

"Good. The third claim Mrs. Taylor makes is that public school teachers may not deny the existence of the supernatural without discouraging religious belief in violation of the First Amendment? Is that correct?"

"I couldn't have stated it more succinctly, your honor," Dexter said as he sat down.

"Mr. Cleaver, aside from the Open Meetings Act claim, I will take argument on the plaintiff's claims as I have described them," Owen declared.

John rose and took three steps to the lectern, reading from his notes. "Thank you, your honor. On the encouragement claim, the plaintiff does not challenge any official curriculum position of the East Grand Rapids public school district. Instead, the estate claims Michelle Taylor's constitutional rights were violated because the district did not disclaim a link between atheism and evolution before teaching her evolution—a disclaimer not a single public school district in this country is offering in any form. If there is one thing the *Kitzmiller* decision teaches us it is that disclaimer statements about religion and evolution are inappropriate for public schools. Certainly, it isn't even a colorable constitutional violation if a public school refuses to get dragged into such a practice. Indeed, for the district to have adopted the statement proposed by Mrs. Taylor after the fact would have exposed it to liability under the establishment clause to some student or parent who objected, as in *Kitzmiller*, to the religious overtones of such statements.

"On the discouragement claim, the teacher is not alleged to have said there is no God; what he said was there is no empirical evidence of a God. Again, this is not an unusual position. All people of faith realize belief in God is a matter of faith. There is no factual proof of God or there would be no need for faith. This court dismissed a similar claim in *Daugherty v. Vanguard Charter School Academy*, finding a teacher's antidotal comments which are not part of an approved curriculum cannot be actionable unless they cause a direct and sharp violation of the First Amendment and the district is deliberately indifferent to the violation. There is no allegation the incidental comments of Mr. Kingston directly rebuff Christianity. Nor is there any evidence the East Grand Rapids school district is deliberately indifferent to any accidental violation of the First Amendment even if clever lawyers after the fact could find such a violation imbedded in those comments. Teacher Kingston's comments were clearly designed to advance neutrality, not hostility towards religion. They did not violate any constitutional mandate. The complaint should be dismissed."

"Thank you, Mr. Cleaver. Mr. Bussey, your turn."

Dexter rose and spoke softly, slowly, without notes: "The holding in *Kitzmiller* supports the estate's position in this case. The court in *Kitzmiller* found intelligent design so closely linked in common understanding with Christianity that for the public schools to teach it would be an endorsement of religion. It permanently enjoined the Dover public school district from teaching the theory. The estate alleges evolution has likewise become so closely linked in common understanding with a religion, in this case atheism, that to teach it without an uncoupling is an endorsement of religion. The estate is in good company in this allegation, since both the original subscriber to evolution, Charles Darwin, and its current chief proponent, Oxford biologist Richard Dawkins, claim nothing less than evolution proves there is no God—that evolution establishes atheism as the one true religion. We will present proofs in this case to demonstrate evolution and atheism are as linked in the common mind as intelligent design is with Christianity. If such linkage compelled an injunction in *Kitzmiller*, it commands some First Amendment relief here.

"Now, unlike the victorious plaintiffs in *Kitzmiller*, the estate does not seek to enjoin East Grand Rapids high school from teaching a cosmological theory, in this case, evolution. The estate asks this court to order the district to simply explain the difference between the science of evolution and the religion of evolutionism, also called 'naturalism.' Given the intentional blurring of those distinctions by evolution's leading proponents and the lofty neutrality mandated for religious beliefs, the estate's request is modest. That school districts across the country are presently not undertaking this uncoupling is no more a defense in this case than the fact that many other schools were permitting daily prayer was a defense in *Jaffree*."

Dexter picked up the pace, "*Kitzmiller* also supports the estate's discouragement claim. In *Kitzmiller*, the court found the contrived dualism in the school district's statement was a constitutional flaw. By contrived dualism the court meant the assumption evolution and monotheism were incompatible. Similarly, the estate alleges contrived dualism in Mr. Kingston's statements wherein he denied the empirical existence of metaphysical concepts such as good and evil—wherein he denied the possible compatibility between religion and science— wherein he denied any evidence that God exists. We can hardly imagine comments more directly or sharply hostile to religion than to deny the objective existence of good or evil, the possible compatibility of religion and science, and most acutely, to deny that the testimonial conclusions of billions of people alive and dead forms some empirical support for the possible existence of God. We are not asking the district to teach that good and evil exist, or that religion and science are necessarily compatible, or that there is empirical evidence of God's existence, but it must refrain from taking negative positions on these matters."

Dexter paused, making direct eye contact with Owen. "Likewise, this court's holding in *Daugherty* supports the estate's position in this case. In *Daugherty*, there was no evidence that the district had been aware of the antidotal teacher comments, much less ignored complaints about those comments. Here, exactly the opposite is true: Mrs. Taylor attempted to resolve her complaints with the principal and formally requested action be taken to counsel Mr. Kingston against further comments discouraging religious thought. The school district expressly refused to disavow Mr. Kingston's comments, subjecting it to declaratory and injunctive relief under the deliberate indifference standard." Dexter paused for another moment.

"We think the *Kitzmiller* court erred in only one regard, your honor. Certain aspects of our cosmological knowledge are so incomplete—such as how matter was originally formed and how and when plant or animal life emerged or how the human brain has come to appreciate metaphysical concepts—that to subject all theories about those subjects to the so-called 'scientific method' is too rigid as a threshold to possible admission into a public school's curriculum. After all, even Karl Popper, the father of the scientific method, considered the theory of evolution to be nonfalsifiable and, therefore, to be a research programme rather than a scientific principle. While we are not asking the court to order the East Grand Rapids public schools to offer intelligent design as a theory as to how matter was formed or how life emerged or how the human brain came to be hard wired as it is, we ask this court to declare that the First Amendment does not preclude a public school biology curriculum from referring to religious speculation on these fronts any more than it prohibits public school teachers from acknowledging that some people believe there is a God." Dexter paused to let his words echo in the courtroom, then slowly sat down.

"Thank you, Mr. Bussey." Owen also spoke without notes: "I am going to deny the motion to dismiss. Taking the complaint on its face, as I must at this time, the district has made official decisions to support the statements of its instructor and to deny the request to make a qualifying statement regarding the difference between the science of evolution and the religious characteristics of evolutionism. Without finding at this stage that the district is obligated to qualify the theory of evolution in the manner requested in order to maintain lofty neutrality, I agree with the court in *Kitzmiller* that if an origins of life theory has been become entwined with a particular religion, a public school district may be guilty of endorsing the religion if it endorses the theory without qualification, especially if impressionable young minds are involved. The estate alleges the theory of evolution has become entangled with atheism, and at this stage, I must accept that allegation as fact. If true, the constitution arguable requires some disclaimer such as requested by the plaintiff.

"Likewise, the First Amendment's edict of lofty neutrality may prohibit the district from permitting its teachers to deny that the recognized struggle between right and wrong is possible evidence of a supernatural being. Again, the court's ruling is not final, but the result of an application of the dismissal motion standard to the complaint. If there are no questions, I would like to close the record and see counsel in my chambers. Mr. Cleaver, any questions?"

"Only one, your honor: Are you going to issue a written opinion?" John asked, signaling his displeasure by jumping to attention using a clipped verbal tone.

"That's a fair question. No, my ruling from the bench will stand as my opinion. My clerk will prepare an order formally denying your motion," Owen responded. "Anything else?"

"No, your honor."

"Mr. Bussey?" Owen turned to Dexter.

Dexter stood. "No, your honor. Thank you."

"Okay. That closes the record." Owen rose from the bench, and Frank timed the opening of door in the back of the courtroom so Owen did not have to break stride to exit.

Dexter turned and took several steps to the edge of the bar. There he found Vicki Taylor, who leaned over the bar. "Things went well, I presume," Vicki Taylor smiled.

Dexter made eye contact and said, "Things could not have gone any better. The trial is on. He wants to see the lawyers in chambers. The judge will want to discuss the time we need for discovery and perhaps set the trial date. This will take half an hour to an hour tops. I need to discuss something with you. Can you stay?"

A sly smiled formed on Vicki Taylor's face. She arched her back seductively. "Of course. I'll wait for you at the Lumber Baron bar in the Grand Plaza Hotel."

"I need to go now. I will meet your there in an hour." Dexter felt a manic rush. He turned from his client and he and Peter strode through the back door of the courtroom.

Once in chambers, Dexter smiled at Sarah and Kelly at their desks. "Mr. Bussey, they are waiting for you," Sarah gently lectured.

Dexter smiled, leaning forward. "Client duty, Ms. Lewis, you know the burden." He turned to Kelly Vandervelde. "I hope I wasn't mumbling, Kelly." Kelly blushed while shaking her head. Dexter made a point of making personal court staff connections, which were invaluable if a favor had to be secured from the court.

Dexter entered the judge's office, finding Owen at the head of the table with John Cleaver and Greg Jones on one side and Mary Lou Shurlow seated on the other, nearest the judge. "Mr. Bussey and Mr. Diamond, please come on in. We were just discussing the Tigers' prospects for the post season. I am afraid Mr. Cleaver and Mr. Jones don't share my optimism."

"John, I'll take the Tigers to get into the post season before the Lions," Dexter wagered.

"After this morning's hearing, you owe me the Tigers, Dexter," John chided, only half kidding.

"Speaking of this case," Owen segued, "Mr. Cleaver, how soon will you be filing your answer?"

"In a week, your honor." John already had his answer prepared but didn't want to let Judge Austin think he expected the motion to be denied. Truth was he had expected Owen to grant the motion and he knew that the school district would be disappointed the case gained any traction and, of course, was now going to increase in expense exponentially. Also, John could feel Jones' hostility, certain Jones blamed John for not sanitizing the meeting minutes by deleting the fatal word "only" as a qualifier to "information." As soon as Jones had seen the minutes he had visited John's office to predict this would be an Achilles heel.

"Good. Let me ask you this?" Owen leaned his face on his hand. "Are you going to deny any factual allegations in the complaint?"

"I don't think so, your honor, but I want to confirm that conclusion with the teacher and district one more time." John could sense Jones tightening.

"I am glad to hear that for several reasons. Most importantly from my perspective, it would appear to largely eliminate the need for discovery. The case appears to center on expert testimony. Do you each agree?"

"Yes, your honor," Dexter jumped.

"I think that is mostly fair, with my caveat," John added.

"All right, I'll require the disclosure of experts in two weeks. I would like expert reports to be circulated two weeks thereafter, including all pre-trial document disclosures. You will each have one week to name a rebuttal expert, thereafter. This gives the month of October to take depositions. Trial will be scheduled for November first. Is that acceptable?"

Dexter and John were stunned, each having expected at least three times as much time, even on a so called "rocket docket." Owen jumped in, not wanting to give either a chance to object, again resorting to the unusual step of using Christian names. "John, I know your client will be concerned about costs. This way costs will be controlled. Dexter, the district is doing you a favor by largely accepting your facts. You both know what you want to establish through expert testimony. I can't think of two finer lawyers for cross examination on the fly. And, if there is any need for attention along the way, this case has my highest priority. Together we can do this."

Dexter was impressed and pleased. The approach fit Dexter's aggressive nature and his personal interests with Kingman Walker. "Okay. The plaintiff will play ball, your honor."

John was mortified. He would have to rearrange his entire schedule to meet this timeline and work longer hours than normal. Yet, he felt as if he was sliding on the wrong side of Judge Austin. He was either going to throw a fit to try to break Owen's momentum at great tactical risk, or go along. A sudden wave of fatigue rushed over him. "East will rise to the occasion, as well," John found himself saying without any conscious decision.

"Very well. I am pleased. Again, I am so happy to have each of you on this file. We will kick out the scheduling order and an order on the motion. Thank you very much." Owen stood, exhausted even though it was barely noon. He quickly pushed away a fearful thought that even this lightning schedule wouldn't get him through the trial.

Dexter and John were surprised at the conference's abrupt ending, particularly given its leisurely start. They hustled out of the judge's chambers, each believing Judge Austin must be rushing to make a luncheon appointment.

As soon as the four lawyers left court chambers, John turned to Dexter. "What in the hell is Austin doing? Doesn't he have anything else on his docket? Have you ever seen a trial date set before the answer was filed? Jesus, you would think he is sleeping with Vicki Taylor."

Although joining in the general sentiment, Dexter, Diamond, and Jones were stunned by the intensity of John's rant. Dexter lightened the moment: "Well, who wasn't thinking about sleeping with Vicki Taylor when she sauntered into the courtroom? Let's face it boys; no one was going to top that performance this morning." Everyone but John nervously laughed. "I agree, John, it is a shocking schedule, but you know, it's the way law used to be practiced. Maybe the old man is reminiscing. It could be fun—like moot court—firing from the hip."

John was in no mood to be trite, but he knew he had already revealed too much. "Okay Bussey, I am going to take up the challenge. No shenanigans, just old fashioned lawyering, agreed?" John stuck out his hand and looked expectantly at Dexter.

"You got it, although don't forget that I am only thirty-eight and haven't a clue as to what you are talking about." Dexter took John's hand, cocking a smile. Even John seemed to enjoy the gentle sleight.

* * *

"John Cleaver is losing his edge," Jones suggested to Bob Holleman, Thomas Sacks, and Rob Simonson, three other firm partners in their late thirties. "It's like in baseball when you don't want the ball hit to you, it always comes and you often misplay it. When you want the ball, you almost always field it flawlessly. John no longer wants the big cases; he no longer wants the action; he no longer wants to expend the effort. The details are slipping by him," Jones explained.

The four lawyers were at Chico's bar after work sharing one beer. Of course, the "one beer" at Chico's, famous only to its patrons, was a thirty-two ounce whopper. The lawyers especially appreciated the elegance of this little white lie. Since Chico's is a blue collar bar, they could be fairly certain that anyone overhearing their conversation would either be unable to interpret it or, in any event, unable to do anything with it.

"The Taylor case is a perfect example: Cleaver has the right strategy. There is a case on point. Bussey is baiting the client into making a decision. Cleaver convinces it not to take the bait and to avoid a decision, but then he doesn't review the minutes. As a result, one word suggests a negative decision. Now Austin has ordered a full federal trial on whether there is evidence of God's existence," Jones pontificated before slugging down half his beer.

"What's up with Austin? Is he showing signs of dementia?" Sacks wondered.

"Have you seen Vicki Taylor?" Holleman answered. "If Austin is of sound mind, he should be angling to get beneath her skirt."

"I've seen her walking down the aisle at the supermarket. There was so much action, the cans were vibrating on the shelf." Simonson chuckled at his own wit.

"So what happens to the East Grand Rapids account now that our firm has failed to finish the case off before it got traction and the district will be handed a huge trial bill?" Sacks asked of Jones.

"Don't worry," Jones responded. "I play basketball with Duncan Smith, the vice superintendent. Bill Reichel, the superintendent, runs the ship, and he's locked at the hip with John. We're good as long as Reichel's there. He's retiring at the end of the next school year; by that time I will have won the case on appeal, even if, God forbid, John loses it at trial. When the heir apparent, Smith, moves in, so will I, and our firm will be set with this client for another generation," Jones explained. "The more immediate concern is what are we going to do with John in January when his term as managing partner expires?"

"Adios, partner." Holleman drew his forefinger across his throat, leaning against the back of his chair, his beer stein emptied, tie loose and eyes starting to water.

"You've got to be kidding," Sacks said incredulously. "Cleaver's done more to build Riley Dickson than any other lawyer. His client book is bigger than all four of ours put together."

"Yeah and he makes almost four times as much as we do," Holleman sneered.

"Look, we are not talking about getting rid of John," Jones eased in Sacks' direction. "We only need to move him out of the managing partner's job. The truth is we would be doing John a favor. He's clearly tired. He has a messianic complex, believing he must pull the full client and firm management load he has carried for years. He's not forty-five anymore. He's not fifty-five. He's pushing sixty. If we don't do something, he will die in the saddle in five years," Jones continued, "No one respects John Cleaver more than me. He's my mentor. I know him better than anyone at the firm. He's estranged from his family and hasn't begun to develop the outside interests he'll need for an active, healthy retirement. He needs extra time to work on those aspects of his life. Who knows—relief from management chores may refresh him, allowing him to come back to his legal work with more drive and energy. We could be extending his career and his bottom line contribution to the firm's financial health."

"I like it," Simonson added. "If we take out the big kahuna, the rest of the senior partners will fall into line. It will signal a changing of the guard. Jonesie, are you ready to take the mantle of managing partner? You've established your bona fides with the older crew while on the comp committee for the past five years. They don't think you'll gouge them, or at least not as badly as they would fare under another Young Turk's reign."

"It is a good time to move; we can also shift the compensation structure to place a bigger premium on production and less on client control. We'll be drinking a year from now at the Lumber Baron's bar in the Grand Plaza, not at Chico's," Jones predicted, subtly shifting the conversation back to their collective interest, his own clearly established.

"Sounds like cause for another Chico's one beer!" Holleman suggested loudly, flagging down the waitress and ordering another round.

"Let's figure out who we can draw from the firm's other departments into what will hereafter be known as 'The Chico's cabal,'" Simonson intoned.

"Cheers!" Sacks offered quickly as the new round of thirty-two ouncers was dropped on the table. He was eager to ensure that the group knew he was totally on board, any concerns about Cleaver's fair treatment assuaged or abandoned.

* * *

"John? This is Robert Johnson," the voice on the other end of the telephone line announced.

"Robert! What's it been? Ten years?" John Cleaver exclaimed, wondering in back of his mind what Robert Johnson of Kingman Walker could possible want.

"I have no idea, John. I think being able to place dates is the first thing to go when you hit sixty. I think it has to be close to twenty years."

John decided to let that past and said, "You are still with Kingman Walker?"

"Yes, and you with Riley, Dickinson and Farhat, I see," Johnson noted. "This is actually why I am calling, John. I want to work with you," Johnson said flatly as he let that declaration settle in.

"Work with me?" John reacted, more than a little puzzled.

"Yes, the Taylor case, for a start." Robert said ambiguously. "I just finished your brief in support of the school district's motion to dismiss. Very well done. Good grasp of the law in the area, well written argument. Highly persuasive. No way Judge Austin should have denied your motion."

"Thank you, Robert. What is your interest in the Taylor case?"

"I represent the Americans for Scientific Studies," Robert answered.

"I know that group. Doesn't Joe Block leave out the 'F' in the acronym?" John asked good naturedly.

Johnson ignored the comment, pressing ahead. "We want to discuss the case with you and how we can help. Then I have another subject to discuss. So, can I book my flight?"

John Cleaver leaned back in his chair and let out a laugh. "It may have been twenty years, Robert, but you haven't changed a lick. I am always open to help on any case, and I am willing to talk about anything, especially with an old friend. I am tied up this week, however."

"Great. How about dinner this Saturday night at seven pm? I went online, and the Chop House restaurant around the block from your office looks delightful."

"I wouldn't be surprised if you have already ordered the wine!"

"John, you know I plan ahead and appreciate the finer things in life—like good wine, a good steak, and good lawyering."

"I will see you Saturday night, Robert." John Cleaver cradled the phone and then his head in hands.

* * *

"Damn! All that talk of Mrs. Taylor's figure and I forgot completely about her!" Dexter exclaimed as he and Peter reached their office building. "I'll catch up to you tomorrow, Peter," Dexter said as he hustled away towards the Grand Plaza hotel.

As he stood in the doorway of the dark, deep, wood paneled interior of the Lumber Baron bar and his eyes adjusted, Dexter spotted Vicki Taylor in the furthermost, most intimate corner of the bar. Between the time he left the doorway and made it to her table, Dexter noticed three businessmen cast lustful glances Taylor's way.

"I am sorry, Mrs. Taylor, it took longer than I expected."

"Please call me 'Vicki,'" she ordered as she put down her smart phone. "And they say that women engage in too much small talk... Give me a briefing and I will see if my suspicion is confirmed."

"The court has placed this case on what we sometimes call a 'rocket docket.' In short, he wants to begin trial on November first. How's that?" Dexter flirted.

"Succinct and to the point. So, what else did you boys talk about for an hour?"

Dexter left that comment alone. "Vicki, I need to tell you something important," he started. "I have been offered a fantastic opportunity with one of the largest, most prestigious firms in Chicago."

"Congratulations." Taylor turned and said, "George!" and raised her glass to get the bartender's attention. When George trundled over, Taylor ordered, "Please bring us a bottle of your second most expensive champagne." She returned to Dexter, "I hope that won't offend you, but if I am going to spend my deceased husband's money on another man, I owe him some concession."

Dexter laughed a little uncomfortably. "I am sorry for focusing on myself. How are you coping? I cannot imagine how I would deal with the losses you have endured?"

"Yes, you can," Taylor said again arching her back imperceptibly and shifting her right leg behind her left to further straighten her posture. "You and I are alike. We are survivors... And are opportunistic..." She stopped as the bartender returned, popped the cork, poured the champagne, and promptly left them alone. Dexter smiled and offered his glass without a toast, knowing his client had not finished with her observation. Taylor met his glass without a toast, took a sip, and continued, "I loved my husband, although imperfectly. I loved my daughter, although not perfectly. Haven't you found that love almost always disappoints, Dexter?"

Dexter artfully dodged. "You have reason to be disappointed; two sudden deaths in two years."

Taylor smirked. "The disappointment began well before their deaths. And I have no doubt that I disappointed each of them. Do you have children, Dexter?"

"One, a little boy."

"Are you married?"

"No, not yet." Dexter replied, surprised at his own response.

Taylor intensified her stare. "Do you think you are a good father?"

Dexter laughed. "I haven't really started yet. He is little more than a toddler."

Taylor did not smile. "I wish I believed a successful man could be a good father, but I don't. Tell me more about your offer."

Dexter took a draught of champagne and paused, looking directly into Taylor's deep blue eyes. "The law firm has clients across the country with sophisticated trial needs and will triple my current salary. They want me to open a new office in Grand Rapids for them and then later head to the home office in Chicago."

"Sounds like a great opportunity, but what about my case?"

"That's the problem, Vicki. The new firm has a major client that is on the other side of cases like ours and would not want me to continue. They also want a decision next week."

Vicki Taylor released a laugh and sat back in her chair.

"What's so funny?" Dexter asked.

"You just told me the judge has put our case on a rocket docket with a trial in November. You can't put off a commitment for a few months? I would have thought that was one of your specialties?" Taylor flirted and met Dexter's eyes. "Let's go upstairs to my room, where we will figure something out."

Dexter paused. Taylor rose, slowly sliding her purse over her shoulder, tightening her firm chest against the soft cashmere sweater under her suit. She leaned forward and sensually whispered in Dexter's ear, "Never meet an attractive female client in a hotel bar, certainly not after having left her idle for an hour." She turned to the bartender, "George, put this on my tab, dear."

Dexter rose and whispered into Taylor's ear, "One lesson learned." They walked out of the bar together.

Chapter Eight

The Philosopher
Wednesday, November 4, 2009
(Third Day of Trial)

Dexter and Vicki Taylor were sitting next to each other a little more than three months later as the third day of trial began with Dexter Bussey calling Alvin Henry to the stand. Alvin Henry was in his early sixties; he was short, and his once-black hair was now silvery and extremely thin on the top. He walked with a limp, as his left side was partially paralyzed as a result of being one of the last victims of polio before the Salk vaccine.

Q.   Good morning, sir. Would you state your name for the record?

A.   Alvin Henry.

Q.   Would you state your educational background and current occupation?

A.   I have a bachelor's of arts degree from Harvard University in education, a master's degree in education from Harvard, a PhD in philosophy from Yale

University, and I am a professor of philosophy at Calvin College here in Grand Rapids.

Q.   Have you taught philosophy at any other college or university?

A.   Yes, at Yale University.

Q.   Have you taught in the public schools?

A.   Yes. I am a certified teacher and taught biology for ten years in a public high school in Boston, Massachusetts.

"Your honor, I propose Alvin Henry as an expert in the field of philosophy and education," Dexter stated, turning to Owen.

"Mr. Cleaver, would you like the opportunity to *voir dire?*" Judge Austin asked, turning to John Cleaver.

The lawyer rose, and before completely stretching his frame, said, "No objection to the professor's qualifications," and then sat down.

"Dr. Henry is recognized by the court as an expert in the fields of philosophy and education."

Q.   Professor Henry, were you present for the testimony of Dr. Devoneau?

A.   Yes.

Q.   How about Dr. Hitchcock?

A.   Yes.

Q.   Are you familiar with the theory of evolution?

A.   Yes. I minored in biology at Harvard.

Q. Would you agree with Dr. Hitchcock that philosophical naturalism holds that there can be no supernatural—no God?

A. Yes.

Q. Would you agree that evolution proves that naturalism is correct?

A. No. Quite to the contrary. Evolution defeats naturalism. It proves that naturalism is almost certainly incorrect.

Q. Can you explain how that could be true?

A. Well, as Dr. Hitchcock correctly observed, natural selection and genetic drift, which are the agents of evolution, are only interested in biological behaviors, not beliefs or cognitive faculties.

Q. Let me interrupt you, professor. Could you define for us what you mean by "cognitive faculties?"

A. 'Cognitive faculties' would be memory, perception, and reason.

Q. Please continue as you were before I cut you off.

A. Under evolutionary theory, the probability that our cognitive faculties would be reliable—that they would deliver mostly true deliverances—is extremely low.

Q. Why is that?

Victor Fleming

A. The brain's principal function is to enable the organism to move appropriately, to succeed in the four "F's" of feeding, fleeing, fighting, and—given the seriousness of the setting, I will say, reproducing. The more successfully the brain moves the organism in those areas, the more certain it is of duplicating. Metaphysical concepts like good and evil, truth, happiness, joy, sorrow, most memory, and poignancy wouldn't matter at all. In fact, any faculty unrelated to our behavior wouldn't be selected.

Q. Can you give me an example that might help us understand this concept?

A. I can try. Charles Darwin himself was on to this problem. Of course, his great contribution to evolution was to link our common lineage to apes and monkeys, but apes and monkeys have never developed any cognitive faculties beyond those necessary for survival behaviors. Thus, a monkey does not know the difference between right and wrong or reason reliably beyond cognitive motor skills related to the four F's. In fact, Darwin fretted that his rational deductions about evolution would not be reliable if they came from the same mind as a monkey.

Q. When did he offer this concern?

A. In a letter he wrote to William Graham Down on July 3, 1881, as reported in *The life and letters of Charles Darwin, including an autobiographical chapter*, which was edited by his son, Francis Darwin, in 1887.

Q. If anywhere, where does this scientific concern lead you?

We Hold These Truths

A. Clearly, sane human beings have the reliable ability to determine the difference between right and wrong. Because our minds could not get there through evolution, there must be an explanation for the reliability of our human faculties other than nature. Thus, philosophical naturalism has been discredited by evolution, which is quite an irony.

Q. Are you saying that we would be insane if evolution was the only factor at work guiding the human intellect?

A. Given the legal definition of insanity, which is the inability to tell right from wrong, that is precisely what I am saying. We would not have the capability to make that determination any more than a dog killing another dog feels guilt or remorse.

A. Are you saying because our cognitive faculties are reliable and evolution could not deliver such faculties, God's existence is proved?

A. Not exactly. In philosophy, we prove things through proving theories false. I am saying evolution discredits philosophical naturalism and an unexplained force has shaped the human mind. That could be a creator; it could be some other process we do not as yet understand and which could be natural. I can confidently opine this, however: evolution as we know it today and the incompatible state of our human faculties together suggest an intelligent designer molded the human race.

Q. Are you the only philosopher, sir, who thinks this way?

A.   Heavens, no. This line of thought is not my own; it does not originate from a former Calvin College professor but from the renowned philosopher Alvin Plantinga, who has taught philosophy at Yale University and has been a professor of philosophy at Notre Dame for almost thirty years.

Q.   What about Professor Dawkins' great criticism that there could be no intelligent designer at the beginning of evolution because design comes later in the evolutionary process?

A.   That is an excellent proof that God did not evolve and certainly did not evolve on earth, to be sure, but of course, no one is suggesting that God evolved on earth, so I don't think it really leads anywhere.

Q.   What about Professor Hitchcock's litmus test that nothing untestable under the scientific method should be taught in the public schools?

A.   Professor Hitchcock conceded science cannot explain what is beyond Planck Time or what existed before the Big Bang. These are examples of science exposing its limits. If the public schools confine themselves to physically testable theories, they miss important truths. The irony of the *Kitzmiller* opinion is if strictly applied, it leaves the public schools unable to explain the origins of a jury's ability to determine right from wrong—the core of our common law system of justice—or unable to explain why we value human equality, a core principle on which the United States was formed.

Q.   I take it that you are critical of the *Kitzmiller* decision's reliance on the scientific method. Is that correct?

We Hold These Truths

A.   There is no testable evidence of human intellect but experience. You cannot dissect the brain and find human reason or the capacity to love, experience joy, or ascertain aesthetic beauty. But those metaphysical concepts exist, perhaps more certainly than what our senses feel and touch.

Q.   How would you define "science," professor?

A.   Science must be linked to some empirical proof, and empirical proof to some objective system for gathering and testing empirical evidence. But we cannot limit empiricism to what we can observe through our senses alone. You cannot discount human intellect and the methods by which the social sciences empirically test through common experience statistically verifiable. What we understand about own faculties is also "science."

Q.   Do you have an opinion as to whether evolution is subject to the scientific method?

A.   If you define the scientific method as Judge Jones did in *Kitzmiller*, I would agree with Karl Popper, the father of the scientific method, and answer, no. He opined that evolution is a "research programme," which is another way of saying it is merely a theory. Evolution is at best only slightly testable. It is impossible to replicate natural selection or test it in any scientific manner. It is only a scientific theory, albeit one based on solid inductive reasoning.

Q.   What about the statement advocated by the estate?

A. I would strongly advocate it. In fact, it is similar to the statement on religion and evolution issued by the National Academies of Science, which I have right here. May I read it?

Q. Please do.

A. Okay: "Does science disprove religion? Science can neither prove nor disprove religion. Scientific advances have called some religious beliefs into question, such as the ideas that the Earth was created very recently, that the Sun goes around the Earth, and that mental illness is due to possession by spirits or demons. But many religious beliefs involve entities or ideas that currently are not within the domain of science. Thus, it would be false to assume that all religious beliefs can be challenged by scientific findings."

Q. What is your understanding, if any, as to why the National Academies issued this statement?

A. It was responding to the common misperception that evolution is inconsistent with religious belief. This misconception left unchecked makes students and their parents hostile towards evolution. That hostility is threatening to science. Correcting that misperception in a fair way, as the National Academies has done, promotes a proper understanding of evolution.

Q. Have you observed this misperception in your classroom?

A. Absolutely. Many Christian students find their spirituality challenged when they appreciate that evolution is scientifically demonstrable because they assume evolution and Christianity are incompatible. Without some qualification, many religious students may have their religious beliefs needlessly shaken.

Q.   Did you teach evolution while you were a biology teacher in the Boston high school?

A.   Yes.

Q.   Did the school district provide any training on First Amendment concerns relating to the teaching of evolution science?

A.   Yes. Every couple of years, the Boston school district held symposiums with First Amendment lawyers, instructing its teachers in the 'dos' and 'don'ts' in walking the First Amendment line between not discouraging or encouraging religious beliefs.

Q.   Did you have an opportunity to apply that training in practice?

A.   Oh yes, every time I taught evolution, which was every semester.

Q.   Have you had an opportunity to review the statement at issue in this case?

A.   Yes.

Q.   Based on your training and experience, do you have an opinion as to whether the statement violates that fine line?

"Objection, your honor!" John Cleaver interjected. "The question calls for a legal opinion that this witness is not qualified to make."

Owen stepped in before Dexter could respond. "I think the objection goes to the weight the court should give the testimony. By training and experience, I think he can offer an opinion even if it is lay in this regard. Overruled. Professor, you can answer the question."

A.   Based on my training and experience, I would conclude that the statement is religiously neutral and walks that line.

Q.   Do you have an opinion as to whether the statement might dispel the common misperception that evolution is incompatible with religious belief?

A.   Yes. In my opinion, the statement's recognition that many experts in both fields find evolution and religion compatible may be of great comfort to many students, allowing them to relax and appreciate both concepts.

Q.   Would you prevent Professors Devoneau and Hitchcock from teaching in our public schools that evolution proves that there is no God?

A.   I think the First Amendment prohibits them from teaching that as fact, as they more or less admitted to you when they admitted that they were hostile to the anti-discouragement clause in the First Amendment.

Q.   Well, isn't turnaround fair play? Wouldn't that same prohibition preclude you from teaching that evolution and that our brain's reliability proves that there is a supernatural designer?

A.   Yes. I agree. What I have said is evolution and the
      reliability of our faculties proves evolution cannot
      explain the modern human brain. That leaves the
      possibility of an intelligent designer or some currently
      unknown intervening natural process as the source of
      our brain's reliability. Such a statement does not violate
      the First Amendment, in my understanding.

Q.   Professor, do you believe that there is no empirical
      evidence that there is good and evil in the world?

A.   Of course not. As I have already noted, the law defines
      human sanity as the ability to differentiate between
      right and wrong—what we would commonly describe as
      good and evil. That humans have this ability is
      empirically verifiable through statistics and through
      observable experience.

"Thank you, professor," Dexter said in a satisfied fashion.
"Mr. Cleaver, your witness." Owen nodded to John Cleaver,
who stood and took the lectern.

Q.   Good morning, Professor.

A.   Good morning, Mr. Cleaver.

Q.   Are you a product of the public schools, Professor?

A.   Through high school, yes.

Q.   Were you taught evolution in public school?

A.   Yes, I was.

Q. Did your biology teacher offer a cautionary statement such as advocated by the plaintiff in this case?

A. No.

Q. Despite that fact, you have been able to discern a difference between evolution and the anti-religious conclusions some biologists draw from evolution. Would that be a fair statement?

A. I have been able to draw this distinction in my post graduate life. To be honest, I can't recall whether I thought evolution was inconsistent with Christianity when I was being taught it in high school.

Q. I appreciate your candor on that point, but since you can't recall your mindset when you first learned evolution science, I assume it is also correct you can't testify that the lack of a warning caused confusion between your new knowledge and your religious beliefs?

A. That's true. I cannot testify to that, although times have changed now.

Q. By change, you are referring to prominent biologists who publicize the religious conclusions they draw from the science, is that correct?

A. Yes.

Q. However, you haven't personally studied the effect this proselytizing might be having or not having on the average East Grand Rapids student, high school or grade school?

A.   True, I have not. I can only offer my opinion based on my discussion with college students.

Q.   And you teach at a Christian liberal arts college, where one might expect students to be more hostile to the religious implications of the conclusions that Professors Devoneau and Hitchcock proclaim.

A.   Yes, I do teach at a Christian college, and my students are possibly more predisposed to being hostile to philosophical naturalism.

Q.   You certainly believe that evolutionary science can be taught without discouraging religion?

A.   Yes.

Q.   The reading of the statement could be used by some Christian teachers to proselytize their Christian beliefs, wouldn't you agree?

A.   I suppose that is possible, but public school teachers are taught to walk the line on First Amendment issues, and if a teacher respects that line, the statement should be easy to administer without proselytizing one way or the other.

Q.   Are you familiar with the term "earth sciences?"

A.   Yes. Those would be biology, chemistry, and geology.

Q.   Wouldn't an earth sciences teacher be more likely to confine his or her discipline to the scientific method?

A.   Certainly earth scientists rely on more testing that employs the physical senses, but that doesn't excuse a failure to understand empirical evidence as a form of verifying proof. It is inexcusable to me that a biologist would conclude that there is no empirical evidence of good or evil when the ability to discern the difference is the legal definition of human sanity.

"Thank you, professor, I have nothing further," John Cleaver said as he slumped back into his chair.

"Mr. Bussey, anything further?" Owen asked.

"No, your honor, nothing for this witness. The estate calls Paul Kingston to the stand."

Paul Kingston rose from his seat in the courtroom and proudly marched to the witness chair. He was sworn in with his head and chin up, and he clearly announced his name.

Q.   Mr. Kingston, you were in the courtroom when Madelyn Wysocki testified, is that correct?

A.   Yes, sir.

Q.   Would you agree with me that Ms. Wysocki accurately described your classroom exchange with Michelle Taylor?

A.   I don't recall every word of her testimony, so I cannot agree with you.

Q.   Do you recall listening in the courtroom and thinking to yourself, her recollection is wrong?

A.   No, not really.

Q.   So, you cannot recall any material inaccuracies?

We Hold These Truths

A.   No, not at the moment.

Q.   We will move along, then. Isn't it true that you were attempting to discourage Ms. Taylor from discussing her religious views of creation in your science class on evolution?

A.   I was trying to concentrate the class on the science of evolution.

Q.   And discussion of creation would be a deviation from science?

A.   Yes. I am a biology, not a religion teacher.

Q.   So you see a conflict between religion and biology?

A.   I see them as two distinct subjects.

Q.   You do not personally believe in a supernatural creator, do you?

A.   No.

Q.   Is that because you are a scientist?

A.   No, it is because I am a skeptic.

Q.   As a skeptic, you require proof, correct?

A.   Yes.

Q.   I will leave it at that. Do you agree there are holes in the theory of evolution?

A.   I agree that the science of evolution is not currently complete.

Q.   The science of evolution cannot explain how the first plant life formed?

A.   Not yet.

Q.   Nor can science currently explain how the first animal life emerged?

A.   Not yet.

Q.   Nor can the science of evolution explain why men and women can determine right from wrong?

A.   There is no scientific proof of right and wrong; those are values affecting group selection or inclusive fitness, which are manifestations of biological self-interest. There is no proof that they are intrinsic to humans.

Q.   So, if there is no proof that right and wrong exist, we should not peg our definition of "insanity" to the ability to discern one from the other, correct?

"Objection, your honor; Mr. Bussey is being argumentative."
"Sustained," Owen responded.

Q.   If there are gaps in evolution, what would be wrong with students suggesting that a spiritual force might fill in those gaps?

A.   The First Amendment.

Q.   You think the First Amendment prohibits even the suggestion that a God may exist in the public schools, is that right?

A.   Yes.

Q.   Is that based on your teacher training from the district?

A.   I don't honestly know.

Q.   What but your training would leave you with that impression?

A.   I don't honestly know.

Q.   Would you agree with me that Michelle Taylor was upset by your classroom discussion?

A.   Yes.

Q.   Do you think in retrospect you could have handled the discussion better?

A.   No.

Q.   Even the statement that premature death was nature's way of weeding out the weak?

A.   Maybe.

Q.   Do you think religion and science are incompatible?

A.   They cannot be compared.

"Thank you, Mr. Kingston, no further questions."

"Mr. Cleaver, any questions?" Owen asked.
"A few, your honor."

Q.   Mr. Kingston, did you intend to cause any distress to Ms. Taylor?

A.   Not at all.

Q.   Did you intend to discourage her religious belief?

A.   Not at all.

Q.   Do you know of any policy at East Grand Rapids Public Schools to discourage religious belief?

A.   No.

"Nothing further, your honor."
"Thank you, Mr. Cleaver; Mr. Bussey, anything further?"
"Yes."

Q.   Mr. Kingston, do you know of any prominent biologists who are religious?

A.   No.

Q.   Regardless of your intent, do you agree your class caused Michelle Taylor great stress?

A.   That was her fault.

"I have nothing further your honor."
"I have nothing further, Judge," John answered after a look from Owen.

"Your honor, other than asking the court to take notice of the facts to which the parties have stipulated, including that the district did not discipline Mr. Kingston, the estate rests," Dexter announced.

"Very well. Mr. Cleaver, are you ready to proceed?" Owen turned to John Cleaver.

"Your honor, at this time, the defense moves for a directed verdict in its favor. As you know, the district's actions carry a presumption of constitutional validity. The plaintiff must prove by preponderance the district's failure to use a statement qualifying evolution violated Michelle Taylor's constitutional rights. Two of the estate's own experts have opined the statement is not only unnecessary but inappropriate. Moreover, the estate has failed to prove the teacher uttered anything more than a few poorly worded comments in the heat of discussion, which cannot rise to the level of a constitutional violation."

Dexter rose to respond, but Owen waived him off. "Mr. Bussey, I am going to deny the district's motion unless you want to talk me out of that decision?"

"I certainly wouldn't want to do that, your honor." Dexter smiled as he sat down.

"Mr. Cleaver, I think your argument might have some merit if it weren't so obvious Professors Devoneau and Professor Hitchcock's opinions regarding the statement are tied to their belief that the First Amendment's prohibition against a discouragement of religion is obsolete. And I might also accept your argument about Mr. Kingston's comments being aberrational if the district had not refused to counsel him regarding the ones that may have crossed the line. I am not ruling that the estate has prevailed. On the motion, as you know, I must construe all inferences in favor of the estate as the nonmoving party, and when I do that, the estate's case is at least colorable. Your motion is denied. Let's break for the day, and we can start with the defense tomorrow, if there are no questions."

Hearing no questions, he rose and exited his courtroom, terminating the third full day of trial.

* * *

"Folks, I am heading home. This trial is a farce." Joe Block threw his notebook out of camera view. "First of all, the plaintiff is hostile to God and her lawyer puts on atheists and only spent ten minutes with the evil teacher on the stand. The school district's lawyer intends to call a Christian biologist to the stand as his first witness tomorrow. The mother is not seeking any damages for her own daughter's death. The parties are merely fighting over whether a sixty second disclaimer is going to be read before the district teaches godless evolution. To top it all off, I think the judge had a petit mal seizure on the stand after the mother testified. He seems totally out of it. Folks, this trial is the theatre of the absurd and I am not going to waste another minute of your time on it. We are headed back to Washington, where we can only hope that the United States Supreme Court will eventually come to its senses and reverse the nonsense in our court system since the godless Justice Douglas—an Eisenhower appointee, for Pete's sake—decided to denude this country of its religious heritage."

With that rant, he cut to station break and his lights went out in Grand Rapids.

* * *

"Did you see the Block show tonight, boss?" Chad Bachman asked Robert Johnson.

"Yes, first time I have ever agreed with him. Your trial has become the theatre of the absurd." Johnson chuckled slyly. "I couldn't be happier. He even discredited Judge Austin, setting the case up perfectly on appeal even if Cleaver is hit by lightning below. Incidentally, how is steady John doing?"

"He is worn out. His killer instinct is gone. His associate and I had to goad him into asking Mrs. Taylor about her religious inclinations. He didn't spring the trap the question laid. I have to admit loving how Joe Block took the bait. Mrs. Taylor is not a Christian, so Block is taking his troops back to Washington. If Cleaver had been left alone, he wouldn't have even elicited this testimony and Block might be hanging around. Are you really thinking of making Cleaver a lucrative offer?"

"Sure. People in Grand Rapids love his 'nice guy' style. Remember, it is the home of Jerry Ford—nice guys with B plus intellects. The new urban law firm model requires outposts in the boondocks referring the sophisticated legal work to the home office in the big city. Cleaver suits that model perfectly. We buy his book of business and broom him when the client transition is complete. Keep up the good work, Chad. We will have you back in civilization in no time."

* * *

"What is wrong with Block? I don't understand why he is quitting this trial," Ross mused as he nursed a vodka and tonic at the Library Bar, a working class bar in the industrial heart of the city.

"I keep forgetting you are supposed to be a good reporter," Riley scoffed.

"What does that mean?" Alex asked, his voice rising.

"The matter is being handled intelligently and evenhandedly. The media can't sell national advertising off a platform like that."

"Why is Kingston Walker helping Cleaver? I heard it was courting Bussey."

Riley gave Ross a long sideways glance and his freckled, reddish face slowly broke into a wide smile as he returned his attention to his whiskey sour.

"So... I am waiting," Ross said. "Remember, you are drinking on my expense account again."

Riley exhaled a laugh. "Do you really want me to tie the value of my information to the level of your expense account?"

Ross stared into his drink.

Riley finally answered, "Kingston Walker represents Americans for Scientific Studies, which considers itself a guardian of the First Amendment."

Ross turned to Riley and stared at him.

Without breaking Ross' glaze, Riley explained, "Kingston Walker, like all big firms, is looking to expand its client base and is considering a footprint in Grand Rapids. John Cleaver would be the perfect anchor for that—solid lawyer and not likely to overstay his welcome."

"What about Bussey?" Ross asked.

"What about Bussey? He isn't long for Grand Rapids whether he lands with Kingston Walker or not."

"Well, I can't say I understand how small town lawyers think, much less the Chicago crowd. So, how do you think Bussey did with his case?"

"For a guy with a small expense account, your questions are insatiable." Riley chuckled. "I thought Bussey was brilliant. Just the right touch. Get it in, get out, and sit down."

"I don't think I can use that on the air," Ross mused.

Riley smiled. "You are as big a coward as Bussey is a loser on this one."

"Really?" Ross wondered. "I'll never understand the law."

Chapter Nine

Gathering Clouds
Friday, September 4, 2009

Two months earlier to the day, Owen Austin rose quickly from his desk to take a bathroom break only to unexpectedly spin and fall, leaving him staring at the molding between the ceiling and the walls in his office. Sarah and Kelly heard the thump and rushed into the chambers. "Frank!" Sarah screamed. Frank was at the far end of the chambers talking about the upcoming NFL season with Jack Gooters when the call came. It took him seconds to fly into Owen's office. There he found a dazed Owen already being helped up to a sitting position by Kelly and Sarah. Frank shuddered at the blank, confused look Owen gave him when their eyes first met, although the look quickly disappeared and the intelligent, old eyes returned.

"Put him gently back down, ladies," Frank ordered as he turned into his shoulder mike and calmly barked, "Fifteen Stat, Eagle 601." His radio broadcast was directed to the marshals on security detail on the first floor, signaling Owen had experienced a medical emergency. It also alerted the actual United States Marshal for the western district of Michigan, William Farr, who was usually monitoring the radio traffic and who now scrambled from his office on the second floor to Owen's sixth floor chambers. Bill Farr started his career as an emergency medical technician with the Kent County sheriff's department before serving two six year terms as its elected sheriff and then being appointed United States Marshal by his Washington Republican friends after his county retirement.

Meanwhile, Owen looked to his side and could see a red well file folder he kicked when he went down. He smiled slightly, realizing his out. "Frank, look at the file. How stupid of me not to lift my leg up far enough. Now, help me up," Owen ordered.

"Can't do that sir. Marshal Farr will be here in a moment. Let him do a field medical check. I don't want you to move until then, your honor." Bill Farr burst into the chambers, swinging his medical bag to the floor next to Owen.

"Sorry Bill, false alarm," Owen offered from his back. "My old prostate required me to get up too quickly and I tripped over an OSHA case file—how's that for an irony?" Owen's joke failed to produce a smile among his staff or the two marshals.

Bill Farr's only reaction was to shine his pen light flashlight into Owen's eyes and place the blood pressure wrap around Owen's arm. He finally backed off, looking into Owen's face. "That may be, Judge Austin, but I don't get to practice my fading emergency medical skills every day, so consider this a practice drill and let me complete my field assessment." Bill Farr was used to giving orders and knew that Owen Austin, no matter how formidable he was on the bench, was not going to wrest control of this situation.

Only after Owen's vitals appeared normal did Farr succumb to Owen's yapping about getting up, getting to the bathroom, and getting back to the opinion he claimed to be writing. Farr and Frank helped Owen back up to the sitting position and Farr repeated his round of vitals. When they too appeared normal, the two men helped Owen to his feet. Frank gently slipped an arm under the judge's shoulders and ushered him to the bathroom in his chambers.

After Owen and Frank emerged from the bathroom, Farr advised Owen that the paramedics and ambulance were present and that he assumed the judge would be transported a block and a half up the Michigan Street hill to Spectrum Hospital.

"Nice try, Bill, but to show you how normal I remain, 'hell no,' I'm not riding in the ambulance to the hospital. It is embarrassing enough to have the marshals fawning over my slip. You think I want my indignity exposed to the hardened emergency room staff as well?" Owen said self-effacingly.

"With all due respect, sir," Sarah interjected. "We are all for sacrificing your pride to make sure you are all right."

Owen laughed, and everyone in the room but Frank smiled.

"Thanks for the generous thought, Sarah, but you can't sacrifice my honor that easily," Owen said with good humor, briefly making eye contact with Frank but quickly looking away from Frank's piercing stare.

Owen slid back into his chair and appeared to examine his paperwork. In reality, he wasn't focused on anything but returning to normalcy. He tried one final stab at humor. "Now that I'm almost seventy, I suppose this is the first of many times you are going to have to 'man your rally stations.' I hope you enjoy the prospects for more courthouse excitement." ·

The staff forced themselves back to their work stations except for Frank, who stood with his hands across his chest, employing the searing drill sergeant stare that must have frozen the wit of hundreds of green minions over the twenty years he fashioned boys into men. Last to leave, he didn't say anything or break his stare. He simply closed the door behind him, leaving Owen alone.

Owen pushed Frank's stare out of his mind. He had larger concerns. The headaches were getting more frequent, and now were occasionally accompanied by dizzy spells. He had a momentary, fearful thought: What if this had happened while he was driving? He pushed the thought out of his head.

When the clock struck three p.m., Owen sheepishly came out of his office. Sarah and Kelly pretended not to notice, but they were carefully stealing glances at their boss. "So, what are you ladies doing for the Labor Day weekend?" He was eager to finish the day on a normal note.

"John and I are taking our kids camping up north and are going to walk the Mackinac Bridge on Labor Day," Kelly said excitedly, referring to the tradition where the big bridge was restricted to foot traffic for the holiday morning.

"That's interesting," Owen replied. "My daughter Megan, her husband and boys are going to walk the bridge as well. How about you, Sarah, what are our plans?"

"I am going to take in an arts and crafts fair in Collins park, then meet some girls for lunch at Rose's restaurant. On Sunday, I am traveling to my sister Ruth's house in Chicago to spend the holiday there with her. Don't you remember? I am taking Tuesday off so I can drive back to Grand Rapids."

"That's right," Owen said. "Of course." Owen was slightly discombobulated because he could not remember Sarah previously telling him her schedule. In order to salve the embarrassment he might have caused by his earlier joke, he decided to offer to escort her to the art fair. "Say Sarah, would you mind if I joined you to tour the arts and craft show? Susan used to love those affairs and would drag me along. I always thought I hated them until she was gone. She is smiling somewhere to hear me say I miss them."

"Yes. Your honor, I would love to have you accompany me. Where and when do you want to meet?"

"How about ten a.m. at the Reeds lake boat launch?"

"Great. What are you doing the rest of the weekend, Judge?" Sarah asked.

"I thought I might take Caesar to the doggie beach in Muskegon for the last time this summer. On Sunday, I am going to Park Church with Megan and the boys before they head up north. Monday, I am going to force myself into boredom so I long for work on Tuesday." He smiled. "Say, why don't we close down the office early today and all start our weekend now?" He said mischievously. Kelly eyes lit up. Sarah was skeptical.

"Let Kelly go. I'll stay and answer the phones," Sarah responded.

"Nope. That's not fair," Owen said. "Either we all go or no one's going—myself included. Look. I am ordering it. What's the point of being chief judge if you don't exercise your fiat now and then?" Sarah still looked skeptical, but Kelly's excited look melted her resistance. "Sarah, call the clerks," Owen added.

Suddenly, Frank was standing behind the three conspirators, startling all three. Owen quickly recovered. "Frank, that includes you, but we have a question: Does it count as 'playing hooky' when the commanding officer orders it?" Frank wasn't impressed with the quip and wasn't playing along. He tucked his business card into Owen's front shirt pocket and leaned over. "Cell phone." He maintained his stare. "Call me if anything comes up." He then backpedaled out the door, not breaking eye contact with Judge Austin.

"What's up with Frank?" Kelly wondered as she shut down her computer and gathered her purse.

"Frank is an old worry wart." Owen reached for his coat. "Let's not let him spoil the holiday mood."

The next day, a beautiful, seventy-five degree sunny Saturday morning, Owen met Sarah at the boat ramp, which Owen thought had not changed since he had fished unsuccessfully off of it sixty years earlier. Sarah clearly enjoyed strolling with Owen along the artists' booths lining the beach. They met several dozen people who stopped to chat with Owen. Each time, he made a point of introducing "my friend, Sarah Lewis." Sarah beamed.

Later that afternoon at the beach, Owen unleashed Caesar and watched him bolt away after a sea gull. Owen could swear that the dog's face was bearing a grin from floppy ear to floppy ear. Owen found a beech log, sat, and kicked out a leg, taking in the warmth of the afternoon sun. To the north, he could hear the shrieks of joy of the children and fathers in the surf, taking in the last reliably good swim of the year. Behind him was a section of beach grass, then towering forested dunes rising two hundred feet or more on an almost forty-five degree incline.

As he looked straight ahead towards Milwaukee, which lay over the watery horizon, his thoughts turned to Michelle Taylor. What a wonderfully substantive young lady to be thinking of the great mysteries of life. What a tragedy to lose your father to such a cruel disease and perhaps suicide, and what a compounded tragedy to terminate your own promising life on what was probably an impulse.

Owen was about to stand up and locate Caesar on the deserted doggie portion of the beach when he saw two bobbing little heads above the beach grass. Where did that Cairn terrier come from? Owen wondered.

"How old is your Westie?" Owen turned to find a trim, handsome woman in her early sixties standing over him.

"Caesar is seven. How about your Cairn?" Owen asked.

"Hedgecock is four." She smiled.

"'Hedgecock,' that's an imposing name for such a little fella."

She laughed and sat down beside him. "And, 'Caesar' isn't?"

Owen laughed. "Touché! Isn't it strange how you don't even think about your dog's name after a while?"

She smiled. "Sheila Blaine" she said as she extended her hand.

"Owen Austin." Owen took her hand after extending his. "Isn't it beautiful out here? I can't believe more people aren't on the beach. What's the point of living in Michigan if you can't escape to the beach every chance you get?"

"I couldn't agree with you more." Sheila nodded. "It's why my husband and I retired here from Ann Arbor five years ago. We bought a place over in the neighboring condominium complex."

"I am envious. I have always toyed with the idea of buying a place there myself... Should I retire."

"You must enjoy your job," Sheila said, her eyes piercing Owen's. "What do you do?"

Owen looked away. Unlike his colleagues, he hated this question. It almost always changed the conversation—like being a minister. "I am an arbitrator." This was one of his practiced, pat answers.

"You're a judge," Sheila said looking away herself.

"You're quick! How did you draw that conclusion?"

Sheila leaned towards him. "You have the look."

They both laughed.

"You scared me for a moment," Owen said still chuckling. "I have a recurring nightmare I will find myself on the street with my robe still on. That's the point they put you away."

"Don't worry. You are disrobed," Sheila teased.

"So where's this husband of yours? You should be enjoying this glorious afternoon together."

Sheila looked away. "He died three years ago. Suddenly. Heart attack."

"Oh Sheila. I am sorry to hear that. I lost my wife five years ago. Not so suddenly. Breast cancer."

"It's not fair, is it? You work so hard so long with the assumption you will be able to someday truly unwind and enjoy a second, carefree childhood. Then, in a blink of an eye, the grand plan is gone," Sheila mused.

"No, there's nothing fair about it. But, what seems more strange to me is that we ever expect it to be fair. After sixty years, shouldn't we understand that life isn't fair?" Owen asked. "This strong imbedded sense of justice people carry never ceases to surprise me."

Sheila smiled. Owen looked out over the long horizon on the lake. The joyous, flirtatious banter and the beautiful setting suddenly weighed him down. He had yet to tell a single person about his terminal illness. Unexpectedly, a wave of grief overcame him, melting his defenses, and emotions bubbled from deep within.

"I'm dying." Owen was shocked to hear himself saying it. Even more surprising were the tears and the sobs springing forth.

Sheila Blaine reached over and put her arm around Owen, comforting him. Owen's emotion was raw and honest, and it exhausted itself within seconds. But he lingered in silence. Suddenly, he began chuckling. Sheila was well aware of the source of his amusement and began to laugh herself. There, next to them were the two terriers sitting side by side as if they were lifelong buddies, perfectly positioned on their back haunches with their front feet straight down, staring at the embraced couple as if trying to figure out what in the world their human owners were doing.

Owen straightened. "Wow!" he said. "I am so embarrassed. I'll bet that's the last time you'll stop to make small talk with a stranger," he said, trying desperately to salvage his dignity.

Sheila stopped chuckling and looked at Owen with compassion. "What is it? Cancer?"

"Yes, Sheila. Brain cancer. About as hideous a fate for a judge as I can imagine. I am so sorry about that breakdown. I haven't told a soul since being diagnosed almost three months ago. I hope you'll accept this as a compliment. I am so embarrassed," Owen fumbled.

"Don't be. I accept it as a form of flattery. An unusual form, but flattery none the less."

"Your husband? What did he do?" Asked Owen, eager to take up where they had left off.

"Professor of biology for thirty years at the University of Michigan," Sheila replied.

"That's truly impressive," Owen responded, "And you? What's your occupational background?"

"Kindergarten teacher for thirty-eight years. " She smiled.

"Well, that explains everything." Owen laughed, pushing away the tears on his cheek. "What do they say? Everything you need to know in life you learn from your kindergarten teacher."

"I'm not sure the teachers get credit in the old saw, but I'll take it," Sheila said as she stood up.

"Listen, Sheila, let me make this up to you. Will you let me buy you dinner at Docker's restaurant, which I think is right in your condo complex, isn't it? I promise you, no more emotional breakdowns."

Sheila looked out at the lake for a moment, weighing something. She turned back and looked at Owen, who opened his face as much as possible. "Okay, Owen. You have yourself a date. What time do you want to meet?"

"Very good. Well... Caesar would like a hamburger at McDonalds, and then he will be fine in the car all evening. It's four-thirty. How about if meet in an hour in Docker's bar? Is that too soon?"

"No, Owen, that is perfect. I will see you then." She scooped up Hedgecock, turned, and walked away. She spun around after a hundred feet and waived, having ensured that Owen was checking her out.

Owen smiled and waved, then dropped to the sand, his head throbbing. He was only going to indulge himself for five minutes, but he couldn't help cursing his fate. He had previously accepted that there would never be another woman in his life after Susan. Now he was experiencing again the exciting, old, familiar feeling, warm if not a touch forlorn under these conditions. God, life was cruel.

He pushed the thought out of his mind, slapping his hand on his thigh. "You have today, Owen," he muttered to himself. "You have until the end of the year. Enjoy, it! Enjoy the moment." He looked at Caesar, who was eyeing him with eager anticipation, his tail wagging—something was about to happen and he was ready for it. Yes, boy, let's run down the beach. Let's wear you out and make the most of this moment. Caesar, you never worry about tomorrow. Hell, you don't even worry about how we are getting home tonight. Yes, Caesar, show me the way.

Victor Fleming

* * *

"It's hard to believe war, mental illness, or lawsuits exist when looking at this scene." Melissa rocked William to sleep in one of the dozens of rocking chairs lining the long porch of Mackinac Island's Grand Hotel. Knowing he was about to become immersed in the Taylor case and feeling guilty about his romp with Vicki Taylor, Dexter convinced Melissa to join him for a last summer hurrah at the Grand Hotel, three and a half hours north of Grand Rapids by car and a half hour trek via high speed ferry from Mackinaw City at the tip of Michigan's lower peninsula. Since Melissa had never stayed on the island overnight, much less at the Grand Hotel, she put up mild resistance.

"This is a most idyllic setting?" Dexter sipped a scotch and soda on a beautiful late summer evening. Not even a breeze stirred. The temperature was an indiscernible seventy-two degrees. The sun was descending behind the majestic Mackinac Bridge, an iron ore freighter passing underneath. Since Mackinac Island permits no vehicular traffic, the only sounds were seagulls squawking, children laughing in the hotel pool, and horses clip-clopping as they pulled guest-laden liveries traveling to and from the hotel perched high on the escarpment.

Mackinac Island is a historic gem—a Michigan state park accessible only by small plane and boat. The only vehicles on the island are a well hidden fire truck and ambulance, which are only for emergencies. With its Victorian buildings, horse drawn carriages, rocky cliffs, eighteenth-century forts, and five mile bicycle path around its circumference, Mackinac Island transports its visitors to the nineteenth century. Ironically, the state built by the automobile is home to the most popular bastion of the horse-drawn carriage era.

Of the all the beautiful vistas on Mackinac Island, the view Dexter and Melissa were enjoying is the best. The porch sits elevated at least one hundred feet above the confluence of Lake

Michigan and Lake Huron in the Mackinac Straits. The Grand Hotel's porch is six hundred and sixty feet long, the longest front porch in the world. To the couple's right, above the mature pine trees and only a couple of miles to the west, the full five mile length of the Mackinac Bridge could be enjoyed. Immediately in front were the hotel's lawn and gardens, brilliantly manicured.

Dexter emptied the bottom of his cocktail and set his rock glass on the wicker table between them. "Let me take the little urchin off your hands," he said as he opened and extended his arms for the sleeping William, who was all dead weight.

After completing the handoff and ensuring that William remained asleep, Melissa saw an opportunity for a segue. "Speaking of our little project, where do you see our relationship heading?" She looked away from Dexter and towards the gardens, afraid of what she might see in his face.

"How do you feel about Chicago, Melissa? I have an attractive offer from one of its largest and most prestigious firms."

"That's a curious answer to my question." Melissa stiffened.

"That's not fair, Melissa," Dexter responded weakly.

"Isn't it? I am looking for someone who will place family ahead of career."

"My 'answer,' as you call it, was a 'question,' and there is a big difference. One of the reasons I wanted to get away this weekend is to discuss this opportunity with you and what it might mean for us. I haven't agreed to take the offer. I wanted this discussion before I made a decision."

"Thank you for saying that, Dexter." Melissa softened. "I guess I hadn't given you a chance to fully respond. And you know I want complete honesty from you. I don't want a relationship with any man who believes he is sacrificing something he doesn't want to give up. For William's sake we need to know our relationship can stand on its own. We may be forcing things for his sake. Until we are convinced we aren't, I don't want to go to the next level."

Dexter leaned over and kissed her gently, slipping his arm around her, while they enjoyed the twinkling lights of the village below and beyond, the stars above.

* * *

"Isn't it amazing how fast a week can fly?" Robert Johnson caught Dexter the next day. Dexter was walking towards the ferry that Melissa and William had already boarded. William had been so excited to hear the idling engines that Melissa had to leave Dexter with the bags after a livery deposited them at the ferry.

"You are right about that, Robert," Dexter offered, surprised his phone had worked since he wasn't getting any email.

"Well, Dexter, I have prepared your name plate. We are busy scouting Grand Rapids office space. I can't wait to see you installed in our new office with a fistful of national work before the first rankings come out in college football."

"I have good news for you, Robert," Dexter said, trying to think of Vicki Taylor's advice but not Taylor. "Judge Austin placed Taylor on a rocket docket and has scheduled trial for November first. So it should be over by Thanksgiving, just in time to see your Bears annihilate our Lions on Turkey Day."

"You are definitely wrong on one count, my friend, and maybe both. Judge Austin did neither you nor himself any favors by denying the district's motion to dismiss. That would have resolved your 'issue' immediately and avoided the negative press Judge Austin has received in Chicago and beyond. Every major newspaper is making him look like a reactionary trying to retry the *Kitzmiller* case, if not Scopes itself. As for the Lions, they may be the only thing Michigan has over Illinois," Johnson argued.

"You mean other than the fact our last two governors are gainfully employed, while in Illinois they are stamping out license plates?" Dexter jabbed, hoping to deflect.

"Touché," Johnson clipped, "but what are your plans for Taylor?"

"I can't abandon the client now, Robert. She has lost her husband, then her daughter—now her lawyer?"

"Better than losing a well-publicized trial exposing the reasons for her daughter's suicide. She cannot win this battle, Dexter. You have delivered your licks and the district is properly chastened. Compromise on the matter, gain some recognition of the anti-discouragement clause, and convince her to endow a chair in cosmology at one of the fine religious-based colleges in Grand Rapids. You will have more than fulfilled your responsibilities to zealously represent her interests."

"She wants this trial, Robert, and I am hard pressed to deny her the day in court Judge Austin just handed her. We are talking three months here, tops!"

"Do you want to give these right-wing blowhards like Joe Block any traction, Dexter? If they had their way, there would be no First Amendment protections for any purpose, including religious."

"Don't tell me AFSS is helping Cleaver out in order to protect religious freedom?" Dexter replied more stridently than he intended.

"I am a crusader for the Constitution for which thousands in this country have died." All amusement was squeezed from his voice. "You are playing a dangerous game, here, Dexter—for the Constitution, for your client, and, I would have thought as importantly, for your career. I told you our job offer cannot wait three months and we will have to pursue Plan B."

Dexter paused, looking at the angry lake under the Mighty Mac, his regrets about his fling with Taylor swelling.

"Don't write me off, Robert. You have to give me more than a couple of weeks to maneuver," he implored.

"No promises, my young friend. Call me when you have a material development. Then we will see if our interests are mutual."

"That's fair, Robert. I appreciate your patience."

"I can't say anything about my patience other than it has been tried. Enjoy the ride back to civilization," he said, and the line went dead.

"Come on, Daddy!" William poked his little head over the front of the ferry. "The captain told me he is going to blow the horn!"

"Can't keep the captain waiting, can we?" Dexter smiled, scampering aboard.

* * *

For Owen, Saturday night was more glorious than the day. Docker's restaurant sits on a dune overlooking a man-made lagoon harboring over a hundred sail and large powerboats. The lagoon strategically empties into Muskegon Lake next to the channel to the big lake. Owen and Sheila were ushered to an outside, candle-lit table surveying the condominium complex, the lagoon and moon tucked behind the sailboat masts at rest in the marina. As on Mackinac Island there was no wind in Muskegon, and the temperature was perfect for the fleece Owen had thrown in the car at the last second.

Owen could tell quickly that Sheila Blaine had been a great kindergarten teacher. She was a wonderful listener, assertive, but also fetchingly shy at times. She wanted to know whether Owen was sure his cancer was terminal and why he hadn't shared the news with his loved ones. He assured her his doctor —despite appearing to Owen to be of college age—was extremely capable, and that he had confirmed the diagnosis, prognosis, and his limited treatment options with an oncologist friend at the University of Michigan medical school. As for not telling his family, Owen explained his rationale of trying to preserve normalcy as long as possible. Sheila seemed to understand without necessarily accepting his reasoning.

In spite of their initial conversation, their dinner mood was enjoyably light. He discovered Sheila was a mother of two boys and grandmother to three little boys and one girl. All lived in the Ann Arbor area, which she visited regularly. Frank Callahan inadvertently added to the light-heartedness when he called in the middle of dinner. Owen and Sheila leaned forward like two conspiratorial teenagers, stifling grins when Owen advised Frank he was fairly sure he wasn't in the hands of an Al Qaeda operative. Owen playfully ended the conversation by advising Frank he couldn't be doing too poorly because he was having dinner under the stars with a very attractive widow who had picked him up on the beach.

The evening ended as surprisingly as their relationship had started. He walked Sheila back to her condo and gave her a kiss that started socially but soon became romantic and ended with Sheila quietly sobbing on Owen's shoulder. It was Owen's turn to be flattered. "Look Sheila, if there is one thing we know from the loss of our spouses it's that life is incredibly short and precarious. We can appreciate every phone call, every sunset, every meal, every laugh, and every smile. I don't have long and maybe very little quality time. I can't ask you to get involved, but I would like to call you again. I enjoy your company."

Sheila looked at him through teary eyes, smiled, and handed him a slip of paper with her phone number. "I was half hoping, Owen, the dinner would be a flop. I am obviously disappointed." She laughed and hugged him again, now tightly. "Please call me. Don't worry about me. I am a big girl—used to seeing my precious kindergartners grow up and move on." It was her turn to look at Owen with an open, pleading face.

"I'll call you tomorrow night, promise." Owen walked away, turning when he reached her car in the driveway and waiving after ensuring she was watching him. The ride home returned old memories. In high school and college, Owen had often taken dates to Lake Michigan for a day of sun and laughter and a night of romance on the beach. It was his good date guarantee. He laughed that it had worked one last time. Caesar slept on his lap as he drove through the night with the window down, closing it only when his cell phone rang.

"Robbie, I didn't expect to hear from you on a Saturday night. How far down your list are you working?" Owen laughed, surprised at his good mood.

"Funny, Judge, but don't quit your day job," the generally good natured Robbie Goldman responded. "I met Joe Calley and Sheila Carter at the Union League Club yesterday, and we were going over the portrait celebration party."

"Robbie, you know how honored I am by the attention, and a party with the former clerks in the Chicago area is a grand idea. Why don't you set up a 'smoker' at the Union League Club and I'll be glad to come down. We can stare at some distinguished old oil paintings, not an unrefined portrait of an old man."

Robbie chuckled. "Judge, no one has used the term 'smoker' for a decade. If we broke out your cigars at the Club, we would all be arrested—and you would make the front paper of the Chicago Tribune for yet another reason."

Owen paused. "Taylor getting a little press, I assume."

"A little? Joe Block started a 'draft Owen Austin for the Supreme Court' movement. You didn't know that?" Robbie paused.

"Of course not. I don't watch Joe Block. I am surprised you do, Robbie," Owen jabbed, trying to keep the mood of the call up.

"You know how worried I get about the religious right," Robbie offered seriously.

"You need not fret about the First Amendment, Robbie. Didn't you once gush that Lady Liberty's steely shoulders are strong enough to withstand the rages of any lunatic?"

"I am not worried about Lady Liberty. I am worried what a lunatic like Joe Block might do to the reputation of a man I respect more than my father."

"You don't have to worry about my appointment to the Supreme Court, Robbie. I am too old now!" Owen noted, tongue in cheek.

"I am worried about you, Judge."

"How many times have I said you worry too much, Robbie?" Owen used a fatherly voice. "Besides, Robbie, what is the worst that could happen? An overheated ACLU member might splatter red paint on my portrait? You have my blessing to turn it into an abstract."

"Just don't pull a Judge Feldman on me," Robbie said, referring to a long-deceased federal judge who had become mentally enfeebled and started holding court on a Lake Michigan beach.

"I guess now would be a good time to tell you that I am driving home from the beach. I was scouting out good locations for the Taylor trial. But thanks for your concern!" They each laughed and spent a few minutes exchanging news about their families. Robbie wished his mentor a good night and good health.

Owen's mood slowly soured as he stared ahead, fully aware of the growing strength of the headwinds into which he was plowing.

* * *

"John, let me be direct." Robert Johnson and John Cleaver settled into their second drink at the Chophouse. "We are the only two people in this restaurant talking business."

John had to laugh at the wry crack, which although completely apropos was not expected from Robert Johnson, who was not known for a sense of humor. Still, it had been painfully obvious to each as they were enjoying their first drink that they stood out in the mid-Labor Day weekend restaurant crowd.

"Well, why don't you be direct, Robert, so you can leave me early, get a good night sleep, get back to Chicago early tomorrow morning, and salvage the last two days of the weekend?"

"Fair enough. I want two things from you. First, I would like to assign a brilliant young lawyer to your Taylor team—at absolutely no cost to your school district—and second, when you finish with Taylor, I want you to leave Riley Dickson and start a local office for Kingman Walker in Grand Rapids."

John did not react. He studied Johnson, who returned the gaze. "Why Grand Rapids?" John eventually asked.

"Grand Rapids is the only city in Michigan that is growing. It has more than its fair share of medium sized family companies ripe for eventual Fortune 500 takeover or public offering. The future of large firms depends on feeder offices. The Taylor case is a good example. This is a national case that should be handled by a firm with lawyers of national skill. It is a pure fortuity East Grand Rapids happens to be represented by a lawyer of that ability."

John chuckled. "As flattering as your rationale might be, I am not sure I could live up to your expectations."

Johnson shrugged. "For Pete's sake, John, you are fifty-nine years old. I am talking about buying your book of business and your assistance for three to five years—your choice. In exchange, I will double whatever you declared on your tax return last year annually for three, four, or five years—again, your choice."

"Let me get this straight: If my tax return shows five hundred thousand dollars for last year, you will guarantee me a million dollars a year for up to five years?" John asked incredulously.

"Provided you bill as many hours as you did last year—and I will take your word on that—and provided at the end of the three or five year period, you have turned over your work to Kingman Walker," Johnson explained.

"What if some clients don't take to a big Chicago-based firm?" John wondered.

Johnson shrugged again. "John, we both know your clients are at Riley Dickson because of you. They will follow you. If we can't justify our value to them in three or five years, we don't deserve their business." Johnson leaned back in his chair.

"How do you know my book of business is worth a million dollars a year?" John asked, skeptically.

"Well, I haven't hacked into your firm's computers if that's what you are thinking. Let's just say I have done my due diligence and am also relying on the handsome finder's fee I paid to a certain fly fisherman we both admire."

That son of a bitch, John thought to himself, not sure if he should be flattered or angered—not sure if Keegan Riley was being more loyal to a friend or more disloyal to the firm he had founded.

"That's a handsome offer. Nonetheless, Riley Dickson is the only firm I have ever known. It isn't perfect, but it has given me everything I have received in the practice of law. There are a lot of people who depend on me there. I like the idea of staying true to the place nurturing me. I think I will pass."

"I admire your loyalty," Johnson said after a half a minute. "But are you sure it's shared? Don't make any decisions before your trial's end."

"What about the Taylor case?" John asked, eager to redirect the conversation. "Why doesn't AFSS just file an amicus brief on the district's behalf? I am sure Judge Austin would welcome your participation that way."

"Simple. We don't want to light up the Joe Blocks of the world. We will file an amicus brief when the case gets to the sixth circuit court of appeals, but for now, AFSS wants to fly under the radar. Besides, if I have someone working at your side we can help you shape the testimony as it is developed."

"I will have to run it by the superintendent of the district. I don't want this to become a political issue, particularly one that could embarrass the district."

"I understand completely. The same sentiment is why we want to fly under the radar and keep our assistance inconspicuous. While I would like to station our associate in your office and have him assist in the preparation of witnesses and perform legal research, we won't file an appearance. His role would be simply to assist you and Riley Dickson as you see fit."

"I am close to the superintendent. I don't anticipate a problem as long as you stay under the radar. I think we can accommodate you there. I wouldn't want you to drive to Grand Rapids, buy me a great dinner, and go home empty handed."

"I wouldn't want that either. And, despite what you may think now, I don't think I will," Johnson smiled.

* * *

"Judge, I called you at ten p.m. last night and you didn't answer. I was worried, sick," Megan chided Owen over the phone at nine a.m., unknowingly waking him from a deep although not restful sleep.

"I'm sorry, honey," Owen tried to reassure. "I turned off my phone after Frank called to check on me last night. That was insensitive. I am running late this morning. I will meet you in the Park Church balcony." Owen was trying to cut off the conversation. He didn't want to have to lie—at least not before church.

Park Church was unusual because its soaring sanctuary started on the second floor. The first floor was efficiently composed of meeting rooms, offices, the nursery, and the restrooms. Owen decided to use the restroom before climbing to the balcony. As he burst through the men's room door, expecting no one because he was already a couple of minutes late for the start of the service, he was shocked to bump into John Cleaver.

John was only slightly less surprised. He had arrived with his family earlier than normal and had been seated for ten minutes. During that time he had worked himself into a lather over the injustice of Owen's motion ruling in the Taylor case. Last night's dinner discussion added to his discombobulation. His excuse to use the restroom was half designed so he could cool off. Providence had now delivered a source of his discontent.

"John!" Owen exclaimed. "I forgot you were a member of Park. Good to see you."

"Judge" was the best that John could muster.

"Please John, in this house I am Owen."

John took that comment to be an invitation. "Owen, what are doing to me?" he blurted.

"To you, John? I am sorry, I don't follow?"

"Surely you must know the Taylor case is frivolous and I advised my client it would never get traction, especially when I saw your name on the file." John was sufficiently astute to throw the last clause in, knowing he was treading on thin ice.

"I have no idea what I am going to do with Taylor on the merits, but the last thing I would call a tragically deceased fifteen-year-old's cosmological quest is 'frivolous.'" Owen's own temperature was rising.

"A quest doesn't belong in court. Such sentiment is beneath you. Don't you realize the effect this is having on your reputation? People are mockingly calling this case the 'Miracle on Michigan Street,'" John sneered, shocked at his own temper and indiscretion.

Owen could have reacted a number of ways, and most judges would have exploded. Owen quieted himself, looked away, and then looked back at John.

"I don't know today's sermon, John, but please listen to mine. I have nothing but respect for you and your law firm and the East Grand Rapids school district. Whether you hang on to the district as a client or what happens to my reputation should have nothing to do with the outcome of this case. Where we came from and where we are going are the two most important questions we can weigh in life. As an intelligent species we spend shockingly little time weighing, much less answering those questions. Now, go back to your family, and when this case is done, take them on a long, lovely vacation."

With that, Owen Austin spun and took three steps further into the restroom. John thought for a moment and quietly exited, recognizing he needed to regain control of his emotions quickly.

After church, Owen treated his family to Sunday brunch at Charley's Crab, a regional sea food restaurant on the river bank in downtown Grand Rapids. After brunch he fended off Megan's invitation to join his two grandsons and his son-in-law on their Mighty Mac Labor Day walk. He was partially afraid the strenuous walk in the wind would stress his struggling immune system. He wanted to reserve his strength for the upcoming Taylor trial and maybe—did he dare think?—for his budding relationship in Muskegon. Truth was he couldn't wait until Megan's family was safely ensconced in their mini-van so he could call Sheila.

"Sheila? Hi! Owen. Were you able to change your plans for tomorrow?" Owen said expectantly over his cell phone. He hadn't yet left Charley's parking lot.

"Yes, my sons bought my lie about not feeling well enough for the trip to their Labor Day picnic," Sheila said excitedly. She hadn't felt this conspiratorial in decades. "How did you fare?"

"Piece of cake. My grandsons were relieved. I think they were worried they would have to carry ole Grandpa the last couple of miles." Owen laughed. "I've got to grab Caesar, and I can be at your place in an hour if that works for you."

"Hedgecock and I will be waiting."

Chapter Ten

Who's Winning?
Thursday, November 5, 2009
(Fourth Day of Trial)

Owen assumed the bench on the fourth day of the trial with the ominous feeling that his last trial was moving too fast. John Cleaver began his case by calling Christian Slagter as his first witness. Christian Slagter was fifty-five years old, six feet tall, athletically fit, and blonde, and his face was tanned and weather-beaten. He looked like a biologist should.

Q. Would you state your name, educational background, and occupation, please?

A. My name is Christian Slagter. I have a PhD in biology from Stanford University and am a professor of biology at the University of Michigan.

Q. Have you ever taught biology in a public high school?

A. Yes. I started my teaching career at Ann Arbor Pioneer high school, where I taught for five years before moving to the University of Michigan.

Q. Do you teach evolution science?

A.   Yes, I always have, both in high school and at the University of Michigan.

"You honor, I propose professor Slagter as an expert in biology and public education."

"*Voir dire*, Mr. Bussey?" Owen asked in response to John Cleaver's proposal.

"Your honor, the plaintiff has no objection to the professor's qualification as an expert in biology and in education."

"Thank you, Mr. Bussey. The professor is qualified by the court as an expert in the fields of biology and public education."

Q.   Thank you. May I ask you for your religious convictions, if any, Professor Slagter?

A.   Yes. I am neither offended by the question nor afraid to give an unqualified response. I am a Christian.

Q.   Do you find your Christian beliefs incompatible with evolutionary science as you know it?

A.   Not at all.

Q.   Are you aware that some prominent biologists consider evolution inconsistent with belief in a supernatural being?

A.   Yes. Certainly Professors Richard Dawkins and Leonard Devoneau would fall into this category.

Q.   Do you consider their atheistic conclusions a logical result of evolution.

A.   No.

Q.   Why not? Professor Devoneau certainly seemed sure of his atheistic convictions.

A.   He certainly did and undoubtedly is. However, many evolution scientists also believe in God. I observed Professor Henry's testimony; he makes a case for why evolution may not fully explain how our human faculties reached their current state. Many biologists recognize micro-evolutionary changes within species but question the common ancestry of all species. Many biologists believe in common ancestry of all animal species but question common ancestry of animals to plants or of plants to minerals. Then, of course, all biologists wonder how the first minerals or first life appeared. The principles of evolution themselves could have been established by a creator.

Q.   Do you mean an intelligent designer?

A.   I would never use that term because it has been co-opted by young-earth creationists to discount and, in many instances, disparage evolutionary science, causing a disservice to the discipline. That qualification aside, the answer is yes.

Q.   Doesn't Dr. Dawkins criticize this view as the reduction of God to the 'god of the gaps?'

A.   Dr. Dawkins has many disparaging things to say about biologists not sharing his cosmological conclusions, but he would have to throw the great Charles Darwin under that bus as well.

Q.   What do you mean?

A. I am not suggesting that Charles Darwin was a Christian. I am fairly certain he wasn't religious, but he certainly did wonder whether someone or something breathed the first life into the evolutionary process. In fact, I would like to quote the last paragraph of *On the Origin of Species*:

> "There is grandeur in this view of life, with its several powers, having been originally breathed into a few forms or into one; and that, whilst this planet has gone cycling on according to the fixed law of gravity, from so simple a beginning endless forms most beautiful and most wonderful have been, and are being, evolved."

Q. Doesn't Dawkins also criticize this view by saying that God as original creator is lazy, letting evolution do all his work?'

A. I find that criticism ironic, because Dawkins makes, in my opinion, the same mistake that the six earthly day, young-earth creationists and other proponents of intelligent design make, which is to assume that God would be creating within the very universe before he created it, subject to the limitations of physical time and energy he was installing.

Q. While all of this, professor, is fascinating, does this discussion belong in the public schools?

A. I am not a lawyer, so I cannot comment on the First Amendment other than as a professional teacher in the public school system who has to apply the First Amendment in my classes. With that qualification, I would say no. No such discussion belongs in the public schools. No one's religious conclusions belong in a public classroom. Instead, as responsible public servants, we should stick to scientific facts that can be empirically verified and leave religious discussion to private settings.

Q.   Have you read the statement that the plaintiff proposed to the East Grand Rapids school district?

A.   Yes.

Q.   As a biologist and an educator, what is your recommendation to the East Grand Rapids school district and to this court regarding this statement's use?

A.   I would recommend against it.

Q.   Why?

A.   For at least two reasons. First, because it opens Pandora's box. As we have seen in this trial, these concepts are complicated and deserve the kind of careful attention the court is giving. To throw out a thirty-second disclaimer and not put these issues in context is not what education is about, and it risks doing more damage when religious questions naturally arise. Second, as the *Kitzmiller* court recognized, no other scientific endeavor has such a qualification, and to require one for biology suggests that evolution is dangerous and needs a warning, which is absurd.

Q.   How would you draw the line, professor?

A.   Almost exactly as the East Grand Rapids biology teacher did. Public school biologists should stick to just the facts, and by facts, I mean those that have been empirically verified using the earth sciences and sensual observation.

"Thank you, professor." John Cleaver looked at Greg Jones and Superintendent William Reichel seated at the defense table, not so much to see if they had additional questions but so that Owen would see them smiling and nodding to John. John purposefully did not visually seek out Chad Bachman. After John let those nods sink in, he turned to Owen and said, "Nothing further, your honor."
        Owen nodded to Dexter. "Your witness, Mr. Bussey."

Q.   Good morning, Professor Slagter.

A.   Good morning, Mr. Bussey.

Q.   Would you agree evolution is being actively used by certain scientists to proselytize their atheism?

A.   Yes. We have seen evidence of that in this courtroom.

Q.   Yes, we certainly have. Can you think of any other scientific theory that has been used to promote any religious view?

A.   No sir, I don't think I can, at least not off the top of my head.

Q.   Many of your students come to class antagonistic to evolution because they assume it is linked to atheism, isn't that true?

A.   Yes, but this misapprehension is the responsibility of intelligent design proponents more than the New Darwinists.

Q.   Putting aside who's to blame, public confusion exists on evolution's implications on religion, wouldn't that be fair to say?

A.   Probably.

Q.   Because of such confusion and the potential damage it is doing to the science of evolution, the National Academies of Science has issued the statement on religion and evolution read by Professor Henry, correct?

A.   Yes, that is my understanding.

Q.   Isn't it true that the estate's statement is not materially different from the National Academies' statement?

A.   There are differences; I don't know if I would call them material.

Q.   Do you see anything in the plaintiff's proposed statement that is untrue?

A.   No.

Q.   Do you see anything in the statement that advocating any religious point of view?

A.   No.

Q.   Since evolution is the only scientific theory that is being actively used to proselytize atheism, since it has been linked with the religion of atheism in common understanding, and given the fact that the statement is neutral and is true, wouldn't you agree with me that there's nothing unconstitutional about the use of this statement in the public schools?

"Objection, your honor. Calls for a legal conclusion," John Cleaver asserted.

"Mr. Bussey?" Owen inquired.

"This is cross examination; the defense opened the door when they took his recommendation on the same subject," Dexter asserted.

"I agree. Mr. Cleaver, you opened the door. Overruled. Professor, you may answer."

A. I think it invites further discussion that may end up being unconstitutional.

Q. But the statement itself is not unconstitutional?

A. I cannot point to a provision in it that is, at least.

Q. And it is possible that the statement may correct the misunderstanding that evolution is inextricably linked with atheism?

A. I suppose that anything is possible.

Q. Thank you. Would you also agree with me, professor, that the teacher's statement that there is no empirical evidence of good and evil in the world is untrue?

A. The teacher's comment is true if you define empirical evidence as testable evidence using the physical senses, which is what I assume he meant.

Q.   Would you confine empirical evidence to the physical senses?

A.   Would I, personally?

Q.   Yes.

A.   No.

Q.   Indeed, as Professor Henry noted, you agree that there is empirical evidence the human mind can discern the difference between good and evil?

A.   Yes.

Q.   In fact, the legal definition of sanity requires such discernment, isn't that true?

A.   Yes. I believe that is true.

Q.   Can you understand how Michelle Taylor might have interpreted teacher Kingston's comment as a discouragement of her religious beliefs?

A.   Again, it is possible.

Q.   So, am I safe in assuming that you would not recommend that teacher Kingston repeat his comment?

A.   His comment was probably ill-advised.

"Thank you, professor. That's all I have, your honor," Dexter said.

"Mr. Cleaver?" Owen asked, wondering if John Cleaver would redirect.

"No further questions, your honor," John said to the obvious surprise of Greg Jones, who immediately looked down and tried to suppress his reactions, lest they be observable to the court.

Owen paused but did not show any reaction. "Very well, court is adjourned for lunch."

* * *

"How's it going?" Tom Sacks asked after poking his head into Greg Jones' office.

"Not as well as it should," Jones exhaled. "John failed to adequately prepare our biologist for Bussey's cross, and then inexplicably failed to redirect him and neutralize some of Bussey's points. Even Judge Austin was obviously waiting for a redirect that never happened."

"More evidence that he's lost his edge," Sacks declared.

"Tom, can you release Greg to me?" John Cleaver suddenly asked, having turned the hallway corner a minute earlier.

Sacks blushed intensely and feebly responded, "Sure, John, I understand you have one witness to go. Knock 'em dead," he mustered.

"Knock whom? Bussey, the witness, Judge Austin, or myself?"

"An expression—that's all," Sacks said as he slinked away.

"How's Stanley Morgan? Is he ready to go?" Jones asked, eager to change the subject.

"As ready as Slagter," John said curtly. "Grab your coat and I'll meet you in the lobby. We can walk to court as a team," he added sarcastically.

In court, John meticulously qualified Stanley Morgan as an expert in the fields of philosophy and education and as a professor of each at Michigan State University. Stanley Morgan was a small-framed African American, only thirty-five years old. He had been a child prodigy, graduating from the University of Michigan when he was fifteen, receiving his PhD in education by the time he was eighteen, and earning a PhD in philosophy from Yale when he was twenty-one.

Q.   Professor Morgan, do you consult with public high schools on curricula?

A.   Yes.

Q.   How many high schools have you assisted in this regard?

A.   Probably close to fifty.

Q.   Have you studied the curricula of public high schools other than those for whom you have consulted?

A.   Oh yes. I have studied the curricula of hundreds of American public high schools over the past twelve years.

Q.   Have you ever encountered a high school in the United States that qualified the study of evolutionary science in any manner?

A.   Do you mean have I ever seen or heard of a high school offering a disclaimer or warning label on evolutionary science such as requested by the plaintiff in this case?

Q.   Yes.

A.   No, I have never seen such a disclaimer in use, nor have I heard of a district using such a disclaimer, other than the Dover, Pennsylvania, school district, whose disclaimer, as we all know, was struck down in the *Kitzmiller* case.

Q.   Have you observed evolutionary science being taught in public high schools?

A.   Yes, many times.

Q.   Have you ever observed any high school students appearing confused or conflicted by the teaching of evolution relative to their religious beliefs?

A.   The short answer to your question is no.

Q.   What is the long answer?

A.   I have witnessed students' challenge the science in a way that suggests that their skepticism may have come from religious parents or religious authorities.

Q.   How did you deduce that?

A.   I have heard comments to the effect that evolution cannot account for the soul of human beings.

Q.   Have you heard skepticism that seemed to be religiously neutral?

A.   Oh yes. It isn't unusual for students to joke about a certain classmate having evolved in one or two generations from a monkey or ape, or that monkeys and apes would be insulted by to be physically linked to a classmate. Comments like this reflect student skepticism that primates are our ancestors.

Q.   Have you read the statement proffered by the plaintiff in this case?

A.   Yes.

Q.   Do you have an opinion as to whether the use of the statement is needed to disabuse high school students of any perceived conflict between religion and evolution?

A.   Yes. I do not believe it is necessary because I believe that students who learn evolutionary science will eventually draw their own conclusions about its effect on their religious principles. This has been my observation.

Q.   Do you believe the statement would be helpful to abate any confusion that exists in the general public about the science of evolution and religion?

A.   No. I think it will create more confusion than it resolves.

Q.   Why?

A.   Well, the present case is an example. Teacher Kingston is accused of violating Michelle Taylor's constitutional rights because he expressed his opinion about a lack of empirical evidence for the metaphysical concepts of right and wrong. Some student will likely consider his or her constitutional rights to be violated no matter which way the teacher travels on such paths. The statement draws the discussion into such a minefield of constitutional dangers.

Q. In your opinion, does this concern explain why most school districts do not offer a qualifying statement such as the plaintiff proposes?

A. Absolutely. Most school districts, particularly after *Kitzmiller*, are petrified by the potential liability of trying to walk the line the plaintiff proposes in this case.

Q. Professor, have you studied East Grand Rapids high school's evolution curriculum in detail?

A. Yes, I have.

Q. Is there anything unusual you find about it?

A. No. It is materially indistinguishable from every other public school's curriculum on the subject.

"Thank you, professor." John turned to Owen and announced, "I have nothing further for this witness, your honor."

Dexter rose and walked deliberatively to the podium.

Q. Professor, are you aware that many public schools were beginning the day with prayer before the *Jaffree* case?

A. Yes.

Q. And just because many were doing it didn't mean it was constitutional?

A. That is true.

Q. Of the public schools that you have observed, how many have considered a qualifying statement for evolution sciences such as the one proposed by the plaintiff in this case?

A.   I am not sure any of them have.

Q.   So, you are not testifying from any personal knowledge as to why those districts are not using such a qualifying statement?

A.   True.

Q.   In fact, for all you know, none have ever considered it?

A.   That is true as well.

Q.   So the "petrifying fear" to which you testified a moment ago was merely your speculation?

A.   No. I have had talks with principals about the dangers of evolutionary science and First Amendment challenges.

Q.   However, those concerns were that a parent might sue the district for teaching intelligent design rather than employing a statement differentiating evolution from atheism, correct?

A.   Yes. That is probably accurate.

Q.   You have never discussed with a principal the utility of adopting a statement such as proposed by the plaintiff in this case?

A.   I have discussed the *Kitzmiller* statement with educators.

Q.   The *Kitzmiller* statement had to do with intelligent design, correct?

A.   Yes.

Q.   The statement proposed by the Taylor estate does not mention intelligent design, correct?

A.   Well, that is technically true, but it mentions an intelligent designer and qualifies evolution the way the *Kitzmiller* statement qualified it.

Q.   Well, let's break that down. Evolution as a science doesn't speak one way or another as to whether an intelligent designer created the process, does it?

A.   I suppose that is true.

Q.   In what way does the proposed statement attack evolution?

A.   It suggests that there are gaps in evolution.

Q.   There are gaps in evolution. Isn't that true?

A.   Yes.

Q.   What provision in the statement is untrue?

A.   I don't know that there is an untrue statement in it.

Q.   What provision in the statement endorses religion?

A. I don't believe there is any one provision in the statement endorsing religion.

Q. Well, if the statement is true and doesn't endorse religion, it cannot be unconstitutional for the East Grand Rapids school district to adopt it, correct?

A. I am not a constitutional scholar.

Q. No, but you offered your opinion. Is it fair to state that you would not advise it for the reasons you stated but that you know of no reason why the district could not legally adopt it?

A. I guess that is fair.

Q. Have you any reason to doubt Professor Hileman's testimony that a majority of East Grand Rapids residents believe evolution and atheism are linked?

A. No.

Q. And you have not studied the effects of the statement on correcting that perception, have you?

A. No.

Q. There is always a constitutional risk that a school district will be sued for a constitutional violation if it teaches evolutionary science, correct?

A. Yes. I suppose this case is an example.

Q. That risk is worth it given the importance of evolution sciences to the field of biology. Would you agree with me?

A. Absolutely.

Q. And the risks of public school being sued after teaching evolution science can be abated by proper First Amendment training of teacher. Would you agree with me on that proposition?

A. Partially, perhaps.

Q. And a school district could decide to include a statement such as proposed here as part of such training, true?

A. I don't know. I would have to think about that more carefully.

Q. Have you ever witnessed students in biology class wonder how the first matter emerged?

A. Yes, I have.

Q. What was the response of the teacher?

A. That science does not yet have an answer.

Q. Have you ever witnessed a student wonder in a public school setting how the first animal or plant life emerged?

A. Yes.

Q. Do you recall the teacher's response?

A.   Something to the effect that science has no answer today.

Q.   In any of those situations, do you think the dialogue violated your understanding of the First Amendment?

A.   No. Not in my understanding.

"Thank you, professor. I have nothing further." Dexter sat down and looked to make eye contact with Owen, who avoided it.

* * *

"What's left for the defense, Professor Riley?" Alex Ross wondered as the bartender poured a couple of scotches lightly braced with soda.

"John Cleaver no longer solicits my advice, but if he learned anything from me he would put superintendent Reichel on the stand tomorrow to empathize with Mrs. Taylor's loss and affirm the district's pledge to stick to the same science curricula as every other public school in the country, and then shut it down. Speaking of shutting down and asking what's left, what's happened to you exposé on teen suicide?"

"What do you mean?" Ross asked sheepishly. "I thought everyone understood that I had taken that as far as I can."

"We don't have an explanation for Michelle Taylor's suicide? Wasn't that the point?"

"Never! What gave you that idea?"

Riley chuckled and sloshed his scotch in a circle.

"You are being paid to analyze the trial, not my methods," Ross remarked, slightly recovering his humor.

"Forgive me. Your compensation keeps me dizzy." Riley turned to Ross and saluted him with his glass.

"So, who's winning?"

Riley smirked. "You are, of course."

"Stop it and behave," Ross instructed.

"Well, Austin is a keen jurist. Cleaver should be winning. East Grand Rapids should be free to teach any curriculum it wants, and certainly one that is similar to every pubic school. The question someone should be asking is whether it is time that the Constitution evolves to eliminate even the quaint concern that biology class might be discouraging religion. If we want to stay ahead of the Chinese, we need to mandate more science, more exercise, and a better diet."

"Who brought in the Chinese, and who are you to be talking about diet while polishing off a scotch?"

Riley laughed. "The Chinese are our biological competition, and whiskey is mother's milk to an Irishman. Any more smart questions from the reporter who quit on his story?"

"You seem on edge tonight, my friend. I think you need some more mother's milk." Ross looked over to the bartender and ordered another round.

Chapter Eleven

Decisions Faithful

Tuesday, September 8, 2009

Dexter was looking out of his office doorway, hoping to make eye contact with his secretary nearly two months earlier. "Amy, where's Peter Diamond?"

"He's finishing a conference call on another case and said he would be ten minutes or so," Amy said at several decibels lower than Dexter's voice, since she was right outside his office door frame.

"How do you do that?" Dexter asked.

"Do what?" Amy wondered.

"Don't act dumb. You know, anticipate I am going to yell to you so you can show me up by locating yourself outside my door?"

"I don't know what you are talking about. By the way, while you are waiting for Peter, how did your Labor Day weekend go with Melissa and William?"

"Very well, thank you. How about yours with Joe and the kids?" Dexter asked.

"Fine, thank you for asking," Amy said. "Aren't we models of decorum? Let me shatter that notion. When are you going to ask the girl to marry you?"

"Holy cow! A little time off and you are running on high octane! But if you must know, when we were on Mackinac

Island we had a deep discussion and she wants to take things slowly."

"Dexter, for all the women you have known and as quick a study as you are on everything else, its mindblowing how little you know about women." Amy shook her head and started to leave the doorway.

"On no, you can't hit and run like that. What are you talking about?" Dexter asked, suddenly concerned. "Are you saying when she says she wants to take it slow, she doesn't mean what she says?"

"Of course. She was hoping you would disagree with her."

Dexter looked down and started rubbing his temples with his fingers. Amy took pity on him. "It isn't complicated, Dexter. When it comes to marriage that's the point with women. We don't want it to be complicated. We want it to come from the heart and so it has to be spontaneous. If you wait until it makes sense, it won't make sense, does that make sense?"

"Oi, Oi, Oi. I understand as much as I can understand Yogi Berea." Dexter continued to rub his temples.

"Dexter, do you want to marry this woman?" Amy prodded.

"I want to be a full time father to my son. I love being a family."

"That's not an answer to my question."

"I love Melissa." Dexter paused.

"Still haven't answered my question."

Dexter looked up. "Yes, I want to get married."

Amy stared at Dexter for what seemed like a full minute.

"Then I'm very happy for you, Dexter," she said finally as she turned and walked out the door.

Peter Diamond passed her in the doorframe and Dexter called out. "Thank you, Amy. You know, things might have been different if you weren't married."

"You are incorrigible." Amy was only half amused as she returned to her desk.

"She's just figuring that out?" Peter asked. "I thought she was the brightest assistant in the firm."

"Hey! Show some respect," Dexter warned, tongue in cheek. "Now, who's our lead atheist, our expert evolutionist?"

"Leonard Devoneau is his name. He is the Coakley professor of biology at Harvard University and is more Richard Dawkins than Richard Dawkins—a true Darwinist of the highest order." Peter Diamond handed Dexter the curriculum vitae he had located on the Internet. "But boss, what makes you think he will testify for you? And how does a lawyer classify his own expert as a hostile witness?" Peter asked, perplexed.

"If he is a true disciple of Dawkins, he isn't hostile to critical elements in our case syllogism. True Darwinists believe science necessarily disproves the existence of God. Darwinists are responsible for the perception evolution is inconsistent with religion. If we establish those facts, the First Amendment will take care of the rest. I've read these Darwinist's bestsellers over the Labor Day weekend. Dawkins and his troupe don't realize they are zealots as surely as the Christian fundamentalists. If Devoneau is a true Darwinist, he'll want to proselytize."

"I don't know, Dex. I am glad you are going to be the one trying to close the deal," Peter said, shaking his head.

"You aren't quite ready to take my place, eh?" Dexter teased. "Well, I have to bring something to this team. Let's ring him up."

Professor Devoneau took forty-eight hours to return the four voicemails Dexter left him, each revealing more than Dexter had wanted, the last indicating Dexter needed him as an expert witness to sustain evolution theory in the Bible Belt.

Finally, Amy pulled Dexter from a firm recruiting committee meeting with the exciting news the professor was on the line.

"Professor Devoneau, thank you for responding to my calls," Dexter said as he slid behind his desk into his desk chair.

"You are a persistent bugger, Mr. Bussey."

"Occupational hazard of trial advocacy, professor. Natural selection weeds out the timid. But I am sure you know all about that, looking at your resume. I see you are an accomplished expert witness, usually for the United States Environmental Protection Agency on wildlife damages caused by the nation's most notorious polluters. Well done!"

"Don't patronize me, Bussey. You don't want me for an environmental case. I googled you before calling you back. What could I possibly offer to your crepe hanging?"

Dexter could feel his pulse rise. This guy was perfect! "You would love my client, professor. She's the type who stays after class to argue with her teachers. As a distinguished educator, you share an objective with her. She believed public school teachers shouldn't be compelled to cut off the discussion on the most important question of all—the cosmological question of whether is there a supernatural creator. You and she may differ on the answer, but you agree the discussion should not be cut off at the pass."

"Is that right? Maybe the newspaper got it wrong. It reported you were trying to put a warning label on evolution, suggesting that evolution doesn't disprove the existence of God."

"Evolution does not obviously convey there is no God. If it did, there would be no work for you or Richard Dawkins. No, that's the factual premise of the other side. You may have to accept a cursory warning label for the near term, but from there you can launch into your belief structure. You need the entry more than the religious," Dexter argued.

Professor Devoneau was thinking. Dexter was encouraged. Dexter decided to press. "Besides, you should hope we win and you are part of the winning team for a different reason. You will be invited to lecture around the country. I'm telling you, professor, lawsuits make even stranger bedfellows than politics." Dexter paused for this to sink in and then continued, "And money is no real object."

There was an even longer pause. "My fee is one thousand dollars per hour," Devoneau answered, "and I will want a twenty-five thousand dollar nonrefundable retainer."

Dexter repressed a laugh. "Where do you want the check sent?"

* * *

Owen ambled up the bleachers to where his teenage grandson Boyd was sitting, iPhone buds in his ears, texting on his phone, oblivious to the football game below in which his older brother Christian was playing. Owen sat next to Boyd and looked over the field.

"Grandpa! Hi!" Boyd pulled his ear buds out as he recognized the older man who had landed next to him.

"Hello Boyd! What are you listening to?"

"The Black Eyed Peas. You wanna hear?" Boyd asked, offering the ear buds.

"Thanks for the offer. I mean it. But I have a headache. This is just a guess on my part, but I think the Peas might exacerbate it." Owen looked directly at the acne-faced teen, smiled, and put his arm around him. "I'm happy just to be in your company!"

"Gee, Grandpa, you haven't been drinking, have you?"

Owen cut loose a belly laugh. "Where are your mother and father?"

"Concession stand. They were starving and wanted a couple of hot dogs."

"How come you didn't go?"

"You've got to be kidding, Grandpa. Do you know what hot dogs are made out of?" Boyd asked incredulously.

"I have a vague idea and it's as much as I want to know about it. You are a smart boy." Owen turned to Boyd, grabbing him gently under his chin and looking him straight in the eye. "Boyd, remember this moment—I believe you can do anything you want and I'll always be somewhere supporting you. Do you understand?"

Boyd frowned, pulled Owen's hands off his chin, and put his ear buds back into his ears. "Cut it out, Grandpa, you're giving me the creeps."

Owen chuckled.

"Hey Grandpa! How's the 'God case' going?" Boyd suddenly lit up.

"The God case?" Owen looked at him, perplexed.

"You know, the case about the battle between evolution and intelligent design?" Boyd looked back down and began texting.

"Oh." Owen paused. "Trial starts in a couple of weeks." Owen rose suddenly to cheer as Christian secured a good tackle from his safety position. "That a boy, Christian! Great job!" Owen yelled. Christian looked up into the stands and did a double take when he saw his grandfather waiving. Christian waived weakly back, turned his back, and returned to his defensive huddle.

Megan and her husband Roy also stopped in their tracks halfway up the stands when they saw Owen present, animated, and cheering in the stands. They slowly completed their trek up the bleachers. "Judge!" Megan said as she took a seat next to Owen on the other side of Boyd. "Didn't expect to see you here tonight."

"Hi Roy! How are you?" Owen extended his hand to Roy, whose face moved from surprise to complete disbelief. Roy shifted his hot dog awkwardly and extended his other hand for Owen's.

"Great night for football, isn't it?" Owen exclaimed, slapping his knees.

"It's going to rain within the hour." Megan stole a closer glance at her father. "Have you been drinking?"

"That's what I wanted to know, Mom," Boyd chirped, not looking up from his smart phone.

"This kid is brilliant." Owen placed an arm around Boyd, hugging him again. "I can't walk and chew gum; he can listen to some rock group called the Peas, text his girlfriend, and keep pace with the adult conversation—truly impressive. Say... I have to go let Caesar out. But I want to make sure that you are going to be at Park Church this Sunday, and I want to take you out to Charley's Crab afterwards. Is that okay?" Owen rose and began walking down the bleachers.

"Sure, we'll see you then," Megan said, the earth returning to its axis now that Owen seemed animated only to make an exit.

"Oh..." Owen turned after descending a few steps. "Meg, I'm bringing someone with me. I hope you don't mind?" Owen did not wait for a response. "I'll call you tomorrow, honey. Bye Roy! Bye Boyd!" Owen looked down to concentrate on the bleacher steps while continuing his waiving.

Roy and Megan looked at each other. "What's wrong with Grandpa?" Boyd asked without looking up from his texting.

"Nothing," Megan said slowly. "Nothing is unusual at all."

Owen made it as far as the parking lot, collapsing on the hood of the first car he encountered. He pulled the brim of his Detroit Tiger's baseball cap down over his face, hoping no one would recognize him. He was nauseous. He had fully intended to stay for the game, having snuck out from work earlier to attend to Caesar, but the bleacher climb left him dizzy. Keeping up the appearances had sapped his reserve strength. He leaned on the car like a drunk for a full five minutes until the nausea half-passed and he could struggle home to collapse in bed.

* * *

Monday, September 14, 2009

"What's your general assessment of Bussey's expert roster?" John Cleaver asked Greg Jones as the two lawyers reviewed the expert trial disclosures.

"Bussey has found atheistic zealots. Leonard Devoneau, the biologist, and Karl Hitchcock, the philosopher, fit that mold in their respective disciplines. The pollster Milton Hileman's role must be to link evolution with atheism in the mind of the masses. Alvin Henry, the philosopher, shares Michelle Taylor's world- and life-view," Jones offered. "I would say Bussey's done well. I don't 'know how he convinced Devoneau and Hitchcock to testify for his side of the case."

John laughed. "Having an unlimited trial budget at your disposal helps, I am sure. I can't wait to ask them how much they are being paid for their testimony. What do you think of Bussey's proposal we stipulate to most of the basic facts?"

"If he wants it my gut says we oppose it."

John sighed. Jones' reaction was typical of today's litigators, who were often mindlessly confrontational. "I actually like the concept, Greg. Although women on a jury might not have liked Vicki Taylor, Bussey shrewdly didn't ask for any damages, so we couldn't ask for a jury. Judge Austin shares with Vicki Taylor the relatively recent loss of a spouse, and his vision doesn't seem impaired. I don't want Mrs. Taylor on the stand for very long. Plus, we have a teacher who will come off as an arrogant know-it-all. The strength of our case is the law. The less time we spend on the facts the better. That's my take."

"Doesn't that give Bussey an opportunity to script the facts his way?" Jones was clearly not convinced.

"There's some truth to that. Why don't you work with Peter Diamond, his associate, and see if the two of you can develop a stipulated set of facts? I trust you will be able to out-negotiate the greenhorn?" John played to Jones' ego.

"What about Bussey's suggestion we skip expert depositions and wing it at trial? I suppose you like that too?" Jones' voice carried more than a little sarcasm.

"Look, Greg, what these experts are going to say isn't hard to figure out in advance, and this case is not going to be won or lost with expert testimony. It's going to be won on the law and the indisputable fact the district's curriculum is completely in line with that of every other public school. I want to keep costs down and the case simple. Whatever surprises the experts have in store for me, I will have twice as many for them when I attack at trial for the first time and they don't have the deposition experience to prepare. So I am going to agree to his proposal on that front as well."

"What did you think of my Christian biologist?" Jones asked, searching for some common ground.

"University of Michigan biology professor Christian Slagter? I like his resume. From the description of your conversation in your memo, he is exactly what I had in mind. Sign him up and good job!" John said agreeably. "What are your thoughts on supplemental experts?"

"I think we need a curriculum educator who can testify the district's approach is standard and respects the 'lofty neutrality' required by the First Amendment. Tracking the *Kitzmiller* plaintiff's team, I think we need someone like the philosophy professor, Robert T. Pennock, to attest to the mandates of the scientific method. I am not sure if we need to counter the statistician they are proposing."

John let Jones' suggestions sink in for a moment. "I agree one hundred percent. If we establish the neutrality of our curriculum, the efficacy of the scientific method, and the basic neutrality of evolutionary science, it doesn't matter what the public perception is. Let's not get dragged into that trap. Find the additional two experts you describe and then let's roll. What happened to the psychologist?"

Jones smirked. "Mrs. Taylor didn't want to let us into the medical records of the Taylor family. Who knows what skeletons we would find buried there? Instead, Peter Diamond advises they will not claim the classroom confrontation caused the suicide."

John nodded his head in satisfaction, although repulsed by Jones' callous smirk.

With the meeting concluded on an apparent high note, Jones left more convinced than ever that John Cleaver was losing his edge and was no longer interested in sweating the intimate details that won big cases. John departed more convinced than ever that the new generation's antagonistic approach to the practice of law was an anathema to the collegiality that originally attracted John to the legal profession. Lawyers might be evolving like everything else, but that didn't necessarily mean progress.

* * *

Dexter and Melissa Connelly looked over the Grand Rapids skyline, such as it is. They were on the twenty-seventh floor of the Amway Grand Plaza Hotel in the Cygnus restaurant. It was only the second time they had been out on true date requiring a babysitter for William.

Dexter thought Melissa stunning, cast in a brilliant blue dress matching her blue eyes, both contrasting with her flowing brunette hair. She was relaxed, enjoying herself, and looking at her, Dexter could not have been happier or more convinced his decision was the right one—for all three of them. After his conversation with Amy, he dove into the project with his typical attention to detail. The results of that planning were about to be displayed. In the corner of his eye Dexter spotted the violinist, who gave him a subtle smile and thumbs up and began unpacking his instrument. Within a minute the violinist meandered over, slowly starting "Somewhere My Love," Lara's song from *Doctor Zhivago*. As the musician reached their table in full swing, Dexter extracted a one carat solitaire diamond ring from his pocket, got down on his knee, and looked Melissa Connelly in the eye.

"Melissa, I love you! Will you be my partner for life, to enjoy the good times together, support each other in the bad, and to put our children and our marriage first forever?"

Tears welled in Melissa's eyes. She didn't speak, gazing at Dexter, weighing the importance of the event. Then, loud enough for the entire restaurant to hear she said, "Oh, why not?" She stood to meet him and chase away his slightly befuddled look. The two embraced in a long, extended kiss, while the other patrons lightly clapped before returning to their dinners.

After the violinist had packed and departed, Dexter and Melissa picked at the meals, neither one having any appetite. Dexter finally leaned over. "Let's go back to my house! I have a bottle of Dom Perignon on ice. We can begin the real celebration and maybe make a second baby!"

"That is a good segue. I have to know something before I can privately follow through on that public commitment," Melissa said, taking a darker tone.

"Anything, my love," Dexter replied, still enthralled in the moment.

"Have you slept with Vicki Taylor?"

Dexter felt his heart compress against his chest, his mind accelerating as fast as it ever had—although not fast enough. The look on his face belied any answer but the truth.

Melissa looked down on the table cloth. If they had jumped through the twenty-seventh floor window the couple's evening would not have crashed more suddenly.

Thirty minutes later, Dexter stared ahead, left hand on the wheel and right hand on the gear shift as he drove Melissa home in silence. He did not dare look at her. Eventually, he felt her hand on his. He glanced over and saw only a gentle smile and rolling tears.

"It was a beautiful evening I will always cherish," she said. "You have broken no promise to me. I know you have your big trial coming up. Concentrate on that and call me afterwards."

Dexter pulled into her driveway. What was happening? He recalled the moment William first acknowledged him as his "daddy." For the second time in a few months, words—his stock in trade—were failing him.

Melissa exited the car and entered her house without looking back.

* * *

Friday, October 9, 2009

"Has Peter brought you up to speed on our experts?" Dexter asked Vicki Taylor coldly after entering the conference room. Peter had already spent half an hour with Taylor identifying the retained experts and their expected testimony.

"Yes." Taylor stared at Dexter, assessing his mood. "I wasn't initially convinced Professors Devoneau and Hitchcock were appropriate, but Peter explained your rationale. I have confidence in you. I keep explaining to my friends that this case is not about establishing some fundamentalist agenda. It is about establishing that life's most serious questions should be available for discussion in a public school."

"Great, you have that theory of the case down," Dexter said impatiently. "Now Peter, if you will excuse Mrs. Taylor and me; I have to prepare her for trial."

"Good day, Mrs. Taylor," Peter extended his hand to Taylor as he hurried out of Dexter's office, wondering what was behind his boss's unusually sour mood and why he was being excluded from the prep session.

As the door closed, Dexter launched into his first instruction: "First, no matter what happens, be polite to me, to the judge, and most importantly, to the other attorney. John

Cleaver is too experienced to attack you directly, but he will attempt to color your motivation. Under no circumstances are you to lose your temper. Do not argue with him. Do not get sarcastic or short. Do you understand? This is very, very important!"

Vicki Taylor stared for a moment. "What's wrong?"

Dexter paused to settle himself. "I apologize. I crossed a professional and personal boundary I have never crossed before. I shouldn't have."

"That may be," Taylor did not break eye contact, "but that isn't what is bothering you at the moment. So, why don't you get to it?"

"It is none of your business," Dexter said without breaking his gaze.

"But it is my business, Dexter. I was listening to you. You just explained that the interactions among you, John Cleaver, Judge Austin, and me are all critical. Now you want me to accept the fact that when you question me there will be hostility?"

"I will be over it by then."

"Perhaps. But isn't that the point of this session—to prepare as if I am testifying?"

"I want to marry someone but she doesn't trust me," Dexter responded without further resistance.

Taylor cackled. "Dexter, anyone who would be worth marrying is smart enough not to trust you. The question for your lady is whether she can accept you."

Dexter looked out the window.

"Don't beat yourself up." Taylor softened. "Freud would love us. We are all id and ego."

"Is it that easy to brush off? You run with your own self-interest? Whatever makes us feel good is right?" Sarcasm dripped from Dexter's voice.

Taylor resisted an inclination to anger. Instead, she turned reflective. "Boundaries are necessary. I obviously made a mistake, because we crossed one and now you are distracted."

She paused. "I don't like thieves or liars, so I won't tolerate such behavior in myself. Other than that, I guess I am not what you would call a 'moral' person."

"What about your marriage to your husband? I assume you weren't faithful."

Taylor smiled. "Chivalry is truly dead."

"I didn't mean it crassly."

Taylor paused to settle herself. "My husband was not faithful. I was not faithful. On the other hand, we didn't have an 'open marriage.' I guess we drew implicit boundaries and accepted a measured level of indiscretion."

"You and Frank agreed upon those boundaries before you entered the marriage?"

"Heavens, no. I never discussed infidelity with Frank."

"Then how could you agree on the boundaries?" Dexter asked curiously.

"We understood each other."

"That's the problem. I think the woman I want to marry understands me too well and is not sure I will change. I don't know if I will change."

"People don't change, Dexter. You should know that. They sometimes redirect their priorities. They sometimes exercise discretion. But they don't change. You have to decide if you want to rearrange your priorities and then maintain them. Your lady has to decide if she can accept the risk you will return to your nature."

Dexter now resisted the impulse to be angry. Instead, he returned to business. "I wouldn't ask you this question, but John Cleaver may: Do you believe in God?"

Taylor smiled, pleased with the conversation and that Dexter had regained his focus. "After the events of the past five years, I certainly don't believe in a loving God—just so you know, if the subject were to come up. Perhaps a vengeful God exists. I could claim evidence of that. I don't know. Someone seems to be writing the rules. There are an awful lot of them—

too many for incompetent humans to have invented. Like most people I know who are honest with themselves, I suppose I am an agnostic. Is there something wrong with that answer?"

"No. The First Amendment is agnostic. Cleaver would rather you were Mrs. Joe Block."

Taylor snickered playfully, "I don't think even Clarence Darrow could reconstruct me as Mrs. Joe Block."

"You are probably right about that." Dexter grinned slightly, his mood lightening. "So, what is your motivation for filing the lawsuit? We have already decided you do not want damages."

"I want only one thing—my daughter's vindication. She wanted to talk about the origins of man and why people are the way they are, and we should be ashamed if such subjects must be off limits in any school, much less a public school."

"Good answer. You are ready for trial," Dexter declared.

"And you are too, my friend. Make no mistake: I am expecting to win this case. I paid for a winner and chose a man supremely confident of his judgment and skills, not someone whining about an error in judgment and bemoaning lines between the professional and personal. I pegged you as a man who figures out what he wants and can get it."

Nothing seemed simple to Dexter Bussey at that moment—least of all how he could have let a preparation session for a client get so completely turned around.

* * *

As soon as he arrived at work, Johnson dialed up Bill Allen, a junior partner in his firm who had been a clerk for Owen Austin a dozen years ago and who, like Johnson, was an early riser. "Bill, did you call Robbie Goldman?" Robert smiled to himself at the lengthy pause on the other end of the line. He knew the answer; Bill Allen had no choice but to have called Robbie Goldman.

"Yes. Robert... The deed is done."

"Did Goldman ask why you were bailing?"

"Of course he would wonder why I would back out of the portrait party for my favorite boss, the man who taught me more than any other lawyer about our profession," Allen spat.

"What excuse did you give him?" Robert smiled again as Allen paused even longer this time, clearly not enjoying any aspect of this conversation.

"I told him I was backing out because of a law firm commitment," Allen replied disgustedly.

"Beautiful. And so true. What was Goldman's reaction?"

"Disappointment. I honestly don't think he thought any more of it than that," Allen offered with more than a hint of spite.

"Give him some time. Thank you, Bill. I will remember this. Don't you forget it."

"I won't forget it, Robert."

"Things are coming together beautifully," Johnson said to himself as he sat back in his chair and enjoyed his view of Lake Michigan, fifty stories above the Chicago River.

Chapter Twelve

What No One Knows
Friday, November 6, 2009
(Fifth Day of Trial)

John had similar thoughts a couple of months later as he focused on the first opinion of his last expert witness. "For better or worse, the scientific method must be a litmus test for the examination of any cosmological theory," intoned Jeremy Hawk, who had been qualified as an expert in the field of scientific study.

Q. Can you describe the "scientific method" for the record?

A. Certainly, Mr. Cleaver. The "scientific method" refers to a set of procedures for investigating theories. To be termed "scientific," a method of inquiry must be based on gathering observable, measurable evidence subject to specific principles of reasoning.

Q. How long has the scientific method been recognized?

A. Aristotle is commonly identified as the father of the scientific method because he identified the difference between inductive and deductive reasoning. The great Muslim scientist Ibn al-Haytham Alhazen, who lived between 965 and 1039 A.D., further developed the concept by adding a reliance on experimentation and peer review. Simple as it may seem now, he was the first to suggest that the truth should be pursued for its own sake. As an aside, Alhazen cautioned that those who are engaged in the quest for anything for its own sake are bound to be misunderstood and persecuted by those whose religious beliefs are challenged by scientific inquiry.

Q.   What are the elements of the scientific method?

A.   Scientists commonly recognize four essential elements in sequential order: Observations, hypothesis, predictions or deductions from the hypothesis, and finally experimentation, otherwise known as empirical testing.

Q.   What is "inductive reasoning?"

A.   Inductive reasoning involves moving from specific to general—making specific observations and then drawing general inferences. An example of inductive reasoning would be as follows: All sheep I have observed are white in color. Therefore, all sheep in existence are white in color.

Q.   Is inductive reasoning used at all in the scientific method?

A.   William Whewell notes in his book *History of Inductive Science* that intuition or induction is required at every step in scientific method. The second step—formation of a hypothesis—is particularly subject to inductive reasoning. However, because inductive reasoning ends with conditions not observable, it is not useful in the third and fourth steps of the scientific method. Thus, in my example one can never prove that the statement that all sheep in existence are white is a true statement. Therefore, other than in the formation of hypotheses, inductive reasoning is not useful. The renowned twentieth-century economist and philosopher Karl Popper denied the usefulness of any inductive reasoning in the scientific method. Popper believed there is only one universal method—the negative method of trial and error. It covers not only all products of the human mind, including science, mathematics, philosophy, and art but also the evolution of life. Beginning in the 1930s he argued that empirical hypotheses must be falsifiable, and thus that all scientific conclusions must be purely deductive. Although there is an absolute truth, it may be mutable and changing—much like natural selection has modified past understandings of biology. Popper's view has become known as "critical rationalism."

Q.   What is "deductive reasoning?"

A.   Deductive reasoning, in contrast, involves moving from general predicates to specific propositions: All sheep in existence are white in color. The specimen in my possession is a sheep. Therefore, this sheep will be white. Since deductive reasoning ends in conditions observable, it is subject to being falsified. It is, therefore, subject to empirical testing. For instance, it is possible to observe that the specimen in your possession is white or is not white. If the sheep in your possession is not white, then you have defeated the hypothesis that all sheep are white. If you determine that the sheep in your possession is white, then you have empirical evidence of the inductive hypothesis that all sheep in existence are white.

Q.   Using the scientific method, can one prove something true?

A.   Albert Einstein asserted the scientific method can never prove something true. It can only prove something false. He once said, "No amount of experimentation can ever prove me right; a single experiment can prove me wrong." I'm afraid, Mr. Cleaver, that at best a scientist hopes experimentation reveals data consistent with his or her hypothesis.

Q.   Is intelligent design subject to the scientific method?

A.   No. It is the product of inductive reasoning. We see order in the world. Order typically comes from an architect. Therefore, we conclude that there is an architect for the universe. That is the reasoning for intelligent design, and being inherently inductive, it is not subject to being falsified. Therefore, intelligent design is not a scientifically based theory.

Q.   How about evolution? Is that subject to the scientific method?

A.   As Dr. Henry admitted, it is subject to being tested and elements may be subject to being falsified. Therefore, it is a scientific theory.

Q.   Is there a relationship between our discussion here and biology class in the public schools?

A.   In my opinion, yes. Evolution is a scientific theory that belongs in biology class. Intelligent design is not a scientific theory and does not.

"Thank you, professor." John looked at Owen. "Nothing further of this witness, your honor."

"Thank you, Mr. Cleaver. Mr. Bussey, your witness."

Dexter nodded and took the lectern without any notes.

Q.   I have a couple of questions, Professor Hawk. First, you would agree with me, would you not, that philosopher Popper opined on whether or not evolution was subject to the scientific method?

A.   Yes.

Q.   And through most of his life he was of the opinion that evolution was not subject to the scientific method, correct?

A.   Through most of his life, that is a true statement.

Q.   The general problem with testing evolution through scientific experimentation is that it takes too many generations to observe random mutation and natural selection—the chief agents of evolution—to work, correct?

A.   Basically, that is what Popper was referring to, yes.

Q.   And at the end of his life, after reviewing some scientific studies regarding micro-organisms, Karl Popper slightly revised his opinion, believing evolution might be "slightly testable," isn't that true?

A. Yes.

Q. Do you agree with Popper's later view?

A. Yes.

Q. So, it would be fair to say that you think intelligent design is not testable and evolution is "slightly testable."

A. If you want to put it that way, yes.

Q. Now, you mentioned that Aristotle is commonly identified as the father of the scientific method, correct?

A. Yes.

Q. Aristotle was a metaphysical naturalist or atheist, is that true?

A. Yes.

Q. That is so, in part, because he believed that the universe has always existed, correct?

A. Yes.

Q. In contrast, his predecessors Plato and Socrates believed that there was a creator of some sort who created matter and life and laws such as physics or metaphysical truths, correct?

A. That is an oversimplification, but as such, it is generally true.

We Hold These Truths

Q.   Aristotle believed that the laws of physics were absolute, correct?

A.   Yes.

Q.   Whereas Socrates and Plato believed that there might be forms or certain truths outside of the universe?

A.   Yes. That is true as well.

Q.   Astrophysics has proved the universe has not always existed, correct?

A.   You are referring to the Big Bang theory?

Q.   Yes.

A.   Yes. Probably.

Q.   And particle physics calls the smallest piece of matter in the universe "Planck," correct?

A.   Yes.

Q.   Particle physics has established something is moving faster than Planck time?

A.   Yes.

Q.   Particle physics theorizes that whatever this something is, it operates outside the laws of physics, isn't that true?

A.   That is a common postulate.

Q. So what I take from your testimony, professor, is that while intelligent design is not testable, evolution is only slightly more, and of the great Greek philosophers, the naturalist as opposed to the intelligent designers is the one who has been proved wrong?

A. Well, Mr. Bussey, I see where you are going. But the fact that you are right proves my ultimate opinion, which is that evolution is scientific and intelligent design is not. You see, Aristotle's and Darwin's works are subject to testing and Plato's works are not.

Q. So what you're saying is that the public schools should teach only things that can be proved wrong and not things that can be proved right?

A. In a manner of speaking, that is exactly what I am saying, since, as Einstein said, nothing can be proved right.

Q. Well, Professor Hawk, if Socrates and Plato are correct, then cosmologically, the public schools will have failed to even acknowledging the most important cosmological fact in the universe—namely, the existence of a supernatural creator?

A. I guess that's the price we have to pay.

Q. For what are we paying that price, Professor Hawk?

A. For the separation of church and state.

Q. That is the question for Judge Austin. Let me ask you this question: Would you consider sanity to be biologically based?

A.   Well, it is a mental condition, but it is obviously a function of the biology of the brain.

Q.   Are you aware of the McNaughton rule?

A.   Yes. You mean the legal definition of insanity. Yes, I am aware of it.

Q.   What is your understanding of the McNaughton rule?

A.   That to be legally sane, one must be able to differentiate between right and wrong and conform one's behavior to what is right.

Q.   What are some of the scientific theories as to how human beings transmit values such as right and wrong?

A.   Inclusive fitness is a theory that suggests that we are drawn to look after those who are biologically related to us. Group selection is a derivative of that: Groups that help each other individually tend to survive more readily. Richard Dawkins has theorized about memes, which is the ability to transmit positive social behaviors by repetition.

Q.   Are any of these theories testable?

A.   Well, only empirically.

Q.   What do you mean by that?

A.   Empirically, such as with the McNaughton rule, the common man understands certain values as right and wrong, and statistically we can measure that perception.

Q.   So that would be an example of inductive reasoning: We understand right and wrong, and therefore, there must be some biological process whereby that perception is transmitted, is that correct?

A.   Yes.

Q.   So while they would not be products of the scientific method, those theories are appropriate for discussion in public school science classes as possible explanations for our biological sanity?

A.   Correct.

Q.   Well, what if I added a fourth potential explanation for our biological ability to discern right from wrong?

A.   You mean an intelligent designer?

Q.   Exactly, professor. You anticipated my question. Is that a possible theory with the others you suggested?

A.   I suppose.

Q.   Is there anything precluding inclusion of this fourth theory when a public school biology teacher is offering postulates to explain the biological reasons for our sanity?

A.   Only the First Amendment.

Q.   How would the First Amendment preclude the simple mention of a possible fourth theory?

A.   It would be extremely difficult to offer such a postulate without either promoting it or dismissing it, either of which would be inappropriate.

Q.   Well, if the Biblical devil exists and is teaching in the East Grand Rapids public schools, certainly you would expect him to describe or even promote the fourth theory without endorsing religious allegiance to the creator?

A.   I guess I wouldn't know.

Q.   Let me put this in terms that might be more familiar. First Amendment law permits public schools to teach comparative religion. Can you think of anything that would make teaching the differences between intelligent design and inclusive fitness as possible sources of biological sanity different from teaching the differences between Islam and Christianity?

A.   I suppose not.

"Nothing further, your honor."

"Mr. Cleaver? Any more questions?"

"None, your honor. If it pleases the court, the district would call William Reichel."

Superintendent William Reichel marched to the stand and turned to look directly at John.

Q.   Would you state your name, sir?

A.   William Reichel, superintendent of the East Grand Rapids school district.

Q. Mr. Reichel, does the East Grand Rapids school district have a policy regarding the First Amendment?

A. Yes. We have an oral policy that we will comply with the First Amendment in everything we do, meaning we will neither encourage nor discourage the practice of religion.

Q. How does that policy come into play?

A. It pops up when we develop curricula, when we consider policies on tolerance and diversity, and when we address extracurricular activities.

Q. Has the biology curriculum for freshmen in the high school been scrutinized for First Amendment compliance?

A. Absolutely. It is one of the more scrutinized classes.

Q. Prior to the proposed statement from the estate of Michelle Taylor, had the district received any complaints from parents about freshman biology relative to the First Amendment and religious freedom?

A. No complaints at all from either side of the First Amendment spectrum.

Q. Has Mr. Kingston been the subject of prior complaints relative to First Amendment issues?

A. None whatsoever.

Q. Has anyone complained that he discourages religious belief?

A.   Not until this matter.

Q.   Are you qualified to speak for the district as to why it rejected Mrs. Taylor's proposed statement?

A.   Yes. I believe I am.

Q.   What is your understanding of the district's rationale for rejecting that statement?

A.   First of all, on behalf of the district, I wish to indicate how sorry we are for the loss of Michelle. The staff of the high school, including Mr. Kingston, was deeply affected by her tragic death, and certainly the board was as well. However, we feel our policy of religious neutrality is legally compliant. We concluded that the statement could threaten that neutrality.

"Your honor, I have nothing further."
"Mr. Bussey, your witness."
"Thanks, your honor." Dexter rose and stayed at the plantiff's table.

Q.   Mr. Reichel, were you in the courtroom when the district's curriculum expert, Professor Morgan, testified?

A.   Yes.

Q.   Do you recall his testimony that he could find nothing false in the proposed statement?

A.   Yes.

Q.   Do you agree with him on that point?

A.   Yes.

Q.   Do you recall his testimony that he could find nothing in the statement that endorsed religion?

A.   Yes.

Q.   Do you agree with him on that point?

A.   Yes.

Q.   So if the statement is true and doesn't endorse religion, how does it threaten the district policy of religious neutrality?

A.   Perception is the reality in this area. It could be perceived as endorsing religion.

Q.   You mean the district is afraid of a false perception?

A.   Basically, yes.

Q.   The district is afraid of being sued by the ACLU based on its misperception?

A.   Or some other interest group, yes.

Q.   Any other reasons for the district's rejection that you can think of?

A.   Not at the moment.

Q. Do you have any reason to dispute Mr. Hileman's testimony that people in East Grand Rapids tend to equate evolution with atheism?

A. No.

Q. Has the district considered whether the statement might neutralize this common mispercepiton of evolution and atheism?

A. No.

Q. So it would be fair to say that when it comes to the statement, the district is more concerned about being sued than in neutralizing the common misperception of linking evolution and atheism?

A. I don't know. I haven't thought about it in those terms.

Q. Maybe not, but I'm asking you to think about it in those terms. Can you answer my question if you do?

"Objection, your honor. The question asks the witness to speculate." John Cleaver's voice rose with his body. He was visibly upset.

Owen stepped in before Dexter could respond. "Overruled. On direct, Mr. Reichel testified he could verbalize the district's reasoning for the issue. Mr. Bussey's question probes the district's concerns. It is proper cross."

A. I guess your statement is true.

"Thank you, Superintendent Reichel."
"Anything further, Mr. Cleaver?" Owen interjected.

"No, your honor, and the defense rests," John Cleaver responded.

"Any rebuttal, Mr. Bussey?" a stone-faced Owen asked Dexter.

Dexter half rose and said, "No, your honor. The estate rests as well."

"Very well. Then there are two ways that we can proceed. I can take your closing summations now, or you could submit closing briefs. It's your case, but my preference is to receive your arguments as proposed findings of fact and conclusions of law."

Dexter rose to respond first, as the plaintiff. "Your honor, I respect your request and we will certainly propose findings of fact and conclusions of law to assist the court. However, I would like to offer a closing summary."

"You certainly have that right, and I will extend it to you. Mr. Cleaver, I presume that you will then follow suit?"

"The defense was prepared to acquiesce to the court's desire, but if Mr. Bussey is to summarize, I would be remiss if I did not."

"Thank you, Mr. Cleaver," Owen responded. "The court will now hear from Mr. Bussey on behalf of the plaintiff, Vicki Taylor as the personal representative of her daughter Michelle Taylor's estate."

Dexter stood, buttoning the top button of his coat. "One hundred and fifty years have passed since Charles Darwin published his history-changing book, *The Origin of Species.* In the ensuing years, evolution has been in constant tension with theism, most particularly Christianity. Over the course of this trial this court has seen this tension in full display. Of the four experts who testified regarding the effect of evolution on religion, two are fully of the opinion that evolution proves there is no God. Despite common perceptions to the contrary, the other two experts suggest evolution may be a part of the best proof there is a God who has guided the development of the human mind.

"I am reminded of *Kitzmiller*'s refusal to permit the study of intelligent design in the public schools because the court found it inextricably bound with Christianity. The public schools don't have that luxury with evolution. It is sufficiently scientific. It must be taught. However, as with intelligent design, schools may not ignore the linkage between evolution and religious thought—in this case atheism, not Christianity.

"The first serious question for the Court is whether there is substantial confusion about the effect of evolution on religion so as to evidence a need for a qualifying statement. That no school has yet ascertained such a need is of no more consequence to this question than the fact that many public schools started class with prayer when *Jaffree* was decided.

"The one hundred and fifty years of constant controversy between the proponents of evolution and many Christians suggests the need for the statement. That the National Academies of Science has issued its own statement, which is similar to the estate's statement, is compelling evidence of a need. That a majority of adults in the East Grand Rapids school district believe the two concepts are incompatible confirms the need. And finally, that evolution has become dominated by radical proselytizers of atheism such as Richard Dawkins, Leonard Devoneau, and Karl Hitchcock should convince the court of the pressing nature of the need.

"The remaining question is whether the First Amendment's requirement of lofty neutrality mandates the statement proposed by the plaintiff, or the National Academies of Science, or frankly, one of the school district's own drafting in order to address this need. The teaching of evolution science by the East Grand Rapids school district in this case leaves no scientific basis for the principle of human equality as expressed in the Declaration of Independence and leaves no scientific basis for our criminal justice system's test for sanity—the reliable ability of the human mind to discern the difference between right and wrong.

Victor Fleming

"The human mind is as much a part of the human body as the foot, the lungs, or the oppositional thumb. Undeniably, evolution cannot explain how the human mind, unguided in its development except by periodic genetic mutation and natural selection, would come to the self-evident conclusion that all men are created equal. Undeniably, some evolutionists find confirmation of their faith in a supernatural being through evolution, while others find confirmation of their faith there is no God in the same science. This truth must be told to place the science in its proper light, unhinged from either the controlling influence of the religious right, which irrationally finds evolution to be an anathema, or the domineering influence of the secular left, which equally irrationally finds it to be the holy grail of atheism.

"There is no dispute there is linkage between atheism and evolution as described in the statement. There is no dispute the statement is true. There is no dispute the statement is religiously neutral. There is no dispute it would not burden the East Grand Rapids school district to offer it. What then opposes it other than stubbornness and an irrational fear of litigation? Even if the statement prevents one student from being dismayed by the misperceptions heaped on evolution from the left and right, it will have served a compelling constitutional purpose. Without such a statement, the science of evolution and theistic religions are needlessly suffering.

"For all their superficial complexity, this case and *Kitzmiller* are not hard. It is easy to see the Dover school district crossed a line and promoted the existence of a creator. It is easy to see Mr. Kingston crossed a line and promoted his anti-creator atheism. The remedy is not to throw the proverbial baby out with the bath water. The remedy is not to stifle cosmological thought or the teaching of different cosmological theories. The remedy is to untether those theories from their religious overtones and present them for what they are—largely untestable hypotheses regarding the greatest mystery of life.

We Hold These Truths

"Our expert Professor Devoneau analogized belief in God to belief in the tooth fairy. That is an exemplar of the underlying hostility of many scientists towards religion. Beyond underscoring the point that de-neutering statements are necessary, analogies such as this point to a broader truth. Over three billion people living on earth now believe what hundreds of billions now deceased believed, namely that we come from an intelligent designer. Perhaps there are a few thousand souls who believe in Big Foot. Yet it is perfectly acceptable for public school teachers to speculate about the existence of Big Foot and not a creator. We can speak of Big Foot and not violate the First Amendment because everyone knows that just referring to its possible existence doesn't mean that the teacher is advocating the worship of Big Foot. Again, however, aren't we making this too hard? *Jaffree* says public school teachers may acknowledge God may exist as long as they don't profess a belief he does exist. If true, why in the world would the courts restrict public school teachers from acknowledging an intelligent designer may have created the universe as long as they don't profess a belief this is what has actually happened?

"In the course of this trial we have demonstrated that the ability of the human mind to reliably value metaphysical concepts such as right and wrong is as likely explained by the work of a creator who set the evolutionary process in motion and then augmented it by breathing values into the human brain as it is by Dawkins' hypothesis that the mind is merely the product of evolution un-augmented by any other force. The simple point is that public school teachers must be free to acknowledge either theory as long as they follow the constitutional edict of endorsing neither. That such teaching requires a little bit of discipline to preserve the First Amendment's lofty neutrality is a small price to avoid the banishment of credible theories with some empirical support. Such denial is reactionary if not medieval and, as demonstrated by this case, can only have evil results."

Dexter let the last sentence hang over the courtroom and then sat down.

John Cleaver then stood and ambled to the podium. He unbuttoned his coat jacket and placed his hand on his hip.

"Unlike the school districts engaging in school prayer, and unlike the Dover school district adopting a statement espousing intelligent design, the East Grand Rapids school district has taken no affirmative act to land in this courtroom. It has not asked for this fight. It has not sought any controversy. It is not doing anything different from any other public high school in the country. It may be that the religious right is disparaging the science of evolution as anathema to their core beliefs, and it may be that the secular left is attempting to co-opt the science of evolution as their own, but neither are defendants in this case. The defendant in this case—the East Grand Rapids school district—is doing neither. It is maintaining the lofty neutrality required of it, and as such the plaintiff estate has failed to carry its high burden of severing the district's curriculum from its presumption of constitutionality.

"This district is not suggesting it would violate the constitution if it adopted the statement. What it is simply saying is that by not adopting the statement, it is not acting unconstitutionally. The statement cannot be forced upon it by the plaintiff. If the statement is good for the science and good for the biology curriculum, the case should be made to the elected members of the school board who are chosen by the community to make such policy and curriculum decisions, not by the plaintiff or by the courts. Thank you, your honor."

John Cleaver returned to the seat without making eye contact with anyone, lost in his own thoughts.

"Mr. Bussey, as the party with the burden, you have the last word," Owen granted and warned.

Dexter stood one last time, "Thank you, your honor. I will say only that the East Grand Rapids school district cannot stick its head in the sand and ignore the passionate efforts of those—

including Mr. Kingston—who have impregnated this neutral science with religious implications and thus corrupted the public mind. Especially when impressionable minds are at risk, the duty to be neutral sometimes engenders a duty to neutralize. With the science of evolution, that obligation is upon the district."

"Thank you, Mr. Bussey," Owen noted. "Thank you both. I will have my decision out after the Thanksgiving holiday. Before I close the record, I want to compliment the lawyers and the parties to this case. I put all through an extraordinary pace to resolve the matter as quickly as possible with a minimum of expense and community conflict. Through their efforts, we succeeded. In my opinion, the *Kitzmiller* case was made needlessly long, expensive, and confrontational. The lawyers in this case, as I anticipated from their excellent reputations, were extremely professional in their preparation and the dignity with which they approached each other, the parties, witnesses, the court, and most importantly, the subject matter. It has been a distinct pleasure for me to preside over this case and to serve this community from this bench. Thank you all."

With that Owen rose to leave the bench. Frank Callahan immediately sprang to attention with the muscle memory of his military bearing and announced, "All rise."

The crowd stood, conversation was beginning to start, and Dexter and John had turned to shake each other's hand, when a hush fell over the courtroom. John and Dexter simultaneously turned to the bench where Owen was standing and staring over the courtroom. From her seat in the back, Sheila Blaine inhaled. From his position in front, Frank Callahan took two steps towards the judge and was stopped in his tracks by the sight of tears welling in the eyes of his boss. Startled and speechless, Frank stood by as Owen turned and swept out of his courtroom.

* * *

"Keegan, I need you." Alex Ross said in panicked voice as he called Riley's cell phone.

"Alex, I am not interested in your personal problems," Riley offered dryly.

"This is serious. I am in the third base side dugout of the baseball diamond at Fuller Park. Do you know where that is?"

"You are not in drag, are you?"

Ross exhaled deeply, revealing the second thoughts he was already having.

"Okay. Okay. Are you alone or is there someone with you?"

"I have someone with me who needs to talk to you."

"All right. You and Madelyn Wysocki stay put, I will be there in fifteen minutes."

"How...?"

Riley cut Ross off. "I told you Ross, never lie to an old trial lawyer."

Fifteen minutes later, after making sure that no one was in earshot, Riley sauntered up to the third base dugout at Fuller Park, where he found Ross holding the hand of an exhausted Madelyn Wysocki, who had cried herself out. Riley suppressed comment and took a seat on the cement wall facing the odd couple.

"Madelyn, this is Keegan Riley. He is one of the best lawyers in Grand Rapids even though it pains me to admit it." Ross pointed at Riley while Madelyn listlessly nodded her head.

"Here's the situation, Keegan: Madelyn is afraid that her testimony wasn't completely honest, and we want your advice as to how she should handle it," Ross said after turning to Riley.

"Madelyn, it is a pleasure to meet you," Riley said, extending his hand and ignoring Ross for the moment. "First, we need to shut up Mr. Ross for five minutes. Alex, do you think that is possible?"

"Fine, the floor is yours," Ross pouted.

Riley lightly laughed. "I want the floor to be Madelyn's alone. Ms. Wysocki, let me first establish this: Do you engage me as your lawyer to answer your concern?"

Madelyn looked at Ross, who nodded his head.

Madelyn turned back to Riley. "Yes sir, I do."

"Good. Now, do you have any cash on you?"

Madelyn looked again at Ross, reached into her pocket and pulled out a crumpled five dollar bill, and was about to study it when Riley grabbed it out of her hand.

"Great, that will do it. It is now official. I am your lawyer. Mr. Ross, will you be my private investigator on this matter?"

"Of course, Keegan," Ross said, puzzled.

"Good, then take this five dollar bill. You are hired. Okay, with that settled, now we are ready. Anything you say to me, Ms. Wysocki, will be subject to the attorney/client privilege. Do you understand?"

Madelyn nodded.

"You are not to reveal what we discuss in this dugout to anyone unless I tell you that you may. Do you understand?"

She nodded again, looking lost.

Alex smiled and patted Madelyn on the shoulder. "I told you he was good."

"Madelyn do you understand how important it is to preserve the secrecy of this discussion?"

"Yes sir, I do."

"Good. Then tell me what bothers you about your testimony."

Madelyn looked at Alex Ross, who nodded in an assuring manner, careful not to say anything. She then looked back again to Riley.

"I told the judge I didn't know why Michelle killed herself, and that wasn't true. I am afraid I know..." Madelyn choked off and began sobbing.

Riley let her unwind for a minute, then abruptly cut in. "Compose yourself, young lady, and explain why you think you know why Ms. Taylor took her life."

"She kissed me and I pushed her away..." Madelyn started sobbing again.

"When did this encounter happen?"

Madelyn could not stop sobbing. Riley reached over and slapped her lightly across the cheek.

"Keegan! Is that necessary?" Ross exploded, standing up.

"Shut up and sit down! I told you to remain quiet!" Keegan Riley's face reddened as he turned on Ross.

They turned to face a now composed Madelyn, who was staring at the two men.

She then continued her story. "While I was at Michelle's house after her biology class blow out, I blew it, Mr. Riley. I mean, I should have known this could happen. I secretly suspected she was attracted to me. I mean, I wondered. I am not that way. It isn't me. I should have asked her about it. I am so stupid, stupid..."

"Take a deep breath. Slow down. So you had never talked about sexual orientation?"

"No sir... No, no. We talked about cute boys, crushes, stuff like that all the time. But it was the way she hated to dress up. She hated make up. She hated to walk the way... You know, like her mother wanted her to... Stuff like that. I mean... I knew. I mean, I should have known..."

"Madelyn... Stop talking." Riley leaned forward causing Ross to rise again until Riley shot him the evil eye. Ross returned to his seat.

"So you suspected Michelle Taylor might have some orientation issues but she never discussed any unusual desires with you, is that true?"

"Yes, sir."

"You went over to her house, as you testified, to comfort her after class, and she was calm as you testified, correct?"

"Yes."

"And everything you told the court about your conversation with her was true, correct?"

"Yes sir."

"What you didn't tell the court was that she surprised you by making a move on you—kissing you, is that right?"

"Yes, sir."

"And I suppose you bolted out of her house like you bolted out of the courtroom, is that true?"

"How did you know?"

"As Mr. Ross implied, I have been around the block a couple of times." Riley saw the empty look on Madelyn's face. "Never mind. I have a knack for figuring things out. Now, let me ask you this: Did you ever discuss suicide with Michelle after this incident?"

"No. We barely talked. It was real awkward for the next week. I blew it. I should have talked to her. I killed her. I blew it..." Madelyn started sobbing.

This time, Riley reached over and grabbed Madelyn's chin, forcing her head up and her eyes into his. "Madelyn, I am only going to say this once, so I want you to look straight into my eyes. Maybe Ms. Taylor was gay. Maybe not. Probably she didn't even know herself. But one thing I am sure of: She trusted your discretion completely. I am certain you haven't told a soul but my private investigator here, am I correct?"

"How did you know?"

"I told you, I know these things. And I know that Michelle Taylor did not kill herself because you rejected her advances. Suicidal currents run much deeper than an awkward moment between two good friends, so put that out of your mind once and for all. Now, let's focus on your legal question. What is it?"

"Well... Isn't it obvious? I didn't tell the complete truth. Am I in trouble, Mr. Riley? Should I call the judge? Am I going to go to jail? Isn't that perjury or something like that? Mr. Ross didn't know."

"He's good at digging things up but has little skill in thinking them through. That's what he usually hires me to do."

Ross initially smiled, frowning only when Riley's serious look didn't soften.

"I recall your testimony on this point quite clearly. Mr. Cleaver asked you if you knew why Michelle killed herself. And your answer was no, you did not. That was a true and complete answer to the question. You don't know. No one does. If you said anything more you would have been answering the question inappropriately. You would be speculating, and that is strictly forbidden. Any lawyer would have told you not to do that. So there is no legal issue here. You are not going to call the judge or the lawyers, nor are you to mention this to anyone else. Do you understand me?"

"Yes sir. I certainly don't want to talk about it to anyone. But are you sure, I did okay?"

"Yes. Mr. Ross was almost right. I am not just one of the best lawyers in town; I am the best lawyer in town."

Madelyn came close to fainting, being near physical collapse.

"Okay. Ross, earn your five bucks and take Ms. Wysocki home. I think she needs a nap. I know I do." With that he stood. "It was a pleasure serving you, Ms. Wysocki. Now remember, mum's the word."

"Yes sir."

Ross stood. "Thanks, Keegan. I appreciate it... I think."

"Don't think, Ross. Thinking gets you in trouble. How many times do I have to remind you?" Riley shook his head, expelled a throaty laugh, and sauntered to his car.

* * *

Sheila was waiting inside his house when Owen arrived shortly after four p.m. For the past few weeks, Sheila had spent many nights with him, which he considered a great gift. He was growing increasingly sleepy as his disease progressed. The headaches were getting more intense and he would typically start and end the day vomiting. Although he slept as much as twelve hours a day, it was fitful and often unsatisfying. He had shed fifteen pounds from a waning appetite. His dexterity was increasingly compromised with daily stumbling. Fortunately, he had not yet experienced the two things he feared most, confusion in thought and impairment of speech.

Sheila embraced Owen when he walked in the side door of his sprawling one story house. "Megan called me today," Owen advised, while Sheila was fixing his cocktail. "Apparently Frank Callahan's suspicions are growing. He called her to suggest I was ill. Frank's observant as a hawk, and my fall six weeks ago didn't help."

"What did you tell your daughter?" Sheila asked.

"A half-truth—that the medication I take for my headaches makes me dizzy and it was nothing she should worry about," Owen replied as he sunk into his leather recliner and Sheila handed him his daily manhattan.

"Owen, this is your call, but if you want my advice—and you are going to get it whether you want it or not—you will bring your daughters into your confidence. You don't want them to resent you for not sharing your illness with them."

Owen took a long sip, staring straight ahead, seemingly ignoring the advice. "Wasn't this trial amazing?" he finally said, changing the subject. "To be honest, after my initial hesitation, it now seems an indulgence to get a trial about life and death on my deathbed. I guess I was afraid I might be convinced by the scientists that life has no meaning. But as the trial unfolded, I was strangely comforted by the subject matter."

"Comforted? How?" Sheila wanted to know.

"I have dedicated my life to the principles of human equality articulated in the Declaration of Independence and the Constitution. This case made me realize you cannot be an evolutionist and hold as self-evident that all men are born equal.

Our understanding of good, evil, and human equality strongly suggests a creator."

"Is that what made you pause at the end of Mrs. Taylor's testimony?" Sheila asked.

Owen's smile slowly emerged. "I hate to admit the truth. But at that moment, I was looking at Judge Drummond's portrait and thinking his contrived countenance was absurd."

"Joe Block said he thought you were having a grand mal seizure."

Owen laughed. "He will soon consider himself prescient. No matter which way I rule, one side or the other, or perhaps both, will consider my opinion the product of a diseased mind."

"Promise me one thing, Owen."

"What's that?" Owen sharpened his focus on Sheila's eyes.

"That you will never doubt the quality of your mind again!"

Owen smiled. "I like you, Sheila Blaine. I'll make you that promise if you promise one thing to me."

"What's that?"

"You will accompany me for Thanksgiving dinner. I am going to rent a banquet room at the Drake Hotel in Chicago and tell my children and grandchildren about my illness. I could sure use your support."

Sheila sadly skewed her head, leaned over, and kissed Owen on the forehead. They walked hand in hand to the living room couch.

"I keep flashing back to significant moments in my childhood, particularly those in my senior year in high school when I had my first date, my first kiss, my first drink, my first job. Now I feel the same overwhelming poignancy because I have seen my last summer, my last Halloween, now my last trial, and soon my last holidays."

Sheila did not know how to respond, so she just hugged him. Together they turned and watched Hedgecock and Caesar as they sat side by side, staring out the back window, watching a squirrel bury his nuts.

"I have another imposition," Owen started, but he was cut off.

"Of course I would be willing to take Caesar," Sheila said as she stood up, slid around behind Owen, and began to gently caress his forehead.

* * *

Dexter opened the side door and waited for a minute. Sure enough, in ten seconds he could hear the pitter patter of the little feet approaching. As William wheeled around the corner of the kitchen, Dexter snatched him under the arm pits and drew him up as the little guy squealed with delight, a big smile on his face.

"Daddy's here!" he exclaimed.

"Yes, your daddy's here. How's my favorite fella?"

"Good. I'm playing with my crane," William announced, his little face inches from Dexter's.

"No, not the crane?" Dexter feigned a look of surprise and concern.

"Yes, the crane. Come and see!" The little boy's face opened.

"Okay, show me the wonderful crane." Dexter gave Melissa a glance and a smile.

"Trial is over?" Was the best that Dexter could elicit from Melissa.

"Trial is over," Dexter declared, not taking his eyes off the crane.

"Any decision yet?" Melissa wondered.

"Nope, but it will be out after the Thanksgiving holiday." He quickly interjected, "Can we talk?"

"We are talking," Melissa said, regretting her words as they left her mouth. She had resolved not to show any hurt.

"I am very sorry, Melissa. I made a major, inexcusable mistake."

"Well, to be fair, we aren't married. You broke no vow."

"Of course I did. I am lawyer. I know about implied agreements. We had an understanding. I violated it."

"Okay. I won't argue with you." Melissa smiled slightly. "Now what?"

"I have accepted a job in Chicago. I would like to stay in your life. Maybe we can step back a second time and regroup once more. No matter what, I want to stay in William's life. I would be happy to take him on some weekends. There's a world for him to see in Chicago."

"That's a reasonable plan, Dexter. No promises except a commitment to our son. I can accept that."

"I will take uncertainty in our relationship—at least for now," Dexter said staring at Melissa, who only briefly returned the gaze. He wanted to say more, but realized this was one setting where less was a whole lot more.

* * *

John strode into his kitchen, glancing at the clock—three thirty in the afternoon. He hadn't been home on a weekday at three thirty since—well, he couldn't remember since when. At least fifteen years. His wife Carolyn turned the corner into the kitchen with a book in her hand and jumped a half-foot when she saw him. "Jesus, John! You almost gave me a heart attack!"

"Sorry," was all John could muster.

"No, I am sorry, I just didn't expect you home after your trial. I figured you would have a stack of phone messages and a mountain of mail."

"I do, but I figure they can wait a day," John said as he poured himself a whiskey and soda.

"How did the trial end, John?"

"No decision, but the last day went better than the day before," John mused.

"What do you think Judge Austin will do?"

"Hard to tell. He's acting strange, very unlike himself, I would say. But it is out of my hands now."

"That's a good attitude," Carolyn offered without any sarcasm in her voice.

John laughed.

"No, I mean it, John. You are a great influence on everything, but you can't control anything."

"I think I like that, Carolyn. Quite profound." John drew a long gulp from his drink.

"Do you want to head out to dinner to celebrate?" she asked.

"No, I would just as soon stay home, share a meal with you, and maybe find a black and white movie on TV."

"How about a walk through the neighborhood before dinner?" Carolyn asked. "A little fresh air may clear out the trial."

"Better than this whiskey?" John smiled. "A long walk is a good idea, and I have one of my own, I think we should book that cruise in the Mediterranean for the first two weeks of the year."

"What about the annual firm meeting? You can't miss that."

"Why not? Nothing significant has happened at that meeting in years."

"Are you feeling all right?" Carolyn looked at him quizzically.

"Never felt better. Something about this trial. I can't put my finger on it," John said, finishing his drink.

"Whatever it is, I think I am ready to try one of your drinks, although I am going to need a little more soda than you use to chase it down."

* * *

Monday, November 9, 2009

"What do you think, Ms. Shurlow?" Owen asked his clerk as she sat down in his chambers, taking one of the leather client chairs.

"Denying empirical evidence of the metaphysical is a step removed from discouraging religion. I don't think the teacher's fragmented comments rose to a constitutional violation, no matter how erroneous. Our district's *Daugherty* case dispels that claim," Mary Lou Shurlow ventured.

"I agree." Owen nodded slightly, his head resting on his hands folded under his chin. He was sitting behind his desk, his coat draped behind him over the back of his large leather chair. "At least as long as those comments don't make their way into approved curriculum. The constitution can forgive a mistaken comment or two. *Daugherty* rightly requires incidental comments to be direct and sharply unconstitutional to be actionable. But how about the guts of the estate's case—the qualifying statement on evolution?"

Mary Lou paused. "That's seems a closer call. I like Mr. Bussey's argument that no religion gets to own an idea, but does that really help his case? If true, atheism doesn't own evolution. I also agree with Mr. Cleaver's argument: East Grand Rapids is just doing what every other public school district in the country is doing. Should the courts intervene and force a policy statement on it?"

"What about the analogy to *Kitzmiller* and the testimony that evolution and atheism have become as closely linked as intelligent design and Christianity?" Owen asked.

Mary Lou paused again. "In *Kitzmiller* and this case, the plaintiffs relied on experts without presenting any students who were confused into thinking the school district was preferring one religion over another in its origins of life teachings. The more I think about it, I think *Kitzmiller* employed the wrong relief. All Judge Jones had to do was delete a couple sentence in the Dover school board's statement to easily purge it of its unconstitutional preference of intelligent design over evolution."

"Interesting," Owen pondered. "So, Mary Lou, you think the East Grand Rapids school district could have adopted the estate's recommended statement without violating the First Amendment, but should not be forced to adopt it?"

"Exactly. Isn't that the exercise of judicial restraint that you consistently teach?"

Owen smiled. "Yes, you are right, Mary Lou. I am proud of you. Why don't you start drafting the opinion. Can you have a draft in a week? I will take it from there."

Mary Lou Shurlow rose and began to leave Owen's office; she then mustered her courage and turned to face him. "I enjoy working with you, your honor."

"Why thank you, Mary Lou. I very much enjoy working with you as well. Now, don't forget to book that warm weather vacation in January." Mary Lou Shurlow smiled and left the office, shutting the door behind her.

Chapter Thirteen

Decisions Fateful

Thursday, November 26, 2009

Owen scanned his gathered family at the Thanksgiving table set in a medium-sized banquet room at the Drake Hotel. Owen knew his daughters were suspicious because of the money he was obviously spending to fly Hal and Mary and their daughters Brittany and Ellen to Chicago and to rent five rooms in the Drake, plus the banquet room for the Thanksgiving dinner. Such extravagance was out of Owen's character. Owen also knew his daughters suspected he would announce his engagement to Sheila. He guessed the possibility had been the subject of much telephonic chatter between his girls in the weeks before the trip. Owen felt some guilt for not quelling this misperception, but was generally relieved his daughters were not focusing their energies on a reason closer to the truth. He took comfort in the irony that but for his illness, he probably would have considered proposing to Sheila in time and arranging some family event to properly introduce her to his family.

At his request, the Drake had set a long straight table. Owen sat in the middle, flanked on the left by his grandsons Boyd and Christian and on the right by Megan and Roy. Across from the boys sat his beautiful granddaughters, who as farm girls were centered and used to hard work. Their male cousins did not intimidate them in the least. For their part the boys, who were the same ages as the girls, were intrigued by their cousins and found them easy conversationalists. The kids were enjoying a healthy banter about bands and reality television.

Sheila sat directly across from Owen, who thought she looked lovely in a navy blue dress. She took an immediate liking to Mary which seemed to be reciprocated. They were engaged in a lively discussion. Not surprising to Owen, Megan was eyeing Sheila more skeptically. Roy and Hal, who had always liked each other, were discussing football, with Hal teasing Roy unmercifully about the woeful Lions and the vastly superior Minnesota Vikings, a debate that was over before it started.

Owen was taking it all in when Megan came up behind him and whispered, "Quite a noisy brood you have spawned, eh Judge? You may need your gavel."

Owen reached over and grabbed her hand and whispered into her ear. "Don't tell anyone, but your sense of humor has always pleased me." Owen didn't let Megan respond; he stood up and said, "Okay gang, let me have your attention, even if Megan reminds me I am without my gavel." He reached over and gently pinched the neck of Boyd sitting next to him until he giggled. "Megan and Roy, Hal usually leads a communal Thanksgiving prayer, and I have asked him to lead it here this year. What we do is all hold hands, and each person has to offer one thing that they are thankful for. We are going to break a little with tradition, however, and undertake the prayer after dinner. So you all have an hour to prepare. Before the great crew here at the Drake serves us, I would like to start with a short blessing. Will you all stand with me and hold hands as I say grace?"

Owen waited until his family was standing, silent and holding hands. "Father, thank you for this opportunity to share this great holiday with you and with each other. Thank you for the bountiful food prepared for us and for the wonderful people who are here to serve us. We pray for them and their families as well. Now bless this food to our bodies. In Christ's name we pray, amen."

Of the many things that pleased Owen about the day, none was more gratifying to him than to hear the spontaneous "amen" from his grandchildren.

As expected, the Drake's staff outdid itself. The meal was sumptuous and leisurely served. Owen paradoxically wanted it to end so he could get his announcement over and wanted it to never end. As the dinner was coming to a natural end, he couldn't help thinking this conflicted attitude had permeated his mindset throughout his life. He liked law school, but couldn't wait for it to end. He enjoyed being a father but was relieved when his kids were safely interested in their friends, then college and family life so his daily concentration could be consumed again by his work. He liked the practice of law but had been eager to leave it for the bench. He had enjoyed the bench but often daydreamed about the outdoor activities he would enjoy when he retired, like hiking the Appalachian Trail or kayaking around Isle Royale. Was this restlessness the source of his drive or just a character flaw? Now that he was facing his mortality, why in the world would he want to push through this last wonderful weekend? No point in self-flagellating now; he reached for another glass of red wine and tried to push all negative thoughts from his mind. Fortunately, he received help in the task. Sheila kicked him under the table, and he looked up to find her smiling at him.

God, how lucky and unlucky he was. What a wonderful gift in his last six months; if only he had more time to enjoy her company. Again, a negative thought he had to repress. Damn it! He was going to relax and enjoy this day. He reached across the table and was happy when Sheila's hand met his. "Thank you," he mouthed. "You're welcome!" she mouthed in return. "Come on gang, let's push away from this feast and give proper thanks to our maker!" Owen declared. With that, he stood and grabbed Megan's hand, pulling her off to the side of the room. His family followed and stood in a circle as the Drake staff scurried to clean the table. Owen paid them no mind. "Hal, would you lead us in a proper Thanksgiving prayer?"

Hal stood tall, his six foot frame extended, holding Mary's hand on one side and Brittany's on the other. "As Owen said, everyone please give one thing you are thankful for over the past year. Let's start with the youngest and move to the oldest. Sorry, Sheila, but we are going to slot you before the judge." Everyone laughed and Sheila said she would graciously accept that position.

Boyd was the youngest, and in keeping with his lighthearted nature, he said he was thankful his parents had not made him play football. Ellen was thankful for the opportunity to share Thanksgiving for the first time with her cousins from Michigan. Christian was thankful his parents had allowed him to play football, bringing laughter. Brittany was thankful she had been admitted to the University of Minnesota, where she was looking forward to nursing school. Megan was thankful for Roy, who was always there for her. Roy reported he was thankful he hadn't been laid off from his job as an engineer at an auto supply manufacturer. Mary was thankful the family was healthy. Hal was thankful for the great growing weather and the resulting bountiful crops this year. Sheila was grateful for the opportunity to make wonderful new friends.

Finally, it was Owen's turn. "Thank you, Father, for Boyd. I love his fun loving spirit and the fact he doesn't need sports to validate who he is. I pray that he will always hold that joyful enthusiasm for life. Thank you for Christian. I love his drive and determination to succeed. I pray you will always be by his side to make sure he slows himself down enough to smell your roses. I thank you for my beautiful granddaughter Ellen, who has the kindest heart in the family, and I pray it will always be as warm and empathetic as it is now. I thank you for my lovely granddaughter Brittany, who embraces hard work and wants to help others. I pray that her hard work for others will never harden her. I thank you for my daughter, Megan, who is always courageous in her convictions. I pray she will accept failures in others. I thank you for my son-in-law Roy, who can fix anything. I pray that if he ever needs fixing, he will find support in this family. I thank you for Mary, who has her mother's grace and compassion. I pray her mother's spirit will always be at her side. I thank you for Hal, for his great strength and his quiet understanding of what is important in life. May he always impart those priorities to this family. I thank you for Sheila, for her compassion and her wisdom and her guidance. I pray her friends will return half the strength and kindness she has extended to me. I thank you for the wonderful life you have given me—a wonderful soul mate wife, the best daughters, sons-in-law, and grandchildren any man could hope for. Now, we pray for your strength, guidance, and love for the year to come, so that next year this family will stand as strong and loving as it stands now. Amen."

Owen quickly interjected, "Before you let go of your hands, there is something I need to share with you. As you know, I have just finished a very interesting trial focusing on the fundamental questions of how we got here and where we are headed. As I listened to the experts, it became clear to me that while our bodies may have evolved over time, our minds have not been shaped by natural forces alone. They are impregnated with certain desires, fears, drives, moral understandings, and a sense of justice and love that reflect our wonderful designer. One of those engrained sensibilities is a love for life, and with it a sense of sorrow when life is shorter than we expected or hoped. But the great irony is that such expectations can never be met on earth. Life here is shockingly short even if one lives to an old age. Every sensibility and sense of justice we carry suggests life must be more than we experience here, even if one's life has been wonderful and full—that relationships never fully actualized here on earth must continue in some world beyond. I believe these things, my loved ones, with all my heart. So while I am very sad to tell you I will shortly leave you, I am absolutely confident that someday we will be united again."

Mary reacted first. "What are you telling us, Dad?" She dropped Hal's hand and placed her hand over her eyes.

"Mary, do not drop Hal's hand!" Owen snapped. Hal gently reached up and grabbed her hand. "I have terminal cancer." To his great surprise and relief, Owen did not break down. His voice was gaining strength. He knew he had passed the critical point and was thankful to his marrow for the clarity of thought and purpose he felt now.

"How could you stand there and let me embarrass myself with thanks for our family's health?" Mary sobbed.

"Because it was true, Mary. We are all slowly dying. This past year was a great year for our family's health. Even I have had a blessed year of health, considering what my body was fighting. You don't know the extent of my fears that I would not make it to this holiday or that if I did make it, how ravaged I might be. God has truly blessed me with strength this year, and with a year's worth of joy with you and your family, with Megan and her family, and with Sheila. I had the most wonderful final case a judge in my circumstances could ever have. No, Mary; I have had a great year."

"But it's so unfair. First Mom and now you, not even seventy years old. We deserve so much better," Mary cried.

Owen almost lost his strength when he realized all of his grandchildren were crying, but a quick look at Sheila and her compassionate smile renewed his strength.

"That's the sense of injustice I was talking about, Mary. But in the grand scheme of things, life is nothing more than a short play. Can you imagine getting a better part than I did, to be appointed by one's country as a federal judge and to have a great spouse like Susan, two wonderful daughters, two wonderful sons-in-law... And who could ask for better grandkids than the four I have been blessed with? Sure, I wish I had another ten years to see my grandchildren graduate from college and get married; to watch you girls become grandparents; to spend more time with my new, wonderful friend Sheila. I can tell you, ten years wouldn't be enough, and what if I was mentally strong but physically incapable in these latter years? There is simply no good way to exit this life, but among the alternatives, I feel I have been given as good an opportunity as a person can get. I have had a great last chapter in my life and I have had this wonderful opportunity to share this moment—painful as it is—with my loved ones. What a great gift!"

Owen never felt stronger and more alive. "Let's do this, shall we? Let's have a group hug and then spend the rest of the weekend enjoying each other's company. Let's make this the best weekend of our lives. I have tickets to the theatre; let's hit the museums; we will eat at the best restaurants. Money will be no object this weekend. The only rule is we will celebrate life, not mourn its passing. Can I count on each one of you?"

The Austin family laughed, cried, and enjoyed the best Thanksgiving weekend they had ever experienced, despite their beloved but hapless Lions getting crushed again by the Green Bay Packers.

* * *

At breakfast on Black Friday, Owen excused himself from his family.

"Judge, where are you going at this hour?" Megan wanted to know.

"I want to see Robbie Goldman, you remember, my old law clerk?"

"The streets will be packed with Christmas shoppers."

"I am not going to walk, Meg, and the day I can't get a cab at the Drake is the day I stop coming," Owen chuckled.

Megan frowned. "What time can we expect you back? Do you have your cell phone?

She was winding up with a third question when Owen looked over the top of his glasses. "Megan... Stop! I assume you will be working your way south on Michigan Avenue, and I will call you when I am done. Maybe we can meet at the river. Robbie's office is on West Wacker."

Fifteen minutes later, Owen stood in the lobby of the glass tower in which Robbie Goldman's office was located. "Hello Robbie, its Owen Austin. How was your Thanksgiving?"

"Great, Judge, how about yours?"

"Fine, Robbie, but I am having a problem convincing the security officers in your lobby that I don't pose a risk to the morning's peace."

"You're in Chicago! What a wonderful surprise! I will be right down."

"Great. Grab a coat and let's go out for a bagel and lox."

Robbie Goldman almost stopped in his tracks when he saw the gray color of his old boss, but Owen's eyes revealed nothing but warmth, and the vigor of Owen's handshake surprised him.

"Robbie, you are a sight for my old eyes. Thanks for taking time for me. I'll bet you are working on some major matter?"

"I am enjoying a break between cases right now, but thought I would catch up on housekeeping matters while the family was shopping. What brings you to Chicago?"

"I have my whole family here, Robbie—even Mary and her family from Minnesota."

The bagel shop two blocks away was packed, but miraculously there was a booth open in the corner of the shop. As they slid in, Robbie asked if Owen wanted to discuss the portrait investiture party between the holidays.

"Yes, I do, Robbie. I appreciate your planning—still have the same roster?" Owen stared at Robbie, whose face revealed a fleeting concern. When Owen broke into a wry smirk, Robbie smiled and knew his old boss had caught him.

"It's a tough season between the end-of-the-year holidays; you could expect a few cancellations, and there have only been a few."

Owen smiled, biting into his bagel.

"I would be willing to review your *Taylor* opinion draft if you would like," Robbie offered, knowing full well the judge would never consult with an outside source, no matter how respected on an opinion.

"I am canceling the portrait investiture party, Robbie," Owen suddenly interjected.

The comment blindsided Robbie. "What? Why?"

"Vanity. I knew I wasn't photographic, but I have learned even a talented portrait artist can't spruce me up." Owen laughed.

"Nonsense, "Robbie smiled, "I like the portrait. It will look awesome in your courtroom."

"There's another problem, Robbie... I am in the latter stages of brain cancer and don't want to be a spectacle." Owen let the words settle in.

Robbie Goldman was speechless. Tears welled and Owen noticed that Robbie's throat muscles were spasming. Robbie could not respond for a minute.

"Owen..." Robbie reached across the table and touched Owen's hand, which was cradling a cup of coffee.

Contrasting feelings rushed through Owen. Robbie had never called him anything but "Judge" or "your honor." Owen hadn't felt that close to a platonic friend in ages, but he also felt a rush of loneliness and regret, realizing the distance involved in being a federal judge had interposed with every person in his life.

"It's all right, Robbie. I am ready to go. I miss my wife and have accomplished more than I ever dreamed."

"Are you treating?"

"No, Robbie. I couldn't go down that path again, but I did confirm with the University of Michigan Hospital that the outcome is not in doubt." Owen was eager to change the subject. "I am anxious for you to read my *Taylor* opinion. The case has been a blessing to me. Despite what you may think about the outcome, I want you to know you influenced my thinking."

"Really?" Robbie recovered only slightly.

"Really... I know how much you love the First Amendment and how vibrant you believe it is. I couldn't stop thinking about that vitality when deciding the case. If it is that resilient, certainly with a little good faith it can facilitate a discussion about the greatest mystery in life."

"I am anxious to read it and will keep that thought in mind when I do."

"Great!" Owen smiled. "It's a book-end to *Kitzmiller*, remember that." Owen stood. "I need to get back to my family."

As soon as they were back on the street, quietly looking over the Chicago river, Owen turned. "Robbie, the most important reason I wanted to see you is to tell you that you have been like a son to me—far more than a clerk and far more important to me than any other clerk."

The festive holiday crowd did not notice as the two men, separated by thirty years in age, shared a lasting embrace.

* * *

Monday, December 7, 2009

John Cleaver walked into the Lumber Baron bar a little after noon, eyeing his target in the corner.

"Johnny boy, I assume you are buying lunch." Keegan Riley smirked.

"Keegan, how could you be so disloyal to the firm you created?" John frowned.

"When did you stop listening to your mentor? Didn't I tell you that law firms are not institutions? Come to think of it, John, it wouldn't matter if they were institutions. My loyalties are to my friends and me. With Kingman Walker, I stoked both interests with one poke. Tell me," he winked, "how much did they offer you?"

"Enough to cover lunch," John said, slowly breaking into a smile.

* * *

December 7 witnessed the first significant snowfall of the season, and three p.m. Eastern time saw the release of Owen's written opinion, which Sarah posted in the electronic record, immediately serving it on the parties and anyone else who paid the access fee. The Opinion read as follows:

> This action is brought by Mrs. Vicki Taylor, the mother of Michelle Taylor, a former freshman at East Grand Rapids high school, which is part of the East Grand Rapids school district. On May thirteenth of this year, Michelle Taylor was attending freshman biology class taught by Peter Kingston, a long-time high school teacher. It is undisputed that Mr. Kingston instructed his students using an approved biology curriculum. As part of that curriculum, the school taught the science of evolution, namely, that man has physically evolved from simpler species through genetic mutation and natural selection. When asked by Ms. Taylor as to whether evolution explained the origin of good and evil, Mr. Kingston reported that there is no empirical evidence of good or evil. When challenged by Ms. Taylor as to whether evolution explained how matter first emerged in the cosmos or how vegetation came from mineral or animals from vegetation, Mr. Kingston reported that science had no explanations for these developments. He also reported that the First Amendment did not allow for speculation as to a possible creator in the public

schools, but rather that this was the realm of religion. He also asserted that science had found no empirical evidence of a God, an afterlife, or metaphysical concepts like good and evil. In the course of further exchange, Mr. Kingston claimed that belief in an afterlife was 'magical thinking' and that religion and science don't mix.

The exchange between teacher and student greatly upset Michelle Taylor and her mother, the latter demanding that the school district discipline Mr. Kingston and force him to retract some of his statements, notably the comment that there is no empirical evidence of God. The school district refused those requests.

Tragically, Michelle Taylor committed suicide several weeks later. Her mother admits that she cannot establish the upset from biology class as the proximate cause of her suicide, and the court will not speculate about the role, if any, that the biology class confrontation caused in Michelle Taylor's unfortunate decision to end her life.

The confrontation and its adverse effect on her daughter motivated Mrs. Taylor to formally present a statement which she demanded the district read before teaching evolution in future biology classes. The statement distinguished the science of evolution and the religion of naturalism. The statement highlighted the inability of evolution to empirically prove the original emergence of matter or of plant or animal life, or to explain the ability of the human mind to discern right or wrong, good and evil, and love and hate—in short, any metaphysical concept. In its entirety, the statement provided:

The theory of evolution, which involves random mutation and natural selection to explain the development of animal species, has scientific support. However, evolution must be distinguished from 'naturalism,' which is a religious viewpoint that evolved nature is all that exists and there is no supernatural creator. Some scientists are naturalists. Some scientists who adhere to the theory of evolution believe a supernatural being or God used mutation and natural selection to unfold the living world and are not naturalists. Neither evolution nor any other scientific theory yet explains the original emergence of minerals, plant or animal life, nor the existence of metaphysical concepts such as love, the struggle between good and evil, and the uniqueness and equality of human life, all of which are commonly understood by human beings. Science can only speculate at present at how the human mind embraces and understands metaphysical concepts. Some postulate that it is the result of imitation and repetition, passed down from generation to generation. Other scientists postulate the brain's ability to differentiate right and wrong and good and evil is programmed by an intelligent designer. Science has been unable to prove, disprove or even test either postulate. The mind's condition remains one of the greatest mysterious in life. The East Grand Rapids school district encourages its students to learn the science of evolution, but also its limitations in explaining the origins of life itself, as well as the existence of metaphysical concepts.

The school district held a closed session in which it made a decision to acknowledge receipt of the statement, but to take no action in response.

Mrs. Taylor, as the personal representative of her daughter, filed suit in this court seeking declaratory and injunctive relief under three counts: an alleged violation of Michigan's Open Meetings Act for making a policy decision in closed session; an alleged violation of the religious encouragement prohibition in the First Amendment of the United States Constitution through the decision not to issue the statement disentangling evolution and naturalism; and an alleged violation of the religious discouragement prohibition through several teacher statements denying there is empirical evidence of metaphysical concepts.

On motion, this court found the school district decided not to use the statement. Because it was made in closed session, the decision violated Michigan's Open Meetings Act. The case proceeded to trial.

The estate presented Mrs. Taylor, Madelyn Wysocki, who was Michelle Taylor's best friend, the teacher, Peter Kingston, and four experts: Dr. Leonard Devoneau, a biology professor; Dr. Karl Hitchcock, a philosophy professor; Dr. Martin Hileman, an expert statistician; and Dr. Alvin Henry, a philosophy professor. The defense presented three experts: Dr. Christian Slagter, a biology professor; Dr. Stanley Morgan, an education expert; and Professor Jeremy Hawk, an expert on the scientific method. The district also called the superintendent of the School District, William Reichel.

The court finds the following facts as a result of the expert testimony in this case:

(1)   The theory of evolution is a scientifically supported theory explaining the physical origins of animal species, including man, through genetic mutation and natural selection [Dr. Devoneau's testimony].

(2)   Evolutionism or naturalism is an atheistic religious world- and life-view believing only the physical world exists and denying a supernatural being or God [Dr. Henry's testimony].

(3)   Many religious believers and naturalists alike believe evolution is incompatible with monotheistic religion. Many leading biologists claim evolution disproves the existence of a God [Dr. Henry's testimony; Dr. Devoneau's testimony; Dr. Hitchcock's testimony].

(4)   The combined, although certainly not coordinated, efforts of these opposed camps have created a contrived and false dualism that evolution and belief in a supernatural are necessarily incompatible. A majority of people in the East Grand Rapids school district ascribe to this belief [Dr. Hileman's testimony].

(5)   Many scientists find the science of evolution compatible with their belief that God created original matter, plant and animal life, and the laws of nature—the original emergence of which

are presently inexplicable by any scientific theory [Dr. Henry's testimony; Dr. Slagter's testimony]. Some philosophers contend that the complete dependence of naturalism on evolution to explain human development disproves naturalism, because genetic mutation and natural selection cannot explain our senses' reliable ability to differentiate right and wrong and discern metaphysical concepts like justice, love, hate, and the equality of all men [Dr. Henry's testimony].

(6)   The court finds evolution barely testable, with no explanation for the original emergence of matter, plant life, or animal life in the cosmos.

(7)   The plaintiff has proved the school district has an official policy refusing to explain the difference between evolution and naturalism [Closed session minutes of school board's July first meeting].

(8)   The plaintiff has failed to prove by an evidentiary preponderance that the East Grand Rapids school district has an official policy that metaphysical concepts such as good and evil lack empirical support. There is insufficient proof on the record that any statements to such effect by its freshmen biology teacher were anything more than incidental, individual comments rather than established school policy.

(9)   The content of the plaintiff's proposed statement is conceded by the defendant's own experts to be factually true [Dr. Slagter's testimony; Dr. Stanley's testimony].

(10) To the extent that it limits science to subjects verifiable by the physical senses and does not also include verification through objective human experience and reasoning, the scientific method entangles itself with metaphysical naturalism, the latter being a religious belief [Dr. Hitchcock's testimony; Dr. Henry's testimony].

(11) Because evolution and metaphysical naturalism ('evolutionism') are intertwined in public perception, the school district's endorsement of evolution without a qualifying, true statement such as requested by the plaintiff had the effect of discouraging the religious beliefs of Michelle Taylor and may have a similar effect on other impressionable young minds [Madelyn Wysocki's testimony; Vicki Taylor's testimony; Dr. Henry's testimony].

(12) The true representations in the statement do not promote religious exercise and are unlikely to induce the public school's promotion of religious exercise, which, if it occurs, can be remedied with other injunctive and other relief [Dr. Henry's testimony; judicial notice].

(13) Michelle Taylor did not suffer any measurable damages as a result of the confrontation in the classroom, and the estate of Michelle Taylor did

not suffer any actual damages from the East Grand Rapids school district's refusal to offer a clarifying statement beyond the possible violation of Michelle Taylor's constitutional rights, which alone is cognizable damage [Vicki Taylor's testimony].

As for relevant law, the establishment clause of the First Amendment to the United States Constitution states, "Congress shall make no law respecting an establishment of religion, or prohibiting the free exercise thereof." U.S. Const. Amend I. The establishment clause applies to instrumentalities of the state, including public schools, through the Fourteenth Amendment to the Constitution. *Wallace v. Jaffree*, 472 U.S. 38, 49-50 (1985). In *Lemon v. Kurtzman*, 403 U.S. 602 (1971), the United States Supreme Court found that a government sponsored message violates the establishment clause if (1) it does not have a secular purpose; (2) its principal or primary effect advances or inhibits religion; or (3) it creates an excessive entanglement of the government with religion. 403 U.S. 612-13. In addition to the *Lemon* test, the Court must also review the government message under the "endorsement test" as laid down by the United States Supreme Court in *County of Allegheny v. ACLU*, 492 U.S. 573 (1989), in which the Supreme Court held that a public governmental message may not lead an objective observer acquainted with the message's text, its history, and its implementation to conclude the government entity endorses religious practice. See *Kitzmiller v. Dover Area School District*, 400 F. Supp. 2d 707, 712 (E.D. Pa. 2005). The duty of the court in evaluating the endorsement test is to "determine whether, under the totality of the circumstances, the challenged practice conveys a message favoring or disfavoring religion." *ACLU v. Black Horse Pike Regional Board of Education*, 84 F.3d 1471, 1486 (3rd Cir. 1996).

Several other legal principles are highly relevant. First, the United States Supreme Court has warned the lower courts to be particularly "vigilant in monitoring compliance with the establishment clause in elementary and secondary schools" because children are "impressionable and their attendance is involuntary." *Edwards v. Aguillard*, 482 U.S. 578, 583-84 (1987). Second, the religion clauses of the First Amendment require the courts to "pursue a course of complete neutrality towards religion" commonly called the principle of "lofty neutrality." *Jaffree*, 472 U.S. at 60. Third, the Constitution "affirmatively mandates accommodation, not merely tolerance, of all religions and forbids hostility towards any." *Lynch v. Donnelly*, 466 U.S. 668, 672 (1984). Fourth, a public school may not establish a "religion of secularism" affirmatively opposing or showing a hostility to religion and thus "preferring those who believe in no religion over those who do." *School District of Abington Township v. Schempp*, 374 U.S. 203, 225 (1963). Fifth, it is insufficient that the school's actions confer an indirect, remote, or incidental benefit on religion. *Grand Rapids School District v. Ball*, 473 U.S. 373, 393 (1985). Sixth, discussion of religion is permissible in the public schools as long as it is neutral, and any incidental comments by teachers that are not part of the curriculum are actionable only if the endorsement or discouragement is sharp and direct. *Daugherty v. Vanguard Charter School Academy*, 116 F. Supp. 2d 897 (W.D. Mich. 2000).

The court finds that that the incidental comments of the East Grand Rapids high school teachers regarding the lack of empirical evidence for metaphysical concepts of good and evil, right and wrong, love and hate, and human equality—although factually incorrect—do not in and of themselves rise to the level of constitutional violations because they do not sharply or directly discourage religious belief. This does not mean, however, that these comments are immaterial to the issue of whether the lofty neutrality requires a qualifying statement to the teaching of evolution.

The court finds many parallels between the present case and *Kitzmiller*. The court finds much of *Kitzmiller*'s analysis applicable here. For instance, the evidence was indisputable in *Kitzmiller* that the intelligent design theory was intertwined in common understanding with Christianity, making it ripe for an endorsement claim. So also, the court finds the evidence is indisputable that the theory of evolution is intertwined in common understanding with naturalism or atheism, which is a religious belief for purposes of the First Amendment. Using the logic of *Kitzmiller*, the theory of evolution is equally ripe for an endorsement claim.

That right and wrong exist and that the sane human mind can distinguish between them is empirically demonstrable using human experience, observation, perception, and reasoning. Indeed, the reliability of these concepts and their discernment define "sanity" and accountability for criminal acts in Anglo-American jurisprudence. Likewise, that the human mind holds a sense of natural justice demanding respect for human equality is empirically demonstrable using human experience, observation, perception, and reasoning. In fact, these metaphysical concepts form the very basis for our Constitution's requirements of equal protection.

Empirical verification of metaphysical concepts is not a difficult concept for teachers and students to understand. They apply it continually. A student's memory of the past few weeks of study in a particular class cannot be touched, smelled, heard, or seen. If the student died and his or her brain was dissected, it could not be located. Yet, despite the lack of apparent physical presence, we test and verify that memory on a regular basis. Accordingly, to suggest memory is not scientifically verifiable would be fallacious.

Similarly, the law recognizes certain prohibitions reflecting only social mores, such as speeding laws. These prohibitions are described as *malum prohibitum*. The law also recognizes that there are other prohibitions inherently wrong, such as robbery or murder. These prohibitions are described as *malum in se*. While the *malum prohibitum* prohibitions are manmade constructs, *malum in se* prohibitions are imbedded in our minds naturally. While evolution may explain the development of our bodies, it cannot explain the embedding of the metaphysical; evolution cannot explain *malum in se*.

A science denying the verifiability of metaphysical truths is a view of science that is necessarily entangled with metaphysical naturalism. This court has received credible evidence that the mind's ability to reliably perceive metaphysical concepts and natural selection's failure to select this ability arguably defeats metaphysical naturalism. From this proposition, it is further argued that evolution and the inconsistent but undeniable faculties of the human mind form powerful evidence of an intelligent designer's presence. While this court does not reach such a conclusion because the estate does not seek an order compelling the teaching of intelligent design, to the extent that the *Kitzmiller* opinion is read to restrict the public schools to a view of science prohibiting the consideration of these proofs, this court disagrees. Such a restricted view of constitutionally permissible subjects would leave the public schools unable to verify the propriety of the legal definition of sanity or the self-evident proposition in the Declaration of Independence that all men are equal.

The question remains whether the teaching of evolution and methodological naturalism (the scientific method) in the public schools without an explanation are concepts distinct from atheism ('metaphysical naturalism') and would endorse secularism and discourage monotheistic religions. Upon this record, the court finds that the defendant's teaching of these concepts as exemplified in the incident involving Michelle Taylor produced such an endorsement and the concomitant discouragement of her Christianity in violation of the First Amendment.

That the East Grand Rapids school district has not created the entanglement of evolution with atheism in the common mind is of no more consequence to the First Amendment analysis in this case than it was in *Kitzmiller*, where the Dover school board had not developed the theory of intelligent design nor linked it in the common mind with Christianity. Simply stated, when a public school incorporates a concept into its curriculum, it assumes responsibility for neutralizing misperceptions that come with that concept. Federal law is replete with similar examples where the federal government has mandated a warning label to address a product's hazards, regardless of whether the party was responsible for creating the hazards.

The court takes judicial notice that all religions center on the existence of good and evil. The East Grand Rapids high school's unqualified endorsement of evolution, coupled with its biology teacher's denial that there is empirical evidence of the existence of good and evil, combined to endorse metaphysical naturalism and exhibit hostility towards religious belief. The supposition that only what we can taste, feel, see, or smell exists and everything else, including God, is a human invention discourages religion.[1] Without qualification such supposition endorses metaphysical naturalism and, by reducing religious belief to the realm of unscientific thinking, evidences an unconstitutional hostility towards religion. The court specifically finds East Grand Rapids high school's unqualified teaching of evolution and its teacher's limitation of science to that which is physically verifiable violated the third prong of the *Lemon* test by excessively entangling the biology curriculum with metaphysical naturalism.

The court also finds the religious accommodation requested in the estate's statement or a facsimile is a reasonable remedy to the public confusion that evolution and atheism are one. Unlike the plaintiffs in *Kitzmiller*, the plaintiff here does not seek to enjoin the

---

[1] The court takes judicial notice that the pre-eminent biologist Richard Dawkins' *The God Delusion* was a New York Times' best seller and that Professor Dawkins and his associates are aggressively and actively proselytizing exactly that evolution proves there is no God.

teaching of evolution, and with good reason—the theory is too scientifically significant and verified to be ignored in the teaching of biology. However, because young minds are impressionable and given the confusion of evolution with atheism, a vigilant neutrality compels a neutralization of the wrongful linkage.

As noted above, federal law mandates warnings and disclaimers in hundreds of settings for the private sector. There is no good reason why the public sector should be immune. Compelling such a disclaimer to evolution will be unlikely to proliferate disclaimers for other subjects. Origins of life discussion is one of the few areas where science and religion interact in a way that is ripe for entanglement or discouragement. Since the entanglement of evolution and atheism involves foundational religious beliefs, namely the existence or nonexistence of God, and since we are dealing with its effects on youthful minds, the First Amendment requires extreme vigilance. A true statement to the effect that some scientists find evolution and monotheism compatible and others do not and that evolution cannot yet explain how mineral became vegetable and vegetable became animal or explain the indisputable cognitive ability of the human mind to discern metaphysical concepts is a modest and minimal antidote to a hostility towards religion that an unqualified endorsement of evolution and a rigid view of the scientific method would otherwise promote. That the National Academies of Science has ascertained the need to issue a similar statement is cogent proof of the compelling need for this context to the teaching of evolution.

The court will not order the defendant to utilize the plaintiff's statement. However, it will order the defendant to introduce to its curriculum a statement that covers three concepts in the Taylor statement, namely:

(1) that competent scientists disagree as to whether the science of evolution is incompatible with or supportive of religious beliefs in a creator;

(2) that neither evolution nor any other scientific theory yet explains how minerals, plants, or animals first emerged in the universe;

(3) that evolution cannot presently explain the human brain's ability to discern right and wrong, good and evil, love and hate, and other metaphysical concepts, not the least of which is the self-evident belief in human equality.

The court gives the school district until the beginning of the next school year to install such a policy statement in its biology curriculum. Adoption of the plaintiff's statement will constitute satisfaction of this portion of the court's order.

The United States Supreme Court in *Jaffree* held it is not unconstitutional for public school teachers to recognize that many people believe in God. Mindful of *Jaffree* and because the physical sciences have no explanation for the emergence of matter or life, this court declares that public teachers do not violate the First Amendment if they advise their students that some people theorize an intelligent designer created matter, plant life, and animal life or infused the human mind with metaphysical values as long as they present the postulate as a speculative theory and acknowledge other theories, including that matter and life have always existed in some form. Such a discussion is not without its risks and tensions, but such is the nature of all subjects protected by the First Amendment. This court firmly believes public school teachers acting in good faith will be able to guide a discussion about the greatest mystery of life—whether we are part of an ageless community on a timeless journey or are separate souls, each on a solitary, temporal path.

The court awards the estate of Michelle Taylor one thousand dollars in nominal damages for the violation of her constitutional rights. Since the plaintiff has prevailed in substantial part on her complaint, she may present her reasonable attorneys' fees for payment by the district.

* * *

Wednesday, December 9, 2009

"Dexter, are you sitting down?" Peter Diamond asked, speaking loudly into his cell phone from a beach in San Diego.

"As a matter of fact, I am in my office talking to Amy."

Peter paid no attention. "I was checking my Blackberry. Judge Austin's opinion was just released. He ruled in our favor! He has given the school district until next September to either adopt our statement or come up with its own covering the salient provisions in ours. He awarded one thousand dollars in nominal damages and, since we prevailed, he also ordered the district to pay our legal fees," Peter gushed.

"Well how about that! Congratulations, Peter! You were the case architect."

"I couldn't have come close to your trial work, Dexter. This feels great!"

"Good. Now hang up and enjoy your vacation!"

"Congratulations, Dexter!" Amy declared. "I could hear Peter as if he were on your speaker phone. May be this should be your life? Moving from one big professional win to another and one big personal score to another."

Dexter cast Amy a dirty look.

"I didn't mean that to sound so facetious. What is wrong with being rich, footloose, and professionally satisfied? It works well for my dreamboat, George Clooney."

"I thought I was your dreamboat?" Dexter looked at her quizzically, then looked out the window somberly. "George Clooney isn't a father."

"Ah... That is the rub isn't it? Well, my departing friend, you can't have it all."

"Can you email the opinion to Vicki Taylor? Then call to verify she still wants us to waive the attorney's fees. If she confirms, then fax out the press release we drafted if we won. You can save the other one in case we lose on appeal," he directed, returning to business.

"You don't want to make that call personally?"

Dexter shot Amy another dirty look.

"Guess not..." Amy closed the door behind her, leaving Dexter staring out the window.

* * *

"Congratulations, Vicki!" Ross Wagner raised his wine glass to toast position.

Vicki Taylor raised her glass in salute. "Thanks; I couldn't be happier with your referral to Dexter Bussey."

They were sharing a celebratory lunch at the University Club on the ninth floor of the Fifth Third Bank building.

"I told you Bussey was smart and stood the best chance of satisfying your desires," Wagner said, probing.

Taylor smiled but did not take the bait.

"I thought you were very gracious in your press release, noting the case was never about personalities, economic damages, or the quality of East Grand Rapids education—only about placing evolution in its proper educational context. I particularly liked the touch about waiving your right to attorney's fees and costs for the public good. That was very generous." Wagner peered over his reading glasses.

"Stop teasing me, I am not in the mood," Taylor complained. "Bussey doesn't mind spending other people's money. I suppose that's a great trait for a trial lawyer."

"You are starting to sound more like Frank each day. Winning the case wasn't enough for you?" Wagner's glasses remained low on his nose.

"You are jealous. I am flattered," Taylor chided. "I am going to miss you."

"Miss me?" Wagner's face dropped. "Where are you going?"

"Chicago," Taylor announced. "I am putting the house on the market. It is time for me to get a clean start. All this serious talk about the progression of life has convinced me at the halfway mark of my life it is time for a new purpose," Taylor explained.

"Don't tell me that you have found religion?" Wagner asked as he sat back in his chair.

"Don't worry about that. It's just time for a new chapter, that's all."

Wagner thought for a moment. "Did I tell you I have a good client in Chicago? I get there once a month or so."

"No, my love, you never mentioned it before." Taylor smiled. "There's always a chance I'll be free when your business calls."

Wagner thought a moment and decided to rest his case. "Good then. I am glad of that." He turned to the menu. "I recommend the shrimp scampi. It's wonderful here. In fact, it's my second favorite guilty pleasure."

"Well then, shrimp scampi it will be." Taylor laid the menu on the table and looked past Wagner to the Calder Plaza and the Gerald R. Ford federal courthouse in the background.

"I have a surprise for you, too," Wagner said as he took a sip of his coffee and looked slyly at Taylor.

Forty-five minutes later they were standing before Michelle Taylor's gravestone in Woodlawn cemetery. Taylor looked perplexed.

"Take a look at the backside of the stone."

Taylor took three steps around the tombstone, and on the backside found the engraving of "statement" and the case citation. Wagner placed his arm gently around Taylor as she wept.

* * *

"Things are working out perfectly," Robert Johnson opened his telephone call to his young partner in Grand Rapids.

"Perfectly?" Chad Bachmann questioned incredulously. "You have to be kidding! Austin ruled against us and I am opening a two-man office in Grand Rapids with steady John, who can't stand me."

"Cleaver just called to advise that the East Grand Rapids school district is moving the case with him to our new Grand Rapids office and has authorized us to appeal. We don't even have to use AFSS's money to finance the appeal. At least in Chicago Judge Austin is now known to be suffering from brain cancer, so this opinion will be met with extra skepticism in the sixth circuit court of appeals. When we get the case reversed our new firm will be the hottest thing in Grand Rapids and we will have cemented ourselves as the go-to firm on First Amendment issues in the Midwest."

"What about Bussey?"

Johnson leaned back in his chair in Chicago. "Surprise, surprise. We thought we were the ones doing an end run. Turns out he has accepted a position with our friends at Weinstein and Strong and will be moving to Chicago."

"Amazing!" Chad exclaimed. "How did he take the news about Cleaver?"

"He acted cool. Expressed surprise. But enough about him. Here is the coup de grace: A public school in Cedar Rapids, Iowa, adopted the Taylor Statement last night, and another one in Montgomery, Alabama, has it on the agenda for tonight. We will have litigation popping up all over the United States. It is going to be a busy year for the firm. The AFSS Trust had a banner year in investments last year, so it is perfectly positioned to fund it all. Yes, things could not have unfolded any more perfectly."

"But you aren't stuck in this backwater with a partner who loathes you," Chad whined.

"How about this offer to cheer you up: I will pay you twenty percent of any savings the firm realizes if John Cleaver quits before the five-year mark. That's a four hundred thousand dollar bonus if he leaves at the three-year stake."

"And I can return to Chicago the minute he resigns?" Chad asked expectantly.

"Done deal," Johnson agreed, and he hung up the phone. He leaned forward in his chair, looked out over Lake Michigan, and smiled, "Yes, things are working out perfectly," he said to himself.

* * *

"At least Austin didn't award any significant damages," Bob Holleman consoled as Greg Jones, Tom Sacks, and Rob Simonson shared a Chico's one beer after work.

"And it was big of Bussey to waive his claim for attorney's fees," Sacks suggested.

"Think the district will appeal?" Simonson inquired.

"Of course," Jones explained. "For East Grand Rapids to be forced to issue a demeaning evolution qualification is beyond the pale to its average overachieving parent. The last thing they want for their beloved high school is to be famous as the school that lost the latest version of the Scopes trial. I received a call from the ACLU in Philadelphia, wondering how we could have screwed up their *Kitzmiller* victory. The decision was on the NBC Nightly news. It's a huge embarrassment for the district and our firm."

"Sounds like you tried a pretty good case," Holleman countered. "Sometimes a judge, even one as good as Austin, goes off the deep end."

"Cleaver blew this trial," Jones retorted angrily. "He didn't repair his witnesses after Bussey's cross. You could see even Austin was waiting for some rehabilitation. He didn't offer one student to testify that he knew the difference between evolution and atheism. He conceded that ground to Bussey. He sat pat on the ACLU's strategy in *Kitzmiller*, even though Bussey had already developed an anti-*Kitzmiller* strategy. No guys, we got out-strategized and out-maneuvered."

"Well, then maybe it is a good thing Cleaver is leaving, but why would Kingman Walker want to hitch its wagon to a broken down old war horse?" Holleman wondered.

"They are only buying his book of business. He'll be gone in three years, and none of the clients he is taking will last much longer. None will be happy with the billing rates of a mega-sized national law firm. You mark my word; they will all be back, including the East Grand Rapids school district," Jones spat bitterly into his beer. "If they win the case on appeal, I will claim it was really my work below. And if they lose it in the sixth circuit, it will be John's and Kingman's loss. Head's I win, tails John and Kingman lose."

"To silver linings and trick coins!" Simonson burped.

Chapter Fourteen

Gravity Quits

Thursday, December 10, 2009

Owen flung his house door open and headed immediately for the half bathroom, expelling his lunch. The pace of the tumor's growth had quickened according to the last CAT scan. His headache was now constant, and he was having trouble lifting his right leg while he walked. He waited an extra minute, draped over the commode. He could sense Sheila's presence outside.

"Owen? Are you okay?" she asked.

Owen splashed his face with water and opened the door. "Fine now, Sheila, thanks." He had to smile; she was standing with a look of great concern totally incompatible with the manhattan she had previously mixed and now held in her hand. Owen grabbed his cocktail and sat at the kitchen table.

"Are you sure you can keep that down?" Sheila said, still unable to shift from a nursing mode.

"If I don't it will be a great excuse for a second." Owen smiled.

Sheila sat down across from him. "How did it go today?" She knew that Owen was going to tell his staff about his cancer.

"They are all in shock. First the buzz of the *Taylor* opinion and then this. I just didn't have the courage to tell them the complete truth."

"What did you tell them?" Sheila said, genuinely surprised.

"I told them I had cancer in my blood and that I was going to take the few weeks through the holidays off, assess my options with my doctors, and develop a strategy," Owen responded.

"I keep forgetting you are lawyer," Sheila deadpanned.

Owen chuckled, trying to marshal a better mood. "You and a majority of the parents in East Grand Rapids, *The Grand Rapids Press*, and *The Wall Street Journal*."

Sheila smiled in return, happy for his humor. "Well, at least you will be popular in church."

"Don't be too sure about that. Remember, I attend a fairly liberal mainline Protestant denomination that is pretty sensitive about the separation of church and state. I could get some strange stares there, too, which is why I am wondering if you will join me on a little trip this weekend?"

"Trip! Come on Owen, don't you think you should rest?" Sheila said, alarmed.

"Sheila, if the naturalists are right, that's all I will be doing shortly. No, I have one more trip left in me and I will be damned if I am going to pass it up," Owen said, suddenly frustrated and a little angry.

Sheila caught herself and relented. "Okay, my intrepid explorer, where to, Chicago again? How about Miami? Some place warm?"

"Mackinac Island." Owen announced.

"You have got to be kidding? Owen, is anything open up there? Aren't the straits frozen? What about health care in an emergency?" Sheila's voice was heavy with concern.

"I called this morning. There are a couple bed and breakfasts still open. The straits aren't close to freezing yet and the Arnold ferry makes a run a day. I knew you would fret about the health issue, and I have the phone number of a medical helicopter in the Sault. They can be on the island in twenty minutes and have us at the Sault's modern emergency room in ten minutes—slick as a whistle," Owen retorted.

Sheila didn't speak for a moment. She just stared at Owen, whose look of anxious but eager anticipation made him appear twenty years younger. This calculating man had to have a rationale for this madness. He had reasons for everything. He hadn't failed her yet; why not give him this one last wish? "I'll start packing. Do the dogs come or not?"

"God bless them, but no dogs. I already called the kennel, and they are expecting them for a complete grooming and a weekend stay."

"You were pretty confident you were going to get your way with me, weren't you?"

"Oh, I only wish that were true!" Owen smiled and threw his arm around her as they headed to the living room.

* * *

"Happy Holidays, Keegan!" Ross held up his glass as his friend sidled up to the bar.

"You're two weeks early and you know I don't celebrate," Riley responded sourly.

"What's with the mood? You had a great year. You assisted your friend in getting a salary he deserves. You did a very good deed in putting a young lady's mind to rest. And I am sure you bagged a couple of brookies in and out of the water."

A stone-faced Riley placed his order with the bartender, finally turning to Ross. "Why are you in such a good mood? I heard a rumor you resigned the cushiest job in the county. Is that true?"

"Yes. I have decided to write a novel."

"Great... Can't wait," pouted Riley as he turned to look for the bartender and his drink.

"Now that you have had a couple of weeks to reflect, what do you think of Austin's *Taylor* opinion? My final story is going to be on the fallout."

"Hogwash!"

"What? Is that a legal analysis of the opinion or a prediction about the quality of my final story?"

When Riley didn't respond, Ross pushed ahead. "I liked Judge Austin's opinion. I think Michelle Taylor would have liked it, and I am glad she is forever linked with it. Let me ask you this: If evolution is right and we only respond to the feeding, fighting, fleeing, and fornicating, why did you help Madelyn Wysocki and John Cleaver?"

"Because it made me feel good," Riley rattled while keeping his gaze straight ahead.

"But why does it make you feed good? After almost a billion years of evolution, why do humans still have a need to feel good?"

"Here's a better question: Why can't a man enjoy his first drink of the day in peace?"

* * *

Twenty-four hours later, Owen and Sheila sat on a bench high above Huron Street, eighty feet above Mackinac Island's main street, overlooking the almost completely emptied town, the straits, and the Mighty Mackinac Bridge beyond. The sky was a leaden gray, overcast, and the entire landscape was almost completely devoid of color. Even the water and spruce trees looked gray. Owen and Sheila were bundled and huddled against the bite of the wind and cold.

"Don't you regret not picking Miami?" Sheila asked, blowing into her hands to keep them warm.

"You know, all my life, whenever I am melancholy, I have looked for a melancholic setting. For whatever reason, forlorn scenery always lifts my mood. It's a trick that never failed me."

"That is perverse."

"Perverse it may be, but I feel more alive and colorful than any of the fixtures around here. And that is pretty hard to do these days," Owen explained as they fell silent for a couple of minutes. "The truth is that I wanted to come here for two reasons. I wanted to experience true peace and quiet one more time after the tumultuous past few weeks. And I wanted to find a place where we could concentrate on each other."

Sheila leaned her head on Owen's shoulder. "Mission accomplished," she said soothingly. They let the silence fall over them again. The only noise was the wind.

"I'm scared, Sheila," Owen announced after several minutes. "What if the atheists are right and there is nothing but silence after we die?"

"I thought you said it best at Thanksgiving. Every sinew in our sense of justice suggests there is more meaning to life than that. Let me ask you this: Do you remember being in your mother's womb?"

"Can't honestly say I do," Owen responded.

"Put yourself back there and imagine you realized you were going to be expelled shortly. You could have as easily wondered at that moment if your separation from the world as you then knew it and the impending severance from the sustaining umbilical cord would be your permanent end. Look how wonderful that transition turned out, even though it could not have been anticipated. Or look at all these dead looking trees. Imagine you are one of those trees today. You could just as easily wonder if you will ever return to life in the spring."

They fell silent again.

"You are incredible, Sheila. Thank you for making my last months so enchanting. You know I wish we had more..."

"Don't say it, Owen. Remember when you convinced me to get involved? You argued that any number of quality moments were worth the pain. You were right. I am thankful for every moment we have had. When I think of how easily we could have passed each other on the beach, I shudder." Another few minutes of silence passed.

"I have one more favor to ask, Sheila: On Tuesday when we return, I want you to leave me." Owen felt Sheila stiffen and he squeezed her with all his remaining might, whispering into her ear. "It won't be long now. You need to be with your family and I with mine over the holidays. I desperately want you to remember me this way. And I have unfinished business with Megan."

Sheila grabbed his hand, and they gently cried together until the sun broke through the clouds and they started walking down Huron Street towards the village. Halfway down the hill, with Owen's arm around her and through still teary eyes, Sheila asked, "Owen, I have always wondered: Where does Lake Michigan end and Lake Huron begin? Is it underneath the Mackinac Bridge?"

"Lake Michigan and Lake Huron are at the same elevation. They are technically one lake. I like to think that Lake Michigan never ends."

"I knew you would know the answer," Sheila said as they turned down Main Street and she slipped her arm around Owen's waist.

Owen sighed, his energy flagging. "I am confident of one thing: If natural selection were the only thing at play, there wouldn't be people as nurturing as the wonderful kindergarten teacher I have come to love." They cuddled closer and smiled as they ambled passed the Victorian hotels and the horse drawn carriages that line Main Street.

Four weeks later, on January fourteenth, Megan let herself into the Austin family home at ten o'clock in the morning, as had become her habit. She heard Owen's CD jukebox stuck on the song which Owen had picked for the father-daughter dance at her wedding, Frank Sinatra's rendition of "Just the Way You Look Tonight." She found him on the couch, his eyes half open, looking straight ahead. The rock glass with his half-finished cocktail from the evening before was on the floor, the ice long melted. Caesar's head was in Owen's lap, and the dog's tail wagged slightly when he realized Megan had entered the room.

Megan reached for her cell phone and dialed the familiar number. "Frank, my father is dead."

"Don't do anything, Megan. We'll be right over."

Megan hung up the phone, sat down on the couch, and leaned into Owen for the last time. "I love you, dad," she whispered softly, and then let their song play one last time.

Chapter Fifteen

Tuesday, June 8, 2010
Landing

In early June, Megan called Sheila and asked her to meet at the beach in Muskegon. An hour later, Megan pulled up behind Sheila's car at the end of Beach Street before it turns away from the water, the curve marking the beginning of the doggie beach. Using her rear-view mirror, Sheila spotted Megan and exited her car, struggling with the energy in front of the two leashes. Megan smiled as Hedgecock and Caesar bolted in different directions, forcing Sheila to bow her legs and brace herself.

Megan exited her car, opened the rear door, and reached into the back seat to pull out the battery-powered drill. She already had the two deck screws in the pocket of her shorts. She reached for the covered oil portrait.

Sheila called out a greeting but did not ask Megan what she had in her hands. Together they set out across the near dune until they were far enough away from the road for Sheila to comfortably release the dogs, who scampered south down the beach. "Megan, let me take the drill," Sheila said as she reached out her hand, and they trudged down the beach. Megan immediately knew she made the right decision to invite Sheila even though the invitation was motivated originally to gain Caesar's presence.

"Where are we headed, Meg?" Sheila asked, still not inquiring about the portrait.

"Up there. Up at the top of the exposed dune where the forest starts—to the large beech tree," Megan announced, pointing to the largest tree at the tallest hump in the dune, well over two hundred feet above the beach—the most commanding feature other than the lake. The two women scrambled up the dune, which was no small task given their cartage and the strong wind that was bending the beach grass down. When they reached the top of the ridge, they turned and sat for a moment, catching their breadth.

"It's a beautiful spot, isn't it?" Sheila said, looking out over the vast lake towards Milwaukee, somewhere over the horizon.

"Dad's favorite spot on earth."

"Did you know, Meg, that we met right there by that large, washed-up beech log?" Sheila said.

"Really!" Megan laughed. "Did you know that the last time I was alone outside with dad, I met him sitting on that same log? This is perfect, then." She stood up and took the blanket off the oil portrait and positioned it against the large tree, asking Sheila for the drill after pulling the first screw from her shorts.

"Are you sure you want to do that, Meg? It won't survive the summer exposed to the elements."

"I'm certain. Dad hated this portrait. But I think he would choose to spend the summer here over the spot he loved and that obviously meant so much to him."

"Drill away, girl, I'm sure you are right," Sheila said encouragingly. With that, Megan drilled a screw above Owen's head and one below the knot in his tie. The two women stood back and looked approvingly as the Honorable Owen Randolph Austin, chief judge for the United States western district court of Michigan, now presided over the doggie beach at Pere Marquette Park.

Suddenly, the women were startled by a rustle in the grass as Caesar emerged. Looking up at Owen, Caesar sat obediently for a moment and stared, seemingly waiting for his master's command. Still looking directly at Owen, he cocked his head, whimpered once, got up, and barked twice. Sheila and Megan stared at Caesar, then looked to each other with amazement. When they turned back to the terrier, he had disappeared as quickly as he had appeared. They could see indications of him descending the dune, straightening the beach grass as it bent against the wind. They watched the ripple of grass reach the top of the fore dune nearest the beach and then, in a blink of eye, he was gone.

About the Author

Victor Fleming is the penname of a Midwestern trial lawyer who has been working in the courtroom for over three decades.